DESTROYERMEN

DESTROYERMEN

CRUSADE

TAYLOR ANDERSON

D0202361

A ROC BOOK

ROC
Published by New American Library, a division of
Penguin Group (USA) Inc., 375 Hudson Street,
New York, New York 10014, USA
Penguin Group (Canada), 90 Eglinton Avenue East, Suite 700, Toronto,
Ontario M4P 2Y3, Canada (a division of Pearson Penguin Canada Inc.)
Penguin Books Ltd., 80 Strand, London WC2R 0RL, England
Penguin Ireland, 25 St. Stephen's Green, Dublin 2,
Ireland (a division of Penguin Books Ltd.)
Penguin Group (Australia), 250 Camberwell Road, Camberwell, Victoria 3124,
Australia (a division of Pearson Australia Group Pty. Ltd.)
Penguin Books India Pvt. Ltd., 11 Community Centre, Panchsheel Park,
New Delhi - 110 017, India
Penguin Group (NZ), 67 Apollo Drive, Rosedale, North Shore 0632,
New Zealand (a division of Pearson New Zealand Ltd.)
Penguin Books (South Africa) (Pty.) Ltd., 24 Sturdee Avenue,
Rosebank, Johannesburg 2196, South Africa

Penguin Books Ltd., Registered Offices:
80 Strand, London WC2R 0RL, England

First published by Roc, an imprint of New American Library,
a division of Penguin Group (USA) Inc.

First Printing, October 2008
1   3   5   7   9   10   8   6   4   2

Photo of the author taken on the Battleship *Texas* (BB-35) State Historic Site—3527 Battleground Rd., La Porte, Texas 77571, with the permission of the Texas Parks and Wildlife Dept.

RoC   REGISTERED TRADEMARK—MARCA REGISTRADA

LIBRARY OF CONGRESS CATALOGING-IN-PUBLICATION DATA
Anderson, Taylor.
Crusade : Destroyermen, book II / Taylor Anderson.
p. cm.
ISBN: 978-0-451-46230-5
1. World War, 1939–1945—Fiction. 2. Time travel—Fiction. I. Title.
PS3601.N5475C78 2008
813'.6—c22   2008012553

Set in Minion Regular
Designed by Alissa Amell

Printed in the United States of America

PUBLISHER'S NOTE

This is a work of fiction. Names, characters, places, and incidents either are the product of the author's imagination or are used fictitiously, and any resemblance to actual persons, living or dead, business establishments, events, or locales is entirely coincidental.

The publisher does not have any control over and does not assume any responsibility for author or third-party Web sites or their content.

The scanning, uploading, and distribution of this book via the Internet or via any other means without the permission of the publisher is illegal and punishable by law. Please purchase only authorized electronic editions, and do not participate in or encourage electronic piracy of copyrighted materials. Your support of the author's rights is appreciated.

AS ALWAYS, TO MY DARLING DAUGHTER, REBECCA RUTH. I KNOW THE TIME MAY COME WHEN DADDY'S NOT YOUR HERO ANYMORE, BUT I'LL ENJOY IT WHILE I CAN. I KNOW YOU GET TIRED OF HEARING THE "HONOR SPEECH," BUT IT'LL SERVE YOU WELL. IT HAS ME.

ACKNOWLEDGMENTS

The list of "usual suspects" is too long to repeat, but their assistance, encouragement, and friendship are no less appreciated. They know who they are. I hesitate to call them a "team" of helpers, even though most of them know one another and each has done something to contribute to the completion of this novel, even if it was just moral support. Maybe a better analogy is a crack gun crew. Each member has a specific task, sometimes performed independently of the others, and when all is going well, their endeavors often resemble a virtual ballet. In that sense, I guess they are a "team," because it requires all of them performing their tasks to perfection to send a single round downrange.

To my previous list, or "crew," I must add the following: Sheila Cox put my Web page together and never complained about all my stupid questions. My folks, Don and Jeanette Anderson, must be specifically recognized as my primary, initial proofreaders and sounding boards for crackpot ideas. My wife, Christine, continues to put up with my foolishness, and recognizes that I was Taylor long before she met me, and there's nothing she can do about it now.

Again, I want to recognize Ginjer Buchanan and all the people at Roc for their patience and support. Ginjer's the best editor anybody could have.

Finally, thanks again to Russell Galen. He's the best agent there is, and a true friend. If this crew has a "Master Gunner," he's the guy.

One last thing. I was *not* in the Asiatic Fleet. I've done my best to describe the situation, hardships, equipment, and conditions of operations it had to endure at the outbreak of WWII, but I'm sure I've made a bundle of mistakes. I want you to know those mistakes are all Jim's fault. (Just kidding—they're mine, of course, but I had to say that.) To all you Asiatic Fleet destroyermen out there, please accept in advance my most profound apologies for those mistakes, and I hope you'll enjoy the story anyway. It is, after all, ultimately—and most respectfully—dedicated to you.

*T*salka, Imperial Regent-Consort and Sire of all India, lounged on his padded, saddlelike throne. The throne was raised upon a triangular platform in the center of a vast oval-shaped stone chamber. An arched ceiling left most of the chamber in shadow for much of the day, and flowering ivies transplanted from the dark jungle floor carpeted all. Only above the throne was there always sunlight. It beamed through a large, ingeniously mirrored opening in the center of the ceiling, and the warm, sensuous rays caressed and illuminated the regent with their favor.

Tsalka idly stroked a small, squirming miniature of himself as it chewed on his long finger-claw. Its sharp teeth were like little needles and its claws and flailing tail tickled his palm. A basket of its nestmates wobbled near the throne. The tiny mewling growls of the occupants struggling with one another provided amusing distraction from thoughts of the disquieting interview he expected. Word had already reached him that a hunting-pack had been thwarted in some way and he awaited details. Details he might have to convey to the Celestial Mother herself. The first reports hinted that the pack had fallen prey and, deep down, a predatory quickening stirred.

He shouldn't have cared less, on a personal level. He was of the Hij, the elevated, and the primordial impulses no longer held sway. He was one of the few who, through birth and achievement, were allowed to advance beyond the Uul, or warrior/worker stage of life. Not many did, and he had few peers. It was from the Hij alone that the Celestial Mother and her sisters took their consorts and provided a gentle stream of hatchlings that might one day gain the awareness to aspire to elevation themselves. Some became engineers and shipwrights. Others became generals, planners, navigators, or scribes. Still others oversaw the making of arms. Some few, like him, became administrators and viceroys of conquered lands. All were ancient by the standards of the Grik. Tsalka was close to forty and a few Hij even labored to the impossible age of sixty or more.

That was the blessing—to continue to exist and achieve a level of awareness the Uul could never fathom. It was necessary that some should do so, and the responsibility for guiding the Uul and shaping a world for them to enjoy was immense. That was also the curse. The Hij could no longer surrender themselves to the joy of the hunt and the ecstasy of battle. Theirs was the role of organizer—gamekeeper, if you will—and they paid for their elevation by stepping aside to let their charges have all the fun. Sometimes, the burden of the curse was heavy indeed.

The philosophy of the Grik was simple: the Great Hunt was the justification for all existence—to chase prey and devour it, ultimately across the world. One is either predator or prey. Only the predator survives and thrives and it must always hunt. Other predators may join the Great Hunt, but if they refuse, they are prey. Worthy Prey perhaps, but still prey. There are no old Grik, besides the Hij. When they slow down, they become prey and are killed by their young. And so it had ever been.

Because of the blessed abundance of prey upon the world, there had also been an exciting variety of predators. Some were merely animals, but others were quite cunning. Grik history was a comforting series of slowly escalating, playful wars (or hunts) between them and other predators that refused to join them. Other predators—even other Grik—were by far the most satisfying prey. Over time, Worthy Prey became scarce and warfare among the frustrated Grik reached disastrous levels. In times such as those, non-Grik predators often became Worthy Prey whether they wanted to or not. Quite regrettable, of course, but family comes first.

And so, ages ago, a very wise Celestial Mother established the tradition of the "Patient Hunt." By this method, it took considerable time to hunt a species of Worthy Prey to extinction so the Grik wouldn't wipe them out too fast and turn on themselves again. When population and instinctual pressures finally grew too extreme, the Grand Swarm was created. Warriors from every region of the empire mobilized to mount a final campaign to eradicate the target Worthy Prey at last. This not only expanded the empire, but often brought them in contact with new Worthy Prey and the cycle recommenced.

For thousands of years, this custom worked extremely well. Wars still raged between the Celestial Mother's various possessions, but they were usually friendly affairs, often arranged by the regent-consorts so their Uul could enjoy themselves. No such entertainment was currently under way, however. Within the last Uul generation or so, the "Prey That Got Away" had been rediscovered. The histories referred to them simply as "the Tree Prey," because instead of fighting like Worthy Prey, they climbed trees to escape slaughter. They were cowards and not true predators, so they were viewed with the same derision as common grass-eating prey. They'd escaped, however, and that still ruffled Tsalka's tail plumage with the shame of those, countless generations past, who'd let it happen.

Now they were found—hiding again—across the bottomless sea. But instead of the stately dance of escalation, there was a mood of urgency to amass the Grand Swarm and finally finish this prey before it fled again. Tsalka was point for that effort. Ceylon was the gathering place for the preparing Swarm, and his task was monumental. Theoretically, his duty was primarily organization. The generals in their white ships would plan the hunt itself, but he was regent-consort and certain strategic decisions had been thrust upon him.

A horn thrummed, echoing dully in the chamber. A tall, scarred, massively muscled Hij general approached from the gloom and sprawled upon the triangular platform at his feet. Tsalka heard the scrape of armor and clatter of weapons and, for an instant, his pulse quickened. Sometimes he wished he'd been a general. They could still sometimes play. But they couldn't lose themselves in battle, and that took great discipline. He breathed. "Rise, General Esshk," he said, hissing a pleasant greeting.

Esshk stood and straightened his short cape. It was the bright red of the Celestial Mother's own house. "The Giver of Life sends her greetings to you, Regent Tsalka, her favorite and most noble consort."

Tsalka bowed, acknowledging the compliment. He didn't let it go to his head, though. Esshk probably said that to all the regents. Esshk was arguably the greatest living general. A nest-mate of the current Celestial Mother and probably royal consort as well, he had her ear and favor. He would command the Grand Swarm when it sailed and was subordinate only to the regents and the Celestial Mother herself. Tsalka didn't want Esshk to see him as a fool. "She is ever in my thoughts," he declared piously. "How was your journey?"

"Tedious, sire. Three ships were destroyed by the great monsters in the sea, but that is of little consequence. I brought many more. Still more will arrive when they are completed. You will victual them?"

"Of course."

Esshk paused and spoke again, in a different tone. "I saw . . . interesting things and heard tales from the Hij at the dock."

There it was. Esshk always came straight to the point. Tsalka sighed. "Indeed. There has been interesting news, and some also troubling. Where would you have me begin?"

"With the troubling, I think."

Tsalka's gaze drifted past the general and focused on another shape being escorted from the gloom. His expression hardened. "Very well,

General Esshk. How convenient. The 'trouble' has arrived. Step forward, Ship Commander Righ. I would hear your words." Righ crept miserably closer. He'd been divested of his colors and armor and was entirely naked. He approached with his head down, tail between his legs, but did not abase himself before the regent, since such displays of respect were appropriate only from one worthy of it.

"My Uul fell prey. I couldn't stop them."

Tsalka bristled. "Of course you could! That's what the Hij are for—to protect and guide the Uul in their charge!"

"Nevertheless . . ."

Tsalka hissed menacingly but waved one of his long-fingered hands. "Nevertheless, it's done. Your crew will be destroyed—such a waste! What will you use for an excuse?"

Righ told of an attack by a six-ship hunting-pack upon a lone ship of the Tree Prey. All went well until a strange vessel appeared, moving magically fast. By no means he had seen, at an impossible distance, it destroyed the hunters on their own ships as well as those fighting the Tree Prey. His ship was severely damaged. In the face of this horror, all fell prey. All. Righ's crew fled without orders and knocked him senseless to the deck. When he recovered, it was night and they'd escaped. Only darkness saved them.

His crew was ruined, however, and could barely function. With no choice, he set course for Ceylon so at least he might report. On the way, he encountered the large hunting-pack that Tsalka had dispatched to raid the place called Java. He expected to be destroyed as prey but instead, after exchanging chart information, he learned that they too saw the terrible ship and fought it! Unlike Righ's, their ships did not fall prey but many were destroyed.

"What was the result of this fight?" Esshk demanded and Righ looked at him dejectedly.

"Victory, of course. They still lived and prey was taken. The strange ship fled, but under such a pall of smoke that it must have burned to the waterline. When the smoke cleared, the ship was gone. The prey they took was strange, without tails or fur or geydt. They offered and I ate."

"How did it taste?" Tsalka asked, genuinely curious.

"Bland, but tender, sire."

"Interesting. I should like to try one."

"You may, sire. The commander of the hunting-pack sent one with me to bring you as a gift. It's alive and fresh. All others were eaten and their skulls sent with the scouts so they might know them if they encounter more."

The infant in Tsalka's lap bit down on one of his fingers again—hard—and he suddenly remembered it was there. He popped it in his mouth and chewed distractedly. Its struggles tickled the roof of his mouth. He swallowed. "Very well, Righ." Tsalka sighed, still deep in thought. "Every hatchling knows defeat is no excuse to fall prey, and a good commander would never have allowed it. Conversely, you've done much to atone. Therefore, if you're certain you've withheld nothing, you have my permission to destroy yourself after you send this new prey to me."

"Thank you, sire." Righ breathed a sigh of relief. It could have been much, much worse. "Thank you!"

Tsalka waved his hand and Righ was dismissed. He cast an uneasy glance at Esshk. "A most unpleasant business," he observed.

The general hissed agreement. "I wonder about this strange ship and the tail-less creatures that drive it. Were they defending the Tree Prey? Perhaps they saw us as poachers?" He flicked his tail. "No matter. They were defeated, if Righ spoke truth. I see no reason to delay the Swarm. If anything, we might move forward more quickly. If there are more of these tail-less prey, numbers would seem the answer to their threat."

"I agree. I was going to suggest that very thing." Tsalka had a sudden insight. "Perhaps the New Hunters might offer suggestions. They may know of them."

Esshk bowed. "We must certainly ask. That brings us to the 'interesting,' does it not? The docks are abuzz—and I can certainly see why! Is it true they've joined the Great Hunt?"

"It is! And long has it been since that occurred!" Tsalka paused. "I ordered they be spared on my authority. If the Celestial Mother disagrees, I will, of course, destroy them."

"Do they hunt well?"

Tsalka snorted. "Very well indeed! As customary, three assaults were annihilated before the offer of joining was made. Only one ship of twenty returned. That is one reason I am glad you arrived with more! But come! Let us walk in the sun! We may view the New Hunters even as we discuss them." Tsalka rose and swept toward the hall adjoining the chamber. Through a vaulted passage they strolled, chatting amiably, until they reached a high balcony overlooking the vast bay below. It was an awesome spectacle. Hundreds of red-hulled ships dotted the purple water and in the midst of it all was something . . . stupendous.

"Is it not grand?"

Esshk bared his teeth and hissed appreciatively. "I would like to meet these New Hunters."

"And so you shall. They are quite amazing, really, if all I hear is true . . ."

Just then, the two guards that had escorted Righ into the regent's chamber appeared on the balcony. Between them was an emaciated, freakish creature with long, gangly arms and legs. It was naked and filthy and had only a stringy tuft of fur on the top of its head and a shorter growth on its face. The rest of its body was as pale and smooth as a just-hatched Uul. Only its eyes did not seem utterly wrong. They were small, but blazed with the universal expression of terrified hate. Both Hij had seen that before. They looked at the creature with revulsion.

To their surprise, it managed to stand up straight. Blinking in the light, it spoke a few scratchy words in its own tongue. It sounded like . . . something . . . "kaphmaan." Then, amazingly, it uttered a short series of numbers! Numbers they understood! Then it promptly closed its mouth and said nothing more.

"Remarkable!" Tsalka exclaimed. "Do you think it knew what it was saying? Or was that a trick Righ taught it on the long voyage home?"

"I cannot say," Esshk replied. "But it will be interesting to find out." He coughed a laugh. "It might provide conversation over dinner."

"Converse with food? What an appalling thought!"

"I agree. But if Righ may be believed, they are at least Worthy Prey, are they not?"

Tsalka snorted noncommittally. "Perhaps, but I have never spoken to any prey—regardless how worthy it might be."

Esshk replied with a hint of humor. "I beg to differ! Did you not just speak to Righ? Was he not made prey? Besides, what is the difference between Worthy Prey and our very pack-mates? One has joined the Hunt; one has not. That is all."

Tsalka regarded the general with keen speculation. "You're a philosopher, General Esshk. I have long thought it so. No wonder you're so popular at court. But that is . . . a dangerous thought. I urge you to keep it to yourself."

They were startled when the filthy, talking prey suddenly made a strangled cry and flailed madly against its restraints. In its weakened condition, it was quickly reduced to a sobbing, sagging shell; until then, it at least showed some courage. They realized it was the sight of the New Hunters that upset it.

"Well!" hissed Tsalka, pleased. "It must know the New Hunters after all! It reacted as prey to its natural enemy! Fascinating!" He paced to the edge of the balcony, clasping his hands behind his back, tail swishing speculatively. The Grik vessels looked tiny compared to the massive, dark gray ship the New Hunters called their home. It was nearly as large as one of the ridiculous Homes of the Tree Prey. Only *this* ship was iron, he was told, and bristled with huge, magic weapons. He wondered what its flag signified—the curious white flag with bloodred streaks radiating outward from the center.

"What do they call it?" asked the general.

"Hmm? Oh, the ship? I'm told it is called *Amagi* . . . whatever that means!" They both hissed amusement.

*T*he morning general quarters alarm woke Lieutenant Commander Matthew Reddy, and he automatically reached for the little chain beside his sweat-soaked bunk and pulled it. The cramped stateroom was bathed in a harsh white light as he sat up, rubbing his eyes. Awareness came quickly, but not instantly. He always took a moment to get his bearings when he'd been having the Dream, and he'd been right in the middle of it. The same one. It came almost every night and he knew it at the time, almost consciously, but he could never remember it when he woke. He just knew he'd had it again. Even while he dreamed, his subconscious seemed to blot out each sequence of events as soon as they occurred so he was aware only of what was happening at that very moment and, of course, the crippling dread of . . . something he knew was yet to come. Sometimes, like now, if he was disturbed before the Dream reached its horrible, inevitable conclusion, he'd carry a sense of it with him for a while. But, as usual, details vanished as soon as he opened his eyes, like roaches when the lights came on. Even now, the last vestiges of ... whatever the Dream was diminished like a wisp of smoke in a gale. All he really knew for sure was that the Squall was involved. The Squall that had somehow delivered them from destruction at the hands of the Japanese, but only by marooning them in this twisted, alternate ... alien world. A world geographically little different from the one they knew, but utterly different in every other conceivable way.

For a while he sat there, struggling to classify the dark, lingering emotional perceptions and taking inventory of the things he knew. They were under way; he could feel the vibration of the warm, dank deck beneath his bare feet. The unusual strain he perceived in the fibers of the ship indicated the "prize" was still under tow. That meant all the terrifying events leading to its capture weren't remnant nightmare threads of the Dream, so everything else he suddenly recalled must have really happened. Damn. He didn't know why the Dream eluded him so. It couldn't be subconscious fear. Nothing could be as scary as the things they'd actually endured since the Squall.

Shaking his head, he stood and moistened a towel in his washbasin. They were already low on fresh water again so he couldn't indulge in a shower. He had to be content with a quick, unrefreshing wipe-down. Finished, he sparingly lathered his face with his last cake of soap and quickly scraped away the stubble. After wiping his face again, he ran a comb through greasy hair and briefly examined the results in his mirror.

"You look like hell," he muttered to himself, then shrugged. "But you've looked worse." There were puffy bags beneath his tired green eyes, and his once embarrassingly boyish face didn't look so boyish now, two months before his thirty-third birthday. A few silver strands had emerged in his light brown hair, certainly due to stress; neither of his parents began to turn gray until their late fifties. The stress was curiously lessened now, however, even if the danger wasn't. They'd fought a battle against a terrifying foe and learned their enemy was even more horrible than they'd imagined. Exponentially worse than the Japanese who had almost destroyed them. But the ship wasn't sinking and they had a steady source of fuel. They had good friends and allies in the Lemurians and if the Grik were a greater threat than they'd feared, the fact they'd finally learned *something* about them, even if it was bad, was a relief of sorts.

When Matt and his crew of Asiatic Fleet destroyermen aboard the old "four-stacker" USS *Walker* (DD-163) had been fighting the Japanese, they'd been outnumbered, outgunned, and on the run. Ridiculously outgunned at the end, when they and their sister ship, *Mahan,* slugged it out with the mighty Japanese battle cruiser *Amagi* right before they'd been swallowed by the Squall. During the two months between Pearl Harbor and their ultimate "escape," Matt's greatest frustration was the way the dwindling remnants of the Asiatic Fleet had been used merely to plug holes in the collapsing Dutch East Indies dike. Even outclassed as they were, the fight needn't have been so lopsided, but an utter lack of air cover, total ignorance of the enemy's strength, dispositions, and intentions, and inept, uncoordinated planning by ABDA's (American, British, Dutch, Australian) multinational leadership had meant they were doomed from the start. They knew they were threatened by an avalanche, but they never knew how big it was or where it would fall.

Until the recent battle, he'd felt much the same frustration about the Grik. They were the Lemurians' "Ancient Enemy," but their allies didn't really know much about them. The incredibly hostile sea had kept them separated for countless generations. After they captured the Grik ship and the wealth of intelligence aboard it, they finally knew what they faced. It was horrible and it was huge, but at least now they *knew.* The Grik were savage monsters, as numberless as ants, and they were coming to wipe the Lemurians out. They were another looming avalanche that made the threat once posed by the Japanese seem almost insignificant. Since they'd lost track of *Mahan,* all that stood in their way was a single battered Great War–vintage destroyer and a flimsy alliance of disparate and often contentious Lemurian "sea folk" and "land folk" who were torn between fighting and running away. Perhaps unreasonably, however, for the first time since they came through the Squall, Matt actually felt guardedly optimistic.

His ship and her crew had a purpose again, other than simple survival, and the men were united in their determination to help their
friends resist the Grik beyond even their earlier determination to resist
the Japanese. After all, the Japanese—hated as they were—didn't eat
those they conquered. With the discovery of a human skull on the Grik
ship, a skull that could have come only from *Mahan*, the war against the
Grik became an American war as much as a Lemurian one. That they
were the only Americans around, besides those they hoped still survived aboard *Mahan*, was immaterial. *Walker* would lead the struggle.
The weary iron ship and her tired iron crew would drag the Lemurians
out of the Bronze Age and build an army and whatever else was needed
to take the fight to the enemy. Some progress had already been made,
but much more would be required before they were ready to begin the
crusade Matt had in mind.

He dressed quickly and pushed aside the pea green curtain that
separated his stateroom from the short passageway through "officers'
country" between the wardroom and the companionway to the deck
above. As he strode to the ladder, he almost collided with Nurse Lieutenant Sandra Tucker as she emerged from her quarters, headed for her
battle station in the wardroom/surgery. They maneuvered around each
other in the confined space, each aware of the electric response that
proximity aroused between them. Sandra was short, barely coming to
Matt's chin, but even with her sandy brown hair wrapped in a somewhat disheveled bun and her own eyes still puffy with sleep, she was
the prettiest woman Matt had ever seen. Not beautiful, but pretty in a
wholesome, practical, heart-melting way.

Sandra and five other Navy nurses had come aboard as refugees before *Walker*, *Mahan*, and three other ships abandoned Surabaya with
the Japanese on their heels after the disastrous Battle of the Java Sea. In
the running fight that followed, the British cruiser *Exeter* and the destroyers HMS *Encounter* and USS *Pope* were sunk by the remorselessly
pursuing enemy, leaving *Walker* and *Mahan* to face *Amagi*—and the
Squall—alone. In the frenzied action with the battle cruiser, the two destroyers were mauled, but they'd put at least two torpedoes into *Amagi*

and when they came through the Squall, she was gone. They hoped they'd sunk her. Also gone, however, were half of *Mahan*'s crew and a quarter of *Walker*'s—including one of the nurses, killed in action.

Three of the surviving nurses went aboard *Mahan* to care for her many wounded and so, like the ship, they were lost to them. Only Sandra Tucker and Karen Theimer remained—on a ship full of rambunctiously male Asiatic Fleet destroyermen. So far, there'd been few problems, other than a mysterious altercation between some of Matt's junior officers over Nurse Theimer's affections, but Matt and Sandra had both early recognized a growing mutual attraction. They had, in fact, finally declared their love for one another just after the recent battle. But both knew, for the sake of morale, they had to remain aloof in front of the crew. The tension aboard caused by the "dame famine" would only be inflamed, they thought, if they openly acknowledged their affection. Matt was convinced there were other humans in this "new" world—there was too much evidence of previous contact—but he thought "taking" one of the only females known to exist for himself might erode the only real authority he had left: moral example. Matt and Sandra would have been surprised and chagrined to know how poorly kept their "secret" was—the men had eyes, after all—but they'd have been equally surprised by how much real authority Matt still possessed. In spite of the dame famine, his crew would follow him into hell. They already had. They'd done it because when they went, he always personally led them there.

As they turned sideway to pass each other, Sandra's breasts brushed against Matt, and he had to restrain a powerful urge to embrace her. Instead, he merely smiled.

"Morning, Lieutenant."

"Good morning, Captain," she replied, her face darkening slightly. As quick as that, the moment was past, but Matt had a springier step as he trotted up the companionway stairs to the exposed deck and climbed the ladder to the bridge above.

"Captain on the bridge!" cried Lieutenant Garrett, the tall gunnery officer. He had the deck.

"As you were. Status?"

"Reports are still coming in, but we're under time."

Matt nodded and went to his chair, bolted to the forward part of the starboard side of the pilothouse. Sitting, he stared out at the blackness of the lingering, moonless night.

"All stations report manned and ready," announced the bridge talker, Seaman Fred Reynolds. His voice cracked. The seaman was so young-looking that Matt suspected puberty was to blame. He glanced at his watch in the dim reddish light. 0422.

"Not the best time, Mr. Garrett, but not the worst by a long shot."

"No, sir." In spite of the fact the Japanese were no longer a threat, it had become clear that other threats were still very real. Because of that, Matt insisted they maintain all wartime procedures, including predawn battle stations. It was during that time when the sky began to gray but the sea remained black that ships were most vulnerable to submarines, because the ship was silhouetted but the sub's periscope was invisible. Matt wasn't afraid of submarines, but there were other, even more terrifying things in the sea and it was always best to be prepared. Besides, even as the men groused and complained, it was a comforting routine and a clear sign that discipline would be maintained, regardless of their circumstances.

Slowly, the gray light came and lookouts, mostly Lemurian "cadets" because of their keen eyesight, scanned the sea from each bridgewing and the iron bucket "crow's nest" halfway up the tall, skinny mast behind the bridge. As time passed, there were no cries of alarm. Ahead, on the horizon, like a jagged line of stubborn night, rose the coast of Borneo—called "Borno" by the natives—and at their present pace they should raise Balikpapan—"Baalkpan"—by early afternoon. Astern, at the end of the tow-cable, the Grik ship they'd captured began to take shape. She was dismasted, but the red-painted hull still clearly reflected the shape of the long-ago-captured British East Indiaman she was patterned after. Bluff bow, elevated quarterdeck, three masts, and a bowsprit that had all gone by the board in the fighting. Just looking at her, Matt felt his skin crawl.

The fight when they took her was bad enough: the darkness, the shooting, the screams, and the blood. He vividly remembered the resistance he felt when he thrust his Academy sword into the throat of a ravening Grik. The exultation and the terror. Exultation that he'd stabbed it before it could rip him to shreds with its terrible teeth and claws; terror that he had only the ridiculous sword to prevent it from doing so. The first Grik he killed on the ship had been disarmed, but certainly not without weapons. They were like nothing he'd ever seen. Fuzzy, bipedal . . . lizards, with short tails and humanlike arms. But their teeth! They had the jaws of nightmare and claws much like a grizzly's. So even though it lost its axe, he was lucky to survive. Then, and many times after. Of course, later it was different. When they chased the remnants of the Grik into the hold of the wallowing ship, they realized that the horror they'd felt before was nothing. Only then did the true nature of the Grik become clear to everyone, humans and Lemurians alike, and he *wanted* to use the sword. The hold was a slaughterhouse, where captives of every sort were butchered for food—while they were alive. Matt had wanted live Grik to study, but that became impossible. He couldn't restrain the Lemurian "Marines" under his command. He didn't even try to restrain himself.

The horrible nature of their enemy should have made their victory that much more satisfying, but when they studied the captured charts and learned the extent and population of the empire they faced, Matt, Keje-Fris-Ar, and ultimately Keje's Sky Priest, Adar, finally realized they must plan boldly or die.

It was light enough now that he could see the distant, hazy shape of Keje's great seagoing "Home." Even miles astern, it still looked massive—because it was. The incredibly thick wooden hull with its ingenious diagonal bracing was as large as one of America's new carriers, like the *Hornet,* and each of the three tripod masts rising around pagoda-like living areas supported immense junklike sails, or "wings," as tall as *Walker* was long. *Salissa*—"*Big Sal*" to the Americans—was typical of her breed of seagoing Homes, but she was now armed with ten 32-pounder cannons that had performed with murderous effect against another Grik ship and all the boarders from three. The cannons were the result of the efforts of the suddenly tireless supply officer, Alan Letts, whom Matt had left behind in Baalkpan to continue overseeing the production of more guns and other things. Also, to keep him away from his other officers, since he seemed to be the one Nurse Theimer had chosen. He hoped the period of "out of sight and out of mind" might help his officers reconcile when they met again.

He sighed and looked at his watch. Speaking of reconciliation and discipline . . . As soon as the men were released from morning GQ, the ship would continue steaming at condition III, as she always did now, with half the guns manned at all times. Some of the men would try to go back to sleep and others would remain to fulfill their morning watch duties. But the forenoon watch, at 0800, would begin with a session of "captain's mast," where he'd have to decide punishment for two of the most valuable members of the crew. For the sake of morale, he didn't want to break them—besides, he needed them too badly. But he couldn't be seen as just slapping their wrists either. He'd have to walk a fine line.

Eventually 0530 rolled around and visibility was sufficient to secure from general quarters. Lieutenant Garrett was replaced by Lieutenant Dowden, Matt's new exec. He'd been at his battle station on the auxiliary conn, aft, before arriving to relieve Mr. Garrett. The former officer to hold his position was James Ellis, but he'd been given *Mahan* after the Squall because most of her officers were killed when a ten-inch shell shattered her bridge. They'd learned from Lieutenant Ben Mallory, U.S. Army Air Corps, and Lieutenant Brister, *Mahan*'s engineering officer, that Mallory's superior, Captain Kaufman, had shot Jim Ellis and taken over the ship. That's why she hadn't been at the rally point after they split up. Mallory, Brister, and Signalman Ed Palmer had arrived in a "found" PBY Catalina after a harrowing escape from the Grik. That was the only reason they knew anything at all about what happened to the other ship. The last information had her off the west coast of Sumatra, heading for Ceylon, a place they now knew teemed with Grik. All they could do at present was hope Jim had survived and managed to retake the ship before the Grik wound up with her. The discovery of the human skull aboard the prize made that seem unlikely. So in addition to their other problems, they also had to either rescue *Mahan* or destroy her.

"May we come on the bridge?" came a hesitant voice from behind him. Matt turned and saw Courtney Bradford standing on the ladder with Sandra. Bradford seemed uncharacteristically subdued. Normally, the Australian engineer and self-proclaimed "naturalist" wouldn't have even asked. *Maybe Sandra made him,* Matt thought. He expected he might have seemed as though he was concentrating on something— which he was—but he was actually glad of the distraction. Bradford hadn't been there for the fighting, but he'd arrived on the PBY flying boat the following day. Since then, he'd spent most of his time inspecting the prize. That was enough to sober anyone.

Theoretically, no one was really in charge of Courtney Bradford. Since the Australian engineer was a civilian, his status was somewhat vague and had been allowed to remain that way because he worked well without constraint. Before the Japanese attacked, he'd been an upper-level engineering consultant for Royal Dutch Shell. That occupation allowed him to pursue his true passion: the study of the birds and animals of the Dutch East Indies. Also because of that occupation, however, stuffed in his briefcase when he evacuated Surabaya aboard *Walker* were maps that showed practically every major oil deposit Shell had ever found in the entire region. There'd been some skepticism that the same oil existed on this earth as the other, but after the success of their first well—exactly where Courtney told them to drill—they were all believers now.

"Of course. Good morning."

"Good morning to you, I'm sure," Bradford replied, stepping on the bridge. Sandra just smiled at him. Matt gestured through the windows at the landmass ahead, becoming more distinct.

"Almost home," he said, with only a trace of irony.

"Indeed," agreed Bradford, removing his battered straw hat and massaging his sweaty scalp. It was still early morning, but almost eighty degrees. Matt had noticed, however, that Courtney usually did that when he was upset or concerned. "I've been studying that map you gave me. The one that was apparently drawn by the Grik captain himself, not the navigational charts with all their incomprehensible references . . ."

Matt nodded. Even though the Grik charts were disconcertingly easy for him to read, since much was, horrifyingly, written in English, Matt knew which map Courtney meant. It was just a drawing, really, that basically depicted the "Known World" as far as the Grik were concerned. It showed rough approximations of enemy cities and concentrations, and it also showed much of what the enemy knew of this part of the world—the part that should be the Dutch East Indies. It was much like what one would expect of a map showing "this we hold; this we want." The farther east it went, the vaguer it became, but Java, Sumatra, and Singapore were depressingly detailed and accurate. There were also tree symbols that represented known cities of the People, and many of those had been smeared with a blot that looked like blood, symbolizing, they believed, that a battle had been fought there. Currently, there was no tree symbol at Baalkpan, but there were two others that didn't have smears beside them. One was near Perth, Australia, and the other was at Surabaya, or "Aryaal," as the locals there called it. The map also depicted a massive force growing near Ceylon and Singapore too, which was believed to be their most forward and tenuous outpost.

"Captain, since only Perth and Surabaya appear on the enemy map, we can only assume the next blow will fall on one or both of those places. I'd bank on Surabaya myself. I'm no strategist, but it seems to me, judging by the dispositions on the map, the Grik are planning a major offensive against that place and it will probably commence within weeks, if it has not done so already."

"That's kind of the impression I got, too," agreed Matt.

"But what are we going to do about it?" Sandra asked, speaking for the first time. Matt shrugged.

"As you know, Keje and I have been kicking some options around and we've come up with some good ideas, I think. But we can't do it alone. A lot will depend on the other Homes in Baalkpan Bay, but most will depend on Nakja-Mur." He grimaced. "Not that I expect much trouble out of Nakja-Mur. He won't leave his city and unlike the seago-ing Homes, he can't take it with him. I think he'll cooperate, but it'll be a tough sell." He sighed. "Lemurians are basically peaceful folks, at least the ones we've met. With a few exceptions, it's hard enough to turn them into warriors—soldiers that can defend themselves. To then send those soldiers far away to defend other people, Aryaalans, who they don't even like . . ." He looked at Bradford. "We need to find out what it is about those people that makes everyone dislike them so. Ever since we first came here, they've tried to steer us clear of Surabaya. Why?"

"I get the impression there are certain . . . frictions between them based primarily on substantially different cultures. There may even be a religious angle involved," Bradford replied. "I don't think it's insignifi-cant that, unlike almost everywhere else in the region, only south-central Java ever had human-based names. Chill-chaap instead of Tjilatjap, for example. Other places are even more obvious. Borno for Borneo. Why do North Java's city names bear no resemblance to human names at all? The Lemurians we know base so much of their culture upon the 'Scrolls' or charts that were rendered from those British ships so long ago. Perhaps the Aryaalans and others like them never had contact with them, or the 'prophet' Siska-Ta who later spread the word?" He spread his hands. "I have no idea."

"We're going to have to find out. We might need them." Matt looked back at "Borno." Even at their crawling pace of five knots, towing the derelict and trying not to get too far from *Big Sal,* they should open Baalkpan Bay late that afternoon. It would be an . . . interesting home-coming. He wondered what the reaction of the people there would be. Joy at first, certainly, that they'd returned victorious. But he wondered what would happen when all they'd learned got out. Several of the huge seagoing "Homes" would probably withdraw from the alliance. Nakja-Mur, Baalkpan's High Chief, would be terrified, but he'd stand firm. He had no choice. Baalkpan couldn't go anywhere. Matt just hoped he'd understand the necessity to implement the plan he and Keje had begun to form. Even Keje had seen that a purely defensive war was hopeless.

Static defenses in the face of the numbers the enemy had could not succeed. They could bleed them white and kill dozens to one, but as the Ancient Scrolls of the Lemurian "People" foretold, no matter how many Grik you killed, there were always more. In a defensive stance, sooner or later they'd be overwhelmed. If they wanted to win, they must take the fight to the Grik.

At the appointed hour, the two miscreants were brought forward to stand before the captain on the well deck behind the bridge. Sonny Campeti, master at arms, shouted for attention. One of the accused, Gunner's Mate 2nd Class Dennis Silva, was no stranger to the procedure and he snapped a sharp salute. If not quite an actual giant of a man, he was only the next size smaller, powerfully muscled and standing six foot three. His hair was still cropped nearly to his skull, but he'd allowed a thick brown beard to form on his face, which seemed perpetually parted in a gap-toothed grin. In addition to a black eye and a swollen nose, there seemed to be a bigger gap than before. Silva was *Walker*'s Hercules, utterly fearless in battle and an expert with any firearm. He'd also shown a surprising proficiency with a cutlass. But he was also, possibly, the most depraved individual Matt had ever known. He gloried in practical jokes, but his "jokes" often got out of hand. Sometimes dangerously so.

Matt turned his attention to the other accused. Chack-Sab-At was a Lemurian, or " 'Cat," as the general consensus had compromised on. Some of the "snipes," or engineering division, still insisted on calling Lemurians "monkey-cats" while equally stubborn deck division "apes" remained adamant about "cat-monkeys." Simply " 'Cat" had become universally accepted, however. Chack, a former "wing runner" aboard *Big Sal,* had been the first to join the "Amer-i-caan" Clan and learn the destroyermen's language. As *Walker*'s Lemurian contingent grew, he'd been duly inducted into the United States Navy, given the rank of boatswain's mate 3rd class, and placed over the Lemurian—essentially second—deck division. He was tall for a Lemurian, topping five-six, and like any wing runner he was incredibly strong. He wore a bright red kilt over his lower body, and a white T-shirt covered the upper. Only his legs, arms, face, and carefully rigid tail exposed his dark, brindled fur. Wide amber eyes peered from an expressionless but highly feline face. His long ears twitched nervously. One eye was puffier than the other and his cleft lips were split and swollen. He'd once been a pacifist, Matt understood, but that was clearly no longer the case. He'd distinguished himself in several fights now, most recently with Dennis Silva.

Besides the wounds they'd inflicted on each other, both still bore wounds from the hellish battle with the Grik. Chack walked with a limp from a badly sprained ankle he got while fighting on the slippery bones and ballast stones in the belly of the Grik ship, and Silva's arm was bandaged from elbow to wrist from a wicked sword slash.

Matt was surprised how many of the crew had gathered to witness the proceedings. He knew all would be curious how it turned out and, because of that, he must not only be scrupulously fair, which he always strived to be, but he must be *perceived* as scrupulously fair. With so many men left in Baalkpan working on essential projects, almost half of *Walker*'s crew were 'Cats. That was one reason he'd sort of rushed the "trial." He feared that if he waited until they reached port, word would spread and create a circus—possibly a highly partisan one—right when they all needed as much unity as possible. The situation had to be dealt with, but it was better to do it now, here, while they could handle it among themselves.

"Since you're both charged with essentially the same offenses and the offenses occurred simultaneously, we'll make this easy. Any objections?"

Chief Boatswain's Mate Fitzhugh Gray and Lieutenant Garrett stepped forward, representing their respective divisions.

"No, sir," they chorused. Matt looked at his exec, Lieutenant Dowden.

"You're the reporting officer."

"Aye, aye, sir. The incident in question occurred aboard *Big Sal*, during the celebration after we joined her with the prize. *Walker* sent over several liberty parties during the course of the evening to participate in the festivities, but neither of the accused had specific permission to be aboard."

Matt looked at them. "How do the accused respond to the first charge: absent without leave?"

Chack began to speak, but Chief Gray stepped forward and interrupted him.

"Captain, Bosun's Mate Chack was escorting one of the 'prisoners' we rescued from the Grik . . . larder." Everyone, even Matt, flinched at the memory of that. The creatures had been emaciated and, for the most part, wildly insane. "One of the prisoners was known to him, and delivering him aboard *Big Sal* was a highly personal act and one that, had I known he was doing it, I certainly would have approved." He looked at Chack. "The accused pleads guilty, but under extenuating circumstances that include not only family but foreign relations." Matt had to smile at Gray's imaginative defense, but his own memory of the event was not amusing. The prisoner Chack escorted was none other than Saak-Fas, the mate of Keje-Fris-Ar's daughter, Selass. He'd disappeared in battle with the Grik many months before and was considered lost. In the meantime, Selass had developed a desperate love for Chack and had expected him to answer her proposal to mate, after the battle. The scene when he returned her mad, barely living mate to her, a mate she'd never really loved, was heartrending.

"In view of the 'extenuating circumstances,' the first charge against Bosun's Mate Chack-Sab-At is dismissed," Matt declared. "Mr. Garrett? Have you anything to say on Gunner's Mate Silva's behalf?"

Garrett looked at the big, grinning man and took an exasperated breath. "Guilty, sir. His only defense is that some other fellas did it too."

"Unacceptable. Mr. Dowden?"

"Uh, the next charge is that both the accused became involved in, well, a brawl, sir, and not only were they at the center of the brawl but they started it by striking one another."

Matt sighed. "I won't even ask who started it. I know I won't get a straight answer. Besides, I have a pretty good idea. If I'm not very much mistaken, I expect Chack threw the first punch—"

"He pulled my tail!" Chack interrupted, seething indignantly.

"Did not! I was just holdin' it. You did all the pullin'!"

"Silence!" Matt bellowed. "Trust me, you both would really rather keep your mouths shut and handle this my way! Silva, your unnatural and hopefully pretend 'relationship' with Chack's sister, Risa, was all very shocking and amusing . . . at first. It's now not only an embarrassment to this ship but a constant goad to Chack's self-control. I know Risa's as much to blame as you are. You're two peas in a pod, personality wise, if not . . ." He shuddered. "In any event, you'll cease tormenting Chack with the lurid details of your fictitious 'marriage' to his sister and you'll *definitely* refrain from any more . . . overt physical demonstrations when you are together. Is that understood?"

"But, Skipper . . ."

"IS THAT UNDERSTOOD?"

"Aye, aye, sir!"

"Very well. It's pointless to dock your pay, but you're both losing a stripe and you're both restricted to the ship for ten days—after we make port. Silva, you're losing another stripe for AWOL."

"But—"

"Shut up." Matt looked at Dowden, who cleared his throat.

"Attention to orders!" he said. Captain Reddy unfolded a piece of paper before him.

"For extreme heroism and gallantry in the face of the enemy, etc., etc."—he looked up—"I'm sorry to you other guys, but I'm still too damn mad to get flowery. Anyway, with my deepest gratitude, I'm proud to advance the following men one grade in rank: Coxswain Tony Scott, quartermaster's mate 3rd, Norman Kutas—" He stopped for a moment and sighed heavily. "Boatswain's Mate Chack-Sab-At and Gunner's Mate Dennis Silva. Most of you deserve it. Chack, you lose one, you gain one, so you're back where you started—except for the restriction. Silva . . ." Matt shook his head. "You're never going to get that first-class stripe if you don't settle down!" Dennis shrugged philosophically and Matt looked at Campeti, who concluded the proceedings. As they walked back to the pilothouse, Matt and Dowden were rejoined by Sandra and Bradford. Both wore broad smiles. "Cut it out," he said, almost smiling himself as he mounted the steps. At the top waited Lieutenant Tamatsu Shinya of the Japanese Imperial Navy.

"Mr. Shinya," Matt greeted him.

"Captain." Shinya was the sole survivor of a destroyer that took a torpedo meant for *Amagi*. Somehow, her survivors in the water had been swept through the Squall with the American ships, but before *Walker* could return to rescue them, they'd been eaten by what was evidently a plesiosaur of some sort, not to mention a ravening swarm of tuna-sized fish that acted like piranhas. They called the fish "flashies" and they were everywhere, at least in the relatively shallow equatorial seas within the Malay Barrier. Shinya alone was saved because he'd been unconscious atop an overturned lifeboat. It had been the first indication to the destroyermen that they were no longer in the world they knew—the first other than the bizarre effects of the Squall itself, of course.

Since then, Shinya, who had studied in the United States, had given his parole and had become a valued member of the crew. He was an excellent swordsman, if not in the traditional Japanese style, and he was a big help to Sergeant Alden, the Marine from the doomed cruiser *Houston*, whom they'd also carried from Surabaya. Together, they were building an army based on historical principles the captain had suggested. Matt had realized early on that the only way they could counter the overwhelming Grik numbers was with discipline—specifically, the Roman shield wall, backed by spears and archers. At least that's what they'd need in an open-field fight. Shinya also understood Latin, which was, amazingly, the language of the Ancient Scrolls of the 'Cats. Not because it was taught them by Romans, but because that's the language the sailing master of the HEIC (Honorable East India Company) ship *Hermione* chose to teach them and communicate in.

Matt suspected the earlier visitors did it to remain as enigmatic as possible, since there was evidence they'd already encountered the Grik, even before one of their ships was taken by them. The rest of the "Tailless Ones" of that long ago visit had sailed into the "Eastern Sea" beyond the "edge of the world" and disappeared from Lemurian history.

Matt suspected they were still out there, somewhere. British Indiamen often carried passengers and deportees, so there was reason to believe they'd survived. Anyway, that's how they first communicated with the 'Cats; Bradford and Tamatsu Shinya spoke the "Ancient Tongue" of the Lemurian Sky Priests.

Valuable as Shinya was, many of Matt's destroyermen still hated his guts simply because he was a "Jap." Matt respected him and trusted his honor, but even he couldn't put Pearl Harbor—and everything that had happened since—completely out of his mind. Chief Gray openly loathed him, despite saving his life in the recent battle. Tony Scott told him something he hadn't even known about the Bosun: his son had been on the *Oklahoma* when she capsized and sank to Pearl Harbor's muddy bottom.

"Where's Pete?" asked the captain, referring to the Marine.

"He'll be along," Shinya replied. Even as he spoke, Alden and Chief Gray arrived on the bridge. Matt noticed that Alden's limp was now totally gone and even the Bosun was in better shape. He was close to sixty, but the once chubby man wasn't even breathing hard after the stairs. After Ensign Bernard Sandison, the torpedo officer, and Brad "Spanky" McFarlane, the engineering officer, arrived, the entire group Matt had summoned for this little conference was present. Ahead, through the windows, Borno grew ever larger and more distinct as the clock on the bulkhead neared 0930. Baalkpan fishing boats began to gather around them, and Matt permitted a single celebratory toot from *Walker*'s whistle. Regardless of the news they bore, he didn't want too somber a homecoming. The people of Baalkpan would need a little happiness to balance the dread to come. Sheets flew on a few of the nimble fore-and-aft-rigged feluccas, and they surged ahead in a turmoil of spray taking the news of their arrival to the city. He motioned to the starboard bridgewing, and the others joined him there. Without further pleasantries, he began.

"When we make port, things are going to be a lot different and they're going to change really fast. We've been trying to ease these people out of the Bronze Age, and despite a lot of bitching and bickering we've made a lot of progress. Not enough. I've already spoken to Keje and Adar about this, as well as a few of you." His gaze lingered on Sandra. "When we dock at Baalkpan we all have to be on the same page with the same message: we're in a crummy spot, but we're going to *win,* and this is how we're going to do it." He smiled a little awkwardly. "I'll go into 'how' a little more in a minute. As for now, I'm not through giving out promotions. I'll have to run a few of these by Nakja-Mur, since they'll impact his people more than anyone's, but he's in over his head." Matt snorted ironically. No one felt that way more than he. "And he trusts us. The first thing we're going to have to do when we get back is call for another 'great gathering.' Way bigger than the last one. Try to get folks to come from everywhere. Right now, there's no real chain of command, so we'll have to get that sorted out. However it shakes out, I expect we'll be somewhere near the top. That means everybody's jobs are going to get bigger and harder." He looked at Pete. "Right now, the Marines are yours. We got that straight with Nakja-Mur from the start. That's close to a thousand well-trained troops," he said with a grimace, "with a fair sprinkling of seriously hard-core veterans. Some of them will get broken up again, to form a cadre of NCOs and even officers, because as soon as we get back, you'll continue to work to build the biggest, most modern army we can field without firearms. I'll talk to Letts about supplying some field artillery at least, but otherwise, keep training them like you already were. It's within my power, I think, to award you the brevet rank of captain under the circumstances."

Pete Alden gulped. "Sir, I'm just a sergeant. I ain't no officer!"

"You are now. Hell, I'd make you a general, but then you'd outrank me!"

"You could make yourself an admiral, Captain," Bradford suggested, but Matt shook his head.

"It's not right," he said softly. "I might take full captain because I bet all *Walker*'s officers would have jumped a grade or two if we'd made it to Perth, and that'll leave me a little room to raise some guys up that deserve it. For example, as of right now, there are no more ensigns aboard this ship. All are now jay-gees. The jay-gees are full lieutenants."

He grinned at Dowden and Sandison. "That includes you two. Start looking for guys, human or 'Cat, that we can make ensigns out of." He looked back at Alden. "Who do you want as your second?" There was really only one choice, but Matt wouldn't force the Marine to make it.

Alden glanced almost reluctantly at Shinya. "You're the guy, if you want it," he said. "I got no reservations, but some of the fellas might. 'Course, you'll be commanding 'Cats for the most part and they don't give a hoot you're a Jap. But there's a few guys you might want to hold off giving orders to."

Shinya bowed. "I am honored to accept. There should be few occasions for me to command any American personnel. If the need arises and I cannot find you, I will try to be conscious of their"—he smiled—"sensitivity." Matt coughed.

"Fine. You'll stay a lieutenant, under Alden. Let's see, for chain-of-command purposes, since Marine captain equals general"—he grinned, much to Pete's discomfort—"first lieutenant means colonel, second is major . . . hell, that won't work!"

"As I was saying," Bradford insisted. "You could still be admiral and make things a lot simpler. No one back home would ever know or care!" Matt gave him a hard stare.

"Why don't I just declare myself king? What's the difference? Where does it stop?" He shook his head. "I don't know what we'll do, but we'll figure something out." He looked at Sandra. "You've made great strides, not only learning Lemurian medicine, which certainly has its virtues, but in teaching them our methods as well. I think both have complemented the other." That was certainly true. The Lemurians had an antibacterial, analgesic paste made, like many other things Sandra had discovered, from the fermented polta fruit that grew wild in the region and was cultivated aboard the massive seagoing Homes. A less arduous and more refined fermentation of the polta also produced the popular intoxicating beverage known as seep.

The 'Cats had learned from Sandra too. Being generally unwarlike, they'd never dealt with anything like the casualties they'd suffered during their recent battles, and her instructions in battlefield medical techniques had been invaluable. She'd already begun forming a hospital corps in Baalkpan. "I want you to keep up the good work, but be ready to really expand your operation. Concentrate on teaching teachers." Sandra nodded grimly. She knew what Captain Reddy planned. It scared her to death, but it seemed the only option.

"That leaves you, Mr. Bradford. Eventually, I want another well site. We'll have to sort out where, but right now all our eggs are in one basket. What if there's an accident or some other stoppage at the site we have? What if, God forbid, the enemy overruns it? I want one that's essentially in a reserve position, building a reserve of fuel. Any ideas?"

Bradford looked thoughtful. "Again, let me consult my charts. I'll come up with some likely areas and you can tell me which is best for your strategic needs. Agreed?"

"Agreed."

Spanky snorted a laugh. "The Mice are gonna hate that!" The others chuckled in agreement.

No single word or phrase was adequate to describe the Mice. "Strange" came closest, but was still almost too specific. By their appearance, Isak Rueben and Gilbert Yager might have been brothers. Both were intense, wiry little men with narrow faces and sharp, pointed noses that contributed much to the rodentlike impression they made. They were irascible, unfriendly and annoying to just about everyone they came in contact with. They never socialized and had always shunned the ship's baseball team. They were quintessential "snipes"—firemen, to be precise—but they took it much further than that. Given a choice, they would never leave the sweltering heat of their beloved firerooms and the boilers they worshipped there. They were painfully insular and apparently just as unimaginative, but Spanky had recently learned there was more to them than met the eye.

Normally, their skins were pasty with a belowdecks pallor they worked very hard to maintain, but now their exposed skin still bore the angry red-brown tans they'd accumulated while operating the first oil rig outside of Baalkpan. A rig they designed based on a type they were intimately, if ruefully, familiar with from their years in the oil fields before they escaped that hated life and joined the Navy. Now they were back at it and not happy at all.

Matt looked back toward Borno. He thought he could just make out the mouth of Baalkpan Bay. "We're all going to have to do things we hate, I'm afraid, before this is over." He sighed. "It's going to be a hell of a homecoming," he added nervously.

As the day wore on and the crew went about their duties, *Walker* towed her prize ever closer to Baalkpan. The nearer they got, the more traders and fishing boats paced her advance. Opening the bay, the old destroyer steamed toward her customary berth near the shipyard and the fitting-out pier. They had been gone less than two weeks, most of that time laying their trap for the Grik scouts they engaged. The battle itself took only a day, and the return voyage took three. The people had known the outcome, however, since the very day after the fight. The radio in the precious PBY was working now, and there had been constant reports. Then the big seaplane had flown out with passengers to examine the prize. Some, like Bradford, stayed with the returning ships, but those who returned on the plane were strangely tight-lipped. No matter. The dismasted hulk trailing in *Walker*'s wake was sufficient proof to the populace that the expedition had been a success.

As always, Matt was struck by the sight of the large, strange, but exotically beautiful city of Baalkpan. The unusual architecture of the multistoried buildings was strikingly similar to the pagoda-like struc- tures that rose within the tripod masts of the great floating Homes. Some reached quite respectable heights and were highly decorated and painted with bright colors. Some were simple, one-story affairs, but all were elevated twenty or more feet above the ground by multitudes of stout pilings. Chack once told him that was done in order to protect against high water and "bad land lizards." It was also tradition, which Matt supposed was as good a reason as any. He'd never seen any crea- tures ashore that could threaten anyone twenty feet above the ground, but he was assured they did exist. He believed it. There was certainly plenty of bizarre fauna in this terrible, twisted world.

Among the pilings, under the massive structures, was what some would call the "real" Baalkpan. It was there, beneath the buildings themselves or colorful awnings stretched between them, that the city's lifeblood pulsed. It was a giant, chaotic bazaar that rivaled anything Matt had seen in China, or heard of anywhere else. Little organization was evident, beyond an apparent effort to congregate the various products or services in strands, or vaguely defined ranks. From experience, Matt knew there was no law or edict that required this; it was just practicality. This way, shoppers always knew where they had to go to find what they wanted. Along the waterfront, fishmongers hawked the daily catch with an incomprehensible staccato chatter. Beyond were food vendors, and the savory smells of Lemurian cooking wafted toward them, competing with the normal harbor smells of salt water, dead fish, and rotting wood. Still farther inland were the textile makers—weavers, cloth merchants, and clothiers. Closer to the center of the city, near the massive Galla tree and Great Hall of Nakja-Mur, one was more likely to find finer things, like ornamental clothing, exquisitely wrought jewelry, and even fine blades. The foul-smelling commerce in gri-kakka oil took place beyond the shipyard, as far from the center of Baalkpan as possible. The rendered oil was sweet, but only after separation from the often rancid tallow.

Matt took all this in: the vibrant, throbbing vitality of a city and people who'd never known threats other than natural ones. They had tails and fur, and if Bradford was right, they were actually descended from giant Madagascar lemurs, even if they looked more like a cross between cats and monkeys—with a little human thrown in, he reminded himself. But regardless, they were people. Many happily rushed down to the waterfront to cheer *Walker* and her crew and gape at the captured hulk of their dreaded enemy. Soon the dock was jammed with wildly celebrating multitudes, making it difficult for the line handlers to tie off. *Walker* remained singled up. Immediately, curious townsfolk tried to storm aboard the Grik ship, but Matt had foreseen this. Fifty hard-eyed "Marines" lined the ship's bulwarks and stood ready to repel them. Matt turned to look back at the mouth of the bay. Keje and his much slower *Big Sal* weren't even visible yet.

At least Nakja-Mur and Naga were aware of the situation, and a hundred guards, led by Lieutenant Alan Letts, arrived from the parade ground in front of the Great Hall. They immediately set up a protective cordon in front of not just the prize but *Walker* as well. The celebrating people didn't seem to mind. Good. If they'd managed to get aboard the Grik ship and have a look around, things might have turned ugly really fast. At the very least, they might have burned it—and he couldn't have that.

He noticed with slight reassurance that some effort had been made to begin fortifying the city since he left. A low earthen breastworks had been started here and there, and trees had been felled a short distance beyond it to make a killing ground. Inadequate as it was, at least it was something, but the People of Baalkpan were about to learn how pathetic their efforts to date truly were.

"The prize is secure and there seems a sufficient guard around it," reported Dowden from the auxiliary conn atop the aft deckhouse. The bridge talker repeated the message to the captain.

"Very well. Cast off the towline. Hoist a signal for Nakja-Mur. Tell him we're going upriver to the fueling pier. We'll fill our bunkers and I'll make a full report tonight, when Keje and *Big Sal* arrive."

"Aye, aye, Captain," replied Riggs. He went to supervise as one of the signalman strikers ran up the appropriate bunting. Matt still had the conn, and he directed the watch to use the engines and rudder to move them away from the pier once more. The rudder hard over, the port engine pushed the stern away from the dock. Then, after the special sea and anchor detail released the final forward line, *Walker* slowly backed clear. Matt looked at the crowd on the dock and smiled.

"Might as well give them a show," he said. With a quick glance to make sure they were clear, he continued, "Right standard rudder, all ahead full!" *Walker* gave a shuddering groan that seemed almost like a sigh of relief that she was no longer burdened with the deadweight of the prize, and her stern crouched down and churned a mighty, muddy froth above the fantail. Even over the rising roar of the blower, Matt heard the excited cries of the crowd's appreciation. Quickly, still on three boilers, the aged thoroughbred accelerated into a wide turn that took her deeper into the bay and, ultimately, upriver to the fueling pier. *We need another one of those down here,* Matt thought. He looked at Mr. Riggs. "Honk the horn!" he said with a grin.

The crowd still milling near the red-hulled ship cheered louder as a cloud of steam and a deep, resonant shriek jetted from the whistle and the amazing iron ship raced upstream, raising a feather halfway up her number, smoke streaming from three of her four funnels.

"Let 'em have a good time for a while," Matt said, his voice turning grim.

"Aryaalans!" snorted Nakja-Mur later that evening, standing on *Walker*'s bridge where she was again tied to the Baalkpan docks. He hadn't waited for Matt to report. As soon as *Walker* returned from fueling, he and the just-arrived Keje tromped up the gangway. "You ask me to risk everything for those unfriendly land-bound . . . heretics?" Matt and Keje had been describing the details of the battle and the capture of the enemy vessel. The account turned to the discovery of the enemy charts, or "Evil Scrolls of Death," as Sky Priest Adar insisted they be called. That led to their theory of an impending Grik attack on the people of Surabaya: "Aryaalans," as they called themselves. Chack was present to interpret, but so far, between Keje, Nakja-Mur's rapid advancement in English, and Matt's slowly growing proficiency in Lemurian, he hadn't been needed.

Matt sighed. "With respect, my lord, it's essential we go to their aid if they're attacked."

"But why? Let them fend for themselves, as do we. They were invited to the last gathering and they chose—as always—not to dampen themselves with the company of sea folk!"

Matt was tempted to point out that Nakja-Mur was, however sensible, the very definition of a landsman. But to be fair, the People of Baalkpan were every bit as sea-oriented as the people of Old Nantucket ever were. They built and repaired ships and they dealt in the products of the sea's capricious bounty. Their livelihood was entirely

centered around maritime toil and commerce. Whereas the Suraba-
yans were . . .

"Just what the hell is it about them you don't like?" Matt asked in
frustration.

"They . . . they are heretics!" Nakja-Mur proclaimed.

"Why?"

Nakja-Mur shifted uncomfortably and paced out on the port
bridgewing. Matt and Keje followed him there, and Larry Dowden
joined them. There was a reduced watch on the bridge since they weren't
under way, but a torpedoman had been tinkering with the director con-
nections. Matt motioned for him to leave them and the man quickly
gathered his tools and departed.

"Why?" Matt asked again.

"Perhaps you should ask Adar."

"I can't. He and Bradford ran off to study together as soon as we
rigged the gangway. Who knows where. Besides, I have to ask you because you're the one whose opinion really matters, in the long run, and
we have decisions to make . . . *you* have decisions to make. I know, tra-
ditionally all 'High Chiefs' are equals here, but surely you know that in
reality you're a little more 'equal' than the others? You have the largest
force and Baalkpan's the most populous city this side of Manila—and
it's on your industry we all depend."

Nakja-Mur grunted, but his tone wasn't unfriendly. "I have heard it
said you're the most 'equal' among us, because of this ship." He patted
the rail under his hand.

Matt shook his head. "Untrue. Without you and Baalkpan, this ship
would most likely be a powerless, lifeless hulk on a beach somewhere
and I and most of my people would be dead. I agree your people owe
Walker much, but she owes you as well. It's pointless to keep score among
friends. We're obligated, bound together, but as great as that combined
strength might be, it's not enough and it'll be even less if Surabaya falls.
We need those people on our side—not filling Grik bellies!"

Nakja-Mur recoiled as if slapped, but then nodded. "The Aryaalans
are fierce warriors," he conceded, "but they do not revere the heavens.

They may worship feces for all I know, but the sky is not sacred. When Siska-Ta went to them to teach the wisdom of the Scrolls, she was cast out and nearly slain." He made a very human shrug. "They are heathens, but their religion is unimportant to me. We are not intolerant of the beliefs of others. Many folk of other lands—even some upon the sea—do not believe as we do and yet we remain friends. Did we not befriend you and your people?" he asked.

Matt didn't point out the probability that they thought then—and probably still did—that the destroyermen had very similar beliefs to their own, and he remembered the scene Adar made in *Walker*'s pilothouse over the charts displayed there. He'd thought they mocked him with apostasy at the time, since the Ancient Scrolls or charts of the Sky Priests are not just maps but holy relics on which are woven the tapestry of Lemurian history in the words of the Ancient Tongue—Latin. Their religion is not based on the Scrolls, but they've become integral supplements—along with a few twisted Christian concepts that may have been passed inadvertently by the previous "Tail-less Ones" almost two centuries before. Matt had picked up a little Lemurian theology and, although it was fundamentally a form of Sun worship, he knew the heavens—and the stars in particular—represented far more than simple navigational aids. Since that first awkward moment, religion had not been much of an issue and he'd concentrated on other things. Maybe he needed to bone up. He would talk to Bradford.

"What confirms the depravity of the Aryaalans, however," Nakja-Mur continued, "is that they often war among themselves! They are constantly at war, one faction against another, and they often repel visitors with violence. I cannot help but wonder, even if we aid them, will they not simply turn on us as yet another enemy?"

"We have to try."

"Perhaps. But it will take another meeting, I suppose, and you will have to be very convincing."

"Sure," said Matt. "We'll have another meeting. We need one, bigger than before. But that's beside the point. Have you boarded the Grik ship yet? Spoken to any of the survivors?" Nakja-Mur shook his head. "You need to do that. Then you'll understand. This is a fight to the death. To the end. Total war and no more goofing around. Even if you could flee, like the sea Homes can, they'll catch you eventually because that's what they *do*." Matt paused. "You told me before we left on the last expedition to find out what we could, that you'd do anything to keep the Grik away. Did you mean that?"

"Of course!"

"Well, then, if we're not going to fight them here, we'll have to fight them somewhere else. Let's do it where we might have some help."

The gathering in Nakja-Mur's Great Hall was even larger than when they'd debated the previous expedition. This time the massive structure was nearly packed. Those present weren't just the High Chiefs of the Homes in the bay either, but their advisors, Sky Priests and senior war leaders as well. Alden, Shinya, along with their Marine and Guard officers and senior NCOs, represented Baalkpan's armed forces. As predicted, some sea Homes left, although *Fristar*, the most vocal advocate of simply running away, sullenly stayed. Others had arrived, as well as delegations from more land folk—one from as far as Maani-la, in the Fil-pin lands to the east. Some had arrived too late for the conference before the expedition; others came because of what they'd heard since. They came because the expedition had, after all, been a success: they'd learned much about the "Ancient Enemy" at long last, and they knew now what was at stake. Adar was determined to make the threat as clear as possible and had suggested opening the meeting to all, but there simply wasn't space. Matt countered that all would quickly know the situation through the many representatives.

A month before, the expedition had returned to Baalkpan with its malignant prize in tow. They were greeted with unparalleled euphoria, for it seemed that this, coupled with their other small successes, meant victory was on the march. Slowly, as the day of return progressed, the visitors and natives of Baalkpan began to learn the truth. Rumors of the horrors within the Grik ship spread like a typhoon wind and so did the scope of the threat. Few had actually seen the blasphemous charts that had been captured, and Matt and Keje tried to keep a lid on it, but somehow the unexaggerated fact that the enemy was numberless took hold of the populace.

The euphoria turned to panic first, but then the few wretched survivors of the Grik larder were carried ashore and, with them, the tale of what they'd endured. Deputations of merchants and townsfolk were allowed to tour the hulk and they came away in shock, but also with an appreciation—at long last—of the terrible choice they faced. They could run or they could fight. There was no other choice available. They might flee and hope to find some far-off land where they would be safe for a time, or they could defend their home against this evil. But if they chose to fight, the time for half measures and preparing only when the mood struck was over. Every waking effort of the entire population, those who stayed, must be devoted to a single-minded goal: fight the Grik and win. The released captives were a grim reminder that defeat did not bear contemplation.

As the days passed, some did leave. A steady trickle of feluccas, hired at exorbitant rates, carried the fearful to the Fil-pin lands. It became known that the enemy maps didn't show that place, and they thought they'd be safe. After the initial flurry, Nakja-Mur even chartered a few boats himself so certain treasures and relics might be carried away for safekeeping. These things were entrusted to the mates and younglings of some of the more talented artisans who were willing to stay as long as their loved ones were safe. Those who remained pitched in with a will—as if their lives depended on it.

The foundry fires glared night and day as every article of copper, tin, and zinc in Baalkpan was rounded up and sent into the crucible. The Bronze Age Lemurian industrial base went from accomplishing the impressive feat of casting one cannon every three to four weeks to the impossible rate of one every four days. McFarlane, Sandison, and a small army of helpers stayed busy at the crude boring machines and hones they'd made. Long lines of people, male, female, even younglings, escorted by Marines against the predators, carried their own weight in sulfur from the volcanic hills to the land home of Sular across the strait on Celebes, time after time. The cargoes were then transported to Baalk-pan by ship. Open leaching pits were laid out to produce nitrates and a vast swath of timber was felled around the city for the charcoal, and to provide a better killing field for its defenders. Smoke hung everywhere and every eye streamed.

Oil continued to flow and the refinery ran around the clock. New storage tanks were constructed and a respectable reserve, at least for a single destroyer's needs, was beginning to accumulate. Alden, Shinya, Chack, and many of the now "veteran" Marines who'd participated in the bloody boarding action stayed busy drilling everyone on the new, larger parade ground that used to be jungle. There was no more complaining, and even the warriors from the Homes in the bay rotated ashore for drill. And in the harbor, the unpleasant, unwanted task of refitting the Grik ship progressed.

Matt wasn't entirely clear about Lemurian funeral conventions, but he knew they preferred to be burned so their life force, or soul, could be carried to the heavens with the rising smoke. There, they would rejoin in the firmament those who'd gone before. He wasn't sure if the People believed they became stars after death, or if the stars guided their journeys there much as they did below. Maybe a little of both. It was clear to him, however, that the 'Cats would *really* have preferred to just burn the thing that they believed still held the souls of Lemurians who'd been tortured and eaten by the enemy. He tried to explain that if all went well, the Grik ship would soon become the second-fastest gun platform in the world. Much as he'd have liked to defer to their cultural preferences, they didn't have time to build another ship of the type. They would start some, certainly, and incorporate many refinements, but for now he was going to need that ship.

The People were aware of the advantages. They knew how fast and maneuverable the enemy ships were, compared to their own lumbering Homes. The idea of arming such a ship with cannon appealed to them as well. They just didn't want to use *that* ship. It was the one instance where Captain Reddy's military plans were met with real resistance. He sympathized, but he wouldn't bend. The crisis was finally solved by Adar, who argued that the trapped souls would surely welcome the chance for revenge, and using the tool of their own murderers to help claim that vengeance would make achieving it all the more sweet. They would clean it out and give it a name. They would re-rig and repair the damage it had suffered, but unlike *Walker*, or *Big Sal*, or, hopefully, *Mahan*, it would never, *could* never truly be a live thing.

Matt was grateful for Adar's assistance. He hadn't been sure which side of the argument the Sky Priest would take. Nakja-Mur's aged Sky Priest, Naga, had begun to defer more and more to Adar in matters of "belligerent spiritual guidance." *Big Sal's* "head witch doctor," as he was sometimes affectionately called by some Americans, had almost visibly swelled in importance and prestige. He didn't flaunt it, and he certainly didn't abuse the power, but he did have greater influence than ever before. His approval had been key. In word and deed, Adar had become the most outspoken advocate of this "total war" no matter what it took. He'd taken to heart his vow not to rest until the Grik were destroyed. At Adar's urging, in spite of their distaste, gangs of workers dutifully, if uncomfortably, toiled on the Grik ship, getting it ready for sea.

Light streamed through the Great Hall's open shutters and motes of dust drifted in the beams. Loud voices and shouted conversations carried on around Matt, Lieutenant Mallory, Courtney Bradford, Alan Letts, and Sandra Tucker, where they stood beside Nakja-Mur and his entourage, as well as Keje and Adar. Nakja-Mur stood, obese but powerful, dressed in his usual red kilt and gold-embroidered cloak that contrasted with his shiny dark fur. Fur with growing splashes of white. Matt thought of it as his "High Chief suit," since he'd always dressed thus when Matt saw him. Adar's purple robe with embroidered stars across the shoulders was an equally constant garment. The hood was thrown back, revealing his almost silver pelt and piercing gray eyes. Matt's friend Keje was dressed in a warlike manner, as Matt had first seen him after *Walker* saved his Home from six Grik ships and, by so doing, joined them in this terrible war. His armor consisted of engraved copper plates fastened to the tough hide of a plesiosaur they called "gri-kakka." At his side was a short, scimitar-shaped hacking sword called a skota, and cradled in his arm was a copper helmet, adorned with the striated tail plumage of a Grik. He also wore a red cloak fastened at his throat by interlocked Grik hind claws. Beneath the armor, as protection from chafing, he wore a blue tunic embroidered with fanciful designs. Other than the Americans, he wore the only "shirt" in the hall. All the 'Cats the destroyermen had met seemed to wear as little as they could manage, usually just a light kilt. Even the females went disconcertingly topless, and their very human, albeit furry, breasts were a constant distraction for the sex-starved destroyermen.

Large-scale addresses were rare among the People, and there was no way to speak directly to such a gathering from within its midst. Therefore, an elevated platform, or stage, had been constructed near the center of the hall where the Great Tree rose through the floor and soared high overhead to pass through the ceiling. Matt had seen the huge Galla tree many times now, but he was always amazed by its size and by the fact that he'd seen only one other like it. The one growing from the heart of *Big Sal*. He supposed other Homes had similar trees, and he wondered again if it was possible they were descendants of the trees the Lemurians had known in their ancient home.

The crowd was growing restless, anxious.

At a nod from Nakja-Mur, he stepped onto the stage. Immediately there was a respectful silence in the Great Hall—a much different reception than the last time he'd spoken to this assembly. Of course, he'd given them a "victory" since then—such as it was. He paced the small platform for a moment, staring at the upturned faces while Chack joined him to interpret. Many of those present had actually learned a smattering of English, but Matt hadn't yet acquired a conversational ability in their tongue and he was slightly embarrassed by that. He'd always thought he was pretty good with languages, but there was something about the strange, yowling words of the People that absolutely defeated him. Bradford, Letts, and even Sandra could jabber away like natives—at least as far as he could tell—but he was just as likely to insult somebody as to tell them it was a temperate day. Maybe it was a mental block, or his mind was too busy. Whatever the reason, he was glad Chack was there.

He gestured at Lieutenant Mallory. "My friends," he began, "as you know, the flying-boat has returned from its scout in the south." He paused. He'd hated sending the PBY and its crew off by themselves, but Bradford and the Mice had managed to refine a small amount of high-octane gasoline. They had done it somehow using salt water, of all things. Also, since Riggs had the plane's radio working, they'd never been out of contact. Ben flew under orders to avoid being seen at all costs, so he didn't have a firm count of the number of enemy ships that invested Surabaya. The only thing he could verify was that the lizards were definitely there. All the air crew could see from ten miles away and an altitude of 13,000 feet—a distance that should have muted the Catalina's loud engines—was "lots of ships." Unrealistically, Matt had hoped Mallory would spot *Mahan*—even though he had instructed him not to specifically look for her. Judging by how long he was gone and how much fuel he'd used, the Air Corps aviator must have covered as much ocean as he could anyway. There'd been no sign. "What Lieutenant Mallory and his companions have reported confirms our fears," Captain Reddy resumed. "Aryaal is under siege." He waited for a moment while the tumult died down. "I must propose that we lift that siege."

This time, many minutes passed before he was able to speak again. There were a few shouts of agreement, but many more cries of incredulous protest. The initial response degenerated into a general roar of discussion and debate. "We have no choice!" he shouted over the hubbub. "If the enemy establishes a permanent base as near as that, Baalkpan is doomed!" He picked out a small gathering of High Chiefs and fixed them with his eyes. "Many of you can just leave. Your Homes aren't tied to the land. But if Baalkpan falls, what then? Where will you replenish stores? With whom will you trade? Who'll repair your Homes? I know there are other lands that will serve that purpose for a time, but how long will it be before they too are lost? If we don't stop them now, one day all that will remain of the People will be scattered clans, alone on the sea, without sanctuary and without hope."

"We have no hope now!" snarled Anai-Sa, *Fristar*'s High Chief. "We should flee. We've seen the charts you took, many of us, and the Grik are as many as the stars above."

"We must not flee!" Adar bellowed, joining Matt on the stage. The intensity of his glare caused many to flinch. "I was in the belly of the Grik ship not long after its capture. I have spoken to the 'survivors,' though such a word mocks them! I have seen the perverted way the Grik twist our faith and use it against us. Speak not of flight! Any who would flee in the face of this scourge is aiding it! They are not only cowards but traitors to their people!" There were shouts of dissent, but some loudly agreed. Anai-Sa brooded in silence.

"Much has happened since we last met like this," Matt continued when the uproar began to fade. "Since then we've accomplished much, in spite of the doubts of some. Most importantly, we've won our first real victory over the enemy. I don't speak of simply destroying their ships. That's been done before. Besides, I agree it's now plain that such small victories are pointless in the face of the numbers the enemy possesses. What we've won is priceless intelligence!" He smiled. "We're no longer as 'ignorant' as we were before, and so we can begin to plan for greater victories. Victories that will make a difference. The first such victory should be the relief of Aryaal."

"How can it benefit us to spill our blood for them?" asked Kas-Ra-Ar, Keje's cousin. The question wasn't confrontational, but genuinely curious. "The Aryaalans have never helped us before."

"If we save them from the fate that awaits them in the Grik hulls, I bet they will then," Matt answered simply. "Don't you see? The Grik are through 'probing.' This is for all the marbles—I mean . . . polta fruit!" He grimaced, wondering how well that would translate. "They've taken Singapore, destroyed Tjilatjap . . . possibly others. Now they threaten Surabaya—Aryaal. This is *it*! The conquest you've feared since you fled them the last time so very long ago!" He blinked appropriately to convey frustration and anger. "Well, I say this time we stop them! This time we throw their asses back!" He stopped and took a breath, wishing he had some water. He was sweating and he knew he was allowing his own frustration over the litany of events that had brought his ship and her people to this moment to color his argument.

Once again, the long retreat in the face of the Japanese was fresh upon him. The terrifying escape from the Philippines, the lopsided battle of the Java Sea, the doomed retreat from Surabaya and the death of *Exeter* and *Pope* and all the others haunted him anew. The fate of *Mahan,* and the horrors he'd seen in the Grik hold. Not to mention the enigmatic human skull. At that moment, emotionally, it all became one. The Grik had become an arguably far more terrible, but just as implacable, surrogate for the naval avalanche that had claimed the rest of the Asiatic Fleet and had begun *Walker*'s nightmare odyssey in the first place. He was tired of running, and he just . . . couldn't do it anymore.

"We make alliance with the Aryaalans by destroying the Grik forces there," he continued with grim resolve. "Then we'll throw them out of Singapore. Once we've done that, we fortify. We build fast, dedicated warships that can blow the hell out of anything the Grik send against us and, in time, we'll kick their asses all the way back to where they came from!" There were enthusiastic shouts of support this time.

"And we'll do that only because we have secure internal lines—an area where the enemy dares not tread. The Malay Barrier will be our defensive wall—but we have to secure it. Java—Aryaal is an essential part of that." He looked out upon them and could see they wanted to believe. "This time we fight! And this time let *their* survivors frighten their children with tales of the fierce creatures that threw *them* out of paradise!"

Nakja-Mur strode onto the stage, holding his hands high to stifle the cheers and shouts and stomping feet. "I propose that Cap-i-taan Reddy, U-Amaki Ay *Walker,* be named War Leader of All the Clans for the duration of the campaign he described!" Matt was stunned with surprise in the face of the roar of acclamation that ensued. He looked at Nakja-Mur with an expression of betrayed . . . gratitude. He'd had no inkling that the High Chief of Baalkpan intended to make such a proposal. But it would certainly simplify things. The Lemurian grinned back at him.

"Aahd-mah-raal!" he said smugly.

*   *   *

The "Allied Expeditionary Force" crept slowly southward under a pale blue, cloudless August sky. Matt doubted the weather would last, however, because Keje had told them they were entering a "stormy" time of year. So far, he'd noticed a few differences between the weather "here" and "back home" and he imagined they had to do with the infinite ecological differences he was slowly growing accustomed to. These ranged from the understandable, such as undredged river fans that created unexpected shallows, to ash-belching volcanic islands that weren't even supposed to be there. Whatever had caused the life on this earth to take such a divergent evolutionary track was still hard at work doing the same with the planet. Therefore, he really had no idea what Keje meant by "stormy." By Matt's reckoning, they should be well into the wet monsoon season by now, when it could be expected to rain all day most days instead of just for a short time. But, for the last couple of weeks it had been drier than he'd have thought.

He reminded himself that "stormy" could mean anything to Keje. He hadn't been impressed by the tempest that raged during their most recent battle when they'd used a "grounded" *Big Sal* for bait. Several times he'd grumped that the plan would fail because no Grik would believe the storm was strong enough to drive *Salissa* onto the rocks. Of course, riding out a storm on *Big Sal* was probably exactly like doing so on one of the big new fleet carriers Matt had seen. *Walker* wasn't so fortunate. She rolled horribly and she was a very wet ship. Any storm seemed severe to those aboard her. The only consolation was that the colossal typhoons spawned in the deeper waters to the east shouldn't be much threat in the relatively shallow Java Sea. He'd never endured a typhoon, but he knew they could make the sometimes large hurricanes that occasionally struck his native Texas coast seem like a spring shower by comparison.

Today there was no storm, by anyone's definition. The sea was placid and the visibility infinite. To the east was the Gulf of Mandar, site of their most recent fight, and to the west he could barely see the tiny dark smudge of the Laurot Islands. The Kangean Islands still lay about a hundred and fifty miles to the south. They were far beyond the usual range of the fishing fleets and it still felt poignantly strange not to see the distant smoke of some wandering freighter or tanker plodding along in an everyday, workmanlike . . . reassuring way. The only ships they had reason to expect now were those of the enemy.

He stood on the signal bridge next to the fire-control platform and felt the firm, cooling breeze of *Walker*'s twenty knots on his face. Beside him stood Greg Garrett, respectfully but companionably silent. Together they viewed the vast panorama of the "task force" arrayed to starboard. *Walker* was steaming a zigzag course several miles in advance of the fleet, screening against enemy ships that might detect their advance. Five miles ahead of *Walker,* the ex-Grik ship, *Revenge,* tacked lazily in the light airs, serving as *Walker*'s advance picket. She was refitted to look just as she had for her former owners, and no Grik would flee from her. She would immediately signal *Walker* if she spotted anything in their path. If she somehow came to grips with the enemy before the four-stacker came to her aid, *Revenge* was well prepared to defend herself.

She sailed under the command of Ensign—now Lieutenant—Rick Tolson, who'd been a yachtsman before he joined the Navy and had even worked on a steel-hulled topsail schooner for a year. He was the closest thing they had to a true sailor, and he had Kas-Ra-Ar, Keje's cousin, as sailing master and second in command. Kas had been hesitant about accepting the title "sailing master" since that's what the great tail-less prophet who had taught Siska-Ta had been called; "Sa-lig Maa-stir." When it was explained to him (and many others) that "sailing master" was a position, not a name, he finally accepted the post with reverence and more pride than if he'd been given command. Matt thought that was appropriate and he suspected they'd helped form the foundation of a proud and unique naval tradition. He just hoped they hadn't set the stage for a blood feud between sailing masters and Sky Priests, since their duties were quite similar. More to the point, however, from a defensive standpoint, Rick's ship was equipped with twenty brand-new shiny bronze guns. They were twelve-pounders, much like the ones they'd made for the Marine landing force, except for the carriages and the bore diameter. Right now the guns crouched, hidden and secure, behind gun port doors that had been cut in the side of the ship. Any Grik that tangled with *Revenge* would be in for a dramatic surprise.

Matt gazed at her in the distance with a strange mix of pleasure and pride, tempered with an underlying sense of revulsion. Her classic lines appealed to the historian in him and her sailing qualities inspired respect—and, of course, he was proud they'd taken her—but he couldn't forget what he'd seen aboard her and what she represented. Nakja-Mur had christened her *Revenge* and everyone considered that an appropriate name. Baalkpan's High Chief had been given the honor of naming her for the simple reason that she was the property of the Baalkpan People. There was no precedent for prize ownership among the People, and it was generally assumed that she belonged to *Walker* and *Big Sal*, even though a large number of Baalkpan warriors had assisted in her capture. Keje and Matt quickly decided among themselves to present the prize to Nakja-Mur as a gift. That action served a variety of purposes. First, it allowed for a much quicker refit, since Baalkpan had far greater resources to devote to the project. (This was mainly just an excuse—Nakja-Mur had long since ceased to stint on anything they asked of him that pertained to the war effort.) There was also the touchy religious angle, which they rightly figured the Baalkpan High Chief could smooth out more easily—with his own people anyway— than either of them could.

Mainly, though, Matt and Keje wanted Baalkpan to have a real piece of the naval war. Most of the landing force were Baalkpans, and most of their supplies came from there. Baalkpan truly was the "arsenal" of the alliance. Despite that, there was no great floating presence that represented Baalkpan in the order of battle, and the way such things were reckoned by their quintessentially seagoing race, the greater share of honor fell to those whose very homes went in harm's way. *Revenge* more than satisfied that requirement of honor, since the plan called for her, the physical representative of Baalkpan, to be first in battle and perhaps even the key to the campaign's success.

Matt turned to stare back at the bulk of the fleet. Five of the "flat-top"-sized Homes lumbered slowly in their wake, screened by forty of the largest feluccas in Baalkpan's fishing fleet. Somehow, they'd managed to arm them all to some degree. The feluccas each carried at least one of the huge crossbow-type weapons that had usually been associated with the main armaments of Homes. In fact, most had come *from* the Homes. A few of the feluccas even carried small swivel guns that Letts thought to cast as antipersonnel weapons. The Homes—*Big Sal, Humfra-Dar, Aracca, Nerracca,* and sulky *Fristar*—were now each armed with ten of the larger guns like *Big Sal* had used to such effect off Celebes. Matt still couldn't believe Letts had pulled that off. He was proud of the former supply officer, who'd become the greatest logistics asset on the planet.

He smiled wryly at the argument Letts put up when he was told he'd worked himself out of a job and was too essential to the war effort to go on the expedition. He, along with a disconsolate Sergeant Alden, would command the Baalkpan defenses at Nakja-Mur's side and continue the good work. Together they would supervise the construction of fortifications and gun emplacements for the shore batteries and mortars that the foundry had turned to once the ships were armed.

The cannons had been an extraordinary achievement, but they had taken time, as had the other preparations necessary to mount the campaign. Two agonizing months had passed—had it been only six months since they passed through the Squall?—and Mallory's weekly reconnaissance flights showed that Aryaal still held, although the noose was tightening. He had also gotten a better idea of the forces involved. Thirty Grik ships, representing who knew how many thousands of invaders, were squeezing Aryaal now. A battle had been under way every time Ben flew.

Against that, the Allied Expeditionary Force carried six thousand warriors and Marines. That constituted almost half of Baalkpan's entire defensive force, male and female. Matt shook his head. He still couldn't get used to that. Instead of crying and waving good-bye from the pier, Lemurian females hitched up their sword belts and joined their "men" with their spear or crossbow on their shoulders. He had no doubt about their ability; he'd seen them fight. But it was possibly the most disconcerting thing he'd seen since he got here. He felt a rueful twinge. Sandra enthusiastically supported the idea of female warriors, once she got used to the concept, and it wasn't like she herself had exactly been sheltered from the dangers they all faced. But in her case, it wasn't as though that's the way things were *supposed* to be . . . He rubbed his chin and gave an exasperated sigh. It just didn't seem *right*. In any event, given the combination of artillery and disciplined tactics, he felt confident they could raise the siege and break through to the relief of the defenders. He just hoped it wouldn't be too late.

Garrett raised his hands and pressed the earphones more tightly to his head. He listened for a moment and then turned to Matt. "Lookout has the Catalina in sight, Skipper." Matt nodded calmly enough, but inside, he felt a supreme relaxation of tension. He hated it every time the plane flew out of sight for two reasons. First, it always carried a crew of bright, talented, and irreplaceable people whose chances of survival were poor at best if the plane was ever forced down. Also, dilapidated as it was, the PBY was the only airplane in this world, and it represented the greatest intelligence-gathering asset he had. It was an asset only if he used it, but that didn't mean he had to like it. The radio usually worked—and that helped a little—although it was strange to talk in the clear without fear of the enemy listening in! But radio or not, he couldn't shake his near-obsessive desire to preserve not just the crew but the plane itself. Important as this campaign was, he knew it was just a single campaign. Maybe it was a reflection of his still-smoldering bitterness over the lack of air cover for the Asiatic Fleet that reminded him you could take nothing for granted. But he couldn't throw off the premonition that if they used up the Catalina now, the day would come when they would really wish they hadn't.

In the meantime, he contented himself with a surge of relief over its safe return from this scout, at least, and he looked forward to hearing what Ben Mallory had seen. "Very well," he said. "Ask Lieutenant Dowden to close *Big Sal* and signal the fleet for all captains to repair aboard her for a conference. Please inform Captain Keje, with my respects; we'll come alongside as soon as they've hoisted the plane aboard. Ask him to rig hoses as well. I want to keep the bunkers topped off."

"Aye, aye, sir," Garrett replied and spoke into his mouthpiece.

Matt watched the PBY grow larger as it neared, its thundering engines loud and reassuringly smooth. Mallory waggled his wings as he roared by the destroyer and began a wide, banking descent that brought him down alongside *Big Sal*. Matt dropped down the ladder to the wooden strakes below and stepped into the pilothouse.

"Captain on the bridge!"

"As you were," replied Matt and smiled as the ship heeled into a tight turn toward the fleet. Juan, the diminutive but supremely dignified Filipino officer's steward, had just arrived with the midwatch coffee, and he was desperately attempting to stabilize the serving tray so the coffee wouldn't slide off onto the deck.

"Juan, Mr. Dowden and I will be crossing over to *Big Sal* at eighteen hundred. Would you present my compliments to Mr. Bradford and Lieutenant Tucker and ask them to accompany us?"

Juan finally got control of the carafe with an exasperated sigh as *Walker* steadied on her new heading. "Of course, Cap-tan Reddy. Might I recommend formal dress?"

Matt thought for a moment, then nodded, a grin stretching his face. "By all means, Juan. As formal as we can manage, at any rate. We must set an example." He glanced around at the quizzical expressions. "We *are* the flagship, after all!"

Lieutenant—now Lieutenant Commander—"Spanky" McFarlane stood in the aft fireroom with his hands on his skinny hips and his eyes closed. He was *feeling* the ship and her machinery around him. The Mice watched expressionlessly, but two of the new "monkey-cat" snipes stared at him with reverential awe, as if they were in the very presence of some diminutive but all-knowing God. He nodded with reserved satisfaction at what he sensed. The limited rehabilitation they'd managed to perform on *Walker*'s engineering plant had done wonders, sure enough. One of his biggest worries, gasket material for the ship's many leaky seals, seams, and steam lines had been laid to rest. A very satisfactory replacement had been found. They'd also replaced corroded fittings with newly cast brass ones, and all the working boilers had been rebricked. He worried about what they'd do when really serious stuff began to fail and their spares were exhausted—things like bearings, springs, etc.—but for now he figured his engines and boilers were in better shape than they'd been in years.

He opened his eyes and caught the big-eyed stares of the new "firemen" before they averted their gaze. He chuckled to himself. Damn, but he liked those little guys! With so many of the destroyer's understrength American crew assigned to such a wide range of projects and responsibilities—from the oil program and the rapid industrialization of Baalkpan to serving as gunnery officers aboard the Homes of the fleet—almost half of *Walker*'s complement was made up of Lemurian recruits. All of whom were duly sworn into the United States Navy. Of course, they had no real idea what the United States was, but their oaths were real enough. They sure weren't like the coolies on the China Station. *Walker* was their Home now, and every one of them felt fortunate to be serving aboard the most amazing vessel in the world. Where McFarlane might see tired iron and dilapidated equipment, they saw only wonders, and they did their work with a zeal and enthusiasm that no engineering officer of a four-stacker had probably ever seen. Those that became snipes certainly suffered, though, confined below in the hellish temperatures with their furry coats. None ever complained, but God, how they shed!

Spanky had figured few of them could take it in the fireroom, even aside from the heat. Lemurians were accustomed to open spaces and freedom of movement, even on their ships. Accordingly, he thought those who'd be willing to toil in the steamy confines below *Walker*'s decks would be few, but he'd been wrong. Ultimately, he turned many away. They *loved* working with the machinery, and no matter how hot it got, the elite few he accepted never grumbled.

They often followed him, surreptitiously, staring with blank fascination at a gauge he'd tapped with a finger or a pipe he'd felt with his palm, trying to divine what magical significance the act had held. He found it difficult not to laugh out loud at some of their antics of childlike wonder, but he always contained himself and maintained an expression of stern forbearance. Partly because he liked them, but also because he *needed* them. They were quick learners and cheerful workers, and even if it felt really weird being the object of semi-deification, he wasn't about to discourage them.

Even the Mice had gained a following, despite their irascible mannerisms. One of the young monkey-cats, a soot-gray female who'd worked at the well site, had followed them into the fireroom. Her name was Tab-At. They had, of course, immediately dubbed her "Tabby" in spite of the obvious fact she was female. Whether it was ignorance on their part or a conscious effort to block her full, rounded breasts from their consciousness was unknown. She followed them around like a devoted pet—which was pretty much how they treated her. Spanky suspected there was more to it than that, at least from her perspective. Chack told him his cousin—for that's what she was—admired their competence and interpreted their inscrutable manner as guarded wisdom. He shrugged mentally. Maybe they were wise; they were good at their jobs, but he was afraid all she'd learn from them was how to be a pain in the ass.

He admitted his suspicion in that regard was mostly due to his prejudice against *any* female in his fireroom. Chack's cousin or not (*all* Lemurians seemed to be related in some way, so what difference that made he hadn't figured out), she was still a *she*, and he wasn't happy about it at all. She worked as hard as any of the monkey-cat snipes, and her size and agility probably made her the best burner batter out of the entire native draft, but there was no getting around the fact that she was, well, a she.

The captain, with some reservations of his own, Spanky suspected, decreed that strict equality of the sexes would be observed at all times with regard to the new personnel. The Lemurians themselves made no distinctions in tasks or duties between the sexes, the sole exception, of course, being maternity. The captain told him that unless they wanted to offend their allies in a very fundamental way, they would do the same. Fine. Half-nude female monkey-cats capering around on deck with the rest of the apes was no concern of his, but this was the goddamn boiler room! Tempers—and passions!—ran high down here in the heat, and the presence of any female of any species only served, in his view, to highlight the frustrations they all felt in that regard.

What made things even worse, if that was possible, was if you could get past the soot-gray fur and long catlike ears, the feline face and clawed paws and feet . . . yeah, well, and the tail too, Tab-At was kind of cute. As soon as that thought registered in Spanky's mind, he realized everyone else in engineering—with the possible curious exception of the Mice—had undoubtedly already thought it, particularly after the much-speculated-upon possible affair between Silva and Risa-Sab-At. He determined then that everyone in *his* division at least, regardless of the heat, would By God wear clothes. If Gray wanted to let them run around on deck with nothing but a skirt, that was his lookout. But not down here!

Spanky had hoped, with a guilty twinge, his decision would make Tab-At strike for a berth in the deck division; there was no question she'd be more uncomfortable. No such luck. The next time he saw her she was wearing a T-shirt that, to his horror, actually accentuated her breasts by concealing the fur, which made them appear even more human! Someone had even gone so far as to give her a pair of trousers with a hole in the seat for her tail. He'd never required that—since a 'Cat's tail made breeches impractical. He realized he was being mocked and finally gave up.

That didn't mean he had to like it, and as he looked at her now, standing with the Mice as they monitored the feed water and the fuel flow, he saw her watching him. She didn't look away like the others, and he didn't sense abashed worshipfulness either. Nor did he detect any hostility over his persecution of her. She wore . . . a look of amused triumph. He sighed, and then grinned at her. She at least knew he didn't know everything.

*   *   *

Matt sat on one of Keje's humble wooden stools in *Big Sal*'s Great Hall. With the exception of Keje, Lieutenant Tucker, and himself, everyone—including Courtney Bradford—lounged comfortably on the overstuffed pillows in a loose group around the ubiquitous table near the base of the great tree that dominated the ornate compartment. Larry Dowden, the only one not seated, stood near a hastily drawn map supported on the table so all could see. Matt shifted uncomfortably on the hard stool and wished, once again, he'd brought a chair of his own. He could've used one of the cushions, he supposed, but that would have made him feel even less at ease. He noted with arched-brow amusement that Lieutenant Mallory felt no similar reservations. The exhausted aviator was sprawled on a particularly deep and soft cushion and seemed to be having difficulty staying awake.

It had been a long day for Ben and his crew. They'd flown out of Baalkpan early that morning to make a final aerial observation of the objective. For the first time, Mallory was allowed to fly directly over the city—and the enemy forces. His observations weren't reassuring. Almost forty Grik ships were now in the bay before Surabaya and they'd dispatched a sizable landing force. Unlike Baalkpan, the defenders had a sturdy wall all around their city, with what appeared to be formidable defenses. But the Grik army was more than large enough to encircle most of the settlement. The only exception to complete investiture was a stretch of waterfront and a portion of the bay between the city and the island of Madura, about three miles from the mainland. A large assemblage of native small craft was concentrated in the passage, and another fortification, as yet unengaged, was constructed on the point of land on the island closest to Surabaya. A dense cloud of smoke from burning buildings—probably set alight by what everyone was calling Grik Fire—hung over everything, and Mallory couldn't see much detail. But this time there was no question whether the Grik saw the PBY.

Matt disliked allowing the plane to be seen by the enemy, but they had to know what they faced. Perhaps the unnatural thundering apparition that swooped low overhead had unnerved the Grik, Matt consoled himself. In order to avoid doing the same to the Aryaalans, Mallory's

crew had dropped hundreds of "pamphlets" over the defenders' main
position. These pamphlets consisted of light wooden shakes etched
with a Lemurian phrase that said: "Your brothers to the north will aid
you. We bring powerful friends. Do not fear." It was all they could do to
assure the defenders help was on the way. With his mission complete,
Mallory returned to join the task force. Tomorrow, he would fly back to
Baalkpan, since they dared not risk the plane in the fight to come. Once
there, he'd stay in radio contact with *Walker*.

Sandra Tucker sat primly at Matt's side, also on one of the stools, and
showed no discomfort whatsoever. He wondered what she was thinking. He'd come to rely more and more on her intuition as time went
by, but he had to admit he also just liked having her around. They'd
evolved an unspoken understanding after they declared their love for
one another. Aboard ship, a wall of strict propriety always stood between them in spite of their mutual attraction. They thought they hid it
well. But sometimes when they were alone, a more . . . comfortable . . .
familiarity existed between them. They both felt compelled to restrict
any further exploration of their feelings, and Matt felt almost guilty
that they shared as much as they did when the rest of the men had
no prospects at all . . . unless you believed Silva and Risa really . . . He
shook his head. Perhaps someday they'd find more people; even the Lemurian legends hinted at the possibility, but right now there was a war
to fight. Terrible as it was, at least it had released some of the pressure-
cooker tension caused by the "dame famine."

In the meantime, for the sake of the men, Matt and Sandra must
control their passions. That didn't mean Matt intended to ignore her
excellent insight. He leaned over and whispered in her ear: "What do
you think of that Anai-Sa?" he asked, referring to the High Chief of the
Fristar Home. The black-furred Lemurian had arrived at the conference late, as usual, and now sat hunched on a cushion in sulky disdain
while the rest of the attendees finished the refreshments that were a
prerequisite to any council.

"I think he only volunteered so he could get the cannons that were
promised to the Homes that take part in the campaign," she whispered

back. "I don't trust him. I hope you don't have to rely on him for a critical assignment."

Matt nodded. Anai-Sa had been the most outspoken proponent of just packing up and sailing off, but to possess the power of the guns was a mighty incentive to hypocrisy. "Do you have any less vague impressions about our other commanders?" he asked with heavy irony.

A quiet chuckle escaped her, but she nodded. "They seem pretty solid for the most part. You know you can count on Rick, on *Revenge*, and Keje, of course." She paused, considering. "I really like Ramic-Sa-Ar of *Aracca* and Tassat-Ay-Aracca of *Nerracca*."

"They're father and son, aren't they?" Matt asked, referring to the pair of Lemurians who sat close together talking animatedly among themselves. There was certainly a strong resemblance. The younger one seemed a virtual replica of the older.

"Yes," she confirmed, "and Tassat is actually younger than Anai, even though you could hardly tell by the way they act." She sniffed. "As far as Geran-Eras of *Humfra-Dar*, it's hard to say." She was referring to the only female High Chief present. "She's been a vocal supporter of the expedition from the start," Sandra continued. "You may even remember her showing rather . . . energetic approval of your plan?"

Matt did remember then, and cringed. Even Lemurian females had surprising upper body strength, and Geran-Eras had actually embraced him after he made his pitch for the relief of Surabaya. He was sure she'd almost cracked some ribs.

"I think, as your Mr. Silva would say, 'she has more than one dog in this hunt.' Adar told me her mate and one of her children were killed in a Grik attack right before they came to Baalkpan. Might've even been one of the ships we destroyed, so she *really* likes you. Also, I imagine she sees this expedition as a chance for revenge. You might need to keep an eye on her."

Matt nodded soberly and glanced around. The refreshments had been consumed and Keje was looking at him expectantly. "Better get started," he said to Sandra, and cleared his throat. "Ladies and gentlemen," he began aloud. "We have a battle to plan."

*   *   *

Standing on *Walker*'s bridge with his binoculars raised, Matt reflected that his return to Surabaya wasn't altogether unlike his departure so long ago. Once again, the clouds above the distant city glowed and flickered with the reflected light of fires caused by an enemy bombardment. This time, the spectacle was all the more surreal. *Walker*'s blowers roared at a pitch consistent with her ten knots, but in spite of that, even at this distance, the loud *whump* and overpressure of Japanese bombs would have been felt and heard. Instead, only an eerie silence accompanied the distant battle. They'd opened the bay from the east at 0120 and picked their way carefully through the Sapudi Islands, which were scattered haphazardly there. The last time Matt traversed these waters, *Walker* had had the services of a fat Dutch pilot, and Matt wondered suddenly where the man was now. Had he even survived? He banished the thought. All *Walker* had this time was a waning crescent moon. Of course, this time there was no minefield either.

As they drew closer, they could discern the stern lanterns of dozens of Grik ships moored in the bay, close to the city. All were ablaze with light and all rode secure at their anchors, never suspecting any threat might descend from the sea. A few, closer in, kept up a continuous desultory bombardment with their catapults, flinging "Grik Fire" bombs toward shore. Sputtering trails of fire arced high in the air and hung seemingly motionless for a moment, then plummeted down near or behind the walls of the defenders. Usually, a red gout of flame mushroomed upward into the sky. The festive, brightly lit ships in the bay provided a stark contrast to the suffering inside the city beyond.

Matt carefully refocused the binoculars dead ahead, watching one Grik ship in particular. Alone among its identical sisters, this one was under plain sail, creeping slowly among its brethren on a light southerly wind. Apparently accepted without fanfare as yet another reinforcement, the ship with the unusual blue glass in its lanterns moved deep into the enemy formation. Matt marked its progress by that blue light that identified it as *Revenge*.

He stepped onto the bridgewing and glanced aft. The Homes were hanging in there, totally darkened, as was *Walker*. He could see the occasional flash of white water alongside them as the hundred mighty sweeps propelled each huge ship forward at close to the ten knots *Walker* was making. He marveled yet again at the strength and determination that took. *Fristar* was lagging behind the others, leaving a small but growing gap between her and *Humfra-Dar,* but otherwise his "battle line" was holding together. The shoal of feluccas brought up the rear. He stepped back into the pilothouse and resumed his post beside his chair.

The bridge watch was silent other than an occasional whispered command, and he felt a tension that was different from any he'd sensed since the battle of the Makassar Strait. Like that night, there was fear and tension, but there was also a certain . . . predatory eagerness. A realization that they'd caught their overwhelming enemy with his britches down, coupled with a determination to make him pay. General quarters had been sounded long ago, and all stations were manned and ready except the torpedo director. Sandison's "torpedo project" to repair the two condemned torpedoes they'd filched from a warehouse in Surabaya was still on hold, and they wouldn't be using any of the three "definites" tonight. Sandison and his torpedomen had filled out the crews of the numbers one and four guns.

Matt turned to Lieutenant Shinya, who was in quiet conversation with Courtney Bradford. "Assemble your riflemen amidships and hold them as a reserve for any point of contact if the enemy try to board," Matt instructed. Virtually everyone topside had a rifle handy, but at their stations, the crew was too spread out to mass their small-arms fire. Shinya saluted him with a serious expression and turned to comply with the order. It would be the first time he'd commanded any of the destroyermen in action, and his self-consciousness was evident. He was directly in charge of close defense of the ship and had half a dozen Americans assigned to his reserve. Matt doubted there'd be any friction. Most of the destroyermen still didn't like him, but his abilities were evident. Some had even begun to consider him just another part of *Walker*'s increasingly diverse extended family. They never would forgive the Japanese, but Shinya wasn't just a Jap anymore. Besides, they were all on the same side now. It even seemed as though Dennis Silva kind of liked the former enemy lieutenant, and if Silva would put up with him, the rest of the crew certainly could.

"Be careful, Lieutenant," Matt cautioned as Shinya departed the bridge.

"Not long now, I should think," commented Bradford when they were alone. Matt nodded. He hadn't really wanted the Australian on the bridge during the action. He would have preferred that Bradford stay in the wardroom with Sandra, but the man had practically insisted. Chief Gray had just as "practically" offered to force him to go below, but the captain allowed him to remain. It was probably better this way. In spite of his peculiar manner, Bradford often made valuable observations, and Matt had to admit it was sometimes refreshing to have a sounding board close at hand who was apart from the official chain of command. It would have been unthinkable for him to ask one of his bridge watch for advice, but since Bradford was a civilian, no one would even raise an eyebrow if he did the same with him. Especially in matters of diplomacy or anthropology. Those were two subjects that, if they were lucky, they might need Bradford's expertise on that night.

They closed to within two hundred yards of the first Grik ship, and Matt couldn't believe they'd remained unnoticed, even as darker shapes against the starlit horizon. Of course, he knew nothing about Grik night vision, but their own lights were certainly enough to spoil a human's, if not a Lemurian's. *Revenge* was so far inside the enemy formation now that her distinctive light no longer distinguished her. Could it be that *everyone* from the ships had gone ashore? Or were they just that arrogant? Certainly *Revenge* would be challenged soon! Almost as if in answer to his unspoken question, a series of bright flashes erupted from within the enemy fleet, and a moment later the sound of a rolling broadside shattered the fragile quiet of the bay. According to the plan, *Revenge* was to sail as close as she could to the city, and very ostentatiously attack the enemy within clear view of the defenders. Failing that, she would open fire as soon as she was discovered. Matt had no idea which had occurred, but regardless, her fire was the signal for the rest of the allied force to attack.

"Signal the fleet!"

A bright red flare soared high above from the fire-control platform and exploded, leaving tendrils of fluttering sparks.

"Inform Mr. Garrett he may commence firing all guns under local control," Matt instructed the talker. "Pointers are to aim at the water-lines and disable as many ships as they can, but make every shot count!" The last was merely repeating what Garrett had already said to his gun crews, but it never hurt to remind them. Soon they'd be able to manu-facture simple solid copper projectiles for the four-inch guns that ought to fire accurately enough on top of a charge of black powder, but they were still quite a ways from producing high-explosive rounds, and the war had just begun.

The searchlight above the fire-control platform sprang to life, its brilliant beam lashing the darkness, illuminating the targets ahead. Grotesque figures raced about on the enemy ships, or just stood, star-ing back at them in blinded shock. The number one gun on the fo'c'sle spoke first, with its door-slamming *crack,* and a large section amidships of the ship directly ahead of them disintegrated when the round ex-ploded. Number two fired immediately after and the shot was rewarded by another explosion close aboard. In the distance, they heard *Revenge*'s twelve-pounders pouring it on. Behind them, the battle line relentlessly advanced.

Walker's job was to blow a hole through the Grik anchorage through which the battle line would follow, pounding ships to either side with their massive guns. The primary objective was the "safe" zone between the city and Madura. There, they would land their troops. The second-ary objective was to kill Grik and sink their ships. Since the secondary objective was essential to the success of the first, *Walker* set to with a will.

The night became a hellish maelstrom of explosions and muzzle flashes as *Walker* slashed through her unsuspecting prey. Tracers arced from machine-gun positions and deluged ships with splinters, lead, and shattered, jagged body parts. The enemy's very bones became projectiles as more and more shocked and groggy Grik surged from belowdecks, adding themselves to the packed targets. The three-inch gun on the fantail pumped star shells into the sky, casting a weird, ethereal light on the battle below, even further terrifying the enemy. Another Grik ship blew up, then another. One exploded violently, its store of Grik Fire probably going up, and furiously burning debris rained down on other ships anchored nearby, setting them alight as well. The gun crews performed their intricate ballet of death, the pointers and trainers madly spinning their wheels to keep each gun pointed at whatever target the gun captain had designated. Matt saw Dennis Silva, captain of number one, bellowing and capering with glee each time a shot went home. Lemurian shell men scampered back and forth keeping the breech fed while others with leather gloves snatched up the precious, still-hot shell casings and collected them in baskets before they rolled over the side. All the while, they whooped and hollered and shouted encouragement to one another in two different languages.

The panic created by the ferocity and total surprise of the attack was complete, at least on the nearest ships. A few cut their cables and tried to make sail, but most were too shocked even for that and they died under the bright glare of the stabbing searchlight or burned to death when their ships went up like piles of dried leaves. And then the battle line struck and the destruction took on a less frenzied but more methodical pace as the larger ships delivered broadside after broadside at point-blank range. *Walker* dashed on, zigzagging through the densely packed forest of masts and hammering anything her guns would bear upon.

"Ahead slow!" Matt yelled from the starboard wing. "Come right twenty degrees!" A Grik ship, sails flapping, had run afoul of its neighbor in its haste to escape, and now the two of them blocked the channel that led to *Revenge*. Beyond the snarl, Matt saw the ship with the blue lights pounding enemies on either side.

"Captain Reddy!" Bradford shouted, pointing. Another ship loomed in the darkness to starboard and *Walker*'s knife-sharp bow was swinging directly for it.

"All stop! Full astern. Left full rudder!"

The ship groaned in protest, the strakes vibrating violently beneath Matt's feet as the turbines were reversed and the screws bit deep to arrest the forward inertia. The gunners on the fo'c'sle stopped firing for a moment and watched as *Walker*'s bull nose swung ever so slowly away from the collision that had seemed imminent. Matt watched too, mesmerized, his knuckles turning white as he clutched the rail. Ponderously, his ship slowed to a stop less than a dozen feet from the enemy's head-rails. Grik stood watching, from a pistol shot's distance, equally horrified. But not for long. As soon as they saw the collision had been avoided, they sprang into action. Crossbow bolts thumped against *Walker*'s plates, gouging the paint and ricocheting into the dark. Red tracers from just overhead played across the enemy fo'c'sle as *Walker* backed away. A man went down on the foredeck, and another.

"Right full rudder!" Matt yelled to the helmsman. "Replacements to the number one gun!"

The number two gun fired into the Grik from a distance of less than fifty yards, and the shell detonated within the forward part of the ship. An instant later, a massive secondary explosion knocked Matt and Courtney Bradford against the chart house bulkhead, shattering the windows on the starboard side of the pilothouse. Large wooden fragments rained down on *Walker*'s deck, and the high-pitched, catlike wail of an injured Lemurian rose from forward. Matt shook his head to clear the ringing in his ears and blinked his eyes. Bradford was staring, stunned, at a foot-long splinter embedded in his left biceps. Jamie Miller, the pharmacist's mate, was below, shouting at a detail of Lemurian stretcher bearers to clear the wounded off the foredeck. Matt lurched to his feet and shouted down at him. "Miller, Mr. Bradford is wounded, but I think he can walk. Please escort him below." He turned and gently helped the disoriented Australian to his feet. "I'm afraid you'll have to go to the wardroom now, Courtney. I'll send for you if I need you."

Bradford's expression was wan and there was sweat on his forehead. He'd lost his hat. "Yes. Of course, Captain. Please do."

Matt looked back at the Grik ship that blew up in their face. *Must've been more of their bombs,* he thought. It was sinking now, quickly, by the bow. "All stop," he called into the pilothouse. "All ahead slow, rudder amidships."

For an instant, Matt was able to take quick stock. The way ahead was still blocked, but the number three gun had turned the tangled ships into so much sinking junk. Soon they could go *over* them, if the water was deep enough. Silva, his T-shirt torn and bloody, was directing replacement gunners into their positions. Aft, the battle line advance had slowed to a crawl as its ships couldn't resist pounding as many of the enemy as they could as they passed. Keje and *Big Sal,* in the lead, were no less guilty of the distraction than the others. Burning and sinking Grik Indiamen were everywhere and the dense smoke made his eyes water as he viewed the spectacle.

From his vantage point, however, he could also see that the enemy was recovering from the shock. Some ships had made sail and were attempting to escape, but others were trying to move in close, in typical Grik fashion, so they could grapple and board. Those that did would be in for a surprise when their under-strength crews went to face Lemurian Guards and Marines, but that wasn't the point. The first priority was to get those troops ashore. Matt spoke to his talker. "Signal *Big Sal* and tell her to step on it. If they fool around killing Grik too long, we're going to get cut off from each other and we'll have to shoot up the lane again. We don't have the ammunition to spare." *I bet it is hard for them, though,* he thought, *to quit killing their Ancient Enemy when it's this easy. They have met the boogeyman, and he is theirs,* he misquoted to himself.

"Aye, aye . . . Captain? The lookout says *Revenge* is in a little trouble."

Matt grabbed his binoculars and scanned ahead, past the quickly sinking "obstacle." *Revenge* was still engaged with ships on either side, both of which were little more than drifting hulks by now. But two other enemy ships had closed with her. As he watched, one threw a firebomb that barely missed. Other bombs were flying now too, and one struck the water off the port beam and whooshed into a wall of flame as it ruptured. An icy tendril of dread raced down Matt's spine.

"Expedite that signal!" he prompted. *If we give the lizards time to get their act together, they'll burn us all,* he thought grimly. Another bomb broke against *Revenge*'s side and a pool of flame spread across her deck. Her guns fell silent as their crews raced to extinguish the fire. "Have Mr. Garrett concentrate all guns that will bear upon those ships nearest to *Revenge!*" he shouted at the talker. The range was just under six hundred yards, and the guns were in local control. Even so, one of the four-inch-fifties hit just under the foremast of a Grik ship that was trying to cross *Revenge*'s stern and throw a bomb down her length. Much like the ship that had blown up beside them, it exploded with an unexpected violence, sending flaming debris and timbers in all directions. The masts slumped toward one another and then teetered into the sea. A plume of flame roared skyward and was quickly quenched as the ship abruptly sank from view. Its lightly damaged companion was trying to perform the same maneuver ahead of *Revenge,* but it fell away to leeward and then heeled hard over and came to a sudden stop as it ran aground.

A bomb landed close alongside *Walker,* and burning liquid washed across her deck plates forward of the aft deckhouse where the number three torpedo mount had been. Matt heard a high-pitched scream. Whipping his head around, he saw a figure, engulfed in flames, stagger to the railing and leap into the sea. "God almighty!" he breathed in horrified prayer. He had no idea if it was an American or a Lemurian, but it didn't really matter just then. Everyone aboard *Walker* was part of her crew. Smoke billowed from burning paint and whatever noxious substance the Grik used in their bombs as hoses played on the fire. The number two gun fired, its muzzle trained far out over the side.

Then, just as *Walker* broke into the clear and began to race through the open lane toward where *Revenge* continued pounding her helpless foes, Matt felt something under his feet that he knew was entirely wrong. It began as a violent bump that shook the ship from stem to stern and rapidly became a sickening vibration that grew with every instant. "All stop!" he shouted, and he raced to the comm, disdaining his talker. Even before he could press the TALK button for engineering, Spanky's voice, terse with stress, came to them over the speaker.

"Lieutenant Commander McFarlane here," he said. "I think we've thrown a blade on the port screw and I've secured the shaft. What happened? Did we hit something?"

Sure enough, the terrible vibration had ceased as quickly as it began, while *Walker*'s speed diminished. Matt hesitated a moment, pondering, before he replied. "I think we probably did. Probably a sunken ship. How soon can I have the starboard engine back?" he asked.

"Right now, Skipper, but just remember we only have one left!"

The captain's lips turned upward slightly in a small grin of relief. "Thanks, Spanky. I'll watch where I'm going from now on." He stepped back from the bulkhead and turned to the bridge watch, his face impassive once more. "Starboard engine, ahead two-thirds!" With an unbalanced, rattling groan, *Walker* resumed her course toward *Revenge*.

The crew of their captured ship greeted them with joyous cheering as they neared, the last of her adversaries still settling to the bottom nearby. They'd made it through the gauntlet. Together, *Walker* and *Revenge* positioned themselves so their broadsides could support the battle line as it emerged to join them. This disposition was doubly suitable to *Revenge*, because it allowed her to deliver murderous fire from her steaming-hot guns into the stern of the helplessly grounded Grik ship. For just an instant as he watched, a tiny fragment of pity toward the defenseless enemy crept into Matt's consciousness, but it was fleeting. The far more powerful and lingering sentiment of visceral loathing quickly banished it, prompted by a mental image of what he'd seen in *Revenge*'s hold the stormy evening they'd taken her. Not to mention the tense apprehension that still consumed him over the discovery of the human skull. To the Grik, there was no question of surrender, and it was horrifyingly clear how they treated *their* prisoners. Suddenly Matt felt vaguely ashamed he was even capable of pitying them.

Clusters of feluccas began to break through, their speed and maneuverability serving them well in their passage through the chaos. The entire bay was awash in flames, the scope of destruction awe-inspiring.

A number of ships continued burning furiously, and many more Grik were so involved in preventing their own ships from catching fire, they were unable to contribute to the fight. Matt knew *Walker* had savaged them and he had no idea how many Grik she'd sunk. The number of burning ships was surprising even so, and he realized some of them must have set fire to each other, flinging their bombs haphazardly in the midst of battle.

The battle line was almost through to them now, their massive guns spitting hate at the Ancient Enemy, blasting great gaping holes in hulls and smashing masts and bodies on any vessel that dared draw near. Some still did, regardless of damage, in the predictable Grik style. The very waters of the bay burned with Grik Fire as bomb after bomb exploded against the stout, scorched sides of the Homes or spilled their burning contents onto the sea. Any fires that were started on the great wooden fortresses were quickly extinguished, and very little had been left exposed that would burn. The decks were soaked before the battle and the huge fabric wings had been stowed, leaving only the massive sweep-oars for propulsion. One by one, the blackened and smoldering but otherwise unscathed leviathans crashed through the final obstacles separating them from *Walker* and *Revenge* and slowly took up positions lengthening the line with their port batteries bearing on the bay.

Even then they continued to fire, without nearly as great an effect at the increased range, but with just as much determination. The surviving Grik that could began to flee. At least half the enemy's fleet of forty ships had been destroyed, and most of those remaining afloat were damaged to varying degrees. Matt was tempted to allow *Walker*'s main battery to continue firing, but he knew he had to conserve ammunition. This was but the opening stroke, and he inwardly cringed at his expectation of what they had expended.

"Cease firing," he said, but the guns had already fallen silent, probably at Garrett's command. After the noise and turmoil of battle, his voice sounded strange . . . disassociated. He glanced at his watch and experienced the usual sense of disorientation when he realized the seemingly hours-long battle had lasted less than forty minutes. The rest of the fleet's cannonade became more desultory as the remaining targets drew away, and a great tide of cheering voices from thousands of throats rose and washed over him.

Larry Dowden appeared at his side. He'd been at his battle station on the aft deckhouse and was black with soot and sweat from the fire that came too close. He stood with Matt and stared at the scene of destruction as the roar of exultation continued. "Even better than Balikpapan . . . in the old war," he finally managed. His voice held a trace of wonder. Matt nodded. The enormity of the victory was beginning to sink in. "This even *feels* better," Dowden continued. "God knows I hate the Japs . . . except Shinya, I guess, but he's the proof. At least Japs are *people*. This feels more like . . . killing snakes."

Matt looked at him and grinned, shaking his head. "Mr. Dowden, shame on you! To insult snakes in such a way!"

"Captain," interrupted the talker, "Mr. Garrett says . . . He says you should go to the starboard wing, sir." Exchanging puzzled glances, Matt and Dowden complied. Several of the watch were already there, staring over the water at the walled city that reflected the light of the burning ships in the bay. It was an impressive sight. Matt had become so accustomed to the strange Oriental-style bamboo architecture of Baalkpan that the far more conventional, even vaguely medieval European design of this world's Surabaya struck him as more exotic than it once would have. He looked at Garrett, who was leaning over the rail above.

"What is it, Mr. Garrett?"

"Listen, sir," he said, almost shouting, and pointed at the city. Matt turned back toward shore and strained his ears to hear over the cheering. He couldn't imagine what it was that Garrett wanted him to hear over—then it hit him. The cheering of the fleet wasn't just echoing off the walls of the city, it was being answered from within! Even at this distance, and in the dark, he saw hundreds of figures standing on the walls, waving banners and weapons in triumph and shouting their defiance to the massive Grik army encamped outside their walls. From that army there came only a shocked, sullen silence.

Matt clasped his hands behind his back and strained to keep his relief in check. Underlying all the concerns he'd felt over the meeting with the Grik had been not knowing how the people here would receive them. They'd still have to guard against friction, but for now . . . "It seems the Aryaalans are glad to see us after all, wouldn't you say, Mr. Dowden?" His statement was met with a few hopeful chuckles.

"Captain!" cried the talker, who'd come as close as his cord would allow. "Lookout says there's a small boat coming up to starboard!"

Matt heard the bolt rack back on the .30-cal above his head. "Hold your fire!" he shouted, looking up. "Mr. Garrett, inform all stations to hold fire!" He turned and peered into the darkness that lay between them and the shore. The blazing wrecks threw a lot of light on the fleet and the fortress, but the space between them was in shadow, cast by the battle line. Even so, he saw what looked like a barge approaching from landward. It was about thirty feet long and broad in the beam. There were six banks of oars on each side and they rose and dipped with admirable precision. "Get Chack up here, on the double," he said, glancing forward. In less than twenty seconds, Chack and Chief Gray were both beside him. Matt was looking through his binoculars and when he noticed their arrival, he handed the glasses to Chack. "What do you make of them?" Chack looked through the binoculars, mainly because he liked to. He didn't really need them to see who was approaching.

"Aryaalans, Captain," he said simply. Then he looked at Matt, inscrutable and expressionless as always, but he was blinking a sequence reserved for surprise. Intense surprise. "And others."

Matt had started to turn and issue an order, but stopped and looked back at Chack. "What do you . . . ? Just a moment." He did turn then. "Signal the fleet 'Well done' and compliments. Also, all battle line captains please report aboard *Walker*. They can send a representative if they have damage or other pressing concerns." His gaze returned to Chack. "What were you saying?"

Chack wordlessly handed the binoculars back. Slightly annoyed, Matt raised them once more. The boat was much closer now, and even as he looked, he heard several exclamations of surprise from some of those crowding with him on the bridgewing.

The first thing he noticed was the Aryaalans themselves. He was struck by how different they appeared from the Lemurians he was used to. Counting the rowers, there were sixteen or seventeen of them on the barge, and almost all of them had dark-colored pelts. It was impossible in the dim light to tell exactly what color they were, but he had an impression of sable. That was unusual enough, since no two Lemurians he'd met were precisely the same color. And yet the differences didn't end there. The People they'd grown accustomed to—Spanky's efforts notwithstanding—wore as little clothing as they could get away with—usually just a kilt. The people who approached were quite well-appointed. Even the rowers wore platter-like copper helmets—not unlike the steel ones Matt's own destroyermen wore at stations—as well as thick leather, knee-length smocks.

What appeared to be "officers" or dignitaries stood clustered on a platform near the back of the boat, resplendent in robes and highly polished bronze armor. Feather plumes adorned their helmets, and unlike their seafaring cousins who generally kept their facial fur cropped short, these creatures sported long, flowing manes that outlined their aggressive features. All of these impressions became a whirlwind of peripheral detail when he noticed the two individuals on the platform with the four potentates.

"My God."

An hour later, they all sat in the hastily cleared wardroom. The casualties were mercifully few, but they'd encompassed the extremes, being mostly either slight or fatal. The victim of the fire had been a Lemurian whose name Matt didn't know, but they'd also lost Andy Powell, ordnance striker on the number one gun. Tom Felts and Gil Olivera were wounded, but so slightly that they'd already returned to duty. Two other Lemurian crew folk had been hurt, and after patching them up and applying the magical antiseptic paste, Sandra bundled them off to their racks. Bradford's wound was a little more serious and had actually required surgery to remove the jagged splinter from his arm. He sat with them now, however, the very picture of the modest wounded hero, with his arm heavily bandaged and in a sling.

Also seated in the cramped compartment were two of the Suraba-yans, or more properly Aryaalans, which was their name for themselves. There had evidently been no assimilation of European chart names here. Whether there had been any early contact at all remained to be seen. The younger of the two was Prince Rasik-Alcas, only son of King Fet-Alcas and heir to the Aryaalan throne. It took a little while for Matt to understand that. He'd picked up a smattering of the 'Cat tongue, but even though Keje assured him the Aryaalans spoke the same basic lan-guage, the dialect was so different he couldn't follow it at all.

Prince Rasik spoke little, however, leaving most of the talking to the older visitor. His name was Lord Muln-Rolak, and he was obviously used to talking quite a lot. Of the two, he radiated a less arrogant air, although he certainly possessed one. To look at him, it had been earned. Unlike that of his young prince, Rolak's pelt was crisscrossed with fur of lighter shades, suggesting a great many battle scars beneath. He looked, spoke, and carried himself like a consummate feline predator. A predator that was getting along in years, perhaps, but was deadly nevertheless.

Keje, Geran, Ramic, Tassat, and Rick were all there, as command-ers of the battle line. Anai-Sa had not deigned to come but had sent a cousin in his stead who seemed to have learned manners from his High Chief. Right now, he merely sat apart from everyone else and peered out the porthole at the fires on the bay.

And then there were the others. Seated at the far end of the table, hands wrapped around two precious Cokes from the refrigerated ma-chine beside the galley door, were Bosun's Mate Frankie Steele and Lieutenant James Ellis, captain of USS *Mahan*. Expressions of wonder were still fixed on their haggard faces.

Except for a few quick, incredulous words of greeting, Matt learned only that *Mahan* still floated and had been here only a short time. Not long enough to accomplish anything like what *Walker* had at Baalkpan. The two men had been joyous but cryptic, and Matt could hardly wait for the current meeting to end, important as it was, so he could learn more of *Mahan*'s tale. Judging by the appearance of Ellis and Steele, it had been a hard one. Both men's uniforms were badly stained and battered, and a dreadful experience of some sort seemed to haunt their eyes. Jim still limped too, and Matt remembered that Captain Kaufman had shot his friend. He returned his attention to Lord Rolak, who was speaking.

"They will certainly attack at dawn." Keje translated for him. "They attack most days, but after tonight . . ." He shrugged in a very human way. "They will certainly come and I doubt they will stop this time. I propose that your"—the Aryaalan lord actually sneered slightly—"warriors join ours in the defensive positions. They should take direction from our captains, of course."

Matt suddenly found all of his commanders' eyes on him as Keje told him what Lord Rolak had said. He answered their unspoken question with a single word.

"No."

For just a moment, after Keje relayed the response, there was an uncomfortable silence. Prince Rasik finally spoke up. "This . . . creature speaks for you all?"

Keje grunted and answered in an ominous tone. "He does. He not only speaks for us, he commands us for the duration of this campaign." He gestured angrily toward the porthole. "In case you did not notice, we swept your little bay clear for you this night. He was the architect of that."

Lord Rolak shifted, and visibly regrouped his argument. "Your victory tonight was impressive," he hedged, "but you are sea folk. Surely you see the wisdom of letting land folk lead when a fight is on land. Aryaalans are a warrior race. The warrior's way is bred into us and nurtured in us as younglings. You sea folk do not even fight unless you have to! We have the experience . . . !"

"It seems to me that you were about to experience defeat, Lord Rolak," Bradford interrupted quietly. "What is your estimate of the forces arrayed against you?"

Rolak was quiet for a moment as he looked around the table. Finally he sighed. "There are, perhaps, fifteen thousands of the enemy." Matt nodded when the translation came. That was consistent with Mallory's estimate of the enemy force.

"How many warriors do you have to face them?" Matt brutally cut to the heart of the matter. If the Grik truly were going to attack at dawn, there was no time for this foolishness. Rolak answered him in a slightly more subdued tone.

"King Alcas has twenty-four hundred warriors in the city, fit for battle. Queen Maraan from B'mbaado Island across the water has sent another six hundreds to our aid."

"She should have sent more!" seethed the young prince, speaking for the second time since his introduction.

Rolak looked at him. "We are lucky she sent anything at all! Do you forget we were at war with her before the Grik came?" Rolak shrugged again and glanced at the others around the table. "War is a . . . pastime . . . among my people. That is why we are so good at it." He paused and his tone subtly changed. "It is different this time. The Grik do not follow the rules. They do not *have* rules. No truce is accepted. There is no parley, no discussion of aims or demands, and . . . no respect for the dead." His tail swished and he blinked outrage. "They eat fallen warriors, you know, whenever we cannot recover them. Sometimes they even stop fighting long enough to feed . . ." Quickly controlling himself, he glanced at all of them, but Matt in particular. "I know it is difficult for sea folk to understand, but perhaps not so much for you, Cap-i-taan Reddy." He gestured toward the far end of the table, where the long-lost destroyermen sat. "We have learned more from your friends than they know. We know that their great iron vessel, so much like this one, is very powerful despite its wounds. We also know your people surely fight each other. How else could it have suffered such wounds but by battling against others like yourselves? To Aryaalans, war is . . ." He smiled slightly, searching for the proper word. "Play?" He tried it, and seemed satisfied with the fit. "I suppose you could say we fight as much for entertainment as anything else. We fight for trade concessions, to elevate our status, for honor. Loot. A contest between honored competitors. Perhaps your people fight for such things, Cap-i-taan?" He blinked rapidly as his mood turned to one of anger. "We do not," he continued harshly, "fight to exterminate one another!"

"We may not always fight for a noble cause, Lord Rolak," Matt replied coldly, "but war isn't play to us." He gestured at the other Lemurians present. "As you yourself have pointed out, entertainment is even less a motivation for sea folk to fight, and yet we are here. Do you know why? Because this *is* a war of extermination! It's *us* or *them* and you're right: they don't have any rules. We, all of us, are nothing to them but prey. You, Lord Rolak, are their *prey!*"

Rolak bristled and stiffened in his chair. For the first time, the formidable fangs behind his lips revealed themselves, but he reasserted his urbane control, recognizing the truth. "Thirty hundreds," he said at last. "That is the total with which we can face them alone, but each is worth many of the enemy."

"I'm sure," Matt replied, nodding respectfully, "but not enough. We have about that many with us. Actually, more. We have artillery—big thunder weapons like those on these ships—and we can have all of it on the ground to help defend your city by the time the sun comes up *if*"—he looked directly at Rolak, unwaveringly—"you understand that any forces we land will be under *my* command, seconded by Lieutenant Shinya. Also, you will agree to join with us in alliance, because after we help save your city, we intend to destroy the Grik forever. We help you, and you help us. That's the deal."

Prince Rasik sputtered and began to speak, but Lord Rolak silenced him. He stared directly back at Matt. "Very well. To the first, I agree. I must speak to my king about the second. I will tell you this, however: if we beat them, you shall certainly have *me* as an ally."

There was a sharp knock in the passageway beyond the curtain. "Come," said Matt, and Sandra and Lieutenant Shinya entered the wardroom. Sandra sat in the empty chair beside the captain, and Shinya stood before him and came to attention.

"You sent for me, Captain?"

Matt forced himself once again not to smile at Shinya's formality. It wasn't an act on the Japanese officer's part, but Matt always thought such "proper" behavior was a little out of place in the wardroom. Right now, with their visitors present, the courtesy was probably appropriate, as much for Jim's and Frankie's sake as for the Aryaalans. The last time they'd seen the Japanese officer, he'd been in chains and guarded by Pete Alden. "Yes, Lieutenant," he said and pointed at the map before him on the table. It was little more than a crude sketch, having been drawn by Mallory from the air. The Air Corps lieutenant had assured him it was accurate in the pertinent details, however. "As soon as this meeting ends—almost immediately, I believe—I want you to begin coordinating our troop landings here, in the dockyard area north of the . . . castle." He supplied that word, lacking any better. He glanced at Keje. "How many of the feluccas did we lose?"

"Most are accounted for, but some are not. I fear we must assume they were lost breaking through the Grik."

Matt nodded somberly, looking at Rick Tolson. "*Revenge* will make a quick search after dawn to see if any are adrift, disabled."

"Aye, aye, Captain."

"Don't take too long, though. I want you back as soon as possible." Tolson nodded. "Mr. Shinya, you will land three-quarters of the Marines and Guards at the dockyard. I'll leave the choice of units to you, but I want you to reserve one-quarter of the force to demonstrate as if they're going to land here"—he pointed at the map—"across the river. Hopefully, we can keep the Grik reserves tied down, prepared to defend against a landing. The battle line will support that impression with a bombardment." He paused. "The main force will assemble at the breastworks that join the castle walls to the beach."

Most of those present were already familiar with the plan, but Lord Rolak leaned forward and peered at the map. "Why gather there?" he asked, puzzled. "It will take time to move your forces within the walls and through the city. Would it not be better to send them in as they arrive?"

"No, Lord Rolak," Matt explained. "The Allied Expeditionary Force won't be going inside."

*   *   *

Shortly, after escorting the dignitaries and the battle line commanders to their boats and watching them scurry to their various commands to begin preparations, they returned to the wardroom. They didn't have much time, but Matt was determined to know, at last, what had happened to *Mahan* and her people. Sandra and Bradford were present, as were Spanky, Gray, and Dowden. By now, the whole crew had heard the exciting news that the lost lambs had returned. As usual, Juan hovered in the passageway prepared to bring coffee, so Matt knew none of them would have to repeat the story to the men.

"So," he said, smiling reassuringly, "I guess it would be a gross understatement for me to say we've been a little worried about *Mahan*."

Jim looked at him and managed to return a ghost of a smile himself. "We've been worried about you too, Skipper." He stared down at a second Coke and rubbed at the beaded condensation on the cold bottle with his thumb. "We . . . we never thought we'd see you again. I don't really know where to begin."

"We know about what took place up until Kaufman tried to send Mallory and the PBY to Ceylon," Matt said gently. "They found us, by the way."

Ellis was nodding. "Yes, sir. We saw it fly over the day before yesterday and we knew it must have. That's how we knew you were coming. 'Powerful friends' is right! When we heard the four-inchers and saw the star shells, I can't tell you how we felt." He paused, controlling his emotions. "We still didn't really think you could make it through," he admitted. "There were *forty* of 'em, for crying out loud! Then we heard the other guns and Rolak came out to the ship to fetch us . . ." His face clouded with shame. "I just wish we could've helped you, but *Mahan*'s anchored around the north point, and the guns wouldn't bear. We've been positioned there as a sort of floating battery to keep the channel between Madura and Surabaya—I mean Aryaal—open." He paused. "By the way, in case you didn't know, unlike 'back home,' the northeast channel is impassable with anything but small boats. Too shallow. There's only one way in and out of the bay."

Matt nodded appreciatively at Nakja-Mur. "Our friends' 'Sacred Scrolls' showed us that. You may have noticed yourselves that our charts don't always entirely agree with the local geography and conditions. They're much more comprehensive than the Lemurians', but not as locally precise. The differences usually tend to be a generally lower water level." He chuckled. "Much as the local temperatures seem unchanged, Mr. Bradford"—Matt nodded at the Australian—"believes this earth might be caught in the throes of an ice age. Farther north and south might be considerably cooler than we're used to." He waved his hand. "Enough of that. I want to know what happened to you. Spotting you on that barge was the biggest surprise I've had since, well . . . since we got here in the first place."

Jim looked like he'd just realized something. "You didn't know we were here, did you? If the PBY saw us, you would've known we knew—" He grinned. It was fragile, but real. "Thank God!" he said with huge relief. "I was afraid all this risk you put *Walker* to was a rescue mission just for us! We didn't know if the plane saw us or not. We heard it, but didn't see it until it was over the island, moving away. The point must've blocked its view."

"Rest assured," Dowden said grimly, "if we'd known you were here, we would've come in spite of . . . all this. And sooner, too!"

"You bet," grumbled Gray. "And we didn't need any help getting through those damn lizards, neither."

"Getting out again might have been a bit trickier," observed Bradford judiciously. "Without the destruction the battle line wrought."

Matt nodded in agreement. "What happened after Mallory left? He said you knew he had no intention of going to Ceylon."

Jim looked at Steele as if he expected the bosun's mate to answer, but Steele merely stared at the table in front of him. Matt had the distinct impression that the putrid green linoleum wasn't what he saw just then, however. Jim cleared his throat. "I was . . . sort of out of it for a while, Skipper. Fever. Thank God we had the nurses or I probably would have lost my leg, at least."

"But I thought *Mahan*'s surgeon survived?" Sandra spoke up. Jim looked at her and lowered his eyes. "He did. But he quickly figured out, like Frankie and I and a few others, that we . . . just weren't in Kansas anymore." He looked back up at Matt and a brief, sad smile crossed his face as he remembered the conversation he and the captain had that morning off the coast of Bali. "He took it harder than most, though. He sank into a depression that nobody could snap him out of. He . . . shot himself."

Sandra gasped, but Matt just shook his head. He hadn't known *Mahan*'s surgeon, but he imagined he knew how he had felt. Under the circumstances, it was probably a miracle they hadn't lost more of the men to suicide. If it had been any other destroyer squadron in the Navy other than that attached to the Asiatic Fleet, they probably would have. Once again, the unique temperament of his destroyermen had proved to be an asset.

"Anyway," Ellis continued, "the nurses pulled me through. In the meantime, *Mahan* creeped up the Sumatra coast, headed for Ceylon. The crew—those who didn't already know it—finally figured out Kaufman was nuts, but there wasn't anything I could do, laying in my bunk. I think what finally made him completely flip, though, was as soon as we made to cross the Bay of Bengal, the lookout spotted an island where there shouldn't have been one. I thought it was one of the Nicobars myself, at first. Frankie and some of the other fellas had taken me on deck so I could get some air."

"Kaufman let you loose?" Spanky asked.

"Yeah. I think he felt bad about shooting me," Ellis reflected. "He wasn't a murderer; he was just nuts. Crazy with fear, I think. Also, once it dawned on him the fix we were in, I think he wished he hadn't done what he did. But he couldn't take it back. Anyway, I saw the island." His face took on an expression of remembered amazement. "Only it *wasn't* an island, Skipper. It was a *fish*! It was *huge*! It looked like one of the ones like *Walker* shelled right after we came through the Squall, that nobody on *Mahan* got to see—'course, we've seen plenty of them since! It was like that, but a hundred times bigger. A thousand! It was bigger than any whale that ever was." Frankie Steele shivered despite the warm, humid air in the wardroom, and Matt realized *Mahan* must have encountered one of the monstrous "mountain fish" Keje had told him about. "I guess we got too close because, all of a sudden, it turned and made for us! I swear, it was big enough to *eat* the ship! Well, we came about and raced back for Sumatra as fast as we could, making eighteen knots or thereabouts, and even then it nearly got us." Jim shook his head, still astonished, and took a sip of his Coke. "I doubt it could sustain a speed like that, but for a sprint—anyway, it finally gave up the chase when the water began to shoal."

"Astounding!" gasped Bradford. "Just imagine! A fish that large!" He turned to Matt. "Captain Reddy, as soon as this current . . . unpleasantness . . . is at an end, I must simply insist that you allow me to study one of these creatures!"

Matt couldn't resist the grin that sprang to his lips. "Sure, Mr. Bradford. You can take the whaleboat." Those around the table chuckled appreciatively and even Steele managed a smile. Ellis spoke again. "After that, Kaufman gave up on Ceylon. There was no way he was crossing any deep water. So there we were, just fooling around burning fuel, day after day in the islands off the west coast of Sumatra. He was scared to death of being spotted by more lizard ships, like nearly got the PBY, but he was just as afraid of heading back this way. Finally, we anchored off Nias. The condensers were screwed up and we needed fresh water so Kaufman led a party ashore to find a source. I think he just wanted off the ship."

His voice became a whisper. "It was a fiasco. I was on my feet again, sort of, and we'd determined to take back the ship. We didn't really even need a plan. With him and his stooges gone, we just armed ourselves and waited for him to return and be placed under arrest. He had twenty men with him, about a third of the crew, as security. They were all armed to the teeth, but we didn't think a shot would be fired when we made our move. They weren't going to actually get any water, just find it if they could and then we'd organize the best way to get it to *Mahan*, or get *Mahan* closer to it. At least that was the plan he told us. I think he was looking for a place to stop—to build shelter and stay."

Ellis's expression became angry. "That would have been fine with me, and good riddance! If only he hadn't . . ." He shook his head. "Anyway, we waited and waited, and they . . . just didn't come back. The whole place was a jungle and we couldn't see a thing as soon as they left the beach. A few times, we thought we heard shots, but it might've been the surf. Night fell and we could still see the boats dragged up on the beach but no sign of anybody."

He looked around at the expressions of those listening and saw their horror. He looked down at the table. "We couldn't go ashore in the dark," he muttered quietly and glanced back up. The horror remained on their faces, but there was also sympathy for him, for the decision he'd been forced to make. A part of his soul might have even felt a surge of relief at the absence of condemnation, but it was far too small a part to provide him any solace. He condemned himself enough as it was. "I left twenty men on board the next day, about half of whom were fit for duty. There was no way I was able to go tromping through that jungle, so I stayed on the beach with Pam Cross—one of the nurses—and one other man. I—" He stopped and looked at the bosun's mate beside him. "Frankie led the party inland."

"Mr. Steele?" Matt prompted.

Frankie looked at the captain with tortured eyes. Sweat beaded on his forehead. He'd been twisting the hair of the beard on his chin— hard—for the last several minutes.

"Uh, we followed the trail they made about three miles into the jungle, kind of skirting along the southern slope of a big mountain or volcano that's right in the middle of the place, see? Hadn't seen a thing up till then but tracks. Then, all of a sudden . . ." He gulped from the cup of coffee that Juan had placed, unnoticed, by his elbow. "There was a clearing, kinda, and one of the guys picks up a canteen and there's blood on it, see?" He closed his eyes. "There was blood all over the place! A boot, a couple o' hats, a few shell casings . . . nothing else but a bigger trail leading toward the other side of the island, with blood on it too, in places." He covered his face with his hands, then ran his fingers up through his hair, knocking off his hat. He didn't even notice.

"But that wasn't the worst of it. I sent one of the guys back to the beach to tell Mr. Ellis what we found and the rest of us pushed on. The island's about eight or ten miles wide there and we never would'a made good time if it wasn't for the size of the trail they left. Close to noon, we heard the sound of surf and eased out to the edge of the jungle overlooking the beach on the southwest side of Nias and we seen . . . we seen them lizard ships! Dozens of them, beating down to southward! You could see they'd been ashore, lots of 'em, and their cook-fires were still smoking." He cleared his throat and licked his lips. When he spoke again, his voice was a whisper.

"I, uh, went out on the beach alone to take a look around and I looked into one o' them fire pits. There was bones in that pit, Captain. Human bones. They were all gnawed up like—" He couldn't continue. He just sat there, twisting his beard and staring at the tabletop. No one said a word, each alone with the mental image Frankie Steele had conjured in their minds.

Finally, the tough, Bronx-born bosun's mate met their stares and his eyes were red and tears threatened to spill. "Them lizard bastards ate my friends," he grated. "I transferred out'a *Walker* to help Mr. Ellis, Skipper, but them guys was still my shipmates." He shuddered. "I want to kill 'em all!"

Matt nodded. At that moment he knew with complete certainty that all the rhetoric he'd used to justify this expedition—this war—to his allies and his own people hadn't been merely rhetoric. It was clear, blinding truth. The things he'd seen in *Revenge*'s hold had been proof enough of that, but ghastly as it was and as much as he liked Lemurians, the war he'd committed *Walker* and her people to had still been mainly the Lemurians' war. There'd always been something of a disconnect, particularly among some members of the crew. Most of the men who felt that way, few as they were, kept their opinions to themselves. All knew they had a stake in the fight, but a few of the more mercurial hadn't been sure exactly what it was—aside from food and fuel for fighting.

Matt had recognized his own hypocrisy when the human skull had elicited a deeper response in him than all the other atrocities he'd seen, but a fair portion of that could be explained by his fear and uncertainty about what that skull implied. Now he knew. If *Revenge* herself hadn't been there that day, she had acquired the skull from a ship that had. As a trophy? A curiosity? Or as something to use as a guide to look for more? Whatever the reason, it was immaterial now. *Walker* was already in it and he'd have supported his allies to the hilt regardless. But now it had become profoundly personal. It was *Walker*'s war now, and *Mahan*'s too, just as much as anybody's. When the details of this conversation filtered through the ship, as he was sure they would, even the few who'd wondered why *Walker* had to get involved would have their answer.

"What happened then, Mr. Steele? Did it look like all of Kaufman's party had been . . . eaten?"

"I don't know, sir," Steele said, shaking his head. "We pulled out pretty quick. The lizards ambushed Kaufman closer to our side of the island, and I was afraid they knew where *Mahan* was, so we headed back in a hurry." A shadow crossed his face again as he spoke. "About halfway back, we came under attack ourselves. Leroy Bennet was bringing up the rear and some kind of lizards, kind of like Griks but different . . . like Grik . . . what's the word, Mr. Ellis?"

"Aborigines," Jim supplied somberly.

"Yeah, Grik aborigines got him. Just tore him apart!" He sighed bitterly. "Well, we got some of them too. I don't know how many, a couple dozen I guess, but they just kept comin'. Behind us, in front of us, through the jungle on the sides. It was a running fight all the way to the beach. We lost four more guys to the bastards before we made it to the boats!" The tears were streaming now and he wiped at them with a tattered sleeve.

"They were armed with bronze swords and hatchets," Ellis said. "I think they were the ones that originally captured Kaufman's party and they sold or traded them to the other . . ." He hesitated and curled his lip with hatred. "More *advanced* lizards.

"Anyway," he continued, "by the time we made it back to *Mahan* with the remainder of Mr. Steele's party, the ships he saw were rounding the point to the south." His eyes gleamed. "We didn't even try to run. We just went right at them! Fire control was still out, but we had the number two and number four guns operating fine in local control. Number one would fire, but the recoil cylinders were damaged and still leak like a sieve." He shrugged. "We also had the machine guns amidships and the three-inch. We probably shouldn't have fought them, but we *wanted* to. In the end, we destroyed five of their ships and crippled God knows how many—at least twice that number." He paused, reflecting, and they could see the satisfaction that that part of the story had given him. "I wanted to destroy them all, but we needed to conserve ammunition. So much of ours had been damaged by flooding." He shrugged again. "So we blew through them and headed south-southeast, making smoke. Finally wound up here and didn't have the fuel to keep on."

His brow furrowed. "The locals didn't receive us too kindly at first. The Surabayans were fighting the Madurans, and when they got over their initial shock both sides thought we were here to help the other. When they figured out that wasn't the case, both sides tried to *get* us to help them against the other and all we could do was sit there and try to stay afloat." He smiled wryly. " 'Course, it was amazing how fast they made up after the lizards got here and they had somebody else to fight besides each other. Both sides started being pretty nice to us after that too, for what good we could do."

"What were they fighting over?" Gray asked.

"Close as I can tell, that snotty little prince that was in here with Rolak wanted to marry, or mate, or whatever they do, with the queen on Madura. They call the island B'mbaado, by the way. Anyway, she's a looker by their standards, I understand, and they call her the 'Orphan Queen' of the island." He grinned. It was a fragile grin, but it was real. "She also thinks Prince Rasik-Alcas is a walking turd."

Sandra shook her head. "The political situation here seems entirely different from what we've encountered elsewhere."

Ellis nodded and looked at Matt. "It's pretty different, from what little I could tell by meeting your 'commanders,' Captain—or should I call you Commodore?" The tentative grin grew. "Admiral? Congratulations on your promotion, by the way."

Matt grunted noncommittally.

"The setup here seems pretty feudal to me," Ellis said, "like Europe five hundred years ago. Lords and ladies and knights and such. Peasants too, of course. There are distinct social classes."

"We can sort all that out later when we have the time," Matt said. "I just hope our people and theirs can get along." He leaned forward. "What kind of shape is *Mahan* in, Jim?"

"Not good." Ellis's grin faded and he raised the Coke to his lips and took a sip. Matt saw that in spite of the conversation and the fact it had veered from the trauma they'd suffered on Nias, Jim's hand was shaking and the mouth of the bottle tinked against his teeth. "She's in no shape to fight, or even move, for that matter. We're real low on four-inch-fifty and ammo for the machine guns. No torpedoes, but you knew that. We still have a full load of depth charges." He shook his head and snorted. "Maybe we can use the explosives in them for something? Anyway, the condensers, refrigerator, radio . . ." He shrugged. "All shot. We've been burning wood in the number one boiler so we keep up enough steam pressure for electricity to run the pumps, but that's about it."

"We can fix that," Matt assured him. "Is the number two boiler still up?"

"Yes sir. I wouldn't let them burn wood in that one—boy, it sure fouls everything up"—Matt avoided Spanky's triumphant glare—"and I guess I kept hoping . . ." His voice trailed off and he paused, looking at Matt with shining eyes. "You mean you have fuel?" He caught himself and looked around. "Of course you do. You're here! But how?"

Matt smiled as he saw hope begin to reanimate his friend. "We have allies, Mr. Ellis, as well as friends. As do you now. *Mahan*'s bunkers will be full just as soon as we can arrange it. I suggest you douse the fires in number one and start cleaning it out as a first order of business, as soon as you can make steam with the other. I want *Mahan* shipshape and ready to move as soon as possible. You'll have all the help you need." He glanced quickly at his watch. "I wish I could come over and have a look at her myself. Battered as she is, she'd still be a sight for sore eyes. But I doubt I'll have time . . . today." He looked up and his eyes held a savage gleam. "Today, I have a battle to fight!"

The sky in the east had begun to take on a pinkish tinge, blurring the stars, when Matt stepped out of the launch onto the long, low dock. His eyes burned and felt sticky with fatigue, but he felt a sense of anxious excitement nevertheless. He'd been awake for more than twenty-four hours, fought a battle, and found *Walker*'s long-lost sister. Still, he felt as though some sort of postponed retribution was at hand. A part of him whispered he was out of his depth, that he had no business directing a land engagement. But he was a historian and he'd studied the great battles of the past. That was probably as good a qualification for this type of fight as any other. What's more, for the first time, he'd be going into a fight with a pretty good idea of what he faced. The Grik were fearsome warriors and if they were allowed to mass, they'd outnumber his force more than four to one. What made him able to feel, as well as radiate, a sense of calm confidence was the fact that the enemy couldn't mass too effectively here on their right flank. They occupied only a narrow strip of land between the Aryaalan fortress and the swampy-banked river. Also, fearsome as the enemy was, they fought as a mob. Today they would face well-drilled and disciplined *soldiers* who were highly motivated to destroy them.

Chief Gray stepped across from the launch behind him and Matt gave the Bosun a wry, grateful smile, then looked around with a confused sense of déjà vu. He had never set foot on Aryaalan soil before, but he'd spent time in Surabaya. Of course, nothing except the longitude and latitude was the same. Even the geography was different. The great wharves and piers that had once altered this coastline into a major seaport didn't exist. The Aryaalans weren't seagoing folk, and there was only this one dock to service their small fishing fleet and the occasional ferry to Madura. The dock and the immediate vicinity were crowded with troops still off-loading from the ships of the battle line.

Feluccas, launches, and small boats of every description came and went as fast as they could, and Lemurian NCOs scurried about, pushing and shoving their charges into some semblance of order by squads and companies. The apparent chaos didn't dishearten him. New to all this as they were, the Lemurian force began to coalesce at least as quickly as he'd seen human troops do before. He glanced at the brightening sky. Now all they needed was a little more time. Behind him, he heard Sandra shouting at her orderlies as they transferred medical supplies and equipment ashore. Her first order of business would be to establish a hospital, or surgery, to tend to the wounded that would be arriving very shortly. She wasn't shouting in frustration or anger, but merely to be heard over the turmoil, and her calm voice helped, as usual, to bolster his self-confidence. Ahead through the throng, he caught sight of Lieutenant Shinya. Lord Rolak and Chack were beside him, and he was gesturing for a company commander to move his troops out of the assembly area toward the barricade that was lost in darkness.

Wide-eyed, furiously blinking Marines and Guards parted before Matt as he strode toward the Japanese officer. Shinya and Chack both braced to attention and saluted as he drew near, and he saw Rolak cast an appraising eye upon the gesture as he returned it. "Lieutenant Shinya, Bosun's Mate Sab-At," Matt said in amiable greeting.

"Captain," they chorused in return.

"How goes the deployment?"

Shinya glanced at Lord Rolak with a hint of exasperation before he spoke. "A little noisier than I would have liked," he grumbled, "but so far there's no sign the enemy has reacted to our arrival. The Second Marine Regiment relieved the locals at the barricade as soon as they arrived and threw out a picket force a couple of hundred yards. The Grik are moving, but they seem to be focused on preparing to assault the fortifications."

"As I said!" interrupted Rolak. "If you have truly come to help us, then I ask you . . . no, I beg you to come inside the walls and help us face this attack!" He gestured around. "With the forces you have brought, Aryaal would be secure and the enemy would pound himself to pieces against our defenses!"

"That may be," Matt said as quietly as he could over the tumult, "but that would only result in maintaining the status quo." He paused, realizing that Chack had stumbled on the term during his translation. "The current situation. We didn't come here merely to help you hold your city, Lord Rolak. We came to destroy the Grik. We can't do that by assuming a defensive posture." He waved toward the blackness of the bay. "How long do you think it'll be before another fleet arrives? Some did escape. They'll return with larger and larger forces until, even with our help, Aryaal will fall. We must not allow that to happen. Not only for your sake, but for our own."

He looked around them at the army as it took shape. A barge had arrived next to the pier loaded with four light artillery pieces— six-pounders—mounted on "galloper" carriages with big wheels and two long shafts instead of a heavy trail so they could be either pulled by draft animals or easily maneuvered by hand. Marines worked feverishly to place ramps so they could bring the guns ashore. Another barge with a similar cargo waited to unload behind that one. Matt had every confidence the training and tactics that Alden and Shinya had hammered into the Marines and the Baalkpan Guard would make the difference against the Grik horde, but eight guns broken up into four two-gun sections advancing behind the shield wall would certainly help.

"You must trust us, Lord Rolak," Shinya said. "This army has been trained to fight in the open. Baalkpan does not have fine walls such as yours to shield her people and so we've not learned to rely on such things. I mean no disrespect," he added hastily, "but by necessity, we carry our wall with us when we fight. For this reason, we can also carry the fight to the enemy."

"But—" Rolak stopped and blinked in consternation. "If that truly is the case, and you're so sure of victory, then what are *we* to do? Aryaalans must be part of this fight! Were you not listening to me before? Battle is not a sport for spectators to enjoy! Even the contingent of B'mbaadans would rail against merely watching you fight the battle we've earned with our suffering these last months!"

Matt grinned at him. "Don't worry, Lord Rolak. There'll be plenty of fighting for all, but you'll have to come out to do it." Rolak blinked at him, a mixture of question and intrigue. Matt summoned a mental image of the map of the city Lieutenant Mallory had drawn. He should have asked Rolak for one with more detail, but he believed the one in his head would suffice for their current purposes. "Garrison your walls as lightly as you can. The initial Grik onslaught will probably fall on you—in fact, I'm counting on it. Gather a reserve force, as large as you can spare, near the main south gate. Did you see the bright red ball of fire that flew high in the air and burst just as the battle began on the bay last night?"

Rolak nodded. "Everyone saw it. It was like when a star falls from the sky, only that one fell upward!"

"It's called a 'flare.' When you see one today, that's when you must come out. You'll know why when it happens, because the opportunity should be clear. You must wait for it, though! Don't come out before you see it, but when you do, don't hesitate or all may be lost."

Lord Rolak looked steadily into Matt's unblinking eyes and he saw the light from the nearby torches reflected there. "I tell you now," he said, "upon my honor and my life, it will be as you say."

By the time the first rays of the sun fell upon the smoking remains of the Grik fleet in the bay, the Allied Expeditionary Force had fully deployed behind the barricaded breastworks that extended from the walls of the city to the harbor. Glistening bronze spearpoints rippled and swayed above the heads of the troops, shining bloodred already in the light of the morning sun. An eerie silence had settled upon the host, almost twenty-six hundred strong, as they gazed over the barrier and across the coastal plain. Matt and the Chief walked behind them, their shoes squelching in the ooze that had been churned in the damp sandy soil by the milling and marching of so many feet. Matt wished he had a horse to ride that would give him an elevated perspective not only of the events that were about to unfold but of the mood of "his" troops as well. It was hard to judge their feelings at that moment, with their inscrutably feline faces. But he'd learned to read Lemurian body language fairly well, and he'd learned to read much of the blinking they used instead of facial expressions.

Most were nervous, of course. Hell, *he* was nervous. But some few were blinking uncontrollably in abject terror. Most of those were surrounded and supported by steadier hearts, however, in a Lemurian way that Matt admired. But the vast majority of the troops poised for battle showed every sign of grim determination, if not outright eagerness. He nodded to himself. They would need all the eagerness, determination, and courage they could muster because across the marshy field before them lay the right flank of the Ancient Enemy.

The only sound was the flapping of the banners in the early-morning breeze. Each of the six regiments of infantry had its own new flag and most were emblazoned with some symbol that was important to the clan that dominated the regiment. The flags were Keje's idea, and at his insistence each also bore the symbol of a tree. It was a sacred sign to all Lemurians and it gave them a unifying identity. It was also the symbol that the Grik themselves used to identify them and to Keje that made it even more appropriate. In the center of the line flowed a great, stainless white banner adorned with only a single stylized green and gold tree. Beside it, also borne by a Lemurian color guard, flew the Stars and Stripes. Keje told him that it was the first flag the People ever fought under, and beneath it they'd tasted victory. It was also the flag of their honored friends and allies, so of course it should be there. Matt felt a surge of pride at the sight of it and he wondered yet again at the irony that had placed it on the field that day.

Across the expanse, the Grik had finally noticed the force assembled on their flank and had begun to react. The mob of warriors facing them swelled, as more were shifted from other parts of the line and others came slowly from across the river on barges. There was no help for it. They had known it would happen before they were ready to strike. Sneak attacks are all but impossible when armies have to assemble and move everywhere they go on foot, not to mention within plain sight of each other. Perhaps their tactics would be surprise enough. Whatever the Grik thought, though, it didn't look like they intended to let this "diversion" take their attention from what they saw as their main objective: the city beyond the wall.

Horns sounded a deep, harsh, vibratory hum and thousands of voices took up an eerie, hissing chant that sounded like some creature being fried alive in a skillet. Accompanying the chant, thousands of swords and spears clashed against their small round shields and the staccato beat built to a deafening crescendo.

"It's even more terrifying on land than sea," admitted a voice beside him. Matt turned to see Keje standing there, resplendent in his polished copper mail. His helmet visor was low over his eyes. "At sea, the noise is muted by wind and distance."

"What are you doing here?" Matt demanded.

Keje grinned. "What a question to ask! I would ask the same of you if I thought I would get a different answer. Adar commands the battle line in my stead," Keje assured him. "He knows what to do and he will be obeyed."

With a great seething roar, the Grik horde surged toward Aryaal, waving their weapons over their heads and jostling one another to be in the vanguard. The beginning of the attack must have been plainly visible to the lookouts high above the decks of the Homes in the bay. Most of the Grik directly across the quarter mile of soft ground from the AEF didn't join in the charge, but continued to face them, securing the flank. Even at the distance, it was clear they were unhappy with the task and a steady trickle was bleeding away to join the assault.

"Now would be about right for him to give the order," Matt said of Adar. As if somehow the Sky Priest heard his quiet words, a bright flash and a white cloud of smoke erupted from *Big Sal*'s side, followed immediately by four more. The heavy, booming report of the big guns reached them a moment later, and by then the sides of all the ships of the battle line were enveloped in fire and smoke. The canvas-tearing shriek of the heavy shot reached their ears, and seconds later huge geysers of mud and debris rocketed upward from the midst of the Grik reserve across the river. Matt watched through his binoculars as troops swarmed over the bulwarks of the big ships and crowded into boats alongside. The guns continued to hammer away, each one sending a thirty-two-pound solid copper ball into the enemy camp. The balls shredded the densely packed bodies and destroyed the tents and makeshift dwellings as they struck and bounded and skated through, unstoppable, to kill again and again.

One of Lord Rolak's aides, left as a liaison, vaulted to the top of one of the brontosaurus-like creatures that had been on the waterfront when they arrived. This particular specimen had bronze greaves on its legs and wore polished bronze plates over its vitals. Besides being beasts of burden, the ridiculous brutes apparently served as Aryaalan warhorses. Matt had noticed the thing when he came ashore, but it never even occurred to him that anyone would try to ride one of the amazingly stupid animals into battle. Now he self-consciously reached up and grabbed the aide's outstretched hand and allowed the powerful Aryaalan to help him swing onto the dinosaur's back. He took a moment to secure himself to the rock-steady platform and then quickly raised the binoculars again.

The camp across the river looked like an ant bed stirred with a stick. Shot gouged through them, but the Grik had begun to assemble on the beach, preparing to attack what seemed to be an imminent amphibious assault. He turned to look at the river. The barges carrying reinforcements into the assault had stopped halfway across and were beginning to return to the far bank with their teeming cargoes. The assault itself had reached the obstacles and entanglements at the base of the wall, and rocks, arrows, and other projectiles rained down upon the enemy. Ladders rose out of the mass and fell against the wall, only to be pushed back upon the attackers. For now. The attack had weight behind it, however, and regardless of the terrible losses they were inflicting, the defenders were too thin on the walls to hold for long. Matt leaned over and looked down at Shinya, Gray, and Keje, who were staring up at him expectantly.

"The army will advance!" he said in a loud, firm voice. He smiled briefly at the irony. It wasn't an order he, a naval officer, had ever expected to give.

The barricade parted before them, and at the shouted commands of their officers, the Marines and Guards from Baalkpan and *Big Sal* and all the other Homes and places that had come to Aryaal's aid stepped through the gaps with a precision that would have warmed Tacitus's heart. For several minutes, they passed through the breastworks until the final ranks had joined the others on the exposed side, with nothing between them and the enemy but a gently swaying sea of marsh grass and flowers. There the army paused for a moment, flags fluttering overhead, as it dressed ranks and waited for the guns to make their more difficult way through the obstacles. Matt patted the Aryaalan aide on the arm and motioned for him to follow. The dinosaur bellowed a complaint when the aide pushed forward on a pair of levers that caused two sharpened stakes at the back of the platform-saddle they rode to jab down hard into the animal's hips. With a sickening pitching motion, the beast began to move and the aide released the pressure on the stakes. Two long cables, like reins, snaked back along the beast's serpentine neck and the aide pulled savagely on one of them, physically pointing the creature's head in the direction he wanted it to go. Slowly, they trudged through the barricade and joined the army on the other side.

"God a'mighty, Skipper! I wish I had a camera!" came a voice from below and behind. Matt looked down. Dennis Silva and half a dozen other destroyermen were falling in on the animal's flanks.

"What the hell are you doing here?" Matt called hotly. "We already have more men ashore than I'd like. You're supposed to be assisting Lieutenant Ellis!"

Silva assumed a wounded expression. "I am, Skipper! But he's a captain now too, you know. What with his own ship and all. He plumb *ordered* us off of it!" He gestured at the other men. "Said he couldn't stand the very thought of us deck-apes foulin' his engineerin' spaces! I think he must'a been a snipe himself once upon a time," he added darkly. "Put us ashore, and made us take these guns"—he brandished the Browning Automatic Rifle, or BAR, in his hand—"to keep 'em out of the workers' way!" Silva shook his head. "No way back to *Walker* now, so we figgered we'd come along over here and keep you comp'ny watchin' this fight."

Matt tried to maintain a stern expression, but an unstoppable grin broke through. "My God, Silva, you missed your calling. Hollywood or Congress, that's where you should be. I've never seen anyone tell such a ridiculous lie with such conviction." He looked at Gray, glowering at Silva. "Chief, put these men on report. They can stay, but they're in your custody and control. They will *not* fire their weapons without my orders. Is that understood?" Matt gestured at the backs of the Lemurian troops as they prepared to move forward again. "The last thing we need is for these people to start relying on our modern weapons to fight their battles. We just don't have enough to make a difference." He smiled sadly. "We could probably do it once, but that would be even worse." He looked squarely at Gray. "Emergencies only. That's an order."

"But, Skipper, beggin' your pardon, haven't we been doing that already? With the ship?" Silva asked, genuinely confused.

Matt nodded. "Yes, we have, but there's a difference. The ship is who we are. She's *what* we are, as far as these people are concerned. She's what's given us the credentials to advise them and help them technologically and be believed. Of course we fight with the ship. That's what's allowed us to give them the confidence they'll need to win this fight— and it'll be their fight for the most part. It has to be."

"But . . . even some of the cat-monkeys have guns—"

Matt's voice took on an edge. "I'm not in the habit of explaining myself to gunner's mates, Silva, but you may have noticed that Sergeant Alden's Marine rifle company isn't here. They're in reserve in Baalkpan." Matt's face softened slightly. "Don't worry. I'm sure you'll get a chance to shoot somebody before the day is out. Maybe you can snipe a general or two, but the victory, if there is one, must be theirs." He waved at the army again. "Won with their arms. Do you understand? That's the only way they'll ever win not just this battle but the war."

Matt was convinced he was right. He just hoped it would turn out that way. Being right in theory wasn't always the same as being right in practice.

"Does that mean we have to sling our rifles and just use these crummy cutlasses, Skipper?" asked Tom Felts from the other side of the dinosaur.

Matt grinned. "No, just don't shoot unless I say so. Damn, I thought I said that."

"Just shut up, you stupid apes," growled the Bosun. "Can't you see the cap'n's got a battle to think about? One more word out of you and I'll drag your asses back to the dock and you'll miss the whole thing!"

Lieutenant Shinya's voice rose above the silence of the waiting army. "Soldiers of the Allied Expeditionary Force! People of the Sacred Tree and sons and daughters of the Heavens!" Others answered his shrill voice, up and down the line. Many didn't hear him over the stiffening breeze, but they heard the voices of those closer to them.

"First Guard Regiment!"

"Second Guard Regiment!"

"Second Marines!"

And on and on, followed by the shouts of company commanders and squad leaders.

"At the quick time, *march*!"

As a single entity, the entire army stepped off with their left feet just as they'd been taught and began to move forward with long, purposeful strides that ate up ground at a surprising rate. The guns went with them, and two dozen artillerymen per piece manhandled the weapons and ammunition right along with the infantry. It was amazing. To Matt's knowledge, the army had never been able to train together on such a scale before, either on the parade ground or in the newly cleared zones around Baalkpan City. But for the most part, the formation held together with almost total precision. Here and there, NCOs called a cadence or shouted instructions for their squads to keep up or slow down, but the overall impression of discipline was impressive. Pete Alden, the man who, more than anyone, had built this army, would be proud. Matt was proud. Despite his inner anxiety, he felt a sudden thrill. He knew then what it must have felt like to be Caesar, or Alexander, watching his well-trained army march into battle against disorganized barbarians. The historian within him continued to whisper insidiously that the barbarians often won, but for the moment, he didn't—wouldn't—listen. The die was cast and the time for strategy was past.

There would be little maneuver; there was no point. When they engaged the enemy, the army would extend from the walls of the city almost to the banks of the river and he was reminded of one of his favorite Nelson quotes: "Never mind about maneuvers. Just go straight at 'em." That was about all they could do in this confined space. When the two forces came together, there'd just be fighting and hacking and killing. His great hope then was that the training his people had received would make the difference. Of course, they did have a few surprises for the Grik even before that happened.

The battle raged with more intensity at the base of the distant walls, and more and more ladders fell against them. Occasionally, firebombs arced up in high trajectories and fell among the defenders beyond his view. Matt surmised the enemy must have some sort of portable machine or catapult that could hurl the apparently smaller bombs than those used aboard their ships. It was difficult to tell through his binoculars how well the Aryaalans were holding because of the odd, jouncing gait of his mount. He heard a different note from the horns of the Grik in front of them, one with a kind of strident edge. He thought, incongruously, that they really needed to come up with some means like that for the Lemurians to signal one another. Their mouths were shaped all wrong to blow on a bugle. They had some woodwind-type horns, but they just weren't loud enough. Maybe the conch-like shells they blew as a warning? Even simple whistles would be better than nothing. He should have thought of that sooner. He wondered how the Grik managed it. The way their mouths were shaped, he couldn't see how they could do anything with them other than tear flesh.

At three hundred yards, a single command echoed up and down the line.

"Shields!"

The tall, rectangular shields made from bronze plate backed with wood that the first two ranks carried clashed together as they were locked, side to side, overlapping one another to form a mobile wall.

Spears came down in unison and rested on the top edges of the shields as the army advanced. It was an impressive display and Matt wondered what the enemy thought. He knew the sight had horrified the enemies of Rome, but he had no idea how the Grik would react. A smattering of crossbow bolts fluttered toward them. Most landed short, but a few thunked into the shield wall. A single piercing scream reached his ears from far to the left. His unlikely mount lumbered mindlessly along with a kind of quartering, rolling motion, following behind the trotting ranks but easily keeping up with its plodding, long-legged pace.

"Halt!" came the cry at two hundred yards, and the advance ground to a stop. For a moment there was a little confusion as the ranks re-aligned themselves. A runner dashed up from where Shinya had stopped with his staff a short distance away. He spoke in carefully enunciated English. "Lieutenant Shinya sends his respects, sir, and asks if he may commence firing?"

"By all means," Matt answered. With a salute, the young runner scampered away. Matt glanced down and saw Keje standing with Chief Gray. The Chief was practically supporting him as the Lemurian wheezed and Matt felt a pang of shame. The advance from the barricade had to have been tough on his portly friend. Keje was strong as a bull, but Matt doubted he'd had many occasions to trot as far as he had. "Keje," he called, "why don't you join me up here? You can sure see better. There's plenty of room."

Keje eyed the beast with suspicion, but gratefully nodded his head. He climbed swiftly onto the platform and settled next to Matt and Lord Rolak's aide. He was still puffing a little. "I grow too old," he said, "and my legs are too short for this fighting on land." He shook his head. "It is unnatural."

Matt glanced behind them and smiled. "But you didn't come much farther than the length of *Big Sal*. Hell, I doubt it was as far."

"Perhaps, but *Salissa* does not clutch at your feet as you run, and her decks are flat and you do not sink into them."

"Batteries, forward!" came the command. "Archers, prepare!" Gaps opened in the shield wall to allow the guns to be pushed through. Their crews immediately raced to load them with fixed charges consisting of thin tin canisters filled with two hundred three-quarter-inch balls on top of a wooden sabot to which was attached a fabric bag of powder. In carefully choreographed, highly rehearsed drills, rammers whirled and shoved the charges down the barrels. Pricks pierced the powder bags through the vents and priming powder was pooled atop them. Other members of the gun's crews stood nearby, blowing on lengths of smoldering slow match in their linstocks.

Around them, bows came off shoulders and arrows were nocked and poised at the ready. Crossbows were cocked and bolts placed in grooves. Before them, the Grik horns had fallen silent. They were close enough to hear the fighting for the walls, but from the Grik that stood refusing the enemy flank, there was no sound at all for the moment. Perhaps it was fear that quieted them? There was no way to know. More likely, it was simple curiosity as to why the machine-like formation that had been coming on so quickly had stopped. They were about to find out.

"Fire!"

Roughly two thousand arrows and crossbow bolts soared into the sky with a whickering crash of bowstrings. An instant later, the deafening, almost simultaneous thundering crack of eight light guns snapped out, belching fire and choking white smoke that entirely obscured the enemy until the wind dissipated the cloud. Sixteen hundred one-ounce balls scythed downrange. Many struck the ground far in front of the enemy, and some of those were absorbed by the damp earth. Many more flew high, missing the target completely and eventually falling, mostly harmless, among the enemy forces hundreds of yards away. Hundreds more went screaming right in among the densely packed, unsuspecting foe and struck like a cyclone of death. Grik were shredded and hurled bleeding to the ground, felled by one or a score of projectiles. Many were hit by shattered pieces of others who were hit. In an instant, fully one-quarter of the blocking force lay still or writhing on the ground. Then, before even their initial shock could begin to register, the arrows that had been fired at a high trajectory began to fall upon them. A high-pitched, wrenching wail built across the field as the plunging arrows pierced armor and flesh.

Already, the second flight of arrows was in the air and Matt saw dozens of shapes collapse to the ground as the deadly rain descended. Fully half the enemy flank was down and some that remained simply fled. Most did not. They charged. With wild, whooping screams, they bolted from their positions and sprinted across the marshy plain, trying to come to grips with this unusual and deadly threat. With staccato thunderclaps, the guns fired again, independently, and were quickly drawn back behind the shield wall, which re-formed where the guns had been. There, the first ranks waited expectantly for the charge to drive home. Less than a hundred wounded, disoriented Grik ran or staggered out of the smoke and slammed against the shields. Their deaths were almost anticlimactic.

As the smoke drifted away, the full impact of the blow they'd dealt began to settle in. The Allied Expeditionary Force had utterly annihilated a force almost as large as its own and had lost less than a dozen to do it. A cheer began to build and soon it became a roar. Flags waved jubilantly back and forth and Matt could see that discipline had begun to fail.

"Silence!" he bellowed at the top of his lungs. Keje joined his shout in his own tongue. Matt beckoned to one of his runners that stood nearby. "Tell Lieutenant Shinya we must push on! We've got to keep up the pressure! This has only just begun." Shinya was already giving those very directions. Runners and NCOs paced the line, outward from the center, yelling for silence and telling the troops to prepare to advance. Matt scanned the wall ahead to see how the defenders fared. It was difficult to be sure, but it seemed like fewer ladders were going up. Either the steam was going out of the attack or a new, more pressing threat had been recognized. The thrumming horns were sounding again, and the notes were clearly different than before.

"A glorious beginning!" said Keje with a tone of satisfaction and clapped him on the shoulder. Matt nodded absently, still staring through the binoculars. He was certain now. The attack on the city was withdrawing as he watched, and a redeployment had begun. There was no order to it, no organization, just a general surge as the Grik army reevaluated its priority objective and moved in that direction. Toward him. "Sure was," he said, confirming Keje's enthusiastic evaluation. "But it's about to get a little tougher."

Lord Rolak impatiently paced the open bastion above the wall near the southeast corner. Risking a bolt from below, he leaned far out over the wall and stared to the north. Past the southeast bastion of the old castle to which this wall was added, great clouds of smoke arose on the right flank of the enemy. He'd known that the sea folk and their Amer-i-caan allies had small . . . gonnes—he thought they called them—like those upon their ships, that they could bring with them to battle on the land. Even so, he'd still been stunned by the sound and effect those weapons had wrought. He had stripped the defenses as much as he dared, just like the green-eyed Amer-i-caan had asked, and then gathered the resultant force in the open marketplace near the south gate. There they waited, nearly sixteen hundreds of them, for him to give the command to sally. He had begun to feel concern when the Grik attack came, and wondered if perhaps he had thinned his defenses too far.

The Grik attacked like the night demons they were—enraged by the defeat they'd suffered the night before and slathering to wreak vengeance upon his city. As the fight raged, he even began to fear the sea folk wouldn't come. They would seize a moment of treachery and allow Aryaal—a city they couldn't love—to fall. All they would have to do then would be to file back upon their great ships and sail away, having accomplished effortlessly what they would never have been able to achieve by arms. He shook his head. But that was pointless. What possible motive would they have for that? Would they really have broken the siege simply to rescue their damaged iron ship? Possibly. He believed the Amer-i-caan, Reddy, would have. But he was sure they'd been surprised by the ship's presence here. He knew nothing of the strange face-moving of the Amer-i-caans, but the sea folk weren't so different that he could miss the genuine shock they betrayed at the sight of the other Amer-i-caans he carried out to them.

Besides, there was just . . . something about them, and the Amer-i-caan leader in particular, that convinced him they were here to help. He cherished no illusion that was the only reason they came, and in fact they'd told him as much. They needed Aryaal's help as much as Aryaal needed theirs. To them, this wasn't just a battle. It was a war. A war of a scope beyond any Rolak had ever heard of. A war in which victory wasn't determined by how much territory or tribute was gained, or by how many trade concessions were wrung from the enemy, or even simply by how entertaining it had been. The sea folk, who almost never fought, had come to save Aryaal so his people could join them in a war to annihilate their enemy. It was unreal. But these Grik . . . they did not fight the old way. They came to destroy his people, not just drive them to their knees. And the things they did to those they took alive . . . He shuddered. No, the sea folk and their strange friends were sincere, and so was he when he gave his own word to help. He had just hoped the Amer-i-caan leader's plan would begin to unfold before it was too late.

Then he had begun to sense a stirring on the far left and had seen the strange banners, which the sea folk had never used before, begin to advance. The fighting for the walls continued unabated, and he began to fear their "allies'" force was too puny to gather the enemy's attention as Reddy's plan hoped. Then he had heard the thunder. Not just the thunder from the ships, which he'd begun to hear already, but the thunder that came from the sea folk land force. That was when he had known it wouldn't be long before they called him, and he stood ready to dash down to the south gate as soon as he saw the flare.

"The wait is . . . distracting," came a soft voice beside him. Lord Rolak turned and looked at Safir Maraan, Queen Protector of B'mbaado. She was dressed all in black, from the leather that backed her armor to the long, flowing cape that fell from her shoulders and fluttered fitfully in the breeze. Her fur was black as well—entirely, without the slightest hint of a past mixture that would attest to any dilution of the royal blood. Her bright gray eyes shone like silver in her ebon face and artistically justified her only concession to the dark raiment, which was a form-fitted breastplate made of silver-washed bronze.

She is perfect, Lord Rolak admitted frankly to himself. He was almost three times her age, but he hadn't grown so ancient he couldn't recognize fact. It's no wonder that young fool of a prince would have them fight a war to have her. That war had ended inconclusively, of course, when the Grik had come. As much as she hated Rasik-Alcas, she'd brought six hundred of her finest warriors, her personal guard, to help defend against them. Lord Rolak rather doubted if Fet or Rasik-Alcas would have done the same.

One of those warriors was a massive B'mbaadan, scarred and old as he, who shadowed Queen Maraan's every move. His name was Haakar-Faask, and Rolak respected him greatly. They had battled often and inflicted their share of scars on one another. After Safir became the Orphan Queen, it was Faask who became her mentor, chief guard, general, and, in some ways, surrogate father. Right now, Rolak wished he would exercise a little more protectiveness. He looked at the warrior and blinked with exasperation, but Faask remained inscrutable. With a growl, Rolak stepped quickly back from the bastion wall, hoping to draw the queen with him. Dressed like that, she had to be a tempting target for the enemy crossbows. Unconcerned, she continued to peer over the side at the roiling enemy below. To her left, some distance away, a great cauldron of boiling water poured down upon the enemy and agonized shrieks rose to their ears. Rolak saw a slight smile of satisfaction expose a few of her perfect white teeth. She turned and stepped from the edge just as a flurry of crossbow bolts whipped over the wall where she'd been. Rolak sighed exasperatedly, blinking accusation at Haakar-Faask. "My dear Queen Protector, you must not take such chances. You must be more careful!"

"Like your own king?" she asked with a mocking smile. Rolak didn't respond. "Unlike the great Fet-Alcas, I am not only the leader of my people in peace, but in war. That is why I am also called 'Protector.' I take that duty seriously. I won't shirk any danger I ask my warriors to face."

"I have not seen you ask your warriors to flaunt themselves pointlessly in full view of the enemy, my dear," Rolak observed with a wry smile as he blinked with gentle humor.

"Have you not? What then do you think they are doing here?" As before, Lord Rolak had no reply.

Shouted voices registered and he looked to the north. To his admitted surprise, the tide of Grik began to ebb, the closer to the harbor it was. The fight below them had not abated, but to the north there was a growing hesitancy. Confusion. The enemy horns brayed insistently, and he ventured nearer the parapet.

"It is working," he breathed. Below him, the Grik were slowly, even reluctantly, backing away from the wall. Some continued to try to raise ladders in their single-minded, berserker sort of way, but the vast majority responded to whatever call the horns had made and began to move, en masse, toward the sea. Rolak turned to face the young queen with shining eyes. "Come! Quickly! If you must protect your people with your life, they will need you very soon!" He motioned to one of his staff. "Stand here!" he commanded. "If we do not see the flying fire, you must tell us when it comes!" He turned for the stairs and, together with their staffs and guards, Lord Rolak and Queen Maraan took them two at a time as they raced toward the southern gate.

Down they went until they reached the cobbled street that threaded through the homes and shops of merchants. The open market area wasn't far and they burst upon a scene of impatiently milling warriors who had been listening to the sound of battle outside and were anxious to join it. Aryaalan warriors fought with each other to get out of Rolak's way and he and his entourage moved through the gap forming in his path with ease. Nearer the gate stood B'mbaado's Six Hundred in their black leather tunics and their shields with the single silver sun device of the Orphan Queen. They also parted so their leader and her chief guard could pass. Before them loomed the great gate, its huge wooden timbers hung upon hinges as thick as an Aryaalan's leg.

Rolak glanced over his shoulder, high over the wall, and waited for the fiery signal. When it came, soaring high above the city, its amber-red trail so different from the firebombs of the Grik, he felt as though a great weight had been lifted from him. All his fears, his paranoia, had been misplaced, and now that those who had come to their aid had done their part—just as they had promised—he felt a surge of eagerness to spring forward and do his. "Open the gate!" he shouted. "All together!"

With a roar, the warriors surged forward, ready to push through the opening as quickly as they could. Lemurians in the gate towers prepared to heave on the windlasses that would cause the gate to swing wide.

"Lord Rolak, you *will not* open that gate!"

Even over the thunderous din, the bellowed command was heard by all. A terrible hush fell over the crowd as all eyes turned to a raised sedan, or shoulder carriage, borne by a dozen muscular guardsmen in immaculate white jerkins that forced its way nearer the gate. Atop the carriage was an ornate golden seat covered with crimson cushions and upon it lounged Fet-Alcas, king of Aryaal. Seated beside him, on the litter itself, was his son, Rasik, and his eyes gleamed with triumph as he stared at Safir Maraan.

"You will not open that gate," Fet-Alcas repeated in a quieter, raspy tone, gesturing angrily with his brown-and-silver-furred hand. The flab that had once been muscle swayed beneath the bone of his upper arm, and the exertion the movement took made his bloated body quiver. Outside the gate, they could hear the turmoil as even the forces arrayed there rushed past, on their way to join the fighting to the north.

Lord Rolak was struck dumb. His first impression was that there had been some mistake. "What did you say, Lord King?" he asked, uncertain if age and his many wounds had finally deprived him of his mind.

Fet-Alcas blinked in consternation as if he was speaking to a stone. "I commanded you not to open that gate, Lord Rolak," he wheezed. His earlier, unaccustomed roar had left him nearly spent. "You will obey me. We will not engage the enemy from beyond these walls."

"But why?" Rolak asked. It was all he could manage for the moment.

"Because I command it!" coughed the king. "I need not explain my reasons to you!"

Rolak's eyes narrowed. "Yes, Lord King, you must. I am Protector of

Aryaal and it is my duty to protect this city. I explained to you the plan this morning. You had no objection then."

"You are Protector, appointed by the king!" sneered Prince Rasik. "You will do as he says."

In a calm, patient voice like one would use with a youngling that had just found a sharp sword and was preparing to examine its sibling's eyes more carefully, Rolak spoke. "Great King, I have made alliance—which is my right—with the sea folk and the Amer-i-caans to defeat the enemy who threatens us. Even now they are fighting at our side as they promised. They have drawn the enemy away from our walls and upon themselves so we can attack from behind. We are moments away from victory, or days from total defeat!"

"It is your right to make alliance, Lord Rolak, but it is my right not to support that alliance if I do not think, in the interests of the people, you have acted wisely." King Fet-Alcas could no longer bellow, but his tone was imperious. "You have not."

"In what way have I not acted wisely, that you did not recognize before our allies committed themselves?" Rolak felt a tension building within him, a tension bordering on rage. He had given his word to the Amer-i-caan leader and even now the sea folk were fighting and dying outside these walls based upon his word. Soon the moment to strike would pass and whatever they did would be too late. Queen Maraan stirred beside him, a small growl deep in her throat. She hadn't been party to the agreement, but she too recognized the opportunity that was being squandered.

The king waved his hand again and glanced at his son. "That is not your concern."

"It is my concern if my honor is at stake, Lord King. I beg you to satisfy my honor and that of your people by telling us what your plan might be."

"That is simple. The strangers refused your offer of honor to join us within these walls and fight at our side. They chose instead to fight alone. It is my order that we let them! They came here unasked for and without my permission—"

"To save us!" Rolak interrupted.

"—with fanciful plans to continue this war far from here. They did not come here to save us, and if they did, what is their price? That we should fight for them as their slaves? No! We will let them fight the Grik and bleed them, and when they are properly and courteously dead and their unnatural smoking ships have gone, then we will destroy the Grik they have left us!"

"No!" Lord Rolak shouted. "Don't you see? The Grik are like the sand on the beach, the water in the sea! The Amer-i-caans showed me a map they took from them. They have conquered the entire world! If we do not stop them now, and push them back, they will return with twice, three times the numbers we now face!"

Fet-Alcas glanced once more at his son. There was fear there, Rolak knew. But what was the greatest source? "You have heard my words!"

"I have heard the words of a coward!" shouted Safir Maraan in a high, clear voice. "And as an 'ally' "—she bared her teeth in contempt— "who came here unasked for and without permission, I choose to go to the aid of another who was foolish enough to do the same!" She turned toward the wide-eyed Aryaalans in the gate towers.

"Open!"

"Do not!" screeched Prince Rasik. "I will have you impaled!" The windlass crews, torn between what they wanted to do and their terror, fled.

Queen Maraan turned and made a follow-me gesture to her guard. "We will go out the north gate, then," she said to her warriors and stared at the royalty of Aryaal with feral hatred. "Perhaps we will only arrive in time to help them retreat, but it would be better to die with honorable strangers than continue to breathe the same air that has been corrupted by such cowardice." Queen Maraan and her Six Hundred began to push through the Aryaalan troops.

"Stop her!" Rasik-Alcas screamed and leaped down from the litter, drawing his sword. In that instant, with hundreds of swords beginning to slide from their sheaths, Lord Rolak knew what he must do. He also knew that, whatever happened, they were probably doomed. He drew his own sword and stepped between Rasik and the queen. The prince stared at him in shock. Then, with a wild snarl, he lunged at Rolak with his sword. The old warrior batted it away with contemptuous ease and then laid the edge of his blade lightly against his prince's throat. He looked over at Safir for just a moment, and nodded.

Another flare soared insistently into the heavens. He watched it rise, pop, and dissipate downwind. Physical shame coursed through his veins as he looked at the now cowering prince. With a growl, he lifted his head to shout. "I, Lord Rolak, Protector of Aryaal, am going to continue as before!"

"Any who follow him will die, as traitors to their king!" screeched Fet-Alcas.

"Who is with me?" Rolak insisted. Hesitantly at first, but then with greater enthusiasm, roughly a third of the Aryaalan warriors gathered around Rolak, shouting their support. Rolak estimated the force, but grimly shook his head. Not enough. They would never be able to break through from the south with so few. With sudden determination, he strode to the Orphan Queen. "My dear Queen Protector, it looks as though we will have to follow your plan after all, if you will have us." He looked around at the troops who had stayed loyal to the king. Many were blinking in shame. "Together, we may still not have the numbers to relieve the sea folk from the south, as we hoped, but we have more than the king can stop with warriors who fear him more than the loss of their honor. With your permission?"

She smiled and nodded graciously and Lord Rolak raised his voice.

"To the north gate, as quickly as you can!"

"Go and die, Lord Rolak!" shrilled the king as he pounded the elaborate arms of his seat. "*Die!* The gates of Aryaal are closed to you forever! All of you! And when the Grik turn their might toward B'mbaado, we will not come! *We will not come!*"

The king's rant echoed behind them as they ran through the deserted inner city. Word of what had happened spread as fast as they ran, and they gathered almost two hundred more warriors who wanted to join them. Some of these came from the east wall, where they could see the battle between the Grik and the strangers who had come to help them. "Hurry!" was all they said.

"They're not coming," Matt muttered to himself, and lowered his binoculars. He was standing on top of the dead brontosaurus to get one last look, to assure himself of the unbelievable. Keje held shields for both of them that were festooned with dozens of crossbow bolts, but so far neither of them had been hit. It wasn't from lack of trying. Rolak's aide had been killed, and the brontosaurus had finally taken what must have been the critical number of wounds to trigger a pain reaction reflex and it had gone amok. Silva emptied a BAR magazine into the thing—without orders, thank God—before it could stampede through the army and decimate a regiment with its death throes. Among other things, that would have immediately lost them the battle. The shield wall was the only thing that had kept them alive this long. Together, Matt and Keje slithered down from the dead beast and the thrumming bolts immediately diminished. Only when they were elevated did they present a real target for the enemy.

"They're not coming," Matt repeated with a tone of wonder in his voice. "My God, how could they be so *stupid*?"

"I told you about them," Keje said grimly.

Matt smiled sadly. "I hate to say I told you so, huh?"

Keje looked at him and blinked. "No, I *did* tell you so."

Matt shook his head.

"Buggers said they liked to fight!" groused Chief Gray.

"Yeah, so did them Eye-talian Marines that time in Shanghai," Silva accused the Bosun. "I still can't believe you put me on report for that!"

"You were pickin' on 'em, damn it! One nearly died!"

Matt almost smiled despite the situation. He and his irrepressible destroyermen, two of whom had taken minor wounds, walked slowly along behind the battle line, shouting encouragement as they went. So far, the fighting at the shield wall had been remarkably one-sided. The Grik just didn't know how to cope with it. They slammed themselves against it, battering with their bodies while the first rank leaned into the onslaught, doing little but holding the enemy back with their interlocking shields. The ranks behind did most of the killing, stabbing, and slashing with swords and spears through gaps and over the tops of their comrades. And how they killed! The ground in front of the shields was piled high with the dead, making the footing difficult for those that came behind. But still they came. Fresh Grik arrived every minute, and the shield wall was beginning to tire.

Occasionally the Grik eased back for a moment and tried to gall them with bolts. Whenever the pressure slacked, the muzzles of the six-pounders poked through and a double load of canister scythed into them, killing hundreds with each blast, so densely packed was their formation. But still, more came. It was insane.

Lieutenant Shinya trotted up with a reduced staff. Matt wondered how many had been killed and how many had been used to fill gaps in the line. Shinya himself was bleeding from a cut under his left eye. "We're getting thin on the left, Captain." He shouted to be heard. "They keep pushing there, trying to roll us back and force a way through by the river."

Matt nodded. "It's the same on the right, but probably not as bad. At least those bastards on the walls will still shoot arrows at them if they get close enough." He paused. "They're not coming, Tamatsu. We're going to have to start pulling back."

Shinya nodded. "It's going to be difficult, Captain. Holding the line together is one thing. Holding the line together and advancing is another. Doing it while pulling back is . . . something else."

"We have that one spot about fifty, seventy-five yards back where the front will be wider," Matt reminded him. "We'll have to extend the line to cover it. After that, particularly as we get closer to the barricade, the land narrows back down and we can thicken things up, I hope. Pass the word; at the next flare, we start to pull back. We've *got* to keep it together." Shinya saluted again and trotted off. Matt looked at the destroyermen around him, cradling their weapons as they watched the battle. All were armed with Thompsons or BARs—probably half the weapons of the type that they had. No choice. "Forget the 'no shooting' order. I want one of you to each regiment, ready to pour fire into any breakthroughs if they occur. We've got to keep this line together at all costs. If it breaks, we're dead. Conserve your ammunition and don't get trigger-happy, but use it if you have to. Now go!"

They all hurried off except Silva, who stood rooted with a worried expression on his face. "But what about you, Skipper?"

"Never fear, Mr. Silva. I have my pistol. If that fails, the Bosun will protect me."

Silva arched an eyebrow and a grin crept across his face. "But who's gonna protect him?"

Gray's face turned purple with rage. "Buzz off, you goddamn weed-chewin' ape! Or I'll let that crazy cook use you for fish bait!"

"Just worried about you, is all," shouted Silva as he loped off down the line. Gray shook his head and stifled a grin. They were standing right behind the rear rank of the Second Marine Regiment. The Second was near the center of the line and it was spear-heavy, all of its members being large and strong enough to stand in the front rank. Those at the rear were methodically shooting arrows over the heads of those in front, and periodically they'd move forward and take the place of an exhausted comrade. It was a good drill and Matt wished the Guard regiments had learned to do the same. Many of those who came to the rear were wounded, some badly, and an increasing number of them were pushed or dragged out of the ranks as the fighting continued. A growing number of bodies, some moving, others not, were gathering behind the lines, waiting to be carried back to the barricade on stretchers to be tended in the field hospital.

"There ain't enough stretcher bearers," Gray observed grimly. "When we start to pull back, things could go bad in a hurry."

Matt recognized one of the wounded Lemurians as he was tossed roughly on a litter. It was that runner of Shinya's he'd spoken to before. He had a terrible slash across his chest and blood-soaked bandages were heaped high upon him. Matt hurried to his side. "Do you understand me?" he asked urgently. The young Lemurian nodded, his teeth clenched with pain. "The hospital must evacuate! Get the wounded to safety." He grasped the runner's hand in his. "Tell Lieutenant Tucker . . ." He paused. He didn't know what to say. "Tell her to pull out now. That's an order." He squeezed the hand.

"I will tell her, Cap-i-taan," the runner replied with a strained voice. Matt nodded and the stretcher bearers raced to the rear with their burden.

Chack-Sab-At gasped with pain as a Grik spearpoint skated off his shield and laid open the top of his shoulder. The thrust had overextended his enemy, however, and Chack drove his own spearpoint into the Grik's throat with a triumphant snarl. An explosive spray of blood and spittle flecked his face as the enemy warrior went down. If it screamed, Chack didn't hear it over the constant roar of battle.

For just an instant, his thoughts turned to his sister, Risa, and he wondered what she would think if she saw him now. It seemed so long ago that she'd virtually shamed him into taking the warrior's tack. How little he'd known at the time; beneath his nervousness and protesta-tion a warrior was what he *was*. Or perhaps, deep down, he knew it all along. Maybe that was why he allowed himself to be bullied and never tried to win the frequent bouts of his youth. Or maybe he was afraid of what he'd become. Afraid he would like it. That day upon the decks of *Salissa*, fighting to save his sister and his people and ultimately his very soul, he'd discovered he had been right to be afraid. He had *loved* it, and much to his great surprise, he had been *good* at it as well.

His warrior-minded sister had seen the change in him when she recovered from her wounds, but she'd believed it was just a sign that he'd grown up at last. She hadn't realized the more fundamental nature of the change. Once, his greatest ambition had been to one day become a wing clan chief. That goal no longer even entered his thoughts. He no longer cared about running *Salissa*'s great wings, or those of any other Home. He still loved *Salissa,* but *Walker* was his Home now and he was a destroyerman through and through. He knew most people believed he was playing a game with Selass, rubbing her nose in her rejection of him for Saak-Fas. But as far as he was concerned, she could remain mated to the mad, broken shell that Saak-Fas had become. The only thing he really felt for her now was pity. He didn't care about anything that once seemed so important—other than his sister, of course, despite her bothersome behavior, and the safety of his people and their strange tail-less friends. All that mattered now was the joy he felt when he was destroying their enemies. A joy he felt even now, in spite of the pain and thirst and exhaustion.

He'd spent most of the fight in the second rank, where his height gave him an advantage, stabbing and thrusting powerfully with his spear. Then the one in front of him, another wing runner from *Salissa,* fell. Chack immediately took his place. He couldn't kill as many of the enemy from the wall, fighting and straining to hold back the weight of thousands, it seemed, but the wall had to hold. Another Grik took the place of the one he had slain, battering furiously at his shield with its sickle-shaped sword. Chack dug his feet into the slurry of sandy, bloody mud and leaned hard into his attacker. He let his spear fall toward the warrior at his back—quite certain it would be put to good use—and drew the cutlass that the destroyermen had given him. He slashed at the Grik's feet under the bottom edge of his shield and was rewarded with a jarring contact of blade on bone.

The pressure eased, but as he stood up straight, a blow from an axe right on top of his head drove him down again. He was stunned for a moment and he'd bitten his tongue. His comrades to the right and left helped support him while his senses returned. Thank the stars for the strange, platter-shaped helmet, he thought. He spat blood between gasps for air. There was frenzied shouting from behind him and he risked a quick glimpse. The muzzle of one of the cannons was inching through the press. He and the others near him shielded its progress until it was right behind them and then, at a shout, they gave back on either side.

Instantly, there was a deafening thunderclap, seemingly inside his head. The pressure turned his bones to jelly and the fur on the right side of his body felt like it had been driven into his skin. A choking cloud of smoke engulfed him and a high-pitched ringing sound replaced the noise of battle. He didn't care. For just a moment, all that remained of the enemy in front of him was a vast semicircle of churned, shattered gobbets of flesh. He barked an almost hysterical laugh and was surprised he couldn't even hear himself. Recoil had driven the gun backward, and the wall closed up tight where it had been. Something caught his eye and he looked up. High in the air, beginning to descend, was yet another flare.

"It's fallin' apart, Skipper," Gray wheezed, his hands on his knees. He had lost his hat and his hair was matted with blood. To their left, they heard the rattle of a Thompson on full auto. None of the guys could have much ammo left, thought Matt as he inserted his last magazine into the butt of the Colt. He glanced at the barricade behind them just a little over a hundred yards away now. They would never make it.

The withdrawal had begun well enough. They'd even made it past the wide spot he feared without too much difficulty. But the enemy had attacked with renewed frenzy as soon as they realized the army was retreating. There was only so much anyone could take, human or Lemurian, and as fresh enemy warriors arrived from across the river, the exhausted troops of the Allied Expeditionary Force had finally begun to break. It started on the left, as he'd expected it would. As the Grik lapped around their flank, the ever-shortening line tried to fold back on itself like it had been trained. But a maneuver like that was difficult even for troops that weren't already almost too tired to stand. The line finally cracked and most of the Fourth Guard had been cut off. They bought the rest of the line enough time to complete a similar maneuver, but there was no way they could break through the enemy and rejoin. The dwindling survivors of the Fourth still fought, surrounded by a seething swarm of triumphant warriors from hell. Determined to sell their lives dearly, they coalesced into a rough square, their proud flag still waving in its midst, but they were doomed.

The rest of the line had no choice but to continue the retreat. There were other breakthroughs, at every point, and many died sealing the breaches. Matt, Keje, and the Chief had gone into the line themselves several times, fighting with swords and pistols until the enemy was beaten back. Matt's expensive academy sword was now notched and encrusted with drying blood. He remembered doubting that he would ever draw it in anger. More irony. With salty sweat burning his eyes, he looked at the sky, at the soft, fluffy clouds and the bright, hot sun that glared down from directly overhead. To the south, twenty-five or thirty miles away, a continuous line of massive mountainous volcanoes loomed indifferently above what transpired on the coastal plain. They stood out, sharp and clear in the distance, their towering peaks lost in wispy clouds. Or was it steam? Could be. The long string of volcanoes that made up the spine of Java were all active as far as he knew. Or they were, anyway, back . . . Well. No matter. The view was so very similar to the one he remembered and yet also so alien. Besides the terror of battle that raged all around and the unfamiliar, embattled city, the very fact that he could see the mountains clearly without the smoke and haze of bombed-out Surabaya seemed strange.

He glanced back toward the bay, beyond the barricade. The battle line continued pouring fire into the enemy across the river, but *Big Sal* had her sweeps out, trying to maneuver into position to shell the barges as they crossed. He glimpsed rapid movement and saw *Walker* sprinting across the bay toward *Big Sal*. She'd been around the point, transferring men and equipment to *Mahan*. That was a sight he'd seen before, he realized sadly. *Walker,* confined in this same bay while events around her swirled out of control. *Less than three hours for it to come to this,* he thought. It had all begun so well. He stared at the walls of the city, forgotten now by the enemy, and wiped sweat from his brow. "Damn you to hell."

Chief Gray fumbled at his side for his canteen and took a long gulp, then handed it to his captain. Nodding his thanks, Matt raised the canteen to his lips and felt the warm water soothe his chalk-dry throat. He'd been shouting for so long, mostly orders but at times with an animalistic rage when he waded into the fight, that he doubted his voice would be audible in a quiet room now. It didn't matter. There was nothing left, really, for him to say. Beyond the diminished line he saw the mass of enemy warriors surging forward, heaving with an elemental energy. Grotesque standards waved above them as densely, it seemed, as the grass that had covered this plain.

A tremendous roar went up from the Grik, a predatory roar of triumph as the shield wall broke yet again. This time, it was as if some critical point had been reached beyond all endurance. One moment, a few Grik were racing through a small gap, hacking and slashing as they came, and in the next, like a pane of glass in a hailstorm, the entire wall around the gap shattered and fell away. Lieutenant Shinya raced by, aiming for the breakthrough, but Matt caught his arm. The Japanese officer whirled toward him, an insane light in his eyes that dimmed just slightly when he recognized the captain.

"Save the guns, if you can," Matt croaked. "Try to form a square around them. If we can make it to the breastworks, we might be able to hold them there." Shinya nodded reluctantly, deterred from his suicidal charge. He ran off shouting for runners. They both knew it was hopeless. Too many had already started to run. But it was all they had left and they had to try.

Maybe not hopeless after all, Matt amended as he wiped his eyes and struggled to see through the developing chaos. The Second Marines and most of the First Guards had already formed a square of sorts. It was a maneuver the Marines practiced often and the Guards had simply retreated into the formation with the Marines. They'd managed to save at least a couple of guns too—suddenly a pair of bronze snouts pushed through and barked spitefully at the Grik that had begun to curve around and try to get between the square and the barricade. Scores fell beneath the billowing smoke and the banshee wail of canister. To the right, the line still miraculously held. But its severed end had curled back toward the wall to form a semicircle at its base.

Separate from either force, however, Matt, Gray, and Keje stood alone as the shield wall in front of them melted away, oblivious to anything but the need to escape. Behind them raged the thundering horde. Matt gauged the distance to the Marine square. Many within it were shouting his name, or Keje's, and waving, urging them toward it. There was no way.

A lone Lemurian gunner, abandoned with her dead crew, stood waiting while the Grik swept down upon her. Crouching behind the axle as bolts whizzed by or spanged off the barrel of her gun, she looked small and frail compared to the monsters coming for her. There was no doubting the determination of her stance, however, and her tail flicked back and forth as if she was preparing to pounce. At the last moment, she touched the linstock to the vent and the gun blew itself apart with a tremendous blast. Grik bodies were hurled into the air or mowed down by fragments of the tube or pieces of the carriage. She must have loaded it to the muzzle, Matt thought, stricken by the act. Of the lone Lemurian gunner, nothing remained.

"Come, my friends!" Keje bellowed, pointing at the Marine square. "We must try!" With a final glance through the smoke at the momentarily stunned Grik advance, Matt and Gray joined Keje, racing toward the square as it resumed a slow, shuffling retreat.

Gray uttered a sudden, startled grunt of surprise and fell to the ground as if he'd tripped. Matt and Keje both stopped and turned toward him. He was lying on his side with a black vaned crossbow bolt protruding from his hip. Irritably, he waved them on. Keje disemboweled a Grik warrior with his scota as it ran toward them out of the lingering cloud and Matt took careful aim and shot another with his pistol. More were coming. Soon it would be a flood. "Go on, damn it! I'll be along!" Gray yelled.

"Shut up," Matt grated as he and Keje helped him to his feet. Stifling a groan, the Chief managed to trot painfully between them as they continued toward the square. Matt shot another Grik and then another as they struggled closer to the Marines, whose formation had started to expand toward them as it moved, hoping to take them into its embrace. Keje deflected a blow from a Grik sword with his small shield and Matt shot the creature as it snapped at Gray with its terrible jaws. His pistol slide locked back. Empty. He tucked the gun into his belt and parried a spear thrust with his sword. He wasn't much of a swordsman, but holding the Chief and fighting with his left hand, he was almost helpless. He managed to deflect the spear just enough that instead of driving through his chest, the sharp blade rasped along his ribs. He gasped with pain but clamped down with his arm so the Grik couldn't pull the spear back for another thrust and Gray drove the point of his cutlass into its eye. It shrieked and fell back, but then Keje went down, pulling them down on top of him.

Matt rolled onto his stomach to rise. All around him he saw running feet, Grik feet with long curved claws that slashed at the earth as they ran. He felt a searing blow of agony in his left shoulder blade that drove him to the ground, out of breath. He raised his head once more. There, just ahead, was the Marine square. He could see the tired, bloody faces of the people he had brought to this, staring expressionlessly back at him, but with their eyes blinking in frustration. He could feel Chief Gray, trapped beneath him and struggling to rise, and he tried to roll aside. *Got to let him up,* he thought. Then something struck him on the side of the head, and bright sparks swirled behind his eyes, quickly scattering into darkness.

"Through! Charge through! Do not stop at the barricade!" bellowed Lord Rolak, waving his sword above his head. He was nearly spent and his old legs ached from unaccustomed exertion. He stopped, gasping for a moment as his warriors flowed past, shouldering their way through the debris of a shocked and splintered army. He stared at the survivors of the sea folk as they stumbled, slack-jawed and empty-eyed toward the dock as if they knew, instinctively, safety for them could only be found at sea. He couldn't believe it. They'd broken, yes, but they had fought against impossible odds for longer than he'd ever expected, and his shame warred with his pride for their accomplishment. Never again could it be said with honesty that sea folk would not fight.

Some fought still. A solid block of sea folk warriors with several flags held high in their midst was churning its way through a mass of enemies back toward the relative safety of the barricade. The block was dwindling even as he watched, but the path they hewed through the foe was out of all proportion to their losses. His sense of failure and shame was only slightly assuaged by the fact that he wasn't entirely too late. It had taken his and the Orphan Queen's forces almost two hours to work their way through the streets of Aryaal, streets that became ever more congested as they neared the north gate. The fighting had caused a general exodus of townsfolk to gather there seeking refuge from the firebombs and hoping that if the city fell they might yet escape to B'mbaado. It was an empty hope, of course, but it was the only hope they had. Then, when they finally forced their way to the gate itself, they found it closed and fortified from the inside as well as out. The king, or his brat, must have foreseen something like what Rolak was attempting and ordered his personal guard to prevent anyone from trying to leave. It was then that Rolak's defiance of his king had sparked a civil war in the city of Aryaal.

He stormed the gate with Queen Maraan at his side. The fight for the towers that housed the gate windlasses was difficult and costly—he himself had overseen their construction years before with that very purpose in mind—but they finally hacked their way to the machinery that opened the massive doors, leaving scores of white-clad bodies behind them. When the gate swung wide, Queen Maraan's Six Hundred and a slightly larger number of Aryaalan warriors—rebels now—swarmed down into the waterfront shantytown where fisherfolk and boat people dwelt. Through the squalid alleys filled with muck they raced, until finally they emerged behind the breastworks to see the disaster their king's treachery had wrought. Tears of guilt and humiliation stung Rolak's eyes as he beheld, at last, the extent of Aryaal's dishonor. The fact that any of those they had betrayed still lived—let alone fought—was proof that if only they'd followed the plan, a great victory could have been achieved. Now all that remained was to save what he could of this valiant army as well as his own people's soul.

"Straight through the barricade!" he urged hoarsely once more as another cluster of soldiers passed. He noticed a group of warriors standing nearby, leaning on their spears and watching the battle beyond the breastworks as the last of his own troops clawed through the gap and slashed into the milling Grik. "What are you doing?" he demanded. One of them looked at him and blinked confusion.

"We are the guard here. This is our station. We have no orders but to defend this position."

Furious, Lord Rolak struck the hapless Aryaalan with the flat of his sword. "You do now!" he bellowed. "Through, now, the lot of you! Or I'll have your tails for baldrics!" More terrified of the raging Protector than of the Grik, the entire barricade garrison hurried to obey. Rolak stood waiting, catching his breath and cursing his age and frailty until the absolute last of the defensive force hurried through to join the battle. He felt a hand on his arm.

"Rest here a moment," spoke the queen of B'mbaado. Her eyelids flickered with concern.

"Never," he said, "will I rest again until the honor that was stolen from me is restored."

She turned her gaze to the battle that raged a short distance away. B'mbaadans and Aryaalans didn't fight in the strange, ordered way she'd seen the sea folk begin the battle, but their tightly massed attack of screaming and slashing reinforcements led by an almost berserk Haakar-Faask had taken the Grik unawares. In moments they had battered a deep wedge through the enemy and were on the verge of linking with the exhausted Marines.

"In that case, Lord Rolak, let us salvage what we may of it while we can!" She flashed him a predatory grin and drew her sword. He nodded and smiled back at her. Aryaalan females never became warriors; it was forbidden. B'mbaadans almost never did, but there were a few exceptions—a noted one stood before him now. Sea folk females fought right alongside the males, and hundreds of them had died that day defending all the people of Aryaal, including its proud male warriors who had done nothing. He knew it was no use trying to make Queen Maraan stay out of the fight. She'd already been in the thick of it at the gate.

"Of course, dear queen, just promise not to outrun me. What little honor I have left would not survive." She clasped his arm tightly this time, and together they charged into battle.

* * *

Matt's eyes focused slowly on the battle lantern swaying above him. He didn't know how long he'd been staring at it, but it seemed like quite a while. It was only now, however, that he realized what it was. He blinked and it felt like sandpaper rasping across his eyes.

"Unnh," he said. It was all he could manage. His lips were cracked and stuck together and his tongue felt swollen and dry. He was lying on his back on what seemed to be a cot. Dingy canvas rippled in a stiff salt-smelling breeze just beyond the lantern and he knew he was beneath some sort of tent or awning. Around him he heard murmured voices, whimpering, and an occasional sob. A sudden sharp, short scream sent a chill down the back of his neck, and the movement was enough to awaken a terrible pain that existed somewhere in his shoulder. "Unnh!" he said again, and was distressed to hear his own voice sound so much like those around him.

Almost immediately, Sandra Tucker's blurry face hovered inches from his own. Her light brown hair had fallen down from where she usually kept it tied behind her head and she wore an expression of grim concern. A cool hand gently caressed the side of his face. Someone else sponged water on his lips and, when they parted, let some trickle in his mouth. The sensation of refreshment it gave him was so intense that he felt utterly wretched. He reached up with his right hand and grasped Sandra's wrist as he stared into her eyes. She smiled at him, raised his hand to her lips for just an instant, and then laid it at his side. "You just lie still for now, Captain Reddy," she said huskily.

"Can't," he managed to croak, and he tried to rise. A searing wave of agony swept over him and he fell back onto the cot with a groan. "Unnh!" he said again.

"If you pull those stitches out, you're liable to bleed to death!" Sandra scolded. "Just lie still! Everything's being taken care of. There are others who can manage quite well for a while without you. You're not indispensable, you know!" She forced another smile while inwardly she railed. *Of* course *he's indispensable, you idiot girl! To you as much as to this whole messed-up world!*

Matt managed a sheepish, lopsided grin, but then drank greedily when someone held a canteen to his lips. Long before he was satisfied, it was taken away. "Aye, aye, Lieutenant," he said, his voice more normal now. "I'll try to behave." He looked around for the first time, as best he could. Many more cots surrounded him and figures moved among them with lanterns or candles in their hands. The flames of the candles flickered with the same breeze that stirred the canvas overhead, and for the first time he recognized it as the fo'c'sle awning from the ship. It was rigged on poles driven into the sand to create an open-sided shelter like . . .

"We're still on shore, right near the dock!" he exclaimed. Beyond the poles it was dark, but other lights moved about on the ground between the jury-rigged hospital tent and the breastworks. "But . . . the line broke! I saw it . . ." He paused and grimaced. "Hell, I was *in* it." He looked at Sandra. "I ordered you to evacuate. Didn't you get the word?"

She nodded. "Yes, but by the time I did, there was no reason to." She didn't mention that she would never have followed the order in the first place—something he'd suspected when he gave it. His mind did a sudden double take.

"What do you mean, no reason to?" he asked carefully. "The battle was lost! A disaster!" He closed his eyes. "My fault."

"No! No!" she said in alarm and sat beside him on the cot. In an instant she knew the torment he must feel after the horror he'd seen—that she knew he'd feel responsible for. She'd forgotten he didn't know what had happened at the end. He'd been unconscious and there was no way for him to know. She took his hand in hers again and, when he opened his eyes, he saw tears running down her face, leaving tracks in the grime. "Captain Reddy," she said, her voice rising slightly so others nearby could hear her speak his name. An excited murmur began to build. "The battle was not lost!" All he could do was look at her in wonder and confusion. "The only ones to know defeat today were the Grik!"

A ragged cheer broke out and quickly spread to the area beyond the tent. It didn't last long, because the voices that made it were exhausted and hurt, but it was real and it was sincere and he knew some-how that her words were true. He closed his eyes in confusion and saw it all again, those last terrible moments when he knew all was lost. He couldn't imagine how they'd escaped disaster, but they must have. Sandra said so. He was alive, so it must be true.

Victory, he thought. "My God." He squeezed her fingers gently.

Long after she felt his hand relax in hers, Sandra sat beside Matt on the cot, looking down at him, wiping away her tears of relief while he slept.

It had been like a terrible nightmare. They'd all been so confident, God knows why. Maybe the string of small victories Matt led them to had made them think they could accomplish anything. After the battle in the bay, that confidence was reinforced. Sandra had watched with the rest as the proud army marched across the field, banners flying, and opened the battle with a terrible, one-sided blow. Even from her vantage point, where she had a better perspective of the horde they faced, she'd still been confident. The battle was unfolding precisely as planned. The Grik reserve was distracted on the far side of the river and the entire force attacking the city had been diverted down upon the Allied Expeditionary Force. And then, like a puff of smoke in a high wind, the grand plan that would have led them to victory, perhaps even with relatively light casualties, was just . . . gone.

The whole thing depended on the Aryaalans coming out and strik-ing hard into the enemy rear, which might not only have sent the Grik into a panic, but would also have cut them off from reinforcements at the ferry landing. She ran her fingers through her hair, scooping the loose locks out of her eyes, and glanced around at the countless wounded around her.

They'd been so stupid! Even in their own world people so rarely did the things they ought to do—had to do!—when the need was so clear! Look at how long Europe had appeased Hitler. How long the United States had tried to accommodate Japan's unspeakably brutal expansion-ism in Asia. Treachery wasn't a unique and alien Aryaalan trait. Nakja-Mur had warned them, and Keje had too, not to count too heavily on the people of Surabaya. But under the circumstances, surely they *had* to see the logic? She snorted quietly. They'd applied their own concept of self-interest to others, she realized, and that was always a dangerous thing to do. It had been the greatest flaw in their plan.

She'd known something was wrong when the second flare went up. The battle line held and held for what seemed an eternity—surely longer than they'd expected to feel the full crush of the enemy assault. All the while, the booming of guns and the drifting white smoke made it impossible to see much detail. The first steady stream of wounded began to arrive, however. Up to that point there'd been a trickle, a few at a time, and most of those had made it to the rear under their own power or assisted by a comrade. Those that came as the battle raged on were carried, and their wounds were almost always desperate. She flew into the fray of spurting blood and severed limbs and directed the surgery with an energy and steady detachment that helped instill calm and confidence into the overworked staff of healers under her command. She was overjoyed when Kathy McCoy and Pam Cross arrived from *Mahan*, but there was no time for a proper reunion. Most of Sandra's medical staff had learned to converse in English, so the two nurses could at least make themselves understood. But they hadn't been part of the "team" Sandra had trained for just this situation. It took a while for Pam and Kathy to integrate themselves and find their most effective roles.

And still the battle raged. The wounded that returned from the fighting were no longer excited and boastful. An atmosphere of exhausted desperation began to prevail. They were fighting like fiends and the field was choked with Grik dead, but something was wrong. The Aryaalans hadn't come. Then came Shinya's runner, horribly wounded but able to tell her the order Captain Reddy sent. By then she half expected it, but it still struck her like a slap. She quickly instructed her orderlies to prepare to move the wounded and raced to the barricade to see for herself. The horror was beyond anything she'd ever expected, or could possibly have imagined.

The battle was much closer now, close enough to see individuals, and she quickly picked out the white and coffee-khaki dress of the captain and the Bosun near the center of the line. Occasionally, she caught a glimpse of other destroyermen here and there and she heard the sound of their weapons when they fired. Beyond the diminishing, wavering line was an endless sea of menacing shapes surging forward with a single-minded, palpable ferocity. She still heard the thunderclap of cannon, but the surflike roar of the Grik and the clash of weapons absorbed the sound of all else except thought.

Abstractly, the struggle before her brought to mind a scene from her childhood. A small green grasshopper had inadvertently landed upon an ant bed. Before it could recover and launch itself again, dozens of ants swarmed upon it, biting and stinging as fast as they could. Within moments, the insect had been completely obscured by a writhing mass of attackers as they continued to sting and sting and slash at their victim with their cruel jaws. Occasionally, she saw one of the grasshopper's legs twitch feebly, hopelessly, but it was doomed. As she watched the battle, to her horror, that mental image was re-created before her very eyes. Like a plank stretched across two points, bowing ever lower beneath a remorselessly increasing burden of stones heaped upon it beyond all sense or reason, the shield wall broke completely with the suddenness of a lightning bolt. She knew she had to leave, to get the wounded out, but she couldn't move—so deep was her shock and terror, not only for herself but for the trio of distant forms that suddenly stood entirely alone in the face of the relentless onslaught. A trio that included the tall, white-uniformed figure of Captain Matthew Reddy. Her heart leaped into her throat and she cried out in anguish—just as a gun exploded and a blanket of smoke billowed outward and mercifully obscured the last moments from her view. She could only stand, stunned and lost, with tears streaming down her face and her soul locked in a maelstrom of grief. All around her, battered, blood-matted troops streamed through the barricade and ran to the rear as fast as they could, but she could think only of what lay within that dissipating cloud of smoke.

Someone bumped against her and she almost fell, catching herself by grabbing the barricade and drawing to the side. It had been a warrior who bumped her, accidentally, of course, but she suddenly realized that this warrior, unlike the others, was racing through the barricade toward the enemy. And then another passed, and another. Within seconds, the trickle became a flood and she watched, amazed, as hundreds more went surging past to join the fight.

The Aryaalans had come at last. She knew it was true when she saw Lord Rolak trot up behind them, bellowing furiously. She could see that he was winded and breathing hard, and he rested for a moment nearby. She wanted to shout at him, to curse him for his tardiness, but all she could do was stare. Then she saw another join him. A dark, exotic beauty she hadn't seen before. They didn't notice her, she thought, although the black-furred female's eyes strayed across her. Their focus was solely on the battle. After a moment more, they hurried past her through the barricade and disappeared into the swirling chaos beyond.

Courtney Bradford found her there, sitting in the mud and weeping like a lost soul while just a few dozen yards away the greatest battle ever fought by the Lemurian people raged. All she knew was that with Matt Reddy lost, all the suppressed loss and grief she'd felt ever since they came through the Squall had suddenly shattered her own fragile veneer of self-control. All the while, as she had tried to be his rock, he had been hers. Now she felt totally bereft. She'd lost her whole world at last.

Bradford gently escorted her back to the hospital tent, where she was met by the shocked expressions of the other nurses and questioning blinks from the Lemurian healers. Wiping her face and forcing herself to concentrate on the grisly business at hand, she dove back into her work, stitching and cleaning the horrible wounds. Forgotten in her misery was Captain Reddy's last command to evacuate the hospital. At some point, Courtney Bradford left her. He'd still been aboard *Walker* when the battle began and she never even wondered why he was here.

She didn't leave the hospital again. She just continued to struggle against the impossible flood of blood and death. Therefore, she hadn't personally seen how the battle came to an end. Despite her concentration on her duty, she could still hear, and she developed a fairly clear picture of what transpired. The Aryaalan and B'mbaadan reinforcements finally managed to batter a corridor through the Grik and link up with the surrounded Marines. Even so, the situation remained grim, and the result would probably have been little more than a postponement of the inevitable had it not been for the timely arrival of the diversionary force that had been menacing the Grik reserve all day. The reserve had long since come across the ferry, and when Adar saw what was happening, he ordered all available transports to take his landing force to the Aryaalan dock. With it came the warrior crews of the battle line as well. Most of the destroyermen, led by Jim Ellis, joined them. They were armed with rifles and pistols and all the working .30-caliber machine guns from both destroyers.

Big Sal's sweeps came out and Adar maneuvered the huge ship as close as he could and began plying her guns upon the densely packed Grik rear. *Mahan* was still helpless, but Larry Dowden carefully conned *Walker*—on one engine!—right up the river until she virtually ran aground on the silty bottom. There, the destroyer unleashed a barrage of high-explosive shells into the raging horde on shore. It was a massacre. Ellis positioned all three .30-cals on the far left flank where the barricade met the sea, and together with the two .50-cals on *Walker*, they poured a solid stream of lead into the enemy flank.

The panicking Grik fought back with renewed ferocity, but they were caught between the heavy reinforcements pouring through the barricade and the wall at the base of the city, where, miraculously, a small group of holdouts from the shattered right flank still held. Added to this was the catastrophic fire from the ships and the machine guns. The increasingly terrified Grik army began to melt away like an ice cube on *Walker*'s midday deck. Once again, just as in the battle for *Big Sal* when *Walker* had first truly met the Lemurians, the Grik broke. It was as though whatever cause, motivation, or collective madness made them capable of fighting with such heedless ferocity and abandon suddenly gave way to a crystal-clear understanding of the danger they faced. At the same instant, whatever it was that drove them, be it blind instinct, courage, or a combination of the two, spontaneously evaporated. Within moments, what remained of the entire Grik horde had transformed from a juggernaut of destruction into a panic-stricken mob of mindless animals consumed by an instinctual, unthinking impetus to escape.

Once again, they trampled or slaughtered one another in their effort to flee, and whatever ability they had for cooperative effort dissolved into blind self-preservation. And once again, through their own surprise and relief, the weary and battle-worn Aryaalans, B'mbaadans, Marines, and shattered Guard regiments, Home clan Guards and destroyermen as well, all sensed the opportunity and pressed their advantage home. It was believed that as many as a thousand Grik might have escaped the butchery that followed.

And Sandra Tucker heard it all. The crash of *Walker*'s guns and the deep-throated roar of *Big Sal*'s. The staccato yammering of the .50-cals on the water and the sharp but almost puny by comparison report of the .30-cals on the left. The triumphant roar when the Grik broke and then the screams and the shooting and the muffled throbbing thud of blades striking flesh—and then, after what seemed like hours, a strange, awkward, almost-silence.

The wounded continued to stream in, however, and their cries broke the spell. She knew, somehow, that they'd won, but her battle wasn't over. Then, like some massive war demon straight out of hell, Dennis Silva swept into the tent. He'd lost his helmet and he was covered with black, drying blood from the top of his stubbly head to his oversized feet. The whites of his eyes and his intermittent teeth shone like beacons through the grime and gore on his face.

"Got a good'un here, ma'am," he said, referring to an equally grimy form slung almost effortlessly over his shoulder. Stunned, Sandra led him to a bloodstained cot and, with surprising tenderness, the big gunner's mate lowered Captain Reddy down upon it. Behind him, Chief Gray limped painfully through the press of wounded, supported by Earl Lanier, of all people. The fat, irascible cook still held a cutlass in his left hand and his expression was hard and deep. Finally, to make the miracle complete, Chack and an exhausted Marine carried Keje between them.

"But I saw ..." she began weakly, then stooped to feel Matt's pulse and began tearing off his blood-sodden shirt.

"A hell of a thing, ma'am," Silva interrupted. "They was maniacs! The whole Grik army swoopin' down on 'em in a rush and it was flashin' swords and rollin' heads!" He turned to look at the Bosun, who still stood with Lanier. His face was a mask as he watched Sandra examine the captain's wounds. "Three rare killers, and I don't care if you hear me say it." He stuck his bloody hand out to Gray.

With an effort, Gray shifted and took Silva's hand in his. "You big idiot," he growled, but his scowl softened slightly when he saw Sandra's upturned face. "It was him and Chack that saved us, ma'am," he explained. "They ran out and fought them buggers off while some Marines dragged us into the square. Tom Felts and Shinya did too."

Sandra began to speak, but she saw Silva's eyes fill with tears that threatened so spill down his face.

"Old Tom's gone, ma'am," he said in a husky voice. "Cut down right when we was almost back in. He was a good'un too." Sandra briefly touched the big man's arm and gave him a sad, thankful smile. Then she returned all her attention to Matt.

Now she looked at his bruised and battered face. The light from the battle lantern cast strange and ghastly shadows upon it. *He's suffered so much for us all,* she thought, *ever since the very beginning.* Most of that suffering was inside, where no one else could see. But she had glimpsed the inner turmoil, even though he kept it hidden. He fought it alone because that's what he had to do. If he'd ever shown an inkling of his concern and doubt to the crew—or their Lemurian allies—they certainly wouldn't be here now, in the aftermath of a miraculous victory. More than likely they'd have been dead long ago, like Kaufman. With indecision, everything would have fallen apart.

She gently touched his lips, reassured by the warm breath she felt. He was getting old beyond his years, with the burden placed upon him, and she noticed for the first time that a few white whiskers had appeared in the stubble on his chin. Maybe he *had* been wrong to trust the Aryaalans, although she would never, ever, tell him so. Maybe even his whole grand strategy to roll back the Grik and create a world where all of them, destroyermen and Lemurians, could live in safety, was hopeless and doomed from the start. She slowly stood so as not to wake him, and stretched her painful muscles. *That may very well be,* she thought grimly, *but it's something that needs doing, and we have to try.* If *Walker* and *Mahan* had been saved from the Japanese only so they could linger in some sort of purgatory of endless strife, so be it. At least she would be there to support Matthew Reddy however he would let her, and patch him up when the need arose as well. And if he believed they could make a difference, then somehow she would believe it too.

*P*rince Rasik-Alcas sprawled on the heap of cushions opposite his father's massive throne in the Royal Chamber of the high, sprawling palace. Blood matted his fur—none of it his—and he idly reflected that the opulent pillows would be ruined, but he didn't care. He was exhausted by the fighting that had convulsed the city, even while the titanic struggle raged beyond the walls. He had, of course, never intended to get as caught up in it as he had, but when some of the palace guard, spurred by rage and shame, actually rose against the king, Rasik had been forced to fight. It was something he didn't much enjoy, strangely enough—at least the physical aspects of it. He was keenly interested in war and strategy and politics and all the heady matters a future king should be interested in, but the actual fighting was something he'd just as soon leave to others. That didn't mean he wasn't any good at it.

And a good thing too, he mused, watching his bloated father nervously stuffing food into his jowly face. The king certainly wasn't much good in a fight. He'd literally squeaked in surprised terror when the guard's sword flashed down from behind. It missed him by the very thickness of the royal cloak it slashed, and Rasik was still amazed that anyone could miss something so fat and awkward. *It just goes to show,* he thought philosophically, *if you're going to retain a palace guard, always choose them from the nobility. Then, if they are treacherous, they will probably be incompetent as well.*

He lifted an eyelid and glanced idly at the only guard currently in the chamber. *A loyal one,* he thought with a smirk. Rasik didn't know the guard's name and didn't care what it was, but he was a formidable warrior. He'd fought alongside Rasik, defending his king and prince from the very beginning of the attempt against them. He had, in fact, been the only one for a time. Now he stood, nervously vigilant, as the occasional sounds of renewed fighting wafted through the broad arched windows that led to the balcony ringing this level of the palace. The coup had failed, but it might be a while before they managed to root out all the traitors. And, of course, there was Rolak. Rasik seethed. He could still feel the cold metal of Rolak's blade against his neck. That one would surely die, he promised himself. And the Orphan Queen as well.

"I told you!" proclaimed Fet-Alcas in a frail attempt at a menacing growl. "We should have let Rolak out!"

Rasik sighed. "No, you didn't, sire."

Fet-Alcas blinked. "Well, he got out anyway," he grumped. "And then those ridiculous sea folk actually defeated the Grik!" His voice became shrill. "That . . . *that* you *did* tell me would not happen!" Rasik lazily blinked unconcern. "And then a rebellion!" wheezed the king, spewing food across the tiled chamber. "Never before in history has Aryaal rebelled against its rightful king!" Fet-Alcas's rheumy eyes smoldered. "And all because you counseled me to deprive our people of their place in the battle! A battle arranged by the rightful Protector himself." He stared out the windows at the darkness beyond. "No wonder they rebelled," he murmured. "The greatest battle ever fought—and a victory!" He glared back at his son. "You *did* that!" he accused darkly, draining a cup of seep. Rasik yawned and blinked irony. "I did not want Rolak to go," the king admitted, "but only because you said the sea folk would lose! We could fall upon the Grik remnants and have our great battle to ourselves!"

Fet-Alcas belched then, and shifted uncomfortably on his throne. "But no!" he continued bitterly. "The miserable sea folk and their friends with the iron ships did *not* lose! It is we who lost!" He stared back into the darkness with a grimace. "The greatest battle ever fought!" he repeated and took a gulp from another cup of seep.

"Do not complain, sire," Rasik sneered. "Our people had their battle after all!"

Fet-Alcas turned to him and began a furious shout, but all that emerged was a gout of blood. It splashed down on his white robe and pooled like vomit at his feet. Both Rasik and the guard rushed to his side and stared at the king as he looked at them in shock.

"The king is ill!" cried the guard in alarm.

"No," said Rasik, as he drove his own sword into the distracted retainer's throat. Blood spurted down the sword onto Rasik's hand and splattered on the king's white robe. The guard fell to the floor and thrashed, describing great crimson arcs upon the tile as his mouth opened and closed spasmodically. His tail whipped back and forth for a few seconds more, smearing the blood still further, and then he lay still.

Fet-Alcas, stunned, looked at the corpse that had fallen almost at his feet. He tried to speak, but yet another gush of blood poured forth and he was wracked with spasms of agony. Silently, for the most part, he continued to retch, but by now the blood had slowed to a trickle. The poison in the seep from the cup he still held was of a type that deadened all pain and sensation while it corrosively ate any flesh that it touched. At least it deadened it for a while. Fet-Alcas looked at the cup in his paw and then dropped it in horror.

Rasik slowly sheathed his own sword and drew the one worn by the dead guard. His eyes were wide with excitement and his tail twitched nervously back and forth. "No," he repeated with a hiss, drawing his thin lips hard across his teeth. "You are not ill, sire. You are dead. Killed by another traitorous guard!"

With that, he slashed down repeatedly across the king's neck and upper chest, grunting with effort as the blade bit deep. Finally, with a gurgling exhalation, Fet-Alcas slid from the throne and joined the guard on the tile abattoir. Rasik stood motionless, listening, while his breathing returned to normal. Laying the bloody sword on the floor, he drew his own again and looked at it wonderingly. Then he dipped the tip into the pool of blood rapidly spreading beneath his father's corpse.

"A king's blood on a king's sword," he whispered, and stepping toward the hallway that led to the chamber door, he began to run. "Murderers!" he screamed at the top of his lungs, flinging the door wide. "They have murdered the king!"

Courtney Bradford stood at the barricade staring through his "borrowed" binoculars at the scene of the previous day's battle. The first rays of the sun were creeping above the horizon, but so far all he could see was a seemingly endless sea of indistinct shapes, alone or massed in piles, across the marshy plain. Occasionally he saw movement. Either a wounded Grik that the searchers hadn't dispatched the night before, or possibly some scavenger darting furtively through the unprecedented smorgasbord.

It was the scavengers he hoped to see. Queen Maraan—a delightful creature, he thought—had told him about skuggiks, which she described as vile little predators about the size of a turkey. They invariably appeared to feast upon the carrion after a battle. They walked on two legs and actually looked a lot like Grik, she said, except they were considerably smaller and had no upper limbs at all. They were walking mouths, for all intents and purposes, with quick, powerful legs and a long, whiplike tail. Bradford couldn't wait to see one.

Perhaps there? he thought, as something seemed to move. He was having trouble holding the binoculars with one hand since his other arm was still in a sling. "Blast!" he exclaimed, lowering his good arm to rest for a moment. He would just have to wait until there was enough light to see. He glanced to his right and was surprised to find a number of Lemurian warriors, on guard against a renewed Grik assault, staring at him with open curiosity. He looked to the left, saw much the same, and felt a twinge of unaccustomed self-consciousness. "I'm a scientist, not a ghoul!" he announced harshly, brandishing the binoculars. They continued to regard him with their inscrutable stares. He sighed and stepped away from the barricade. Most of these wouldn't understand English, he realized, since the majority were Rolak's or Maraan's people. They had made every effort to retrieve all of their own few wounded and many dead throughout the night, but some would undoubtedly remain. The idea of him watching in fascination while some scavenger chewed upon anyone besides Grik—and maybe them too—might be a less than popular morning activity.

With as much dignity as he could muster, he stuffed the binoculars into his sling and strode away from the breastworks toward the guttering torches that surrounded the hospital tent. Marine guards ringed the area, nearly dead on their feet. After the treachery of the day before, they'd been reluctant to allow the Aryaalans and B'mbaadans to take their place on the barricade, but they were exhausted and Adar ordered them to rest. They weren't about to trust undependable allies with the security of their wounded comrades and leaders, however. Battle-weary Marines rotated the duty throughout the night. Bradford knew now what had happened, and he personally felt nothing but gratitude for the warriors that came to their aid, but he could sympathize with how the Marines felt.

There were many, many wounded lying on the ground in the vicinity and he carefully picked his way through the sleeping forms. Many, he suspected, would never awake. Most would, however, and that was largely due to the efforts of Lieutenant Tucker, who he now saw step tiredly from under the awning into the gray morning light. He realized she'd probably brought little in the way of medical science to the Lemurian people. In many ways their medicines were more effective than those she knew—the strange antiseptic paste for one—but she had introduced the idea of battlefield triage and the associated patch-and-splice that went with it. That was something the local healers had never considered. The sea folk didn't need it because they so rarely fought anything like a major battle, and the locals, who fought all the time, had just never thought of it. Perhaps it was because even they had never fought a battle such as this, in which the sheer numbers of casualties were so high. Unlike anyone they'd met so far, the B'mbaadans and Aryaalans understood the concept of surrender, at least among themselves. Maybe they had never let things go this far before one side or the other just quit. Whatever the case, the exhausted young nurse had done heroic work that night. He picked his way toward her.

"You should rest, my dear. You are destroyed." He spoke quietly so as not to disturb those nearby whose sleep was only temporary. She nodded at him and smiled weakly. "But you know that, of course."

"Yes." She sighed. "The healers we brought are a wonder. I couldn't have managed without them." Her face brightened somewhat. "Pam Cross and Kathy McCoy came from *Mahan* to lend a hand. God, I'm so glad they're safe!" She gestured under the tent and shook her head. "They're in there now. Last night was bad, but they sure had a rough time on *Mahan*. Everything from constant fear for their lives to attempted rape. With Kaufman in charge"—she snorted—"pretending to be in charge—there was chaos. They told me things . . ." She didn't finish, but instead looked in the direction of the barricade and what lay beyond. "Beth Grizzel went ashore with Kaufman. Did you know that?"

Bradford nodded and gently patted her arm. "Mr. Ellis told me last night."

Sandra shivered, but continued to glare at the barricade. "Damn Kaufman!" she muttered fiercely. "So much misery because of him. I hope he roasts in hell!"

Bradford felt his eyebrow arch, but decided now wasn't an appropriate time for the response that leaped to mind. Pity. "I'm quite certain he did, my dear." He guided her to a bench and hovered near her as she sat down at last. "And how then are the captain and his extremely lucky companions? I still can hardly believe they survived, from what I hear."

She stared bleakly at her hands on her lap. "As you say. Lucky to be alive. Keje has a concussion, I think, but other than that he didn't get a scratch. The Chief had an arrow in his hip, but it struck the very edge of his pelvis and went down instead of up. Lucky. If it went up, it would have perforated his bowel. God knows if that Lemurian paste would have any effect on peritonitis. It'll hurt when he walks for a while, but he should be fine. Matt?" She closed her eyes tightly and tried to control the relief in her voice. "His cheekbone is cracked, at least, and he has a deep gash in his side, down to the ribs. Besides that, he was stabbed in the back, through his shoulder blade and out his chest with a spear." She laughed bitterly. "At least it was a 'clean' wound. Not many bone fragments or other debris. Those Grik spears are sharp!" The tears came then, in spite of all she could do.

Bradford sat beside her and put his good arm around her shoulders. "You care a lot for him, don't you, my dear?" He spoke in a kindly voice.

"Of course I do," Sandra whispered, answering his question before he could himself, for once.

"Of course you do," Bradford repeated, oblivious to her response. "As do we all."

The sun finally rose and showed for all to see the results of the Battle of Aryaal. By late morning, the skuggiks had arrived in force, and soon there were so many even Bradford couldn't watch them anymore, so sickened did he become. Beyond the barricade and across the plain, all the way up to the base of the wall that surrounded Aryaal, a seething mass of raucous scavengers feasted on the thousands of Grik corpses underneath the brilliant sun and cloudless sky. The ground itself came to look like one huge corpse, working with maggots as the light gray skuggiks capered and hopped among the bodies, gorging themselves on the remains. The smell was overpowering, but the sounds the creatures made while they ate were even worse.

Jim Ellis walked, still limping a little from the wound Kaufman had given him, up to the awning that served as a hospital tent. There he found Rolak, pacing anxiously back and forth while Chack stood in one place and spoke quietly to him. Jim had met the Lemurian bosun's mate only the night before, but he didn't feel the least bit ridiculous return-ing the sharp salute Chack gave him when he joined them.

"Good morning, sir," Chack said. There was a blood-soaked ban-dage on his shoulder, and he wore his battered doughboy helmet with a jaunty air. Over his other shoulder was slung a long-barreled Krag-Jorgensen and a Navy cutlass was belted around his blood-spattered kilt.

"Good morning, ah, Mr. Chack." Ellis gestured at Rolak, who had stopped his pacing and was now looking at him. "What's with him?"

"He is anxious to see the captain."

"Me too," Jim said with feeling. He glanced at his watch. "I guess we'll get to in about fifteen minutes. I got word there's an officers' call at twelve hundred hours."

Chack nodded. "Yes, sir, but not in the tent. It's down at the left flank of the breastworks, close to the water. I'm directing everyone there as they arrive."

Jim Ellis looked at him in surprise. "You mean they carried the cap-tain over there in the shape he's in?" he demanded.

Chack blinked. "He walked."

Matt was seated stiffly on a stool near where Ellis had placed the .30-cals the day before. His left arm was bound tightly to his side so he couldn't move it, even accidentally, and risk opening his wounds. His sunken eyes and the purplish-yellow bruise that covered the left side of his face made his pain clearly evident in spite of the clean uniform and fresh shave. Behind him stood Lieutenant Tucker, wearing a dis-approving frown, and Chief Gray, supporting himself with a pair of crutches from *Walker*'s medical locker. His hat was back on his head. Someone had found it while retrieving the wounded and dead and had returned it to him. Lieutenant Shinya stood beside him, wearing a slightly bewildered expression. Somehow, throughout the battle, he'd received only a few superficial wounds, even though he'd been in the thick of it from the start. Often his gaze drifted to the field beyond the barricade, where the scavengers now reigned, and his hand strayed to the hilt of the modified cutlass at his belt as if he wanted to reassure himself it was still there.

The gathering, or "officers' call," was quite large. All the battle line "captains" were there, including Rick Tolson from *Revenge*. Matt had already praised him and his brave crew, and he and Kas were about to burst with pride. So were some of the *"Revenges"* that accompanied them. Chack was now the de facto commander of the Second Marines, since the CO of that regiment had been killed the day before. In fact, almost all of the original regimental commanders had fallen and been replaced by their second or third in line. The Fifth Guards had a sergeant in command. There was no representative present for the Fourth, since it no longer existed.

Keje was there, also on a stool, with his head bound in a bandage that resembled a turban. Nearby stood his daughter, who stared at the striking, black-furred queen of B'mbaado with expressionless eyes. If Safir Maraan noticed the scrutiny, she gave no sign. She was immaculately groomed, which alone was enough to set her apart from most of those present. Her black cape and brilliant armor had been just as muddy and bloodstained as anyone's the day before, but since then it had been either cleaned or replaced. Now she cut a most imposing figure as she stood, slightly aside, with Haakar-Faask and four of her elite personal guards in attendance. They were not quite as resplendent as she, but they had groomed themselves. Adar was speaking softly to Keje, who nodded without thinking and winced at the pain from the sudden movement.

Larry Dowden and Lieutenant Garrett were the only officers from *Walker* that weren't there and Matt watched nervously as they slowly, carefully, backed his ship from the mouth of the river just a few hundred yards away. Slow maneuvers in any kind of current were difficult for the old four-stacker, but going backward on one engine in a confined space . . . It was positively nerve-racking for him to watch. Jim Ellis shouldered through the crowd to stand next to him and Matt glanced at his watch. It was on his right wrist for now.

"I guess everybody's here that's coming," he said.

"Sorry I'm late, Captain," Ellis apologized, although it was only just now 1200. "I went over to check how repairs to my shi—" He grimaced guiltily. "I mean *Mahan*—are progressing. I was only told the meeting had moved when I came ashore."

Matt made a dismissive gesture with his good hand. "You're not late, Jim, and *Mahan is* your ship. No apology necessary."

"Thanks, Skipper," Jim said in a tone of relief. He wouldn't have been surprised to be relieved. After all, he deserved it. He cocked his head toward *Walker* and made a wry face. "She's still my ship too. You don't think maybe I . . . ?"

Matt shook his head with an assurance he didn't feel. "Nonsense. Lieutenant Dowden's a fine officer. He'll have no trouble. Now then . . ." He turned his attention to the gathered officers, who had silently watched the short exchange. There was a sudden commotion in the ring of onlookers and Matt vaguely recognized Lord Rolak as he pushed his way through to stand before him. His fine helmet was dented and the feather plume was gone. Unlike Queen Maraan, he hadn't refreshed himself in any way since the battle the day before. He stood squarely before Captain Reddy and his eyes blazed with inner torment. He drew his battered sword.

In an instant Gray had his pistol pointed at the Protector's face. In the shocked silence, there were several metallic rasps of bolts slamming home as other destroyermen reacted to the threat. Matt raised his hand. Slowly, never taking his eyes from Matt's, Lord Rolak went to his knees and laid his sword on the ground at Matt's feet.

"My sword, my life, my honor—which is all that I am—is yours," he said in a keening monotone.

Astonished, Adar hurried to him and knelt at his side. "I am Adar, Sky Priest to *Salissa* Home and councillor to Keje-Fris-Ar," he whispered urgently. "I know little of your customs, but of this I have heard. Must you do this? I know the Amer-i-caans well and I assure you this gesture is not required."

"It is not a gesture, Priest!" Rolak growled harshly. "If you know what I have done, then tell him. I gave my word and it was broken."

"It was not your doing. We all know that!" Adar hissed.

"Nevertheless. The word of Muln-Rolak will have meaning!"

Adar stood, blinking in consternation. He turned to Matt, who was looking at him with a puzzled expression. "I am sorry, Cap-i-taan Reddy," he said. "But if I am not mistaken, Lord Rolak wishes to make a"—he quickly sought a word besides "gesture"—"representation, regarding his remorse over yesterday's, ah, change of plans."

"Unnecessary," Matt promptly replied. "We're indebted to Lord Rolak and all who fought with him for coming in spite of his leader's orders to the contrary." He shrugged with one shoulder. "He saved my life and many, many others by doing so."

If it was possible, Adar looked bemused. "I told him you would react this way, but it's already too late."

Without thinking, Matt used the Lemurian blink of surprise in response. "Too late for what?"

"He has already done it. He has proclaimed a debt of honor and has given himself to you, as a slave if you wish. Do not be angered. He does not know your ways! But regardless, his life now belongs to you."

"But . . . !" Matt was speechless and he looked at the elderly, kneeling Lemurian before him. "Tell him no! He can't be my slave! Tell him thanks, but *no*!"

Adar sadly shook his head. "I knew you would say that too. In that case, you must kill him. It is the only way his honor can be restored." Adar held his hands out helplessly at his sides.

"What? *Damn it!* I don't need this today! I'm not going to do that!" Matt clenched his eyes shut in pain from his own outburst.

"Very well. I will tell him," Adar said. "But if I do, it's my understanding he will immediately kill himself as being so without honor that he is not even worthy of being a slave." Adar shrugged again. "Strange folk, as I have said." He started to turn to Rolak.

"Wait!" Matt said sharply. "Don't tell him that! Tell him okay!" He sighed. "Tell him to pick up his sword and stand ready to answer some questions. We'll sort this out later!" Adar complied, and with supreme dignity Rolak retrieved his weapon and stood. He looked around at those assembled. Not really knowing what to do next himself, he stepped back.

Matt stood, and his face paled when his slashed muscles tensed. Sandra was caught by surprise and seemed unable to decide whether to support him or try to force him back down. Ignoring her, Matt spoke to the faces that watched in silence. "I guess we won."

A spontaneous cheer erupted from those who understood his words, and the others joined in when they were told what he said. The roar of approval and relief continued for several minutes, startling the skuggiks on the other side of the barricade and echoing off the walls of Aryaal. At the tops of those walls, grim-faced defenders watched in silence. Matt waited for the cheering to subside.

"We won the battle and I've heard how each of you distinguished yourselves. I'm proud of you all, and I give thanks to my God for your bravery and mourn your sacrifices as well as those of all who fell." His face became grim.

"It was a costly victory and you have my apology for that." There were shouted protests. He knew none of them expected him to assume responsibility for their losses—but they were his fault regardless of what had happened. It had been his plan and he was in command. In the face of that surprise and disagreement, he remorselessly tallied the casualties. "Almost four in ten of the brave soldiers, sailors, warriors, and Marines who began the battle were killed or seriously wounded. Seriously enough that most of them are out of this campaign, at least." He looked at Safir Maraan. "Her Gracious Highness, Queen Protector Maraan of B'mbaado told me her losses were similar. I imagine the same is true for those who followed Lord Rolak. Let no one here doubt for a moment their courage and honor. It wasn't they who betrayed us, but King Fet-Alcas, who still sits safe behind the walls we preserved for him." There were angry growls. "But let's put that aside for now. I think Her Highness has an announcement to make." He nodded at Adar, who whispered something to the queen. She stepped briskly forward, her cape flowing behind her. When she was in the middle of the circle, she looked around and began to speak in her husky, self-assured voice.

"B'mbaado is proud, grateful, to have fought beside such warriors as yourselves. Never has there been such a battle, and never have warriors achieved so much against such odds." She listened to the appreciative murmurs. "B'mbaado is a warlike nation," she continued matter-of-factly. "We war often. With Aryaal, or the other nations up the coast, so fighting is not strange to us. But this war is unlike anything we've faced. The Grik are Evil. They are not even People. They do not fight for, or with, honor but only for death. Beyond that? Territory perhaps. We do not even know. We do know what happens to those they vanquish." She took a breath. "For the first time, when the Grik came here, B'mbaado faced a war it did not want, was not prepared to fight, and knew it couldn't win. We even tried to join forces with our most bitter rival, Aryaal, because we knew that only together might we have a chance." She paused. "But it was to no avail. They were too many. We knew it was just a matter of time until Aryaal fell, and then B'mbaado would be next. I brought the Six Hundred, my personal guard, to help delay that day as long as possible, but in reality all hope was lost." She turned to look directly at Matt.

"Then you came. Not for loot or conquest, or for anything from us at all. You came to *help!*" She shook her head and blinked with remembered surprise. "Sea folk!" She glanced quickly at Jim Ellis. "The other iron ship had been here for a time and we knew it had great power, but in our shortsighted, uncurious way, neither Aryaal nor B'mbaado had any use for it or its people once we knew it would not help either of us against the other." She blinked apology at Jim. "Besides," she said, "it was badly damaged. Every day I expected to look out and see that it had sunk. When the Grik came, it tried to help us against them, but it couldn't move. All it could do was use its power to keep a passage clear between Aryaal and my home." She bowed to Jim Ellis. "For that, I thank you."

She looked back at Matt, and again at the surrounding officers. "But then you came, with yet another iron ship, and the great Homes of the sea folk. You *erased* the Grik from the bay! It was the greatest thing I ever saw. I am sure that were it not for Fet-Alcas's treachery the battle for Aryaal would have been just as one-sided, and just as complete."

She paused and blinked significant resolve. "I have come to realize that this war you fight to destroy the Grik forever is not just a war for honor, as we've so often fought, but an honorable war—and one we must be part of." She looked around. "Until the end," she added grimly. Then she straightened her back with an air of solemn dignity and spoke once more.

"I, Safir Maraan, Queen Protector of the People of B'mbaado, beg you will accept my nation and my warriors into your Grand Alliance to destroy the Grik menace once and forever."

There were appreciative howls and stamping feet, and the humans that could clapped their hands together. Matt stood and watched while the queen bowed formally, acknowledging the praise, and he managed a smile. Behind it, however, as he so often did, he was considering ramifications. The B'mbaadans were considerable warriors. Much like the people of Madura were reckoned in the world he came from. The question was how best to integrate them into the shield wall. They would have their own ideas how to fight, and he hoped they wouldn't prove too difficult to teach the new way of fighting, as they'd done with the others. If the battle had taught them anything at all, it was that the tactics Matt had suggested and Shinya and Alden had drilled into their troops worked. The last thing they needed was a gaggle forming part of the line.

Surprisingly, Queen Maraan immediately answered the question for him.

"I was, of course, impressed by the skill and courage with which you fought," she said. "As an ally, might I presume you will teach us these skills of war?"

Matt stirred with relief when Adar told him what she had asked, and he cleared his throat. "Certainly, Your Highness. I'm sure something can be arranged." He waited until Adar began telling the queen what he'd said. "Lieutenant Shinya?" he whispered quietly.

Shinya stepped up beside him. "Sir?"

"See to it, if you please. Set up an abbreviated drill for our new allies. Or if they're willing, maybe we can integrate the B'mbaadan troops directly into our existing regiments, at least for now. Sort of a 'jump right in' form of basic training. God knows, we need the replacements after yesterday." While he spoke, he noticed the queen of B'mbaado staring at Chack with as close to an expression of interested speculation as her face was capable of. Perhaps Adar had mentioned him? Maybe she'd asked about the powerful young Lemurian who stared brazenly back at her from beneath the jaunty angle of his dented helmet. "I know you've learned to speak 'Cat pretty good, Lieutenant," Matt said in a thoughtful tone, "but use Chack as your liaison. If you want him to keep the Second Marines that's fine with me—hell, he helped train them—and that'd be a good outfit to put their officers in to work them up."

Lieutenant Shinya nodded. "That was my thinking exactly, Captain."

Matt looked at the battle line commanders for a moment before addressing them. "All of you are not just captains but also heads of state. You have an equal say in this matter. Do any of you object to this alliance?" There was only a respectful silence from the Home high chiefs, although Anai-Sa of *Fristar* seemed oblivious. "Good." He turned to Safir Maraan. "Your Highness, as commander of the Allied Expeditionary Force, it's my honor to accept your nation into our alliance on behalf of its other members, with my gratitude." There was another short cheer, and Queen Maraan bowed graciously once more. Matt took a breath and regarded Lord Rolak, who stood watching what transpired with a tired, wistful posture. "Lord Rolak."

The Aryaalan seemed to clear his thoughts as he quickly knelt before the captain. "Yes, Lord?"

Matt understood that much of the People's speech, and he rubbed his eyes with his good hand and peered down at the Lemurian, cursing the fact that he'd never found the time to become fluent in the tongue. No time, he asked himself then, or just too lazy? Maybe too arrogant? He honestly didn't think so, but it was high time he learned to speak without an interpreter. "Adar," he said, "please try to explain to Lord Rolak that he's not a slave. I know what he did—what he risked and what he lost—in order to keep his word. I don't doubt his honor or his courage, and no one else should either. I admire it. Tell him that. Then tell him I'd be grateful for his service, and the service of all those who followed him and fought so well at our side. Not as slaves or vassals, but as friends."

Matt carefully lowered himself until he was kneeling on the ground. As Adar spoke, Rolak lifted his gaze until it rested heavily and searchingly upon Matt's face. With an encouraging smile, Matt extended his hand. Rolak looked at it, unsure, until Adar quickly explained the human custom. Then Rolak slowly, almost tentatively, extended his own hand. Matt grasped it between them and pumped it up and down.

Seeing Matt's difficulty in rising, Shinya and Sandra helped the captain back onto the stool, where he sat, puffing slightly and watching the Aryaalan.

Rolak stood and brushed sand from his knees. "We are friends then, yes," he said, talking to Adar. "But that in no way absolves me of my honor debt. If anything, it makes it a greater burden. Sometimes friendship can be the cruelest slavery of all, but in this case I accept it gladly. Tell Cap-i-taan Reddy he is my lord, as Fet-Alcas once was, and my sword, my life, and my honor are still his, but they are freely given as a friend and not as a slave."

Matt listened to Adar's translation and sighed. It was probably the best compromise he would manage for now, given the dire nature of Rolak's original pledge, and he was grateful that, however it happened, the alliance had grown still more.

"Now," he said, holding himself as still as possible while the pain of his exertions subsided, "that's over with. I've heard your reports, but this meeting is to get everyone on the same page regarding our current situation. Mr. Shinya, would you describe the disposition of the enemy?"

"Yes, sir." Shinya shifted and spoke so his voice would carry to all those present. "As far as we can tell, they're gone. Our original estimate of their embarked force seems to have been . . . a little off, and several hundred of them, at least, escaped at the end of the battle. There is no indication that they retreated in any semblance of order, though.

They just fled. I would recommend that when the Catalina flies in from Baalkpan this afternoon, Lieutenant Mallory be requested to fly a quick search pattern, fuel permitting, to ensure that the enemy has not reconstituted himself nearby."

"Do you think that is likely?" Keje asked. He spoke very carefully because he, like Matt, was trying to remain as still as he could.

"It's possible. I do not think it likely, however." Shinya paused and his brow furrowed in thought as he tried to decide how best to explain himself. Before he could, Courtney Bradford spoke up.

"If I may, Lieutenant?" Shinya nodded and the Australian cleared his throat. "Well. First of all, when the Grik finally broke, it was quite spectacular. Quite spectacular indeed! They just ran in all directions, like bees! As if they'd entirely lost their minds. Although I wasn't, um, actually in the very thickest of the fight, I saw the end from what might have been a better vantage point than most. Their demeanor couldn't have been more different from one moment to the next. It was as though one just pulled a cord and flipped a light." He looked owlishly at Keje. "It was like the deck of *Big Sal* all over again, the day we first really met. Many hundreds—I couldn't possibly count them—were slaughtered without attempting to defend themselves at all. It was as though the solitary thought in all their heads was escape. Quite spectacular indeed. Even if they did at some point recover themselves, I doubt they'd have the slightest notion how to reassemble into anything like a threatening force. Besides"—he grinned with what could only be described as anticipatory glee—"I am reliably informed that Java is populated with quite a variety of fascinating predators. Perhaps not as terrifying as some inhabiting the inner reaches of Borneo, but . . ." He looked around and arched an eyebrow. "Well. Certainly we should mount an expedition to go and see?"

Sandra leaned forward and whispered in Matt's ear. "Sometimes I wonder if everything that's happened since we came through the Squall has been God's attempt to overwhelm Courtney's curiosity."

"Never happen," Matt whispered back, then raised his voice. "Perhaps at some point, Mr. Bradford, but first let's win the war. Speaking of which, could you tell, from your 'vantage point,' what broke the Grik? What caused their extraordinary behavior? They still had us pretty badly outnumbered, as I recall. Mr. Shinya? You were speculating on the remaining enemy force. We should have a better idea now how many lizards there were to start with?"

Shinya looked grim, but that same expression of bewilderment returned as well. He opened his mouth, closed it, and finally waved at the plain beyond the barricade, black with skuggiks and enemy dead. "It's impossible to say for sure, Captain, but our best estimate is almost nineteen thousand enemy dead. More than we thought they even had." His face became a stony mask and there was a sharp intake of breath by some of those nearby. "No prisoners, of course. No wounded."

"Of course." Matt already knew their own losses had been more than seven hundred killed, with almost twice that number seriously wounded. Five more of his precious destroyermen had died as well, and a knot appeared in his throat when he remembered their names. Tom Felts, Glen Carter, Gil Olivera—the ordnance division had certainly had a bad day. Loris Scurrey and Andy Simms had made it almost as tough on the first deck division. He could see their faces in his mind—all of them—and he felt he'd failed them too, just like Marvaney, the first man they lost after coming through the Squall. He would have to try to forget for now, to push them away. There'd be plenty of time later, in the darkness of his quarters, for them to demand his full attention.

"Ten to one, Skipper," said Gray, sensing his mood. "Them Romans knew a thing or two, I guess."

"Not all Roman," Matt replied absently, then blinked and shook his head. "Very well. I'll ask you again, Mr. Bradford. Why?"

Courtney tucked the hand of his unwounded arm in his belt and stood on the balls of his feet. "Captain Reddy, you cannot possibly appreciate the position you have placed me in! To speculate upon such behavior based upon so little—"

Adar interrupted. "You already have a theory, one we have discussed. Otherwise, instead of bouncing on your toes, you would have removed your ridiculous hat and wiped your hairless scalp." Adar had sensed the need to lighten the mood. He may be a Lemurian Sky Priest and no type of real preacher, parson, or holy man, in any of the destroyermen's eyes at least, but he'd gained tremendous respect for his wisdom—hell, he could talk English as good as Chack! He could predict the weather better than anyone alive, and he definitely had a sense of humor the men could appreciate. A lot of worse fellows calling themselves priests came aboard back before the War.

"Grik Rout," Bradford confirmed. "We saw it once aboard *Big Sal* and again, well, yesterday. I don't think it's a phenomenon we can feel certain enough of to base any strategy upon."

"What *do* you think it is?" growled Chief Gray.

Bradford shrugged. "Some kind of massive, instinctual panic attack that renders them totally incapable of concerted efforts—such as war. Be lovely to turn it on and off again at will, but so far the only things I've seen do the trick are massive doses of automatic weapons, heavy artillery, and having their assault stopped cold by what were, at least briefly and locally, superior numbers that attacked *them* with mindless ferocity." He beamed at Lord Rolak.

Matt frowned. "So, in other words, pretty much the same thing that has stopped every other attack in history."

"Indeed. But the *effect* was still significant, don't you think?"

"It was certainly significant," Shinya confirmed. "And if we could learn how to create it at will, even strategic perhaps." He turned to Matt. "But Mr. Bradford is right. We cannot 'plan' for it. We have fought the Grik enough now to know that it does not always happen. In fact, sometimes their 'rout' can make them even more dangerous." He was remembering the losses they'd taken in the hold of *Revenge* when they scoured the last of the Grik from below. Slowly he brightened, his hand still resting on the pommel of the cut-down katana/cutlass Sandison had given him. "But they are gone from here now!"

"Good," said Matt with a genuine smile. "At least the 'land' lizards no longer seem a threat." There were a couple of chuckles from the destroyermen nearby. "What's the condition of the task force?"

"All is well, Cap-i-taan Reddy," Keje said, but then he put a hand to his forehead and closed his eyes. Adar continued for him. "No serious damage yesterday, or in the fighting with the Grik ships. Ammunition is depleted. We expended more than half of what we brought. As you know, weight and storage is not a problem, only production. We brought what we had. As more is made in Baalkpan, it will be sent."

Matt nodded. "What about those feluccas we couldn't account for?"

Rick Tolson spoke up. "We found one, Skipper. Hard aground in the shoals around those crummy little islands off the southeast coast of Madura. Everybody got off okay, but the ship was a total loss." He shook his head. "Lucky we didn't lose a dozen of 'em in there. No sign of the others. Lizards must've got 'em."

"Poor bastards," muttered Gray. Matt glanced at him, then looked at the bay where *Walker* had finally backed clear of the river. Even as he watched, her horn tooted exultantly, and Matt grinned in spite of himself. Dowden must have known he'd be as nervous as a cat. He had every confidence in his exec's seamanship, but he still felt tremendous relief.

"Well, now that it's clear our exuberant Mr. Dowden has saved my ship from further exposure to freshwater, I guess I'll report that she came through the fighting with no damage except for some scorched paint, some busted glass, and the loss of one of her propeller blades."

The Lemurian sea folk all nodded seriously at the news. They'd never seen *Walker*'s propellers, of course, but they'd seen drawings of the magical things that moved the iron ship so swiftly. Also, they'd seen the propellers on the PBY and knew the principle was the same. Matt had been taken aback that an airplane's propellers weren't harder for them to understand. If a PBY had shown up among his own ancestors two thousand years ago, he figured they'd have thrown spears at it or started a new religion. They certainly wouldn't have acted like "Oh, yeah. Pretty neat. *We* can't make one, but it makes perfect sense."

The fact that their culture—at least that of the sea folk—revolved around the reality of moving air, or wind, must have given them a pretty good grasp of the idea that air had substance whether you could see it or not. There were enough creatures that flew to prove flight was possible too. So from there, the notion that people might fly in a machine of some sort wasn't as big a stretch to them as it probably would have been among Bronze Age humans. Anyway, it was just another example of how sophisticated Lemurians could sometimes be. He didn't know why it surprised him anymore.

"That brings up another matter," he said, addressing Jim Ellis. "I want *Mahan* to make for Baalkpan as soon as possible. We don't have a dry dock, of course, but there are facilities there. Whatever we decide to do next, *Mahan*'s in no shape to fight. If we can get her to Baalkpan, at least we can start to change that." He paused and grimaced. "Before she leaves, though, I want one of her propellers if we can manage it."

Jim whistled. "That's a tall order, Skipper. How are we going to get at them? Hell, we can't even go in the water."

Matt was relieved that Jim didn't show more resentment at the prospect of crippling his ship further. He hated to ask it of him, but he didn't see any choice. If *Walker* couldn't run on two engines, it would seriously hamper any plans they made for further offensive operations.

"I don't know, Jim, but we'll think of something. I'll get with you after the meeting and we can hash it out. We'll work out a schedule to get *Mahan* as seaworthy as possible too. Now"—he looked back at Rolak—"what's going on in the city? I see guards on the walls, but no one's answering the door."

"Civil war," growled Rolak through Adar. "Warriors came out during the night, warriors loyal to me. They told of fighting throughout the city and . . . horrible deeds." He cast down his eyes. "It seems that by trying to save my city's honor, I may have caused its destruction. None have come out since morning, though, and I don't know what's happening now. My best guess is that the king's loyalists have retaken control of the main gate."

"What happened?" Matt asked gently.

Lord Rolak sighed. "As you know, when Fet-Alcas refused to allow us to strike the enemy rear, as we agreed, my forces and those of Queen Maraan swept north through the city and came out through the north gate. We had to fight to get out even there. Apparently, word spread of the specifics of the disagreement and many were appalled not only by the king's treachery but also by the fact that they had been deprived of participating in such a great battle. I know it may be hard for some of you to understand, but to watch such a fight from behind stout walls and do nothing, regardless of the honor at stake, would be difficult for Aryaalans to bear. Fet-Alcas has never been a popular king. He assumed the throne upon the death of his brother, who *was* popular and widely respected. Even, I think, in B'mbaado."

Safir Maraan nodded. "Tac-Alcas was a worthy opponent," she agreed without reluctance. "We warred with him often and he was difficult, difficult, but my father respected his courage, as well as his honor. As did I. Tac-Alcas would never have betrayed us as his brother did."

"In any event," Rolak continued, "there were already factions, political ones, long before the Grik came." He spoke the word "political" with a sneer. "I suspect most of those who actually supported me and my decision to come to your aid managed to make it out during the night. Any fighting still under way is probably between the king and other factions within the nobility that, like skuggiks drawn to carrion, have seen an opportunity. I imagine my return would be as unwelcome to any of them as it would be to the king."

"We must talk to them, nevertheless. Whoever's in charge," Matt observed.

"Indeed. Many of my warriors who would wish to join you still have families within those walls. None of them are bound by my friendship with you, although most will consider themselves so. I will storm the city myself, if necessary, to get their families out."

"Hopefully that won't be necessary," Sandra said in a fervent tone.

Heads nodded in unison and Matt cleared his throat. "Well. That's pretty much how things sit, I believe. The way I see it, we have, almost in spite of ourselves, won a major victory here. It was costlier than it should have been and we're not in as good a shape as we'd hoped to be at this point. But that doesn't change the ultimate strategy of our campaign. We've got to keep up the pressure and move against Singapore as quickly as possible. The intelligence we gained from the captured charts suggests the enemy has only an outpost there so far. While we can presume that the force we destroyed here probably at least stopped off at Singapore, there's no indication in the charts that they dropped off any sizable force. That being said, I expect that's probably where the ships that escaped the battle in the bay retreated to, but they left their troops behind. With the addition of Queen Maraan's troops, and those of Lord Rolak, we should have sufficient forces to evict them—if we act before they reinforce." He looked at the gathered faces and wished again that he had some inkling of their thoughts. "Therefore, our priorities are these: first, bring the B'mbaadan and Aryaalan troops up to speed as quickly as possible." Matt let his gaze rest on Queen Maraan and Lord Rolak in turn. "That's going to take considerable cooperation from both of you. Your people are proud warriors and they may resist training in the new tactics, particularly since their instructors will be 'mere' sea folk."

"They won't resist," Queen Maraan assured him. "Not after yesterday."

Matt hoped she was right and he tried to hide his skepticism. He knew how difficult it had been for Europe to accept the lessons of modern war that Americans learned during their own Civil War. "Second, I want every felucca in the fleet either transporting supplies from Baalkpan or scouting the coastlines for any further incursions by the enemy. If they've established other outposts—at Tjilatjap, for example—we must know about it immediately. We'll also reconnoiter toward Singapore. Rick Tolson and Kas-Ra-Ar will assemble a small squadron of the fastest craft around *Revenge* for that purpose." He looked at Rick. "Don't push too hard. They have to expect us to check them out, but I don't want them to expect an attack."

"Understood, Captain."

"I also want the wounded out." He looked speculatively at his battle line commanders. "We should move them aboard a Home. Decide among yourselves which one it'll be." Matt had no doubt they would choose *Fristar*. Even now it was clear that the High Chiefs of the other Homes were avoiding Anai-Sa. His Home had lagged throughout the Battle of the Bay and had shown no initiative with her fire the following day. Adar told him that he doubted she'd fired a dozen times—as if Anai-Sa was hoarding his ammunition. "Whoever it is," Matt continued, "must deliver the wounded and return here as quickly as possible with as many more warriors as Baalkpan can spare." He took a deep breath. "Finally, we have to resolve the situation in Aryaal. I hope we can do that peacefully, but when we move on Singapore, I expect we'll be taking as many B'mbaadan warriors as Her Highness can spare from her island's defenses." He looked at Queen Maraan and blinked a question. She nodded slowly in reply. He had no idea if she was reluctant or merely contemplative. "Since we can't afford to leave a sizable force here to secure our lines of supply and communication—or to protect B'mbaado from an opportunistic Fet-Alcas trying to reunite his people against a common enemy—we must ensure that we aren't leaving a hostile presence in our rear."

There was considerable murmuring over that, as he'd expected. The sea folk harbored absolutely no moral qualms over battling the hated Grik to extinction, but the idea of fighting other Lemurians—no matter who they were—was anathema. It was what had always set them apart, in their view, from the people of Surabaya. He let them continue to talk among themselves a few moments more, but then silenced them. "Mr. Shinya, the Second Marines and half the remaining artillery will deploy in front of the north gate, and the rest of our forces will guard the barricade in case old Fet-Alcas starts feeling adventurous." He looked at the others.

"If there's nothing else, we all have a lot to do over the next couple of weeks. That's all the time we can spare, so make the most of it. If any of you have questions, I'll be back ashore tonight"—he stopped, and his eyes became hooded and his voice grew quiet—"for the funeral. Right now, I'm going back to my ship."

The meeting broke up and the attendees drifted off, some talking excitedly among themselves, others silent. Matt summoned his reserves and stood up from the stool once more, casting an impatient glance at Sandra when she tried to help. She shook her head and stayed back, but the displeasure was clear on her face.

"I want you out of here as quickly as possible, Jim. How soon can you get under way?"

Ellis visibly calculated how long it would take to accomplish the necessary preparations. "A week or two, Captain . . . I think." He assumed a troubled expression. "But I'm not sure how we're going to manage the propeller trade. That might slow things down."

Matt nodded. "I know, and I'm sorry to do this to you, but it can't be helped. *Mahan* can't steam any faster on two engines than she can on one. We'll fix that as soon as we can, but right now we need at least one of our ships to be fast." He grinned. "At least by local standards."

They began walking slowly toward the dock at a pace set unobtrusively by Sandra to minimize any chance of the captain stressing his wounds. Chief Gray hobbled along on his crutches, joined by Chack and Lord Rolak, a respectful distance behind. With so much to do, Matt flatly refused to return to his hospital bed, but no one was about to let him run around on his own. They reached the dock and waited for *Walker* to complete a wide, easy turn out in the bay that would eventually bring her alongside the pier. After a long silence in which each of them stared at the slender, light-gray ship with different and sometimes conflicting thoughts and emotions, Jim Ellis cleared his throat.

"Captain?" he said. "Matt?"

Matt arched an eyebrow and looked at his former executive officer. Jim was his friend, but even so, the number of times he'd addressed him by his first name could be counted on the fingers of one hand. In the past, he'd done it only when he wanted to speak to him *as* a friend and not as a subordinate officer. "There's something I've got to say. I wanted to, night before last, after the battle in the bay, but everything moved so quickly and besides"—he shrugged and gestured at the destroyer, which had completed her turn and was slowly approaching the dock—"I was just so glad to see you and that old 'can, the last thing I wanted to do was argue." He frowned. "But that was before yesterday." He glanced at Sandra for support and then looked to see if anyone else was in earshot. There was a general commotion and bustle all around, but the only ones close enough to hear were Gray, Rolak, and Chack. Currently, however, the Bosun and Matt's new . . . whatever he was . . . were deep in discussion, with Chack translating for them. He sighed.

"Skipper, I really don't think you should let yourself get caught up in any more desperate land battles, and I'd take it as a personal favor if you'd refrain."

Both of Matt's eyebrows rose then, but he managed a chuckle. "I had to be there, Jim. Nakja-Mur and all the High Chiefs put me in overall command. It would have looked pretty lousy if I wasn't willing to face the same danger as those I was supposed to be leading. Hell, Keje was there."

"Keje was there because *you* were there, and he almost got killed too," Sandra pointed out.

"Well, you're the one who so forcefully assured me I'm not indispensable," Matt reminded her with a gentle smile.

"I lied," she retorted. She wasn't smiling. Matt's grin faded and he looked at her intently for a moment. Jim seemed to be considering his words. When he spoke, at first it appeared he was changing the subject.

"When's the last time the men got paid?" he asked. Matt blinked at the apparent non sequitur.

"Before we left the Philippines," he answered guardedly.

"What do you suppose would have happened, before the War, if they'd gone that long without pay?"

Matt made a "what next" gesture, wondering when Jim would get to the point. But instead of Jim, Sandra spoke up. "What he's trying to say is you *are* indispensable! After everything that's happened; the War, the Squall, making an alliance with the Lemurians, and now this battle, *Walker* and her crew have continued to carry on and follow orders and do what you asked of them regardless of the fact that, besides her, and now *Mahan* thankfully, the United States Navy doesn't exist anymore.

Not to them. Even the country they fought for is gone. The only thing that's kept everything together up to now is you. The possibility that the crew might not continue to follow orders never became an issue because you didn't let it. You just continued ruthlessly on, as you always had, and made it clear you expected everyone else to do the same. The United States is gone, but *Walker*'s their center, their core, their cause to cling to, and you're the one who made that happen." She rubbed her tired eyes. "Do you have any idea how fragile that is?"

"She's right, Skipper," Jim said solemnly. "If anything happened to you, it would probably all fall apart. I'm only beginning to learn what all you've managed to accomplish in Balikpapan. I mean, *fuel*, for Christ's sake!" He took a deep breath. "I might be able to carry on for a time—at least I hope I could. I kind of doubt it, though. My command experience so far has been less than stellar. Or maybe Dowden or Letts could swing it for a while, or Bradford could keep things going. But if you're lost, the unique relationship you've forged between *Walker* and the people here would be lost too. What effect would that have on this war against the Grik? Do you think it would even continue?" He waved around, a gesture that encompassed those close by as well as the walls of the city. "Hell, most of these people wouldn't even talk to each other before you made them. Do you think they still would if you were gone? They see you as an honest, impartial broker. One who's not caught up in their petty disputes. The way I see it, you're the glue that's holding this alliance together, and even adding to it." Jim grunted in frustration. "Hell, when I got here with *Mahan*, I couldn't even get the locals to *talk* to me.

"Besides," he continued, "from a purely selfish perspective, think what it would do to the crew. You're the last visible vestige of supreme authority they have left to cling to. The last physical connection to the world they've lost—to normalcy, I guess, and duty. They still follow your orders because you're The Captain, and that's the way it's supposed to be. Even here." Jim looked down at his feet for a moment, and then met Matt's eyes again. "I like to think I could fill your shoes on the bridge someday, as far as seamanship is concerned. Believe me,

I thought about that a lot over the last few months. Then I look at *Walker,* with her new paint job and fuel oil burning in her boilers and I see . . . guys . . . like Chack over there, filling out her crew. I see a ship that was *whipped* but has since become the most powerful ship in the world, more than likely." He sighed. "I compare that to *Mahan,* which hasn't done half of what you have since we split up, and she still looks whipped."

"We were lucky," Matt murmured.

"Maybe so, but that wasn't all." Jim stopped and rubbed his temples, but when he spoke again his expression was pained. "I don't know if I could've stopped Kaufman or not. It never dawned on me that he'd try to take over the ship. Then, when he did, I never thought anyone would obey him, but they did. After what *Mahan* went through, it was hard to blame them, I guess. He sounded like he knew what he was doing when nobody else did, even me. But I've seen what happens when chaos and fear set in and a ship loses all sense of purpose and hope. I don't want to see it again."

Spanky McFarlane stood on *Walker's* fantail, hands on his skinny hips, peering down through the portside propeller-guard tubing at the water below. Occasionally, small waves lapped against it and disrupted the almost perfect, wine-bottle blue-green clarity of the bay. That itself would prove to somebody who just woke up that this wasn't the cloudy, oily, Surabaya/Madura Bay they remembered. Through the occasional ripples, the sandy bottom was visible about thirty feet below, and between it and the surface, the growth-encrusted propeller shaft and support protruded far out beyond the line of the deck on which McFarlane stood. The only thing glaringly wrong with the view was the decidedly queer appearance of the now two-bladed screw. That, and the malevolent silvery shapes that glided and darted hopefully about.

McFarlane was surrounded by half a dozen helpers, snipes and deck-apes together. All stared at the water as if it were fresh molten lava oozing from the ocean floor. The most persistent shark had never received as much attention as the smaller but infinitely more numerous "flashies" did. A short distance away, so close the 'guards almost touched, floated *Mahan,* with a similar assembly peering at the water between them with identical expressions. Noisy sounds of difficult labor and coarse shouts echoed from the other ship as repair parties worked to make her seaworthy, but on *Walker*—just a few yards away—men and Lemurians almost tiptoed around, ridiculously making as little noise as they possibly could. The Skipper was asleep and the titanic racket from the ship alongside had no bearing on their stealthy efforts. If somebody woke the captain, it wasn't going to be any of them.

Machinist's Mate Dean Laney looked from the water to Spanky's hard, solemn face with wide eyes. "I ain't goin' down there, boss!" he said, with just a trace of panic.

McFarlane never even took his eyes off the damaged propeller. "If I say you're goin', you're goin', Laney. Even if I have to throw your worthless ass in." Nobody even mentioned that Laney had fifty pounds on the engineering officer. If Spanky wanted Laney in the water, one way or another, Laney would wind up in the water. "You and Donaghey are the only ones qualified in the diving gear 'sides me, and I'm too important to go. If we can't figure out a better way to get this done, we won't have any choice."

Wisely making no comment on Spanky's perception of his own importance compared to how Laney rated his, the machinist's mate tried sweet reason instead. "Why can't we just flood her down forward? Then we can take it off from a raft."

Spanky shook his head. "Won't work. I already thought of that. We'd have to sink the whole forward part of the ship plumb to the bottom to get those screws out of the water." Laney looked at him with an expression that seemed to ask, "So?" Spanky sighed.

Dennis Silva had joined him at the rail. The big gunner's mate spat in the water and watched as the white bubbles dissipated.

"Why not see what a grenade'll do? A stick of dynamite works pretty good in a lake."

Spanky looked at him and opened his mouth. Then he closed it. "Go get one."

Silva grinned. "Campeti don't just leave 'em in baskets outside his door."

"Tell him I said you could have one." Silva's sheepish expression gave him pause. "Shit. How many times have you told Campeti somebody said you could have a grenade? Never mind, I don't want to know." He took out his notepad and scribbled something on it. Then he tore out the sheet and handed it to Silva, who glanced at what he'd written.

> Sonny: Give Silva a grenade.
> I swear to God it's for me.
> You can ask me later, or bring it yourself.
> To the fantail.
> Spanky

"Looks like a po-eem," Silva said, admiringly.

"Just go get a goddamn grenade!" Spanky raged.

"Shhhh!" cautioned Laney. "You're gonna wake the Skipper!"

Spanky's angry expression changed to a worried frown. "Say, you know, a grenade'd probably do that too. Damn it. I better go talk to the exec. See what he thinks. If he says okay, I'll pick one up myself." He started forward, but then stopped in the narrow space between the rail and the aft deckhouse. He turned and looked at Silva. "Gimme that note back, you." With an expression of purest innocence, Silva passed him the small rectangle of paper and Spanky wadded it up and threw it over the side.

Twenty minutes later, he returned with two hand grenades hooked on his belt and a sour expression on his face. "Skipper wasn't asleep at all. He was on the bridge." He cast an accusatory glare at *Mahan*. "Bastards over there kept him awake, I'll bet, with all their damn noise." He plucked one of the grenades like a pear and held it in his hand. "He said to give it a try." Without another word, or a warning of any sort to the men clustered near *Mahan*'s stern, he pulled the pin and dropped the grenade over the side. The spoon flipped away as soon as it left his hand, and with a sullen *kerplunk!* the grenade was on its way to the bottom of the bay. Seconds later, there was a dull flash and the sea between the ships turned opaque white. Even as the surface heaved, they felt a jolt through the deck plates beneath their feet. A geyser of water erupted skyward and the prevailing wind carried the bulk of the spray down upon the men on *Mahan*'s fantail, who gestured and cursed.

Cheers and happy, good-natured jeering broke out on *Walker*, and even on *Mahan*, since the man most thoroughly inundated was Al "Jolson" Franklen. Franklen had once enjoyed a measure of celebrity throughout the squadron before the War. He did a really good Al Jolson impersonation and he wasn't shy about performing. But even before Pearl Harbor, his act had begun to sour—for a variety of reasons—and most of his fans became distant. Then, of course, he was one of the few *Mahan*s still alive who'd supported Kaufman's mutiny. He only agreed to resume his duties with a full pardon—which Jim Ellis had been obliged to give because of how shorthanded his ship was. In any event, he wasn't a celebrity anymore and the jeering continued long after he strode forward, stony-faced and soaked to the bone.

Ignoring the noise, Spanky, Laney, and Silva too were staring intently at the water. Dead flashies, belly-up, appeared at the surface. Many trailed bloody tendrils but most were unmarked. The other crewmen on both ships quickly forgot their momentary indignity or amusement and joined them in their scrutiny of the grenade's effect. A large flashy swirled and bumped gently against the side of the ship. It twitched. It twitched again. For an instant, they thought it had resuscitated itself, but then it jerked violently and a dark cloud spread around it. Within moments, the surface of the water around and between the two destroyers' propeller guards boiled and seethed with ravenous flashies as they gorged on the bodies of their schoolmates. Laney looked at Spanky, his face a pale, waxy green.

"Fire in the hole!" Spanky warned this time, and dropped the second grenade. The effect was similar to the first, with the exception that the *Mahan*s had time to scramble under the aft deckhouse overhang before they were drenched again. This time, there was only the briefest calm before the roiling frenzy redoubled.

"Oh, well," Spanky grumped, regarding Laney with deadpan remorselessness. "Back to plan A."

"Captain, Lieutenant Mallory's on the horn," reported the radioman, Clancy. "He's crossing Madura—I mean B'mbaado—now, sir."

"Very well," Matt acknowledged. "Tell him to watch out for wrecks in the bay when he sets down."

"Aye, sir," came the reply and Clancy disappeared back down the ladder.

"Too bad we can't just roll a depth charge over the side," Steve Riggs said, resuming the interrupted conversation. "We still have a full load of those."

Garrett shook his head. "A depth charge is not a hand grenade. If we did that, we'd blow the stern right off the ship." Matt nodded agreement. He was sitting in his chair on the bridge sipping "monkey joe," the local equivalent of coffee, which actually looked and tasted somewhat like coffee except for the greenish foam. He mostly just listened while his officers and senior NCOs brainstormed about the propeller problem.

"I can't send a man over the side," Spanky said. "He'd be torn to bits."

"Maybe we could beach *Mahan,* take off her screw, and then refloat her with the tide," Dowden suggested doubtfully. "Then do the same with *Walker.* If one ship gets stuck, we can pull her off with the other."

"That's something to consider," Jim mused. "How high do the tides run around here? The charts ought to say, but it's awful risky this close to the equator. I doubt they run more than a couple feet. Besides, more ships than I like to think about have been lost trying to pull stranded vessels off a bank in confined waters. What was that cruiser, twenty years ago or so, that tried to pull that sub off a shoal? The line parted and the cruiser went aground. Total loss. What was her name?"

"*Milwaukee,*" answered Spanky.

Gray grunted. "That's all we need. Our own little Honda Point." He referred to the 1923 catastrophe when seven four-stackers ran hard aground on the California coast in a dense fog. "A fine stupid mess we'd be in then."

Matt shook his head. "I have to say, that's my least favorite option so far, gentlemen. Nobody wants to deliberately beach his ship."

"Maybe we could build a cage of some sort," Sandison speculated. "Lower it over the side next to the screw and let the divers take it off through the bars."

Spanky looked at the torpedo officer with surprise. "Hey! That might work. We've only got the one little crane aft for handling the depth charges and it won't lift a screw, but we could use it for the cage and then rig a boom off the main mast to raise the propeller, I bet."

"Keep working on it. I know you'll get it figured out," Matt said. Then he frowned and looked at his watch. "I'm afraid Mr. Ellis and I have to leave you now. We have . . . a couple of funerals to attend." He glanced at Garrett and Chief Gray. "You too. The men we lost were in your divisions. Have the burial party turned out as sharply as they can manage." He sighed and stood carefully from his chair, groaning slightly. "I'll meet you ashore at, say, sixteen hundred. The Lemurians have some sort of funeral planned for dusk, I believe. We may have to be flexible, but I want to bury our people as close to eighteen hundred as we can."

"You sure we shouldn't just bury them at sea?" Gray asked quietly.

Matt took a breath and grimly let it out. "I'm sure. I hated putting Marvaney over the side and I've never felt right about it. Not like I probably would . . . back home. Not like I *did* when we buried all the people we lost in the fight running away from this damn place. But that was different—at least we thought it was." He shook his head, but his frown remained. "Besides," he finally added, "these guys fought for this crummy place . . ." He didn't continue. There was no need. The following silence was broken by the lookout's report that the plane had been sighted.

"Sixteen hundred, Mr. Dowden," reminded Matt as Riggs replied to the lookout. "Carry on here. Show the flag at half-mast, if you please, and I'll want one to take ashore. I doubt we have enough to cover them all, so we'll just have to make do." Instead of departing as he'd intended, he remained a moment longer with a thoughtful expression. In the distance, the droning engines of the PBY could be faintly heard. "What happened to our flag they carried during the battle?"

"The Second Marines, Skipper. They have it," Gray answered.

Matt nodded with approval. "Good. We'll use that one instead."

"Aye, aye, sir," they chorused.

Freshly shaved and dressed in his less than pristine whites, Matt appeared at the place he had specified for the burial services to commence. Sandra, Ellis, Bradford, and Shinya accompanied him. Together they waited amid a growing crowd of curious Lemurians and stared somberly at the Marines guarding the five small graves. There might have been six as far as Matt was concerned, had the 'Cat they lost during the Battle of the Bay not gone over the side. The location of the new cemetery caused considerable controversy. Matt insisted on the flat, high ground right beside the road from the waterfront and just a short distance in front of the hasty breastworks they'd thrown up facing—and in clear view of—Aryaal's main gate. From which, there had still been no word at all.

Lord Rolak joined them, as did Queen Maraan. Rolak had polished his armor and replaced his missing plume, but in spite of his expressionless eyes, his deep frown left no doubt he was troubled. He spoke to Captain Reddy through Courtney Bradford. "My lord," he began hesitantly, "I am yours, as you know, and will do as you command. But since you've placed the burden of friendship upon me, it is my duty to counsel against this act." Matt turned cold eyes upon him as he continued. "If we and the sea folk agree on one thing, it is that the souls of the dead belong in the heavens, where they are taken by the flames of the pyre. Not planted in the ground—from which they may never ascend." Rolak had little experience upon which to base his perception of human expressions, but Matt's darkening mood was clear enough. As a credit to his courage, he continued. "Please. Do not take offense. I understand you have different beliefs, as do we differ from the sea folk regarding where those souls ultimately reside. But to do this here, like this, can only breed resentment among those beyond the walls who wish us ill."

Matt nodded calmly enough, but when he spoke, his quiet words were iron. "On land, burial is the way of our people. We believe our God can find our souls wherever they are. The men we're going to bury here today died to save your city—the same as the sea folk and the people who followed you did. I'm going to bury them in the shadow of that city, so, from now on, people who live here will see their graves and remember the sacrifice they made for a people who—with a few noble exceptions—didn't lift a finger in their own defense and then betrayed those who did. Tomorrow, we'll talk to whoever rules behind those walls whether they want to or not, and you'll tell them what I said and why we're doing this. You'll also tell them that if I ever hear these graves have been desecrated in any way, or the memory of the men we bury here is ever given less than the respect it deserves, I'll steam here in *Walker* from wherever I am and reduce this city to dust. No offense."

Adar arrived beside Matt while he spoke, and he wore a different robe than the one in which they usually saw him. This one was black instead of purple, and golden stars covered it entirely instead of the usual silver ones upon the shoulders. "Not until this moment," Adar said, "did I truly realize how different your people are from mine, Cap-i-taan. I knew from the beginning that we worshiped differently, of course, but I always believed that, in the end, we only sailed a different wind to the same destination. Your 'charts,' as you call them—when I first saw them, I was angry. I believed you didn't treat them with proper respect, but I made that judgment from within the context of my own belief. When I came to know you, I lost my anger, particularly in light of the kind of people I now know you to be. I believed you were heretics, yes, and misguided, but certainly not nonbelievers." Adar sighed, looked at Matt, and blinked compassion. "But you are." He held up a placating hand. "Do not be angry! What I mean is, I now know you do not believe *at all* the same as we, and I suppose I am relieved." There was a rattling growl deep in his throat that was a kind of chuckle. "You're not warping the True Faith as I feared. Any similarity between your practices and mine are entirely coincidental. You do not disrespect my faith either intentionally or otherwise—you don't share it at all! This 'burying' of souls in the ground is proof enough of that!" He stopped and glanced at Rolak. "Although, if it must be done, I find it highly appropriate for you to do it here."

Matt looked at his friend with new respect. With a human Bronze Age priest, this would have been about when the torches would be lit.

"You're not angry that we don't share your beliefs?" Sandra asked.

"Of course not," Adar replied. "No one can be forced to accept the True Faith. It would not then be True, would it? I was only . . . uncomfortable . . . when I thought you mocked it." He looked darkly at Rolak. "As the Aryaalans do."

Rolak sniffed. "A lie," he said pedantically.

Matt was looking at the Marines and the graves they guarded. "You might be wrong, Adar. My people sail many winds to reach the same destination, but once there, I believe the place might yet still be the same. Perhaps the same as yours." A commotion grew behind them and they saw the approach of seven destroyermen dressed in whites. They had probably scrounged both ships to find so many bright, clean outfits. All of them carried Springfields on their shoulders and they marched in step well enough, despite being more than a little rusty. Matt swelled at the sight, as well as when he saw the battle-scarred American flag that had been rescued by the Second Marines leading the way. He was surprised to see who carried it. Walking slowly in front of the riflemen, also dressed in whites with gaiters laced on above his bare feet and with his battered helmet on his head, was Chack-Sab-At. His eyes were grimly set and focused before him and his tail was held erect as it swayed back and forth behind him as he walked.

The firing party halted beside the graves and the flag fluttered in the breeze between them and the walls of Aryaal. "I have to go now," Matt said quietly, and stepped quickly through the Marine guard to stand before the graves, facing the growing crowd with his back to the city. He reached into his coat pocket to retrieve his small Bible, but found himself faced with the difficulty of opening it with one hand. Sandra rushed to join him, opening the book to a page where he had inserted a small piece of paper. He looked at her and smiled.

"Please stay," he said. She returned his smile with a supportive one of her own and took her place beside him. A column of thirty destroyermen was moving toward them, swaying in step from side to side. Between each group of six was the body of one of their comrades, sewn in his mattress cover. Chief Gray led the procession, hobbling on his crutches. When they drew even with Ellis, Jim joined the Chief and the column followed the pair to the graves. Matt noticed that almost half of the party who bore the bodies of his crewmen were Lemurians, in spite of what might be a religious aversion toward what they were doing. He felt a surge of affection for them, mingled with a sadness that the original crews of the two destroyers had dwindled so far. When the bodies were deposited beside the graves, the bearers stepped back.

To Matt's further surprise, the final member of the procession was a stony-faced Dennis Silva. Before him in his hands he carefully carried Mack Marvaney's portable phonograph. He stepped into position beside Chief Gray where a bugler would have been if they'd had one, set the phonograph on the ground, and opened it. It had already been wound and he merely released the brake and positioned the needle on a record as the turntable began to spin.

"Atten-*shun!*" barked Gray.

Sounding tinny and forlorn, emanating from the open louver in the side of the small machine, "The Star-Spangled Banner" began to play. Instinctively, all the destroyermen, human and Lemurian, snapped a salute to the flag that floated over Chack's head. The recording was an upbeat, cheerful, even sort of jazzy rendition like Matt had heard played by a lot of dance bands before the War to start things off. For a poignant moment he could almost smell the perfume of a girl he'd danced with in San Diego when he was on his way to the Philippines to take command of *Walker*. Many of those in the gathered crowd gasped at the unexpected music, but Matt felt a sudden tightness in his throat and a strange pressure behind his eyes. He blinked.

Looking sidelong at Sandra, he saw a sad, wistful expression and as the anthem ended and Silva leaned down to turn off the machine, he saw tears streaming down the gunner's mate's face. Tears for Tom Felts, or Mack Marvaney, or any of the dozens they'd lost, there was no way to know. Or maybe he was just thinking about all they'd left behind.

"Pa-*RADE, REST!*"

Matt cleared his throat and looked at the book Sandra held open for him. Then he shook his head. "I never was one much for church," he apologized, "and I guess we've all missed a few services lately." Some of the men chuckled quietly, in spite of themselves. "It's not my way, or my place, I think, to preach a sermon here today. I do want to say a few words about these men we are burying, as well as all the rest of you destroyermen. Like all of us—except maybe Juan—Tom Felts and Glen Carter, Andy Simms, Loris Scurrey, and Gil Olivera were a long way from home even before the Japs bombed Pearl and Cavite. For some reason, all of us are even farther away now. Tom was from Arkansas. Glen and Andy were both from Ohio. Gil was from New York and Loris was from California." He paused for a moment, collecting his thoughts.

"Mr. Ellis is from Virginia and so is Lieutenant Tucker. Sonny Campeti is from New Jersey and Frankie Steele is from Brooklyn. Chief Gray and Dennis Silva are from Alabama. I miss Texas as much as any of you miss the places you're from . . ." He shrugged. "We might be stuck here, however it happened. My guess is we probably are. But no matter how far we've come from those places we yearn for, they'll always be with us—part of us—deep down. And no matter how far apart they were from each other, those places had one thing in common. They were part of the United States of America, and that made us all Americans." He looked out at the faces of the firing party and the bearers, and some of the others who had come ashore. He saw out into the bay where *Walker* and *Mahan* floated side by side in the distance and, for the moment, those who'd stayed aboard them lined the rails and the flags flew low. "We're all still part of that no matter how far we've come. We were still Americans in the Philippines, and by God, we're still Americans here."

He paused for a long moment before continuing. "A few of us have gone even farther than the others now, but it's my belief that, in so doing, they've gotten closer to home, not farther away. I believe there's one God, above all things, who made the world we came from and this one too. Has to be. Only God could've figured out anything as complicated as *this* situation. I think He can probably manage to sort things out and put us where we belong when we die. I believe the men we bury here today in this strange but familiar place are with their loved ones that went before them now just as surely as if they'd died at home in bed." He stopped again to let that sink in. He really believed it was the truth, too. At least he hoped it was. The idea of their very souls being banished to this strange world as well was more than he could bear.

"But they didn't die at home," he said, "or in bed. They did die fighting for the same principles they fought for back home. For Duty, Honor, and Country. For freedom and liberty and against aggression." He grimaced. "A more horrible aggression than we've ever known. Most importantly, though, in some ways, they fought for *you*. They fought for their ship and their shipmates. Old and new. They died in a fight we didn't want but we have to win if we or our friends are ever going to be able to live here in peace and freedom from the evil that sweeps this world." He glanced at Sandra and saw her looking at him with an expression of pained concentration. Then he looked out at the Lemurians, most of whom couldn't understand him, but were getting a quick translation.

"You know, it just came to me that maybe I *do* know why we're here after all. Back in our world, our two ships, *Walker* and *Mahan*, were expendable. Hell, they'd already been expended. Their loss or survival didn't make any difference at all to whether the United States won or lost the war. Here, they *do* make a difference. *We* make a difference." He looked at the graves that lay in the center of the gathering and when he spoke again, his voice was a husky whisper.

"*They* made a difference."

Quickly, he reached into the Bible in Sandra's hands and took out the piece of paper there.

"I am the resurrection and the life, saith the Lord," he resumed in a wooden voice. "He that believeth in me, though he were dead, yet shall he live: and whosoever liveth and believeth in me, shall never die . . ." He continued on in a dwindling voice until the passage was complete, but quite a few of the others echoed his words from memory.

"A-tten-*shun!*" bellowed the Chief's raspy voice.

"Firing party, *pre*-sent, *arms!*"

Most of the Lemurians had seen what was coming, but they flinched anyway when Gray commanded the riflemen to fire three volleys. Matt then stumbled through the committal, clumsily substituting "the earth" for "the deep" and ended with a harsher command than he'd intended for everyone to bow their heads. He was surprised and a little embarrassed to see quite a few of the Lemurian troops follow his order. Now that it was over, he thought it had been a hokey speech, right out of a B movie, but he couldn't help it. It was how he felt. Sandra took the piece of paper from him and squeezed his hand gently for a moment. Then she placed the page back in the Bible and closed it.

There was no one to play taps. Silva crouched down beside the phonograph and removed the platter that bore the national anthem. Beneath it was another record. They all stood still and listened while a very old and melodramatic choir performance of "Rock of Ages" oozed from the louver. There was no telling why Marvaney had it, or why Silva hadn't sent it with him when they buried him at sea. Toward the end, the spring began to wind down. Matt cleared his throat uncomfortably and Silva applied the brake.

"Mr. Ellis."

"Sir?"

"The flag will remain uncased. It'll fly here as long as we remain. Signal the ships to resume normal duties. The burial party will proceed with the interment. Afterward, those who wish to do so may remain to witness the Lemurian ceremony. The firing party will remain as well."

"Aye, aye, Captain." Ellis hesitated.

"Yes, what is it?" Matt replied distractedly, wiping sweat from his brow with the sleeve of his good arm.

"You did all right."

"Never was much good at public speaking," he demurred.

"You did all right, Skipper," Ellis repeated.

"Yes, you did," Sandra agreed. "And you know? Maybe you're right. About why we're here, I mean."

"Makes as much sense as anything," said Jim. "And if it's true, it proves God sure is an imaginative guy."

"What do you mean?"

"The way the war was going back home, and in the shape our ships were in, *only* God could've found a use for them. Even if we'd managed to get out of our fix without the Squall—which I doubt—they wouldn't have been any good to the Navy anymore."

"God works in mysterious ways, huh?" quoted Matt with a small smile of his own. "What an understatement."

The crowd dispersed, many to attend to their military duties but most to continue preparations for the Lemurian service later that evening. Labor parties resumed tearing down the wooden warehouses that lined the wharf to use them for fuel for the pyres. Others swarmed over one of the Grik hulks that had been driven ashore during the battle and were quickly reducing it to its skeletal framework. The ghetto housing, such as it was, was left untouched. The allied commanders were unhappy about the necessity of destroying the warehouses—or any property at all—but since there was no suitable timber nearby, they had no choice. They needed all the wood they could find to send this unprecedented number of souls to the sky. At least the warehouses were mostly empty, their contents having been moved into the city when the Grik arrived.

"An . . . unusual ceremony," remarked Keje to Adar and Rolak, referring to the Amer-i-caan funeral they'd just seen. Keje had arrived late and had been supported by his disapproving daughter. He was still dizzy from the blow on his head.

"Unusual," Adar agreed thoughtfully. "Short, too. And very somber. Their grief was quite clear."

"They see death more as an ending than we do, perhaps. As if they do not expect to meet their lost ones again," Keje speculated.

"I think not," countered Adar. "Cap-i-taan Reddy told me to hear his words and I might better understand their faith." He shook his head. "I listened, but my understanding is no less uncertain. I think he was right, however, that we may only sail a different wind to the same destination. They certainly *hope* to meet again those who go before them, as do we, but perhaps they are less certain their God will find them here, so far from their home."

"Even more reason not to hide their dead underground."

Adar looked at his lifelong friend but shook his head at Keje's obtuseness. "You know as well as any novice priest that the souls of those lost at sea will rise to the heavens as surely as those sent by the pyre. The smoke of the pyre is symbolic. The ashes of the dead that rise within it settle back to the land or sea, in time. No," he continued, "their customs may seem bizarre, even distasteful. But the meanings behind them are not so different as they may at first appear. I will have to speak more with them about this, but I think we must consider: they are willing to fight and die with us despite a fear that if they *do* die, they will be utterly lost. I believe our service for the dead would be considerably more somber if that concern lingered in our minds." He hesitated. "Although I must confess I feel less positive about this ascension than I have in times past." He held up a hand to forestall the shocked blinking of his companions. "No, I've no doubt the souls we free tonight will find their way, but I do grieve that there are so many. Their concerns are over, beyond those they may retain for us. I do not begrudge their contentment in the heavens . . . but we will regret their loss in the battles to come. Do not think I've forgotten my oath," he said.

The three Lemurians lingered in silence a short while longer, watching as the mixed human and Lemurian burial party proceeded with their chore. Shovelfuls of soil disappeared into the rectangular holes with soft thumping sounds.

"It was surely a ceremony for warriors," Rolak stated. "Except for the part when they are buried."

The Lemurian "service" was just as alien to the human destroyermen who witnessed it as theirs had been to the Lemurians. Matt watched the initial ceremony accompanied by Jim, Sandra, and Courtney. Except for the firing party, whom Matt had ordered to remain as a show of honor and respect, most of the other members of the funeral party had returned to the ship. He'd ordered Gray to go, ostensibly to help coordinate repairs but mainly to get him off his feet. To his surprise, all the Lemurian destroyermen returned to the ship as well. All except Chack, who had remained behind along with the equally surprising Dennis Silva. Silva sent the phonograph back with Stites but stayed ashore talking quietly with Chack, waiting for the Lemurian funeral to get under way. Matt doubted they had ended their feud, but they appeared to be observing a truce for the evening, at least. Matt joined them briefly, out of curiosity.

"Chack?" he said.

"Sir?"

"Why did the other people . . . your people, go back to the ship? I thought I made it clear they were welcome to stay."

Chack looked at him and then glanced out at the deepening gloom of the bay, beyond the pier, where the two ships lay. Nearby, and lower down, the dark silhouette of the PBY floated now as well. The Lemurian ceremony was about to take place on the west side of the point, nearest to Madura, where *Mahan* had been anchored almost since she arrived. A power cable had been rigged between the destroyers, and portable lights and lanterns glowed harshly on the decks, contrasting brightly against the dull glow in the western sky where the sun had slipped away.

"They grieve, Cap-i-taan," he said. "But they are Navy men, yes? They are destroyermen."

Matt nodded. "Yes. They are."

"*Walker* is their Home. You are High Chief for *Walker*. You are High Chief of all the Amer-i-caan Navy here, so *Mahan* is their Home too. Both Homes need us now, more than the dead, and so they want to work." He paused. "I am here because I do not know what you want me to do."

Matt was taken aback. "What do you mean, Chack?"

"When I came to *Walker*, Keje-Fris-Ar was my High Chief. *Big Sal* was my Home. When I joined the Amer-i-caan Navy, I thought *Walker* was my Home. I was Bosun's Mate," he added proudly. Then he sighed. "Lieutenant Shinya tells me now that I am to be Chief of the Second Marines. What does that mean? I have become a good warrior," he said matter-of-factly, "which is something I never expected, and I . . . *am* good at it. But is *Walker* no longer my Home? Do I not *have* a home?"

Matt was perplexed for a moment; then realization dawned. "No! I mean, yes, *Walker* is certainly your Home, Chack, and you're still a bosun's mate! Good grief, I'm sorry if I made you think otherwise!" Matt scratched his chin in thought. "The way things are, a lot of us— you included—have to do more than one job, though. Do you think Lieutenant Letts and Tony Scott—and all the others we left in Baalkpan doing other jobs—have lost their Home?" Grudgingly, Chack shook his head. "Then don't worry about it. I'm glad you're here, though. It's appropriate that you should be. The Second Marines fought well. Hell, the battle would have been lost without them, and a lot of the credit for that goes to you. You helped train them and you fought with them and they trust you to lead them well. We all do. And your being here now is one of the duties of command."

Later when the funeral finally got under way, Matt imagined as he watched that Chack probably was beginning to contemplate some of the consequences of command.

The great pyres, three of them, were erected in a triangular pattern between the city walls and the sea. In each case, a huge bed of timbers had been laid on the ground with the dead gently arranged upon them. Above them all, a carefully erected A-frame latticework of timbers was created that gave the pyres the appearance of three stranded Homes. The air was thick with the ripening reek of the dead and the fishy stench of rendered gri-kakka oil that the dreary structures had been painted with. No living Lemurian had ever seen such a large pyre before, let alone more than one. None had ever seen anything like the battle that forced the need for them. Chances were, Matt grimly reflected, this wouldn't be the last time the People would send so many souls to the sky.

At the base of the triangle, Adar stood alone in the twilight. Torches were arrayed nearby and the golden stars of his robe twinkled and shimmered, reflecting the light. In a new touch, he was flanked by the proud, hopeful flags of those who'd fought and died. In the center, behind him, flew the lone-tree flag that Keje had fashioned to represent them all. The only flag missing was the Aryaalan flag, even though Rolak had begged one from the city. There had been no reply. The American flag still flew over the American dead, but not very far away.

Rolak had also tried to acquire an Aryaalan priest, but again there was no response. Queen Maraan had been satisfied by Adar's assurance that his service wouldn't stress the differences between their religions. From what little Matt knew, the differences weren't extreme, but like any religion, he supposed, the devil was in the details. In a nutshell, Bradford softly explained while they waited, land folk and sea folk both believed that something like a soul was carried into a heavenly afterlife. The main friction stemmed from what the two peoples believed the souls did after they got there. The sea folk, Adar told him, carried on in a peaceful, idyllic existence as, or among, the stars (this was still unclear) where they helped guide the lives and seagoing paths of those on earth. Kind of like angels, Bradford explained. The sun, of course, was the benign, gentle creator and nurturer of all things. In other words, sun-god worship with a twist.

To the land folk, however, the heavens were like a utopian Valhalla. Full of willing servants and lovely females, food, drink, and great, glorious battles in which nobody ever died. The dead paid no heed to those who remained behind because they were having too much fun to notice. The sun was God, under whose judgmental gaze one had to perform the great deeds that earned a place above. Other than that, as an arbiter of who got to play forever and who didn't, the sun was just a big lightbulb—at most, a spectator. Most distressing of all to the sea folk, however, to the Aryaalans and B'mbaadans the stars were just "up there." Matt understood why the stars would have much greater importance to a people who used them for navigation, but he found it difficult to imagine anyone being incurious enough not to think of them at all. That was a tough difference to bridge and he knew major religious wars had been fought throughout human history over less profound differences. Matt had to admit that the sea folk's religion was probably closer to what he'd been brought up with—profoundly different, of course, but still closer than Rolak's or Queen Maraan's. Although, he admitted wryly to himself, he could understand the attraction of the land folk religion to its adherents. At least to the males.

He looked at Sandra and saw the torchlight reflecting off her gold-tinged, sandy hair and fresh-scrubbed face. Her nurse's uniform was immaculate and exotically feminine compared to the dungarees she wore day to day. He couldn't help it, but a deep sadness, unrelated to the day's events, swept over him and he looked away so fast that his throbbing shoulder made him wince.

She looked at him with concern. "Are you all right?" she asked anxiously. It had been a long day for him, emotionally and physically, and she'd not be surprised if he passed out at any moment. Triumphant maybe, considering the dark predictions she'd made all day about the consequences to be expected if he overtaxed himself, but not surprised. "Just a little sore," he whispered, forcing a smile. Most of the crowd had grown silent as Adar prepared to speak.

"Now what?" asked Jim Ellis irritably as they stared at Aryaal's petulantly silent north gate. Arrayed before it was the newly expanded Allied Expeditionary Force. Expanded by membership anyway, if not by actual numbers. An acrid haze from the funeral pyres that had burned throughout the night served as a constant reminder of why there had been no net increase in force levels. Another reminder of the long, strange "funeral" was the pounding headache that Matt's former exec was enduring at the moment. A mass celebratory drunk to rival Dennis Silva's wildest dreams had followed Adar's sermon and subsequent igniting of the pyres. Adar's requiem for the fallen had progressed from praise for their deeds to, ultimately, an almost envious bon voyage to the departing souls as they swept to the heavens atop the roaring flames. What followed then was an insane "wake."

The seep flowed from casks brought ashore from the ships of the battle line in such abundance that Matt was frankly stunned they even had an army in the morning. At one point he questioned Adar about the wisdom of prostrating half their force on the doorstep of a possibly hostile city and the by then already sozzled Sky Priest had assured him that even the most depraved Aryaalan would never attack them while they were in "mourning." Matt was fairly certain the Lemurian meaning of the word conveyed a few subtle differences. Adar then sternly pressed a cup of seep into his hand and solemnly asked him to celebrate the "rising" along with his friends—if he didn't think his own God would be too terribly put out.

Matt took a few sips of the bittersweet brew under the watchful stare of Sandra Tucker. He finally even allowed the rest of those present, with the exception of the firing party, to imbibe as well. The unfortunate firing party was retained as an impromptu shore patrol to make sure everyone got back to the ship. Besides, in spite of Adar's assurance, Matt felt compelled to maintain at least a small armed and sober force ashore. Letting them drink, with weapons at hand, didn't even bear thinking about. Silva became a vocal convert to the Lemurian faith, although the denomination he embraced was unclear. Courtney Bradford was carried to the ship.

Now Matt had to admit his worst fears had been for naught and at least the majority of the AEF had stood to when called. With the dawn also came a return of the army's positive nature, as if the smoke and flames of the night before had lifted much of their gloom. The smoke had eliminated the stench of the diminishing Grik carrion beyond the barricade and the seep had washed away their dread. He shook his head. A different wind, certainly, he thought. And maybe even a better one as far as warriors were concerned.

Jim Ellis pinched the bridge of his nose and clenched his eyes shut when the roar of the PBY reached them from the bay. Lieutenant Mallory was departing on a belated scout and Matt swiveled his head and watched the battered flying boat skip across the choppy morning wavelets and claw its way into the sky.

"You drank too much seep," he accused good-naturedly, turning back to look at the gate. Many figures were atop the wall above it, but there had been no response to their hails.

"No," Ellis denied, "but I guess I drank enough." He nodded toward the gate before them. "And I repeat, what now? If they won't even talk to us . . ."

Matt snorted. His wounds were healing, thanks to the mysterious paste, but the pain was pretty severe and he had to guard against a tendency to snap. On the slope before them, Lord Rolak continued to pace back and forth, haranguing the inhabitants of the city to send somebody out to talk. "I guess we're just going to have to make them." He turned to Lieutenant Shinya, who stood nearby with his hands behind his back. "Mr. Shinya, have Chack carry a message to Lord Rolak to deliver. Tell him to instruct them to clear an area around the gate if they don't want to be killed."

Shinya nodded. "Aye, aye, Captain. *Chack!*" The new commander of the Second Marines ran to join them and Shinya passed on Matt's instructions. With his dented helmet on his head and rifle slung muzzle down, Chack hurried to where Rolak stood, radiating impotent rage. Matt noted with interest that Queen Maraan's gaze never left the burly Lemurian bosun's mate.

"What are you going to do?" Keje asked, stepping closer. Unlike Jim Ellis's, his head seemed much better after last night.

"I'm going to blow the gate in," Matt answered stonily, gesturing at the two fieldpieces in the center of the line, directly opposite the entrance to the city.

"But if any inside are killed . . ." Keje began. Regardless of his own frustration, the idea of killing other Lemurians came hard to the High Chief of *Salissa.*

Matt turned to face him. "We can't leave Aryaal to threaten our rear, or our allies." He nodded toward Queen Maraan. "If we have to storm that city—and we will if they force us—there's no telling how many will die. My hope is if we knock down that gate it'll show them how vulnerable they are to our guns and maybe we can talk sense into them."

"But surely they saw the effect of the guns against the Grik?"

"Sure, but they're pointed at *them* now, and my guess is they don't think we'll do it."

"Cap-i-taan Reddy speaks truth," said the B'mbaadan queen through an interpreter they'd assigned her. "They know sea folk do not war among their own race." She grinned predatorily. "But we did not think you would fight the Grik either. If you 'knock down' that gate, they will wonder what else they were wrong about. In any event, they know I would have no qualms taking *my* army inside!"

When Rolak delivered his ultimatum there was, again, no response. The sentries atop the wall above the gate did surreptitiously ease away from it, however. Matt lowered his binoculars.

"Damn," he muttered after twenty minutes passed. "If we wait any longer, they'll start to go back. Mr. Shinya? Proceed." A moment later the two guns in the center of the line fired almost simultaneously. At a range of only a little over two hundred yards, it was impossible to miss. With a thunderclap roar and a billowing rush of white smoke, the guns leaped back and the brief, ripping-sheet sound of two solid shots was drowned by their impacts on the heavy wooden gate. The effect was spectacular. One shot struck near the center, blowing a large jagged hole and sending splinters in all directions. The second struck near the top hinge on the right-hand gate and it slowly toppled inward, tearing the bottom hinge as it fell. There was a muted scream from within.

"Again!" Matt commanded, his lips set in a hard line. The second two shots obliterated the left-hand gate. "Mr. Shinya! The Second Marines will advance!"

"Second Marines! Forward . . . march!"

As a solid rectangular block, the veteran unit stepped forward toward the gap made by the guns. Matt was suddenly struck by how eerie it was to see such a mass of troops move with such precision without even the beat of a drum to keep the cadence. The regiment had been whittled down to only three hundred now, but they weren't like any warriors that had ever approached those gates before. They were a battle-hardened killing machine. Matt also knew that none of the Marines now marching toward Aryaal wanted to fight fellow Lemurians. They would, though, if it came to that. He was certain. He just hoped his bluff wouldn't be called—because it wasn't one. Most of those present thought it was, probably even Keje, and he didn't know how they would react if fighting actually began. Just in case, he'd detailed Queen Maraan's Six Hundred as the follow-on force. Unlike the Marines, the Orphan Queen's guard had been reinforced from across the water and actually had six hundred members. Also unlike the Marines, they'd seen their dreams come true when the gates of Aryaal fell. There was no question that they would fight, and the Aryaalans had to know it.

Chack strode ahead of the Marine regiment as it approached the gate with his Krag at port arms. The long bayonet he had been given was fixed, and behind him the Marines formed their shield wall, with spears bristling from it. After what the Arylaans had seen that force do just a day before, this reorganized, grim, and fresh-looking block of warriors must have been a horrifying sight to the dazed and deafened defenders. Not quite halfway there, Chack called his troops to halt when a group of Aryaalans hurried out. They were waving a white flag—just as Rolak had been instructing them to do all morning if they wanted to talk.

Matt lowered his binoculars again with the beginnings of a relieved grin.

"Would you have let them go on?" Keje asked quietly.

Matt looked at him. "For what we have before us? Yes. The stakes are too high."

Keje nodded sadly. "That is what I thought."

"Would you have tried to stop me?"

"No. As you said, the stakes are too high. We must win. I just hope we do not destroy ourselves to accomplish the victory."

Matt nodded his understanding, and together they went forward to treat with the Aryaalans.

"So. Fet-Alcas is dead," noted Safir Maraan with some satisfaction. "Why is it only now they are telling us this?"

Bradford grunted. "Evidently there were . . . irregularities surrounding his demise. Prince Rasik has of course assumed the throne, and they would have us believe that everything, even the delay in speaking to us after the battle, was caused by confusion while they hunted the murderous conspirators."

Matt shook his head. "Sounds awfully Byzantine to me—or Soviet."

Courtney Bradford laughed out loud. "I don't believe we need look to Uncle Joe Stalin for examples of a dirty and complicated rise to power. Our own shared English history is replete enough with those, Captain."

Matt smiled. "I'm Irish American, with a fair measure of Scot. O'Roddy—Reddy—you know."

"Hmm."

They were aboard *Walker,* in the wardroom again, and it was full as usual. They were engaged in an informal discussion of the situation, but nearly every faction was represented, except the Aryaalans, so whatever they decided would have the effect of policy. Nearly two weeks had passed since they blew down the north gate of the city, and in that time Matt had spent precious little time on his ship. He was glad to be home. *Revenge* had sailed with a small squadron of feluccas to scout the enemy and Mallory flew every other day, either probing north toward Singapore or carrying news and people between Aryaal and Baalkpan. So far there was no sign that the Grik intended to renew their offensive. The ragtag remnants of their fleet had gone to ground at Singapore, but no other forces had joined them there. Given everyone's reluctance—the Grik included—to cross the menacingly deep water of the Indian Ocean, it seemed unlikely the enemy would use any other avenue of approach.

Sergeant Alden came to help Shinya integrate the B'mbaadan forces into the AEF. His envy of the Japanese officer regarding his role in the battle had been palpable. He managed to contain it, however, and the burgeoning friendship between the tough Marine and the former enemy lieutenant wasn't in danger. Alden was gone again, but the news from "home" was welcome, and good for the most part. The Baalkpan defenses were strengthening every day and the cottage arms industry was beginning to flourish. Matt knew *Walker* missed all the people they'd left in Baalkpan, Letts most of all, but he was glad the fair-skinned supply officer was there. Letts, Alden, and Brister, together with Karen Theimer, had been working miracles. Besides, with the dame famine still under way, keeping Letts's and Theimer's affair out of the local eye was certainly prudent—even now that they had two more nurses for the guys to ogle. It was one less latch on the pressure cooker. Some tension still existed regarding Silva and Risa's apparently ongoing trans-species relationship and there was little doubt now that they had one. But it now seemed more platonic than anything and few really took it seriously anymore. They were clearly great friends, and ever since captain's mast they hadn't been as blatant about "it" anymore either, whatever "it" was. Both were popular characters—not to mention dangerous—and as long as they maintained a semblance of dignity their "friendship" was ignored beyond the mild humor it inspired. Mostly. Occasionally there were still words.

One "relationship" Matt thoroughly approved of seemed to be flourishing as well. He looked at Queen Maraan with a puzzled expression. "Queen Protector, I just realized you spoke to us in English."

"Yes," she confirmed with a toothy grin and a series of blinks that indicated pleasure. "I spoke . . . Did well?"

"You sure did," Jim Ellis confirmed.

She looked across the table at the commander of the Second Marines. "Chack teach," she explained.

"Well. Yes." Matt arched an eyebrow at the young Lemurian. "He's a remarkable fellow."

"Re-maak-able," said the queen, testing the word.

"The question is," Jim said, returning to the subject, "how long are we going to let Rasik yank our chain? They stopped us from taking them down when they waved the white flag, but nothing's really changed."

"I'm not so sure about that," Matt disagreed. "I haven't really wanted to push things since we're not ready to move yet. But Rasik's announcement that he was king included assurances that Rolak's people were free to leave. He also swore undying loyalty to the cause we're fighting for—"

"Which we know is a lie," interrupted Chief Gray harshly. "Beggin' your pardon, Captain."

"No, you're right, Chief. I'm pretty sure it's a lie. But what can he do? Their little civil war about wiped out the last core of solid warriors in the city. He's in no shape to cause much trouble now even if we do leave him behind. I doubt he'd even be much of a threat to the 'old men and boys' militia Queen Maraan has proposed leaving to defend B'mbaado. Lord Rolak's troops are the only viable Aryaalan infantry left and they could probably retake the city on their own—especially with the new training they've had. Rasik doesn't *want* them back. They're solidly in our corner and they hate him as much as they did his dad. I'm pretty sure he'll make good on letting their families out. Right now he thinks he needs the security of being their 'Protector.' "

"That's not what I mean, Captain. He's been 'protecting' our friends long enough."

"I know, but I don't think we have much to worry about from him for the time being. I hope I'm not underestimating him, but I imagine he'll be too busy sewing up his power base for the foreseeable future to spend much time causing us trouble."

"So, when do we move, Skipper?" Garrett asked from the far end of the green table.

"Spanky says he'll be ready to pull our damaged screw in a couple of days. If it works, he hopes to get *Mahan*'s off by the end of the week and then *Mahan* will leave immediately." He turned to Jim Ellis again. "You ready for sea?"

"Just say the word, Skipper."

"Good. Then if all goes right, we should be ready to resume the offensive in three weeks. I'll want increased recon, of course, and that'll give us plenty of time to finish training up the troops as well. When we move on Singapore, I want to land on it like an avalanche."

"I sure hate to miss it," Ellis grumped. "Seems like *Walker*'s always doing the heavy lifting and *Mahan* gets a pass."

"You call what you went through a pass?" Matt asked derisively. "You were lucky to survive."

"Sure," Jim responded defensively, "but she hasn't been much help in *this* fight. I haven't either."

"Don't worry about it. Get her fixed up and she'll get her chance. Alden took a set of prints back with him and they're going to cast a new screw in Baalkpan." Matt grinned. "He also said there're more volunteers for the 'U.S. Navy' than he could shake a stick at. It won't take long to bring her complement up."

Ellis nodded with a strange expression on his face. He was still not used to that idea. The Asiatic Fleet had a long tradition of employing native auxiliaries to fill out its crews—mostly on the China Station—but "native" had meant something else entirely back then. From what he'd seen, *Walker*'s new destroyermen were more competent than the Chinese coolies he remembered, and a hell of a lot more loyal.

"We take this . . . Sin-Po-Ar . . . war end?" asked the Orphan Queen.

Matt sadly shook his head. "No, Queen Protector. It won't even be the beginning of the end," he said, quoting Churchill. "But it'll be the end of the beginning."

"My God!" exclaimed Bradford. "I wonder what dear Winston would think to hear his words used in this context?"

"I bet he'd find it appropriate," Matt responded thoughtfully. "And pretty familiar too—except I don't really believe the Krauts eat their prisoners."

"Ready to go!" announced Spanky over the intercom at the auxiliary conn on top of the aft deckhouse. His voice was more gruff than usual with repressed tension as he watched the slack go out of the cables that trailed past the propeller guards. A vicious squall had marched across the bay late that morning, threatening to delay the operation. It passed quickly enough, however, leaving the sky bright and clear and the water almost dead calm. Now the only thing marring the otherwise perfect Java day was the customary oppressive heat and humidity—and, of course, the critical nature of the task at hand. *Walker* and *Mahan* had maneuvered into the middle, deepest part of the bay. Now they were poised stern to stern with lines trailing down to *Walker*'s port side shaft support and across to *Mahan,* where they were carefully secured to the propeller they planned to pluck. The low angle was necessary so they would pull the screw straight off, without putting an upward bind on the shafts—not only so the screw would come off easier, but to avoid warping either of the shafts themselves. They needed the deep water so when the propeller came off, it wouldn't plunge down and damage itself on the bottom of the bay. The "practice run" had been a success. That was when they used a reverse arrangement to pull *Walker*'s useless propeller the day before.

Spanky spared an unusual sympathetic glance at Dean Laney, who stood beside the starboard depth-charge rack, shivering, in shock most likely. He was black and blue with bruises, and Silva, just as uncharacteristically, had draped him in a blanket as soon as he came out of the suit. They'd hoped to use a welded-steel cage to lower the machinist into the sea, but there was one problem they just couldn't solve. It had to be tight enough to keep out the smaller flashies, but still let Laney work through it to secure the cables and remove the huge nuts that held the screw in place. Ultimately, they resorted to the ancient technique of passing one of *Big Sal*'s coarse, heavy sails under the hull of the ship and securing it tightly wherever it came in contact. This created a flashy-free pocket for Laney to work. Captain Reddy told them sailing ships had often used the same strategy in shark-infested waters to make repairs, or just to have a place to swim or bathe in safety. It worked like a charm—until the swarming predators figured out something was inside the pocket.

It may have been noise or movement, but even though they sensed nothing edible, they began bumping aggressively against the bulging canvas with their hard, bony heads. Often, of necessity, Laney was right behind it and they very nearly beat him to death. Somehow he managed to finish the job in spite of the pain and terror. Spanky cringed to think what would have happened if any of the blows had broken the skin. Even through his suit, enough blood would have entered the water to drive the damn things nuts.

Now Spanky stood, watching intently as the lines Laney had secured grew taut. Captain Reddy himself stood at the auxiliary conning station, looking over his injured left shoulder with his right hand on the wheel. Now was the critical moment. If the maneuver wasn't performed or the current judged just right, the cables might foul the rudder or the other, turning, screw. Besides that, they had to pull *straight* back. Spanky squinted hard. The line looked good to him.

"Let her buck, Skipper."

Matt nodded, his face a mask of concentration. "Starboard ahead slow," he said to Dowden, who relayed the command to the engine-room throttle station. Almost imperceptibly at first, the distance between the ships began to grow and Matt carefully adjusted the wheel to counteract the thrust of the single screw. Then, in a rush, the cables went completely taut and began to strain against the anchored ship astern. *Walker*'s fantail rose high enough that the prop wash from the starboard screw flashed white on the surface and all forward motion came to a stop. A deep, tired groan emanated from the ship as she strained against her sister.

"Starboard ahead two-thirds!" The frothing wake reappeared at the surface and the vibration increased dramatically. A slight fishtail began to manifest itself and Matt compensated accordingly. Still the screw refused to budge. "Somebody wipe this sweat off my face!" he ordered tersely. It was beginning to run down and burn his eyes. He couldn't do it with his left sleeve since that arm was still immobilized against his chest and he didn't dare let go of the wheel with his right. With nothing else at hand, Dowden sopped at the sweat with his own sleeve.

"Starboard ahead, *flank!*" Matt grated. Dowden looked at him for an instant, but relayed the command. He glanced past the captain at Spanky, who was clearly concerned about the cables, but the engineer only shrugged. The prop wash from the starboard screw erupted into the air, inundating Laney, Silva, and the others who were poised on the fantail with axes, ready to cut the cables. A considerable spray even reached the auxiliary conn. The ship writhed in protest. The rattling groan was so loud now that it wasn't possible to be heard below a scream. For two whole minutes it seemed the ship would tear herself apart while the captain fought the wheel. Smoke from the overworked boilers piled straight up into the still air in spite of the violent expenditure of energy, creating a surreal effect. The crew, human and Lemurian, exchanged worried glances.

"Back her down!" Matt finally yelled. "Two-thirds!"

Slowly, so rudder control could be maintained, the commands came to throttle back. When the engine stopped and the deck grew still, it seemed as if the ship herself was panting with nervous exertion, along with the crew, as steam pressure vented from the stacks.

"That didn't work too good," Matt said with a tired, wry smile. Juan appeared with a carafe of ice water and cups for those on the aft conning station and he received grateful thanks.

"What now, Skipper?" asked Dowden, wiping his mouth and handing his cup back to Juan.

"Well," said Matt, "we tried pliers. Let's see if the old 'door and string' will work."

Slowly, *Walker* eased back until the cables went slack and dipped low into the depths of the bay. More slowly still, until the jackstaffs on the fantails of the two ships were nearly crossed.

"The cables will never bear it," Laney whispered nervously to Silva, standing beside him leaning on the rail. "And if they do, they'll tear the shafts right out of us both."

Silva looked at the machinist's mate and then slapped him on the back of the head.

"Hey . . . !"

"You idiot snipe! You tryin' to jinx us? I guess the Skipper knows what he's doin'! Here, gimme that blanket back!" A short Lemurian ordnance striker named Pak-Ras-Ar, hence of course, Pack Rat, stood behind the pair and Silva threw the blanket at him. "Here, Pack Rat. You have it. I ain't sleepin' under no damn snipe-sweaty blanket!"

Pack Rat held the blanket at arm's length and wrinkled his nose. "Smells mostly like Silva sweat to me," he said.

"Goddamn little hairball."

On the deckhouse, Dowden took off his hat and ran shaking fingers through his greasy hair. The captain's expression was like stone as he calculated the angle. How could he be so calm? What he didn't see was Matt's left hand shaking at his side and the typhoon of acid roiling in his stomach. His right hand was on the wheel, the only thing that kept it still.

"Signal to *Mahan*: Hold on." Matt waited a moment while the message was passed. A high, fluffy cloud passed overhead, dulling the glare of the sun on the water and he looked quickly forward to check the angle of his ship once more.

"Starboard ahead full," he said quietly.

Black smoke chuffed skyward from the aft stacks and *Walker*'s stern crouched down. Vibration quickly built as the old destroyer leaped from the block.

"She's comin' up!" Silva bellowed unnecessarily as the cables raced from the depths once more. Fifty, sixty, seventy yards—the distance quickly grew. There was a hundred yards of cable. Suddenly there came a tremendous, wrenching groan and it felt as if *Walker* had slammed into a wall of rock. Crewmen were thrown to the deck and the bow heaved to port, nearly spinning the wheel out of the captain's hand. Then, as quick as that, *Walker* lunged free and resumed her dash away from *Mahan*.

"All stop!" Matt cried.

Dowden passed the word and then ran to the rail. Below him, Silva and Laney were trying to heave on the line that trailed over the side. "Do we have it?" he shouted down.

"Aye, sir! And it's heavy enough! I hope we didn't yank *Mahan*'s shaft and turbine too!" A cheer built as men and 'Cats picked themselves up and word quickly spread forward.

Dowden pounded the rail in triumph. "Quit fooling around with that line, men. You'll never lift it without a winch!"

"Ain't tryin' to lift it, sir, just want to feel if it hits bottom. We got three hundred feet of line and three hundred twenty feet of water—we think."

Dowden's face grew troubled. "Well . . . let us know."

Walker's momentum bled off until she coasted to a stop about a quarter mile from her anchored sister. At rest, she had a slight list to port, caused by the weight of the screw. Silva was the last to let go of the cable. "Swingin' free and easy, Mr. Dowden," he announced.

Spanky sighed with relief and turned to relay the report from the engine room. "Seals are fine, Skipper. No more water coming in than usual."

"*Mahan* reports the same," Riggs said from behind them as he watched *Mahan*'s signal light with a pair of binoculars. He lowered them to his chest. "Thank God."

Matt nodded, keeping his hand on the wheel so it wouldn't betray him. "Thank Him indeed," he said. "Good work, Mr. McFarlane. Pass the word to all hands: Well done." He grinned. "My mother always used to say it's easier if you just yank it out! Works for teeth, sticker burs, and apparently destroyer screws." There was a round of appreciative chuckles and the crew had begun to cheer again now that they knew the precious propeller was safe.

Spanky gulped another cup of water and hitched his breeches up on his skinny hips. "Now, sir, with your permission, I'll see about landing this fish."

"By all means. Mr. Riggs? Send a message to *Mahan*. I'd be obliged if Captain Ellis would join us this evening." He turned to Juan. "Something special tonight, if you please. I think a celebration is in order."

As night fell, the two destroyers were moored side by side once more, but this time they were snug against the Aryaal dock. Men and Lemurians capered from deck to deck to shore and a party atmosphere reigned on land and sea. Many stopped to gawk at the dingy brown screw that floated aft of the ships, lashed securely to a large raft. Paul Stites was spinning records on Marvaney's phonograph and broadcasting the music on the shipwide comm. Silva had done it for a while, but Stites spelled him so his friend could "cut a rug." On deck, he glanced around for Risa, his usual dance partner, but she was nowhere in sight. He emitted a sonorous belch as though it was a mating call, but there was no response other than nearby laughter. Alcohol was still strictly prohibited on board, but kegs of seep had been tapped on the dock and there was a steady stream of destroyermen and Lemurians going ashore and tanking up before returning to party on the ship. His second (and by captain's decree, last) mug of seep now glowing in his stomach, Silva watched wildly gyrating Lemurian forms try to imitate the dances the Americans showed them. Most gave up and reverted to dances they knew, but it didn't matter. They had the beat.

Silva caught a glimpse of long blond hair leaning on the cowl vent by the engine-room access trunk. He realized with a jolt that it was one of those nurses from *Mahan*. Pam Cross. That was it. She was watching the dancing with an amused expression on her pretty oval face and keeping time to the music with her chin. He suddenly, desperately, wanted to talk to her—just to hear a dame's voice—but for the first time in his life Dennis Silva felt unable to throw a line. Any line. In fact, because of the dame famine, it'd been so long since he'd even *seen* a woman other than the captain's, he wasn't sure he could speak at all.

"What's the matter with you?" he growled at himself. "Just go talk to her. Damn." He sauntered through the dancers and found himself standing beside and slightly behind her. His mouth opened.

"Buzz off, sailor boy," she said over her shoulder. Obviously, she'd noticed his approach. The words came in a harsh Brooklyn accent and were intended to send him slinking away. Instead, a slow grin spread across his face. Everything would be fine now, he thought. If she'd been as sweet as she looked, he probably would have been stuck.

"Hey, doll, that's no way to talk," he said in his best wounded tone. "It's just, you standin' there, you reminded me so much of my girl back home." He feigned a sad, faraway look. "Gone forever, now."

She rolled her eyes and swiveled her head to stare up at him with a mocking expression. She barely came up to his chest. "In the Asiatic

Fleet? I bet you haven't had a girl without black hair and dark skin since you came aboard this bucket."

He leered down at her. "My third-grade sweetheart had hair just like you."

She locked an iron-hard stare upon him for a full ten seconds before her stiff facade dissolved into an uncontrolled giggle. "Jeez," she said. "We must be twins."

"The spittin' image," he confirmed. "Wanna dance?"

She shook her head, still smiling. "Can't. You're cute, but I'm not supposed to."

"Cute?!" Silva demanded, puffing out his mighty chest. He stepped back and struck a pose that displayed his massive biceps to good effect. "The Great Dennis Silva is *not* cute!" he bellowed in mock outrage. Those nearby stopped for a moment at the outburst, but quickly recognized one of Silva's playful spectacles.

Pam Cross laughed out loud. "Okay! Okay! So you're a great big hulking stud! But you're still an enlisted stud, and I'm an officer!"

Silva flung himself on his knees at her feet—which still left the top of his head almost even with her chin.

"Aww, c'mon! You're an ensign, right? That's only barely an officer." He leered again. "I'm a gunner's mate . . ." He had to think for a moment. "Second class! That's an *awful lot* of enlisted man!"

She laughed again, and then peered around. "Oh, all right, you big goon! It's not like it matters anymore anyway. What are they gonna do? Throw me out? Come on!"

And Dennis Silva, for a while, was in heaven.

They started out with a rusty jitterbug that might have looked worse, but Dennis wasn't the rusty one; Pam was. It came out all right, though, because Dennis didn't so much as dance with her as pose her while he danced around her. There were hoots of glee for the first couple of dances, until they fell into a third dance—a waltz this time. Inevitably, it was "Ramona" and Stites never should have spun it because it always made the guys misty-eyed at best. At worst . . . a much bruised, sharpened, and put-upon Dean Laney tried to cut in between Silva and Cross.

"Ease up, ape!" he said. "Jeez, you two." He glanced a sidelong appraisal at Pam. "Come up for air! Why don't you spread it around, Ensign?"

This struck Silva *and* Cross as particularly uncalled-for, since they were only, in fact, dancing.

"Ease up yourself, Fatso," Pam snarled at Laney. "I don't belong to you or nobody and I'll dance with who I want."

Laney glared at Silva. "Let her go, Silva. She ain't yours." He smirked. " 'Sides, you already got a dame. We all ought'a have a turn."

"What she does ain't up to you, you filthy, stinky, chickenshit snipe. You heard her just fine and if you don't get your rancid, slimy grabbers off her I'll put your greedy eyes in the bilge. You got me? 'Sides, dancin' with you'd be enough to put her off guys at all. The rest of the crew would hang you!"

It was then that Laney swung.

Inasmuch as their frequent bouts usually went to Silva, mostly because of ruthlessness and experience, the two men were physically fairly well matched and Laney's blow landed like a pile driver on Silva's cheekbone, staggering him for the merest instant. It might have even been enough for Laney to finish him on a better day, if Chief Gray's bearlike forearms hadn't descended around him like a tractor tire and held him helplessly immobilized while Silva shook it off.

"Lemme go, goddamn it!" Laney bellowed desperately, wriggling like a mackerel.

"Yeah." Silva smiled at the unexpected opportunity, rejected it, then began to consider it again as his cheek began to sting. "He's got one comin'."

"Break it up!" Gray snarled. He glared at Silva over Laney's madly ducking head, while the taller man took his time, aiming for a shot.

"He cold-cocked me, Bosun," Silva said conversationally. "We didn't even square off."

"Finish it later," Gray growled in a lower tone. "We got problems."

Silva's face went flat. The party continued unabated around them, tinny ragtime strains on the comm replacing the waltz. His eyes flicked to the couple of other faces who had arrived with the Chief and he noticed Chack, Donaghey, and Campeti from *Walker*. Steele and the new 'Cat bosun's mate from *Mahan* were there as well. He sensed a hell of a lot of body language from the humans and the 'Cats.

"I take it these ain't 'officer' problems?" He didn't point out that, as acting exec of *Mahan*, Steele was an officer now. That's not the way it worked.

"If we can keep it that way," Donaghey agreed. Silva looked at Pam Cross, who was watching, wide-eyed. Gray cursed.

"Don't worry, fellas." Pam poked Silva in the ribs with her elbow. "As this big dope just told me, I ain't much of an officer. I can keep a secret."

Gray exhaled. "Right. We need a nurse anyway." He looked around and glared at the few curious faces nearby until the party resumed full force and the small gathering was forgotten.

"Okay, a few at a time, without a word, we'll ease on shore. Meet up by the seep kegs—hell, get another cup, then walk on up to the cemetery."

"What's this all about?" Laney almost whined. Gray had been holding his arms so tight and so long, he was beginning to lose feeling in his hands. Gray let him go, but spun him around.

"I guess you'll find out a lot of things tonight, Machinist's Mate Laney, and you'll keep every goddamn thing to yourself, is that understood? We're trusting you to be a man, but you don't get to be a kid again. Hear?"

Laney was startled, but he didn't hesitate. He knew what he was being asked.

"I won't blow."

There was a fair-sized gathering near the cemetery. Human and Lemurian chiefs and senior NCOs, for the most part, all eerily silhouetted against the star-picked clouds that floated above the American graves. Two Lemurian Marines armed with Krags, sergeants both, glowed in the light of the small fire that burned to illuminate the tattered American flag. The flag would remain under the protection of the Second Marines for as long as it was uncased on this hallowed ground. The fire would also draw distant attention away from what transpired nearby. A few others were armed, too. Russ Chapelle was holding a BAR when he nodded the group through the small cordon to join the others. There were perhaps sixteen all told.

"Campeti'll make sure we're not noticed away from *Walker* for a while," Gray mumbled.

"*Mahan*'s taken care of," agreed Steele.

The two men led the newcomers over the small rise and down onto the beach where *Mahan* had been tied up for most of her stay in Aryaal. She might have never been there, for all the evidence remaining, except for the small shelter that had been erected for Ellis's meetings with the suspicious natives. Sealed now from outside view, the shelter served another purpose.

Gray paused before entering and addressed Pam Cross. "There's two patients in there for you, Ensign. One needs you pretty bad." He paused. "The other won't need you at all, directly, but you might make sure he's not going to bleed to death or pass out before we're through."

Wide-eyed, but less shocked than she expected, Cross nodded and stepped inside. Silva, Chack, and Laney followed.

In one corner of the "tent" was a young female Lemurian. She looked about the size and maturity of one of their "teenage" younglings, although she was dressed as a warrior in one of the Guard regiments. At least she wore the remnants of such garments. She was stripped almost entirely, only her shin greaves held where the lashings had survived the knife. Anywhere else her clothing or armor might have resisted, her fur was matted with blood.

Risa held her like her very own child, sobbing right along with her, stanching the blood that welled from her face and a nearly amputated upper lip. She gave Silva the slightest nod and then her eyes flashed daggers when she glared into the other corner.

Gagged, trussed in leg irons and even bloodier was *Mahan*'s quartermaster's mate second, Al "Jolson" Franklen, and Silva knew they were in a hell of a lot of trouble. Franklen was an ugly bastard, even when his face wasn't beaten nearly off, but he'd always enjoyed a degree of popularity because of his uncanny Al Jolson imitations. Sometimes when a bunch of the ships were in Cavite, he'd even put on blackface and stage a show. Do it up right. Some of the other fellas might throw in and it was better than a movie. Usually.

Sometimes it got ugly.

The thing was, in the Asiatic Fleet, the men were steeped in the diversity of centuries of empire and trade. It was not a real "melting pot" in the American sense of the word, but the men were in constant contact with Chinese, Filipinos, Malays, Arabs, Javanese, Indians . . . And that was just in the cities. Almost every island had its own distinctive culture. Regardless how they felt about them, eventually they at least got *used* to the locals. Even the most hard-core racist sometimes found his prejudices at least tempered to some degree, if not washed away entirely. Until the Japs came.

But Franklen wasn't like that. He was a Kard-Karrying Klansman from Michigan who thought the U.S. should have thrown in with the Nazis—at least until the Japanese bombed Pearl Harbor. As far as he was concerned, only white humans were even people. Now with the dame famine, the booze, the party—and the fact the *Mahan*s hadn't had near the contact with Lemurians that the *Walker*s had—Al "Jolson" Franklen had gone and done something he was probably going to have to die for.

They should have been more on the lookout for something like this. Silva reflected guiltily that he might even have contributed to it, but it made no difference. The unthinkable had happened. Sexual assault had been perpetrated upon a Lemurian by a human, and somehow, tonight, they had to sort it out.

It was obvious to Silva what was going on. They couldn't report it. By morning, in the aftermath of the "great party," news of the atrocity would spread. The captain would come down like the end of the earth, but the damage would already be done. Lemurian females did not ordinarily give their favors indiscriminantly, Silva's real relationship with Risa notwithstanding. And that's what they were: *favors*. Jealously guarded and given with care. They would not be *taken,* any more than from a human female. That they had been—and so brutally—could breed resentment and hate. This one would have to stay with the chiefs—if they could keep it that way. Possibly nothing less than the alliance, and maybe even the war, was at stake. All because of one selfish, perverted, racist bastard.

A lot was up to the girl. They'd allowed Pam a few minutes to assemble a bag and without even a glance at Franklen she rushed to the young victim and began a quick, softly murmured examination. As she and Risa began to ask quiet questions, the grim-faced men turned to the prisoner. Chack crouched beside him in the sand, resting his chin on his cutlass guard, staring at him from inches away, his inscrutable eyes somehow radiating malice.

"Pull his gag," Gray instructed. He looked at Chack. "If he does anything but quietly answer questions, kill him." He peered hard into Franklen's eyes. "You got that? You answer questions and keep a civil tongue, you might just survive this night."

In spite of himself, Franklen snorted and blood bubbled from his shattered nose. The Bosun shrugged and nodded at Donaghey, who yanked out the nasty, bloody rag.

Franklen coughed and spat for several minutes before his spasm subsided enough that he might be understood. Finally he spoke.

"You gonna kill me any-ay, Chee. You ne'er 'iked me." Black blood and wrecked lips made him almost unintelligible.

"Not so. I thought you were funny as hell. When you're made-up, you're not near as ugly. You can act and talk as much like Al Jolson as anybody I ever seen, and you can tell the funny stories like he can. You just wouldn't leave well enough alone. Hell, a lot of the coolies and Filipino guys got treated like crap for days after one of your shows. Not to mention the mess attendants." He snorted. "Besides, I got news for you: you can't whistle and you can't sing . . . and your big Hollywood role model—who loaned you the only popularity you ever had—is a Jew!"

"Das a damn lie!"

Gray rolled his eyes.

"An for de others," Franklen went on, "they was just lyin' Tagalog Bastards. Flips. Like Nigras back home. Takin' jobs in de fact'ries from hardworkin' white men just 'cause they'd work for less." He looked around and sneered as best he could. "And now these goddamn 'Cats puttin' on airs like real destroyermen. Real soljers!"

Gray slapped him hard. He couldn't help himself.

"Like real people, you mean? You don't even think of 'em like that, do you? You figure you can just have your way with one like one of your farm animals back home. Is that about the size of it?"

Franklen stared at him defiantly. "You're one to talk." His tiny eyes squinted around. "All of you, I bet." They fell at last on Silva. "And you most of all, you 'Cat-lovin' traitor!"

Gray and Donaghey almost weren't quick enough to stop Silva from drawing the long bayonet at his side and ramming it into the top of Franklen's head. Chack stood up, though, and watched Silva's reaction with interest—as well as that of his sister, who came partly uncoiled from around the victim Pam was tending. With both a shudder and a sense of wonder, he realized their "carrying on" couldn't be quite entirely a joke after all. Whatever it was, he was certainly getting a major contrast lesson in Silva and Risa's relationship as opposed to others that were possible.

"We can't get anywhere with him." Donaghey sighed emotionlessly. "He just don't get it."

"I'll get through to him," Silva said softly, resheathing his bayonet and dropping to his knees in the sand. The two 'Cats who'd been holding Al fought his struggles, but were replaced by Laney on one arm and Chack on the other. For quite some time, Silva stared across the tent at the intensity of the eyes that glowed back at him from the females. One was filled with a murderous passion and the other . . . similar, but with a measure of devastation he'd seen only once before. In the belly of *Revenge* when they took the ship from the Grik and rescued the "provisions" there. He'd never been the sensitive sort and he'd used women like toys himself, but this . . . He almost felt ashamed to be a man. And to add a measure of icy mercury to his shame and his resolve, it suddenly dawned on him that this was the first time he'd ever seen a Lemurian teenage female seem just like a vulnerable, devastated, teenage girl. He was filled with a smoldering rage like he'd never known. Pam's frequent glances in his direction weren't much different from those of the Lemurians.

"I'll tell you something, Al. I like these 'Cats. A hell of a lot better than I like you. And I do think of 'em as 'people.' Hell, maybe even human. They're a lot more human than you are; that's a fact. I've fought with 'em and worked with 'em and spilled my blood alongside 'em. We've helped them and they've helped us." He pointed at the crumpled child. "I don't recognize her after what you done, but I bet I've fought alongside her!" He looked intently at Franklen. "The way I hear it, you never fought alongside anybody. Why don't you tell us what you've done for 'us humans' since we got here, Al, 'cause by all accounts, it ain't much. You supported Kaufman's mutiny against Mr. Ellis, and look how many died because of that . . ."

"Pardoned," Franklen gummed, but Silva went on.

"Let's see, how many battles *have* you fought against the Griks that are swoopin' down? You'll at least agree they're worse than 'Cats, won't you?" There was no response. Dennis started counting on his fingers.

"Well, let's see. I seen—helped—the 'Cats fight like hell to save *Big Sal* from a gob as big as the one Mr. Ellis fought through. Which you was in the brig waiting for Captain Kaufman to come back aboard if what I hear is true. Skipped that one, didn't you? Even stayed in the brig as 'insubordinate' the whole time the ship was laid up here and made no effort to give a hand."

"We were screwed, Silva, you dumb son of a bitch! Just look around yourself! The stupid 'Cats around here wouldn't talk to us. They didn't even care about the Griks until it was too late. All they cared about was fightin' each other." He spat a gobbet of blood. "Ellis weren't no officer. He couldn't get anything sorted out between 'em. And I did too agree to work on the ship."

"You agreed to work on the ship—for a pardon," Gray glowered, "because the ship was so shorthanded. Mr. Ellis should'a hung you. Instead, your skipper *forgave* you and let you loose. Figgers 'let bygones be bygones and we're all together now.' My God, after seeing that field in front of the city how could you *think* anything else? But you sat out the battle on shore. Again. Even when it started to fall apart and everybody went to fight."

Silva raised his eyebrows. "So on top of everything else, you really are a coward." He shook his head. "Except where little girls are concerned. All you could think of, the first time nobody's really watchin' you, was grabbin' up some . . . child and tearin' her up like that. What were you gonna do next? You couldn't have let her live."

There was a sharp intake of breath and suddenly everyone in the tent knew Silva was right.

"Nah, Silva," Franklen gushed. "It wasn't like that! I wouldn't'a really hurt her . . . I just wanted a piece—like you got!"

Risa practically leaped across the distance separating them and grabbed him by the hair in iron claws.

"Silva no have 'piece,' you piece of *shit*!" Her glare moved to encompass her brother as well. "He have *friend*. We make big joke, scare Chack. Scare Captain too, have big laugh . . . but we more than friends too." Now she was talking directly to her brother. "Okay with you, the Captain." She glanced at Pam. "Or anybody, that's fine. Not okay?" She blinked sublime unconcern. "Still okay with Risa."

"Now see," Franklen whined, "I got no problem with that! That's what—" He was almost dead before Silva and Chack could pull Risa off him and move her back across the tent.

Gray, Donaghey, Laney, and Steele were kneeling over the unconscious form as if deciding what to do with a dead snake, when Silva and Chack returned. Silva didn't come right out and say "Sorry about that," but his body language did. He did apologize for "using up all the air so far."

"Hell. You just said what everybody was thinking," said Gray. "Make no mistake. This is a trial. He's admitted what he done, and you pointed out it would have been a lot worse if he hadn't got caught."

"Who caught him, anyway?"

"Steele. Sheer luck. He was runnin' a final check before he went on deck for the party and heard her cries. Damn, he's got good ears! Franklen had her down in *Mahan's* steering engine room to show her the 'machines.' Hell, they can't resist that. It's like offerin' 'em candy."

Silva felt another uncharacteristic twinge of guilt.

"How much of me and Risa 'carrying on' mighta, you know, contributed?"

Several faces became unreadable.

"I don't reckon any," said Gray at last. "For one thing, nobody really knew *what* you were up to, and I guess we still don't. I'd just as soon keep it that way. 'More than just friends' can mean anything. Outside this tent, they still won't know that much." His eyes bored into Laney's. "Besides, whatever it was, it sure wasn't . . ." He spit on Franklen as the man groaned and began to come to. "Like this."

"So," Chack said at last, "what shall we do with this creature?" For the first time in a long time, he didn't appear to be thinking about Silva when he said the word "creature." Maybe he'd started to think over what his sister and friend had said—or maybe their "relationship" had finally been put in perspective for him. "We've already decided we can't make an example of him, which is actually a shame. There are more than a few of my people who don't think of humans as 'people' either."

"That's changing fast enough. We've spilled enough blood together. Besides, most of the ones who feel that way are on the other side of that wall, yonder, or they've run off." Franklen was fully conscious again when Gray finished. "And pretty soon, there'll be one less of ours who feels like that."

"Let's ask the girl," Laney suddenly blurted. They were the first words he spoke. Donaghey nodded.

"Yeah. Let's see what she wants to do with him." Franklen began to thrash and moan, but the bloody gag went back in his mouth and Chack and Laney held him again. Having made the suggestion, Laney was more than willing to let others carry it out. The last thing he wanted to do, in his heart of hearts, was speak to a teenage rape victim of any species.

She looked better as they approached her. She was covered now, by what must have been clean linens from the ship. The blood had been cleaned from her fur and in its place was the viscous healing paste. Pam was still gently applying stitches to her lip, but she didn't seem to notice any pain. Silva was uncomfortably aware that, like "Tabby," the 'Cat "snipe" the Mice had taken on as apprentice, or whatever, this one was young and, well . . . stacked. After so long without female companionship, it was easy to understand how passions could flare. But rape was rape.

"She speak English?" Gray asked. A small, dark-furred head briefly nodded.

"Surprisingly well," Pam said, glaring at the prisoner. "Most of the Baalkpan Lemurians I've met, and the ones from *Big Sal* too, are all pretty talkative. Kind of like they *want* to be *our* friends."

Franklen spit out his gag. "The nastiest cur-dog will lick your hand before it bites it off!" He began to scream before he was silenced again.

"Shut up, you!" Gray roared loud enough that Silva was half convinced they'd hear him on the ships. Gray turned back to face the Lemurian and when he spoke again, his voice was softer than butter. Dennis's mouth hung open, shocked by the Bosun's transformation into something so . . . unsuspected.

"What's your name, child?" he asked.

"Blas-Ma-Ar," she whispered. "*Nerracca,* Body of Home clan." She straightened slightly. "Striking for the Second Marines. I was in the square," she added proudly. Gray smiled.

"I happen to know the acting CO of the Second Marines and I'll have a word with him this very night."

The young female's facial fur stood out in a 'Cat blush when she looked over at Chack. Gray's voice became more serious. "Now, all that aside, a man's life is at stake. I've heard about all I want to hear out of him, but you have to tell me your side of the story."

Blas hesitated and Pam and Risa practically melded into her with their caresses and reassurances.

"It will be difficult," she said in a distant voice.

"I know, sweetie," Gray whispered back. "I know."

*   *   *

When she was finished, Gray nodded. It was about what he expected. It was also very detailed and disturbing. Since Lemurians had virtually no concept of modesty, no detail was left to his imagination and since, conversely, Blas-Ma-Ar (he'd taken to thinking of her as Blossom) had experienced the assault much like any teenage human girl might, with the same outrage, terror, and even guilt, Gray found himself controlling his killing rage with difficulty. He looked at Franklen and was surprised to see him dozing. Oh, well. He looked back at the "girl." No, "girl" wasn't right even before tonight. She was a proven warrior who'd fought for her people. More than Al Franklen ever really had.

"You understand why we have to keep this between ourselves for now?" he asked gently and she nodded. "People *will* know, and it won't happen again. But word will spread slowly and it will add power to the words. That's why we have to do things like this sometimes."

"Captain no have power for this?"

Gray shook his head. "No, sweetie. The captain has *too much* power for this right now. His anger would overcome everything else, and then others would get mad, and others, until everything was just about this. We might even forget to fight the Grik. You don't want that."

"No," she whispered softly. "I don't want anything like that. I want to be a Marine." She paused, looking at Franklen, who had awakened and was looking back. "And I want to eat his eyes."

Donaghey glanced at his watch. "Whatever we do, and whatever she eats, we better get on with it. Sooner or later *some* officer is going to figure out there's a hell of a lot of Indians running around without any chiefs to tell 'em what to do."

"Right," agreed Gray. "Call 'em in and we'll sort this out."

Except for Russ Chapelle and the Lemurian Marines, everyone else managed to squeeze in the tent. They made solicitous comments as they passed by "Blossom," but had only hard stares for their former shipmate.

"We ain't gonna have no jury," Gray said. "The 'accused' was caught in the act, admitted what he done, and invited Mr. Steele to 'get some' himself. No one has since heard him deny he raped and brutalized one of our young female allies. He *is* guilty, so I won't even call for a vote. The only thing we have left to decide is punishment."

Steele sighed. "We're kind of in the same boat there. There's only one punishment for what he did, and he probably would've done worse before he was finished."

"I never figured chiefs had so much power," Laney whispered. "This ain't in the book!"

"No, it ain't," Gray growled. "There're lots of things that ain't in the book. This world we've wound up in, for one. But chiefs have always 'handled' things." Gray looked at Donaghey. "And this ain't the first time we handled somethin' like this. Sometimes problems just have to go away and Franklen's turned himself into one of those problems tonight. With all that's at stake, we can't dump this on the captain."

"It will even look better from our point of view," confirmed Chack, speaking very close to Franklen's ear, "if news of this . . . event comes forward over time. It will show your people honor your leader and the alliance, but you also honor a youngling's virtue enough not to wait until the 'time is right' to sort things out." Blossom bristled at the "youngling," but Chack blinked reassuringly. "You are still a youngling—I am scarcely beyond that myself—but you are also a Marine."

"So, how are we gonna do it?" Silva asked, ever practical and to the point. "I'd kinda' like to get some more dancin' in before the party winds down."

"We can't shoot him, for obvious reasons," Donaghey mused.

"Easiest thing is to take him down to the water and just throw him in. Let the flashies have him," said Silva. "Where'd ol' Al Jolson go? Hell if I know. Musta' got drunk that night at the propeller party and fell in the water. Yeah, seen him swipin' everybody's half-empty seep cups when they was dancin'. Serves the bastard right."

Gray looked thoughtful. "Say, that's just how we'll work it. You're a fiend, Silva, but you're a pretty good acting chief so far."

Throughout this exchange, Franklen was unable to speak, but his eyes had begun to move rapidly back and forth. They were talking about killing him, right in front of him, matter-of-factly, like he wasn't even there.

"You— You can't do that!" protested Laney. Franklen leaned against him in relief and began to sob.

"What do you mean?" Gray asked menacingly. Laney gulped, but didn't look away.

"I mean, kill him, sure. The bastard deserves it." He shivered and held the quivering form farther away. "But don't throw him in the water alive. And"—he looked almost apologetically at Blossom—"don't let her eat his eyes."

"Don't worry. We won't throw him in the water alive, and that girl is sure not gonna eat his eyes. We've got rules during these illegal get-togethers, Laney. That's the thing that makes us different from the Grik and from guys like Al. We've got rules of decency, of honor to follow, even when we're breaking the rules of the Navy. And it's because we take those rules so seriously that we're breaking them in the first place. To protect the honor of our Navy, our ships and our people. See?"

"So how *are* we gonna kill him? We ain't gonna hang him—not in here," Silva persisted. "I don't mean to sound all insensitive, but the bastard's gotta die, and we prob'ly oughta' quit sankoin' along."

"He's right," said Steele. "Let's get on with it. Lots or volunteers?"

"Oh, for cryin' out loud," said Silva in an exasperated voice. "Somebody draws a short straw, or long straw, you gonna *make* 'em kill him, Frankie? What if he can't do it? Whoever kills him is gonna have to use their hands. What if they ain't strong enough? Might as well sell tickets for that." He turned to Laney.

"Would you like to kill him, Dean?"

Surprised, Laney looked around, then looked at the ground. Anywhere but at the prisoner or his victim. "No, Dennis, as a matter of fact I wouldn't. Not in cold blood. I'll do it, but I wouldn't like to." He looked up. "I guess I just ain't the killer you are."

"Few are," agreed Silva equably. "Thing is, I shouldn't have to kill him either, even though, for reasons of my own, I'd really kind of like to. But we all been told a chief's job is to lead. Well, we're all of us chiefs, or acting chiefs or petty officers now, but some are higher than others. I been here before, even if I never got The Hat, but I never could keep it because I didn't want the responsibility." He walked over and looked Gray in the eye. "A *lot* of responsibility comes with that chief's hat. You got time in grade on everybody. You're 'in charge.' Maybe Frankie out-ranks you now, but there ain't no officers here. Right here, right now, you're it. So lead, Bosun. You either got to pick somebody to do it or you have to do it yourself."

After a long moment, Gray nodded. "You would'a had The Hat a long time ago, Silva, if you weren't such a maniac. Come on, we'll do it together."

With Laney and Chack still each on an arm, Silva grabbed the burly quartermaster's mate around the chest. Wide-eyed, he struggled and moaned through his gag.

"I'll pull this gag and let you have some last words if you'll keep 'em quiet and decent," Gray offered. Franklen went slack. Taking this as a sign he agreed, Gray pulled the bloody rag. Instantly, Al began scream-ing at the top of his lungs. Gray grabbed his head and began to twist and the screams abruptly ceased.

"You hear that kind of weird crackin' sound, Al? Sounds like it's right under your skull? Just grunt if you do." Franklen made a noncom-mittal sound. In Fitzhugh Gray's very best Al Jolson voice (which wasn't half bad) he spoke the real Al Jolson's signature line: "You ain't heard *nothin'* yet!"

Rasik-Alcas, King and Protector of Aryaal, paced back and forth before the large arched window, his rich, supple gown flowing as he walked. Barely visible in the distance beyond the north wall, bonfires, lighted ships, and muffled sounds of merriment goaded him into a dangerous, seething rage.

"Yes, my Lord King Protector," confirmed Lord Koratin with a ner-vous glance, "the invaders revel."

"Why?" Rasik snapped.

Koratin bowed his head. "I am not sure, lord. Some needed repair, he could atone to some degree by telling tales of real virtue and clear morals to the young. "You begin to believe your own fables," Rasik accused. Koratin remained silent. "As long as the sea folk war against the Grik, we won't be rid of them," Rasik repeated, returning to the subject at hand. He resumed pacing, deep in thought. Then he stopped. "But what if the war was over?"

"What do you mean, Lord King?"

Rasik's eyes had become predatory slits. "Tell me, Lord Koratin. Do you think those silly sea folk would have the courage to fight without the iron ships?"

"No, Lord King," Koratin answered honestly.

"Do you believe they'd even consider carrying on without them?" Koratin felt a chill.

"No, Lord King," he whispered.

Rasik barked a horrible laugh. "So simple!" he said and resumed his pacing, but for the rest of the evening, his mood was much improved.

Courtney Bradford was drunk again. His civilian status and eccentric behavior outside the chain of command were still tolerated, as long as he didn't push it. Sometimes he did, usually by covertly exceeding the strict limitation on alcohol intake. He sat in one of the chairs around the wardroom table idly fingering a freshly stripped Grik skull, retrieved from the battlefield, while Juan Marcos and Ray Mertz cleared the dishes left by the dinner party. It had been a fine meal, mostly Americanized local fare, but a few purely native dishes had been presented. Bradford wasn't accustomed to the unusual Lemurian spices and, for the most part, he just stuck to salt. At least salt hadn't changed, thank God. His morbid trophy hadn't elicited the excitement he expected when he flourished it at the beginning of the meal. He'd been politely but firmly asked to place it out of sight until everyone had eaten.

Now, most of the diners had returned to their duties or joined the party on deck, leaving only the captain, Sandra, Jim, Keje, and Bradford himself. Without fanfare, the grisly thing reappeared upon the table.

long delayed, is the word I hear. We have few spies among them yet." Rasik-Alcas began to scold his senior and currently only advisor for taking so long to build a network of informants, but he hesitated. Lord Koratin represented one of the oldest houses in Aryaal, and the creature was politically savvy. He was urbane, vain, and quick to take offense— but fear would prevent him from challenging his new king. For now. Rasik was fairly sure that Koratin harbored firm suspicions as to how Fet-Alcas had died, but for now the Aryaalan noble seemed willing to let the matter stand, and even to help. It made Rasik uncomfortable to rely on Koratin for anything, particularly anything critical to his con-solidation of power, but he had no choice. "Perhaps when their repairs are complete, they will go away," Koratin speculated.

Rasik growled. "Of course they will—to fight the Grik."

Koratin blinked. "Then that is good! They will be gone from here and things will become as before." He paused. "We are weakened, true, but we can stand against B'mbaado. In time—"

"No!" shouted Rasik. "Don't you see? As long as they war against the Grik, they will have a presence here! They will never go away as long as the war continues!"

"Is that so terrible? What if the Grik return?"

"Return?" Rasik snorted. "With what?" He gestured eastward. "Have you not seen the carrion beyond our walls? Mere bones now, but the bones of *thousands*! It will be generations before those losses are made good." He shook his head. "No, the Grik menace is gone. They won't return in our grand-younglings' lifetimes."

Koratin was not so sure. He proceeded carefully. "I have heard it said they are not like us—in more ways than are obvious. They breed quickly and their kingdom is vast. Some say they are the Demons of Old, come to harry us again, and what they sent here is but a tithe against what they are capable of."

"Nonsense! You really should let your females tell stories to your young." Koratin's devotion to his younglings was no secret, and he often recited tales to them—and others—in open forum. He enjoyed per-forming, and while he recognized his own failings, he secretly hoped

he could atone to some degree by telling tales of real virtue and clear morals to the young. "You begin to believe your own fables," Rasik accused. Koratin remained silent. "As long as the sea folk war against the Grik, we won't be rid of them," Rasik repeated, returning to the subject at hand. He resumed pacing, deep in thought. Then he stopped. "But what if the war was over?"

"What do you mean, Lord King?"

Rasik's eyes had become predatory slits. "Tell me, Lord Koratin. Do you think those silly sea folk would have the courage to fight without the iron ships?"

"No, Lord King," Koratin answered honestly.

"Do you believe they'd even consider carrying on without them?" Koratin felt a chill.

"No, Lord King," he whispered.

Rasik barked a horrible laugh. "So simple!" he said and resumed his pacing, but for the rest of the evening, his mood was much improved.

Courtney Bradford was drunk again. His civilian status and eccentric behavior outside the chain of command were still tolerated, as long as he didn't push it. Sometimes he did, usually by covertly exceeding the strict limitation on alcohol intake. He sat in one of the chairs around the wardroom table idly fingering a freshly stripped Grik skull, retrieved from the battlefield, while Juan Marcos and Ray Mertz cleared the dishes left by the dinner party. It had been a fine meal, mostly Americanized local fare, but a few purely native dishes had been presented. Bradford wasn't accustomed to the unusual Lemurian spices and, for the most part, he just stuck to salt. At least salt hadn't changed, thank God. His morbid trophy hadn't elicited the excitement he expected when he flourished it at the beginning of the meal. He'd been politely but firmly asked to place it out of sight until everyone had eaten.

Now, most of the diners had returned to their duties or joined the party on deck, leaving only the captain, Sandra, Jim, Keje, and Bradford himself. Without fanfare, the grisly thing reappeared upon the table.

"This is the face our own world would have taken if whatever killed the dinosaurs . . . hadn't," Bradford announced muzzily, interrupting the conversation at the other end of the table.

"Probably," Matt agreed. They'd had this talk before. He began to resume his conversation with Jim.

"But have you considered," Bradford plowed on, "that maybe this is the way it *should* have been? Just look at this thing!" he demanded. "Similar brain capacity, large eyes, wicked, wicked teeth! Obviously a far better-adapted natural predator than we!" The rest of the group reluctantly turned their attention to the Australian. He was on a roll, and even drunk, whatever he said was bound to be interesting.

"Well, there's no doubt they're intelligent," agreed Ellis grudgingly, "and they're certainly better fighters on land than at sea. I don't see how that makes them 'better natural predators' than us. We beat them."

"Ah," said Bradford, controlling a belch, "but we beat them with our minds, not our bodies. Only superior technology won the day, in the end. Consider: as far as we know, humanity has not risen on this world. We may be its only poor representatives. Where we come from, man is the greatest predator, but here that's not the case. Here"—he tapped the skull—"this creature—or similar races—might predominate all over the globe." He shifted his bleary stare to Keje. "Even on the islands that the People control, there are Grik, are there not? You've said so yourself." He paused. "We've seen them," he remembered. "Primitive, aboriginal, but plainly related to the more sophisticated enemy we face." Keje nodded, peering intently at the man.

"What's your point, Mr. Bradford?" Sandra asked quietly. The Australian's fatalistic tone was giving her the creeps.

"It's quite simple, my dear. We all, myself included, have from the beginning considered the world we came from to be the 'normal' one— the 'right' one—and this world the aberration." He blinked. "No offense, my dear Captain Keje." The Lemurian blinked acknowledgment. "But if you compare just the sheer physical lethality, there's no way we humans would ever have evolved to become 'top dog,' as you Americans so aptly put it, if these creatures had anything to say about it—" His belch finally escaped. "Back home, that is. Here, we would have been an evolutionary impossibility . . . excuse me, please."

"But what about the 'Cats?" asked Matt. Bradford shrugged.

"They apparently evolved more recently, in an isolated environment—Madagascar, I am quite sure. Two sentient species rising independently, but necessarily separate or it could never have taken place." He stared at the skull. "At least I don't think so. I'm convinced that my poor, lost Fritzi—a standard poodle—was more intelligent than most people I've met." He shook his head. "In any event, the existence of Lemurians in no way alters my thesis. They are dodos."

"What is a Do-Do?" Keje asked.

"A large, flightless bird that looked quite a lot like a skuggik." Bradford beamed. Keje started to rise from his chair, his tail rigid with indignation.

Matt put a hand on his shoulder and whispered, "He's drunk, my friend, and he means no insult." Then he continued in a louder voice. "Dodos were birds, as he described. I can't remember where they lived—"

"Mauritius," Bradford supplied. "Not too dreadfully far from Madagascar, in fact." He blinked. "How odd!"

"Anyway," Matt resumed, "dodos lived on an island with no natural predators and they thrived despite being extremely vulnerable creatures. When humans discovered the island, several hundred years ago, they were killed for food. To make matters worse, some animals, livestock animals called hogs, escaped and went wild—destroying the eggs and nests of the dodos. Soon, they were extinct."

"I have heard this word, 'extinct.' It means 'rubbed out,' 'gone,' correct? That's what the Grik mean to do to us." Keje turned back to the Australian and fixed him with a hard, expressionless stare. "If that is the case, then what are you Amer-i-caans? Dodos too, you think? No. We are not this stupid bird that couldn't fly. We can fly. We *did*! We flew to safety when the Grik came to destroy us and we've not lost our wings! One day, we'll fly back to our nest, across the Western Sea, and it will be the Grik who are extinct. Not us!"

*   *   *

Tsalka stared at General Esshk in abject disbelief. "Impossible!" he gasped.

"Impossible indeed. But true." Esshk himself still seemed shaken by the news. They were standing on the quarterdeck of the *Giorsh,* flagship of the fleet. Above them a bright, loosely woven awning fluttered in the mild breeze. It reduced the glare but still allowed the warming rays of the sun to wash upon them. It was also the only thing on the entire ship that wasn't painted a bright, sparkling white. Tsalka often took his late-days beneath the awning on the quarterdeck even though it was inconvenient for the crew to rig. He had no command authority, having accompanied the fleet on a lark, but he was the highest-ranking Hij in the Eastern Empire and if his comforts caused annoyance, no one dared to say. A short time earlier, a dispatch vessel from the New Conquest had closed the flagship to report. A report that General Esshk had just related.

"All of them?"

Esshk hissed a negative. "Not all, Lord Regent . . . but most. A few made their escape to the New Conquest and not all fell prey. Some were not involved and managed to avoid the hunt—a simpler thing on a ship. Those that did fall prey have already been destroyed."

Tsalka paced the width of the quarterdeck, stunned. "An entire Pride-Pack of hunters made prey!" he whispered.

"Not all—" began Esshk.

Tsalka waved a clawed hand impatiently. "As near as makes no difference! It was bad enough when the hunting-pack fell prey, but *this!*"

"We often lose ships, Lord Regent."

"Lone hunters!" Tsalka snapped. "Scouts! Victims of the sea, as often as not. A Pride-Pack has not been lost to prey . . . ever!"

"We have lost that many and more to other hunters, sire, while we still considered them prey."

Tsalka glared at the general. "You have spoken thus before, I recall. Have a care." He hissed a sigh. "What is the world coming to when prey do not know their proper place?" He shook himself. "What caused the calamity this time? How did the Tree Prey resist?"

"The same as before, sire," Esshk replied. "They had the aid of the smoking ship."

Tsalka turned to face him. "I did not think to hear of it again. If Righ yet lived I would give him the liar's death!"

"Perhaps he did not know. It was the report of others that he passed."

"All the same," Tsalka mused, "I should probably destroy his mates when we return." He resumed his pacing, but stopped near the rail. Beyond it, the sea was covered with red-hulled ships as far as the eye could see. Here and there were the white hulls of generals. Far away to the east and west were the lands that bordered their path. The drawings of the world called it the Malacca Strait. The sight stirred him in spite of his elevation. He knew he shouldn't concern himself, but it was an inauspicious beginning, this latest tale of disaster. He consoled himself that in the end it would scarcely matter. Nothing could stand before the Grand Swarm.

What difference would it make if the contemptible Tree Prey had allied themselves with some Worthy Prey? It would only make the hunt more exciting. With an amused hiss, he glanced far astern, where the "new" hunters that had joined the Grand Swarm struggled to keep pace. He knew little about them; their language was unspeakable, but they were fearsome hunters. They were so like his tail-less pet—Kaufman— in form, and yet different enough that they could not be the same race regardless they both used iron ships. They were different enough that his pet was terrified of them, clearly natural enemies. That was the main reason he had given his pet to them as a gift, and he still remembered the shrieks as they carried it away.

He turned to face forward and rejoined General Esshk. What if the Tree Prey did have strange new friends? So did the Grik.

*T*he day after the party, just as the forenoon watch came on, Matt and Sandra stood on the starboard bridgewing alone. He wasn't sure exactly when the nurse had achieved unlimited bridge access, but by now it was a fait accompli. She never abused the privilege, but nobody ever questioned her when she arrived. Others lined the starboard side as well. From his vantage point, Matt saw Silva leaning against the rail next to the number two gun. On his face was an uncharacteristically thoughtful expression as he stared out to sea. Beside him, Paul Stites made some kind of crack about Silva's "dame running off" and the big gunner's mate didn't even respond. *Strange,* Matt thought, wondering what that was about.

He looked into the east and watched *Mahan*'s distant shape steaming down the bay toward the island gate that led to the Java Sea. To have searched for her so long, only to have her leave once they found her, left him with mixed emotions. It was different this time, though, wasn't it? She would return in a couple of months and rejoin her sister, wherever that might be. By then she'd be a different ship. Better, with a full and willing crew. She would finally become an asset instead of a liability, and together again, the two old destroyers would sweep the Grik from the sea. His optimism couldn't stop him from worrying, though. They'd made her as fit for sea as they could, under the circumstances, but she was still in sorry shape and she was still shorthanded. Even more so this morning, since Jim had actually reported a man missing. He was known as a malcontent malingerer and chances were he'd turn up in a day or so. Where could he go?

Matt suddenly realized that Sandra's small, soft hand had found its way into his own. Clearing his throat, he released her fingers so he could ostentatiously adjust his hat. He glanced around, but the bridge watch all seemed preoccupied with their duties.

"It's hard to watch them go," Sandra murmured beside him. He nodded. To the south and east, the sky was clear and the harsh glow of the morning sun touched the wave tops with fire. To the north, however, the sky seemed smeared with a muddy brush. He stepped away from Sandra, heading toward the opposite wing, glancing up through the windows as he walked, until he saw the sky beyond the city in the west-northwest. Across the horizon, a great black mass was forming, as dark as the blackness of night. Wispy stringers of gray and white crawled across it like snakes, or worms. In spite of the morning heat, he felt a chill as Sandra joined him.

"Keje said this was the stormy time of year," he whispered nervously.

"What's that?" she asked.

"Something bad."

Rick Tolson was having the time of his life. He'd always loved the sea—even as a kid, having run away aboard a fishing schooner when he was ten. He hadn't enjoyed that life, to be honest, but it taught him a lot about the sea and sails and how to be a man. When he returned as a prodigal son, his father arranged for him to spend the summers with the crew of a sixty-five-foot racing yacht named *Bee* that belonged to a wealthy Chesapeake-area business associate of his. All through high school, the summers found Rick converting the wind into raw speed. While other kids his age worked at gas stations and soda fountains, he got paid (a meager salary) to play, racing against the other sleek play-things of the rich.

He learned everything, and by the time he went to college he'd com-manded *Bee* in several high-stakes races and won, always against newer and faster competitors. In college he didn't have much time for racing, since he took summer classes as well, but he always had a place aboard the *Bee* when he went home on weekends. He also joined the Naval Reserve Officer Training Corps—against his father's wishes—and that was how he'd wound up here. He was glad.

Not in his wildest boyhood fantasies had he imagined that a Navy life would put him in command of what was, for all intents and pur-poses, a square-rigged frigate. Like Stephen Decatur, Isaac Hull, or Por-ter before Valparaiso, he was living the life of his childhood heroes with the greatest assignment any frigate captain could ask for: independent command. It was a fantasy come true, and he was loving every minute of it. *Revenge* was fast—by Lemurian standards—and surprisingly well made considering her builders. The Grik had taken her draft directly from the lines of the stout, fast-sailing British East Indiamen, and it was obvious now that they'd captured one centuries before and used it as a pattern—scaled up or down—ever since. *Revenge* had one major dif-ference, of course. She was armed with twenty guns. More a ship-sloop than a frigate, in the old scheme of things, where a ship's class was reck-oned by how many guns she carried, but "frigate" sure sounded better.

Rick's crew was entirely Lemurian, with the exception of an ord-nance striker named Gandy Bowles, fresh off of *Mahan*, who'd been jumped to "master gunner." The rest of the crew couldn't love their ship, remembering constantly what she represented. Despite every-thing they did to eliminate it, the cloying scent of her previous owners and what they'd done aboard still lingered, and that didn't help. They loved the *idea* of her, however, and they were ecstatic about what she could do. She was faster and more maneuverable than the stolid, plodding Homes—and faster than any other Grik ship they'd encountered. They'd encountered several. Rick remembered each action with a warm glow of excitement. All had been stragglers or scouts and showed no concern as *Revenge* drew near. She was one of theirs, wasn't she? All were destroyed.

Revenge's speed was due primarily to some innovative rig improvements that Rick and his crew came up with, and he liked to think his racing background helped. Also, in spite of her guns, she wasn't as heavy as other Grik ships. Her crew was smaller and she didn't carry a regiment of warriors and their supplies everywhere she went. That might be a problem if the enemy ever grappled, but so far, *Revenge* had destroyed her surprised victims from beyond the range of even the enemy's shipboard bomb throwers. Whatever the reasons for her success, *Revenge* had been a wolf on the prowl for the better part of three weeks now, earning her name in spades, and the enemy had no idea she was even there. Rick felt like Robert Louis Stevenson had written this part of his life and he couldn't wait to see what happened next.

"Good morning, Cap-i-taan," greeted Kas-Ra-Ar as the Lemurian joined him on the weather side of the quarterdeck.

"Morning, Kas." Rick smiled. "A brisk day and a stiff wind." He glanced aloft at the single-reefed topsails overhead.

"When should we expect the plane, do you think?" Kas asked. Every four days, the PBY flew out and rendezvoused with them so it could carry a report of their sightings back to Surabaya. The latitude wasn't prescribed for the meetings, but the longitude was. That way, the Catalina could just follow the line north until they met. In theory. *Revenge*'s consorts tried to stay in line of sight, and they would signal her with any sightings they made as well. Once, amazingly, they encountered a Lemurian Home headed north into the China Sea. They closed to speak to her and had nearly taken a fusillade of the giant crossbow bolts for their efforts. They finally managed to convince the Home they weren't Grik (an understandable mistake) and they passed them the news of the war. That news came as quite a shock, since these people hadn't even known there *was* a war. They told Kas they might go to Baalkpan, or they might not. They did turn around and head south.

"Sometime this afternoon, I think," Rick replied to his sailing master's question. "We're farther north than they probably expect us, but not close enough to Singapore for Mallory to worry about being seen."

"Will the plane try to find us if there is a storm?" Kas asked, nodding toward the horizon. Rick had been watching the growing clouds since dawn.

"You've got me there. If it gets bad, no." Rick snorted. "If it was me, I wouldn't let them fly the only bloody airplane in the world if the wind was over five miles an hour." He glanced at his second in command and then pointed at the sky. "Do you think it'll get bad?"

Kas cocked his head to one side and blinked. "It is difficult to say. Possibly. This *is* the stormy time of year."

"So everyone keeps saying," grumbled Rick.

A silence stretched between them, but it was broken by a high-pitched cry from the maintop. "Deck there! Sail!"

Rick snatched a speaking trumpet. "Where away?"

There was a short pause while the lookout pondered the best way to translate the bearing. "Two points the left . . . the *port* bow!"

Rick scrambled into the port main shrouds and secured himself as best he could. Then he raised his binoculars. Yes! There she was, running toward them under all plain sail. Probably trying to escape the storm building behind them, Rick mused. "Shake that reef out of the fore-tops'l!" he shouted. "We'll wait till they get closer. Act like we're turning to run, too. We'll rake him as we turn!"

He beamed down at Kas-Ra-Ar. "One way or another, it's going to be an interesting day!"

"Captain, the launch is alongside."

Matt nodded. "Single up all lines and prepare to cast off."

The rain was falling in sheets now, and he could barely see past the fo'c'sle. He was accustomed to the dense squalls of the region, but this was different. He could feel the power behind the thing. He wondered fleetingly if this would be the event that snatched them back where they belonged? For some reason, in spite of everything, he caught himself hoping it wasn't. Jim was right. Back home, *Walker* was just another over-age 'can. If they didn't break her up and scatter her crew through the fleet, she'd probably spend the war towing targets for newer, more capable ships to practice against. Here, she and her people could make a difference. They had already begun.

"The work detail is back aboard and the launch is hooking on," Dowden reported as he entered the pilothouse. Water coursed down his saturated clothes and drained away through the strakes at his feet. The work detail had been winching the screw onto shore, raft and all, so that working against the dock wouldn't damage it.

The talker spoke again. "Radio says Lieutenant Mallory's about to turn north, but it's getting pretty boogery up there—his words—and he wants to know if you still want him to rendezvous with *Revenge*."

"No sense. He can't set down even if he spots her. Tell him to make for Baalkpan. Fly around the storm if he can—he should have plenty of fuel."

The attention of the bridge watch was diverted by another figure entering the pilothouse. It was Keje. He must have come over on the launch that delivered Courtney Bradford, Sandra Tucker, and a few others to *Big Sal*. Matt sent them with the explanation that it wasn't wise to keep all their eggs in one basket. Also, since they weren't critical to the operation of the ship, it made no sense for them to endure a major storm aboard *Walker*—given her less than sedate performance in heavy seas. It would result only in unnecessary suffering. Bradford went with an appreciative smile, but Sandra had been reluctant. Matt finally traded heavily on her professional concern for the wounded that remained on *Big Sal*. Most had been shipped home on *Fristar*, but not all. As to her suspicious concern regarding his own injuries, he blithely reassured her that he'd take it easy.

"Good afternoon, Cap-i-taan Reddy."

"Hello, Keje. I'm glad to see you, but we're about to cast off. It looks like we're going to have some of that 'stormy' weather you talked about."

Keje nodded agreement as he wrung water from his fur. "Indeed. Quite stormy."

"Well." Matt paused, unsure how to continue. "Shouldn't you be with your ship?"

"Unnecessary. Both her feet are out," he said, referring to the giant copper anchors, "as are those of the other Homes. This is a wide, deep bay. They will ride comfortably. The feluccas have all run upriver and, as long as the surge is not too great, they will be fine. We usually moor when a Strakka comes, but it is my understanding you prefer to face them in the open sea. How exciting! I thought, with your permission, I might enjoy this one with you."

Matt looked at his friend for a moment, expressionless. "That's fine, Keje," he said at last. "Glad to have you. I don't think I've ever heard that word, though. What's a Strakka?"

Keje waved his hand. "I don't know if there is a proper word to describe Strakka in Amer-i-caan. The closest I can think of might be . . . typhoon? Is that it?"

"You know what a typhoon is?" Matt asked with surprise. "Those are storms we only used to get in deeper waters than the Java Sea."

"Yes. Mr. Bradford described the typhoon very well. It did sound like a Strakka, but on a different scale."

Matt smiled. "Yeah, a typhoon's as bad as they come. But you're in for a heck of a ride aboard *Walker* in any kind of storm!" There was knowing laughter in the pilothouse.

Keje looked at him and blinked. "No. You misunderstand. A typhoon is bad, but a Strakka . . ." He smiled tolerantly. "A Strakka can be much, *much* worse!"

The Mice had wedged themselves between the forward air lock of the aft fireroom and the access-hatch ladder. Nearby, clutching the grating as if the ship itself was trying to shake her loose, Tabby continued the dry retching that had wracked her small body since the storm began. Isak's and Gilbert's stoic expressions belied the real concern they felt for their furry companion. The monumental cacophony of sound was stunning even to them. The blowers howled as they sucked the sodden air, and the tired hull thundered and creaked as the relentless sea pounded against it. Condensed moisture rained from every surface to join the nauseating sewer that crashed and surged in the bilge as the ship heaved and pitched. The firemen on watch weren't doing much either, just holding on as best they could and trying to supervise the gauges and fires.

"Reckon she's gonna die?" Gilbert Yager asked, peering through the muck that streaked his face. As close as they were, he still had to shout for Isak Rueben to hear him. Even Tabby's soggy tail lay still—he'd never seen that before. Her ordinarily fluffy light-gray fur was almost black, and plastered to her body like it had been slicked down with grease.

"Nah," Isak Rueben reassured him after a judicious glance. "Poor critter's just a little seasick, is all. Must be sorta' embarrassin' for her to be seasick after spendin' her whole life at sea." He was thoughtful. " 'Course, on them big ships o' theirs, I don't reckon it ever gets quite this frisky. Don't carry on so. You'll make her feel worse."

Gilbert looked at the exhausted, wretched, oblivious form.

"Okay. She wouldn't want us coddlin' her." He paused. "Damned if I ain't feelin' a little delicate myself," he admitted, glancing around the dark, dank, rectangular compartment. He could certainly *feel* the violent motion of the ship, but the only visual evidence was the sloshing bilge and the way the condensation sometimes fell sideways. "Now I know how those idiots who go over Niagara Falls in a barrel feel."

The air lock beside them opened, but the "whoosh" was lost in the overall din. Spanky McFarlane spilled out onto the grating, nearly landing atop the afflicted 'Cat. He crawled to his feet, holding on to the catwalk rail.

"What's the matter with her?" he shouted.

"Seasick, we figger," Isak told him.

"What's she doin' here? If she's that sick, she ought'a be in her rack." Spanky remembered then that he hadn't seen Tabby for a couple of days.

"She was," Gilbert confirmed. "She crawled down here today.

The roll's just as bad, but there ain't so much pitch. Maybe she'll feel better."

Spanky hesitated. "Well, try to get her to drink something. She'll get dehydrated."

The Mice nodded in unison. "Say, how're things topside?" Isak asked, uncharacteristically interested in something besides the fire-room. Spanky blew his nose into his fingers and slung the ejecta into the bilge.

"It's a booger," he said. "It's startin' to taper off a little now, though. I just came from the bridge and, I'm telling you, that was a ride! It's a miracle we haven't lost anybody overboard. Even the lifelines have carried away!" Spanky was thoroughly soaked, but that alone wasn't proof he'd been on deck. The Mice were soaked too. "Skipper's been up there ever since the storm hit and he looks like hell. Lieutenant Tucker would give him a shot to put him out if she was here—and if she had one. The man needs rest, with his wounds and all. Other than that, the damage ain't as bad as you'd think. Antenna aerial's gone. Took the top of the resonance chamber with it so the radio's out." He saw their blank expressions. "You know that big pointy cylinder on the back bridge rail, right next to the main blower vent? Looks like a great big bullet?"

"You mean that's what makes the radio work?" Gilbert asked, amazed.

". . . Yeah. Anyway, the launch is wrecked too. Hell, it crashed on the deck right over your heads." The Mice looked at him and then up at the deck above. They hadn't heard a thing. "The life rafts are gone—not that I'd ever get on one of those things on *this* ocean—and we've lost just about everything else that wasn't bolted down." He patted the railing under his hand. "But the old girl's doin' okay—on one engine too. I think Skipper's more worried about *Mahan* than anything. As usual. If she got hit as hard as we did . . ." He grunted. "Anyway, that Keje's up there too." Spanky grinned. "He's havin' the time of his life."

"Where are we?" Gilbert asked and Spanky shrugged.

"If we run into something big and rocky, we'll know it was one of the thousands of pissant islands scattered around out there, but that's as close a guess as I'd care to make."

"You've been out in a 'can like this in the North Atlantic, ain't you?" Isak asked and Spanky nodded, accustomed to the Mice's abrupt subject changes. "Is this as bad as that?"

Spanky just looked at him. "Son," he said, shouting above the turmoil, "I was on the old *Marblehead* in a typhoon in the Philippine Sea back in '36. That storm tore up a 'can like this and a fleet oiler too, like they were paper cups. It wasn't a patch to this one. We're doin' fine." With that, he shook his head and crept away, lurching hand over hand along the rail to resume his inspection of the engineering spaces.

"Well," Isak said, "dudn't feel that bad to me. Maybe we ought to get out more, Gilbert."

"Well," said Captain Reddy as the bow buried itself under a roller, "now I know what a Strakka is." The entire ship shuddered with effort as it came out the other side. Gray-green water sluiced down the deck, submerging the number one gun and erupting upward against the pilothouse. After *Walker* spent two days running east-southeast before the wind while the nightmare storm hammered at the ship with a ferocity Matt had never seen, the raging vortex had climbed all over it and then, apparently, passed it by. The trailing edge of the storm was still quite lively, and the chaotic hash it had made of the Java Sea was rougher than any sea *Walker* had steamed through before. Not as big as it might have been in deeper water, but certainly rougher. Still, they'd been able to bring the ship about and begin the difficult—and even more nauseating—task of working back in the direction from which they'd come.

"How much longer before things quiet down?" he asked through set teeth as *Walker* dove under another, lesser, wall of water. In spite of Keje's fatigue—which had to be almost equal to Matt's—the Lemurian still radiated a vague exuberance. He had absolute faith in Matt's skill and *Walker*'s iron construction, so the whole thing had been just an exciting adventure to him.

"A day. Maybe more. Strakkas move swiftly, as you've seen, and they usually leave as quickly as they come."

"Thank God for that!" Dowden gasped. The youthful exec had the conn and was struggling mightily against the forces of the sea and the thrust of the single propeller. "I'd sure hate to see what a deepwater Strakka's like!"

"There are greater dangers in deep water than a Strakka," Keje reminded him darkly.

"So you say," Dowden wheezed. "Mountain fish and such. But that's a creature. Captain, I thought Mr. Bradford said creatures were the only things different here, but he's talking like storms like this are common in the Java Sea."

"Only at this time of year," Keje reminded them. "And I have to admit, this was an unusually intense Strakka. Of course, it might have just seemed so since we are on such a small ship." Matt grunted and Keje grinned. "No offense, Cap-i-taan, I assure you! Never have I been so exhilarated! It's very like the gri-kakka hunt, in a small boat, but even more exciting and prolonged—at least when the lance strikes true. Gri-kakka die quite quickly then." He peered at the captain with his large reddish-brown eyes. His tail twitched with mischief. "You must try it sometime."

The worst of the storm passed Baalkpan by as it roared down in a great semicircle of destruction from the South China Sea, across the Java Sea, and then pounded the Lesser Sunda Islands on its way toward Australia. Borneo had been struck a glancing blow, by comparison, but tornados, pounding rain, and lashing winds hadn't left Baalkpan unscathed. Lieutenant Mallory had brought the Catalina in just before the whitecaps on the bay would have made it suicide to set the plane down and, together with hundreds of guards and volunteers and the help of the engines, they heaved the big plane out of the water and up a steep, muddy ramp that wasn't yet complete. Once ashore, the plane had been lashed down securely. The PBY weathered the storm, but it had been a near thing. Now, all that remained of the storm in Baalkpan was an incessant deluge that drummed on the plane's sloping wings and ran off the trailing edge in sheets. Ben Mallory, Alan Letts, and Perry Brister were gathered under the port wing with Pete Alden and Tony Scott. Together, they watched the Strakka slowly die.

"I wish this would quit," said the coxswain in a loud voice so he could be heard above the rumbling aluminum overhead. His fear of water didn't encompass rain, but he was heartily sick of it nonetheless. Mallory nodded and glanced at the fuselage. Ed Palmer was in there, still trying to raise *Walker*. They'd heard nothing for two whole days and were beginning to worry. Both destroyers and *Revenge* had been in the path of the biggest storm they'd ever seen.

"Yeah," said Letts, whose thinking mirrored Mallory's. "How's the plane doing? Engines okay?" he asked.

The pilot hesitated. "Sure," he answered in a defensive tone. "The oil we're getting isn't quite up to spec, but we change it every time she flies. Other than that, she's better now than when we got her." He grinned and gestured at the rain. "Cleaner too." He pointedly didn't remind them that "when they got her," the PBY was full of holes and half sunk on a beach.

"Good," Letts murmured, looking carefully at the aviator. He turned to Brister. *Mahan's* former engineering officer had become the general engineer for all of Baalkpan. Captain Reddy and Pete Alden had designed the city's fortifications with an eye toward successful historical port defenses. Alden added a few things based on local conditions. Also, with an infantryman's eye, he'd stressed additions based on the possibility that the enemy might make a landward approach. In addition to his other duties—which now included direct supervision of the massive (by local standards) foundry—Lieutenant Brister was responsible for making the dream come true. The result might very well be the most formidable defensive works this world had ever known.

Instead of the stone walls that Aryaal enjoyed, a huge defensive berm had been thrown up around the city, the approaches festooned with entanglements and sharpened stakes. Moving the vast amount of dirt had also created a wide, deep trench that had subsequently filled with water and become an impressive moat system. The jungle was pushed back at least five hundred yards on all sides, except where the ground sank into swamp. Some of the wood was stockpiled for later use—much of it was fine hardwood after all—and some was used to shore up the breastworks and put a roof over the heads of the defenders to protect them from plunging arrow fire.

The pièce de résistance was the twenty-four heavy guns that pierced the berm at regular intervals through stout embrasures, mostly facing the harbor. These were carefully concealed. The thinking was that, since the harbor was their most heavily defended point, they didn't want to scare the enemy away from it—now they'd had a taste of cannon. If the Grik ever did attack Baalkpan, the defenders wanted them to do it in the "same old way" because the waterfront was where they would smash the invaders' teeth. Still more guns were situated in a heavily constructed and reinforced stockade named Fort Atkinson, overlooking the mouth of the bay.

Again thanks to Alden, the landward approaches hadn't been neglected. One hundred crude mortars were interspersed among the defensive positions. Little more than heavy bronze tubes, they could hurl a ten-pound copper bomb as far as the extended tree line. A little farther if you were brave enough to put a dollop more powder beneath it. The poor fragmentation characteristics of copper had been improved by casting the things with deep lines that ran all around and up and down the spheres—just like a pineapple grenade. When all was said and done, there wasn't so much as a copper cup or brass earring in Nakja-Mur's entire city, or anywhere they could quickly trade with. But what they had, hopefully, was a slaughterhouse for the Grik.

"How have the defenses held up in the rain?" Letts asked.

Brister snorted. "A little rain won't hurt anything. Pack it all down a bit, is all. I may not be a combat engineer by trade, but when I put something together, it stays put together."

Letts grinned and looked at Ben. "All right. As soon as this lets up and you think it's safe, I want you back in the air. See if you can find our people."

"There's an awful lot of water out there," Mallory replied thoughtfully.

"True, but as the storm winds down, *Mahan* should head here and

Walker ought to head back for Surabaya. I figure they were both carried a good ways east-southeast, so throw a horseshoe in your search.
You can refuel at Tangalar," he said, referring to a small outpost they'd
established for that purpose on the southern point of Celebes. "That is,
if it hasn't been washed away. Then head for Surabaya."

"What about *Revenge*?"

Alan grimaced. "If she was northeast of Bangka, like you said, she
could be anywhere by now, with just wind power." He shook his head.
"If she didn't sink, or wind up scattered all over some beach, she might
be in the middle of the Java Sea by now."

"If they're out there, I'll find 'em," Mallory promised.

Letts turned to Tony Scott. "If the rain slacks off later today, take the
launch and check out the refinery. Make sure it came through the storm
okay. Take some help. All we had out there was a couple of caretakers. If
anything cracked, fix it if you can or come get Mr. Brister. Take a look
at the wellhead while you're at it. It was shut down during the storm,
but the Mice'll have a fit if a tree fell on that mechanical dinosaur of
theirs."

Tony kept a straight face, but gulped at the thought of the boat trip.
"Aye, sir," he said. He knew it was a necessary trip, but he sure didn't
want to go.

Tony Scott was no coward—everyone was well aware of that. At the
height of the Battle of the Stones, when they captured *Revenge*, he'd
proven his courage beyond question by jumping *in* the sea to rescue
Lieutenant Tucker. This was the ultimate proof, because he had become
profoundly terrified of the water—and all the creatures that lurked
there. Anyone who might have scoffed at his newfound fear was silent
after that. But nothing changed. There was no revival of his old spirit,
no catharsis. No feeling of being back on the horse. He was no longer
worried that he might have become a coward in general, but he was still
afraid of the water.

It was morning before the rain paused long enough for Scott and
his half dozen 'Cat roughnecks to embark on their inspection jaunt
upriver. It took a while to bail out the boat, and while they worked they

watched those on shore maneuvering the heavy Catalina down to the water. Tony shuddered as a group of line handlers actually waded out up to their waists. He knew, philosophically, that they were relatively safe. There were fewer flashies in the bay than in open water. There were fewer still in the shallows, and after a storm there'd be almost none inshore. Still . . . The launch's motor started on the first try and for a while he concentrated on performing the tasks that once had made him happy. As the boat nosed away from the dock, the PBY floated clear and Tony waved his ever-present Thompson gun at the army pilot as the man climbed on top of the wing to supervise the final preparations. Mallory waved back.

A decent guy, Scott thought to himself as he spun the wheel and pointed the bow toward the distant river mouth. Sure wouldn't want *his* job. Flying around in that beat-up plane over miles of empty ocean. Nothing but water below, packed with millions and millions of voracious . . . He shook his head to keep from shuddering again. The captain had left him here as a mercy, and maybe even as thanks for saving his dame—although that probably didn't figure too consciously in the skipper's mind. *He's giving me a rest so I don't lose my nerve completely,* Scott decided. *He knows all it might take is one more trip across that deep, dark sea to send me absolutely ape.* It would wreck him. Even if he came back to his senses, it wouldn't matter. Everyone would *know.* Tony Scott, coxswain, was helplessly afraid of the water. The pity would be worse than jeers. He'd blow his brains out. Thank God he could still handle the bay.

Behind him he heard the clattering roar of engines as the PBY thundered across the bay and took to the sky. He looked over his shoulder as a fleeting ray of sunshine flickered on the rising plane. *All that water,* he thought. It was bad enough in the bay, where few of the monsters were present, but . . . out there, where the plane was headed and most of Tony's pals might even now be slipping down into the dreadful embrace of the sea, so far from land. The safe, dry land.

He fought the current upriver and dodged the dead trees and other debris that had washed down from the distant mountains. Crocodiles floated by, disoriented or dead, and he knew the river must've been something at the peak of the deluge. It was still out of its banks. The damp world had begun to reawaken, however, evidenced by the flocks of lizard birds that rose amid raucous cries and riotous colors to greet them as they churned upstream. Finally, after another hour of enduring the buckshot of bird shit that peppered them constantly from above, the fueling pier came into view around the bend.

The willing hands of the caretakers caught the rope, and Tony gratefully leaped up to the dock and onto the shore. His relief at feeling the motionless earth beneath his feet was palpable, and his mood brightened immediately despite another round of drizzle. "Everything all right?" he asked the first Lemurian caretaker/guardsman that joined him.

"No pro-bleemo," mimicked the 'Cat, proud of his English.

"Anything come apart?" Tony asked the other one, who he knew could speak much better.

"Don't think so. Everything fine here. Won't know for sure until the pump is back on."

"Okay," Tony said. "I'll go check it out. In the meantime, why don't you fellas try to get the fires lit? God knows it'll be a week before any local boats can make it up that river and bring the rest of the crew. I'll have to ferry 'em up in the launch." The idea of spending the better part of the next two days on the water didn't appeal to him, but at least for now he could bask in the safety of the shore. He stuck his hands in his pockets and, whistling, followed the pipeline cut into the jungle.

He didn't whistle for long. The ground was mucky and the grade was steep. Soon he was gasping, trying to suck a few molecules of oxygen past the moisture that hung in the air. There was absolute silence except for his breathing, and the humidity deadened the sound of that almost before it reached his ears. Halfway to the wellhead, he stopped, huffing, and contemplated sitting on one of the wet, mushy tree trunks that had been moved to the side of the cut.

"Out of shape," he scolded himself, still in a good mood in spite of his exertion. He began unbuttoning his trousers as he stepped to the side of the trail to relieve himself.

Over the sound of his rasping breath he thought he heard something. Something else . . . breathing. He peered into the misty jungle. There, directly before him amid the tangled tree trunks, two trunks didn't quite match the others. His eyes went wide and his hand flew to his shoulder for the sling of the Thompson—which at that moment lay behind the control station in the launch, ready to protect him from the horrors in the water.

"Shit," he whispered as the gaping jaws descended upon him.

Ben Mallory had coaxed the reluctant aircraft up to three thousand feet, all the while listening intently to the engines. So far, so good. The steady, throbbing drone of the Pratt & Whitney R-1830-92 Twin Wasps seemed healthy enough. Contrary to Lieutenant Letts's suspicions, Mallory really thought the engines were fine. Of course, it was hard to tell over the excessive rattling and violent vibrations the rest of the aircraft made. Everything except the engines on the hard-used plane was falling apart. He tried his best to take it easy on the old gal, but metal fatigue was beginning to take its toll. Sooner or later, good engines or not, the battered flying boat would fold up like a paper kite and fall out of the sky and the only airplane in the entire world would be no more. He shrugged mentally. When it happened, it happened. Until it did, he would fly.

He spared a quick glance at his "copilot." The young sable-furred 'Cat on his right was peering through a pair of precious binoculars through the open side window at the ocean below. His name was Jis-Tikkar, but he seemed to like "Tikker" just fine. He'd been a good companion on the long flights between Baalkpan and Surabaya and he was still fully enraptured by the wonder of flying high above the world at a measly 110 miles an hour—oh, how Ben missed the glorious P-40E! Whatever Ben called him, Tikker wasn't quite ready to assume all the duties of his position. For one thing, he could barely see over the instrument panel.

On a couple of occasions, Mallory had allowed him to take the controls for a little "straight and level," but it would be a while before he did it again. The second time the little devil had his hands on the oval-shaped wheel, he'd nearly put the big plane through a barrel roll. It was all very exciting and the flying lessons abruptly ceased. For now, the "copilot's" duties had reverted to observation and keeping Ben awake on the long flights with his irrepressible humor.

The rest of the flight crew consisted of Ed Palmer, and two more far-sighted Lemurians in the observation blisters. Ed sat in the compartment directly behind the flight deck, still trying to raise *Walker* when he wasn't keeping track of their navigation. The young signalman had been studying under Bob Flowers to raise his grade before the lieutenant was killed. In his short time aboard *Mahan* he had, for all intents and purposes, been the navigation officer. He wasn't a pro yet, but he was a quick study. As long as there were landmarks he could identify, he hadn't led them astray—and they were forbidden to fly at night. Besides, they'd made the trip often enough now that the Makassar Strait was pretty familiar. Ben liked having someone to bounce his reckoning off of, though.

They broke out of the dreary overcast at last and the sky ahead was bright and clear. The trailing edge of the storm was still visible far to the east beyond Celebes, and a few petulant squalls marched about at random. Below them, evidence of the storm was still apparent from the lingering whitecaps. Three hours of flying had them in the general vicinity where they'd captured *Revenge,* and nearing the way point where they would either turn southeast and prepare to set down and refuel or head due south on the next dogleg that would complete the bottom of their horseshoe search.

Ben glanced at the fuel gauges. More than enough. The flying boat had a theoretical range of over twenty-eight hundred miles, and the search pattern Letts had suggested would consume less than half of that. Mallory intended to cover more area than the plan called for, but there'd still be ample fuel. He decided to forgo a visit to their remote gas station on Celebes. Every time the plane touched down there provided potential for an accident, particularly on the still-rough sea. Besides, there were no pumps at the station and they would spend half the day hoisting and pouring the two-gallon jugs. He much preferred idling up alongside *Big Sal* and letting the fuel run *down* into the plane.

He called Palmer forward. "We're going to zigzag south across the Flores Sea on hundred-mile legs, west-east, west-east. But I want to check out those islands north of Sumbawa. Keep track of our turns so we don't miss the damn things. I'd rather catch them headed east so we can cross them twice. There must be a hundred of them."

"Most of those islands aren't much account," Palmer replied.

"No, but if somebody got driven east by the storm there's a good chance they might've wound up on one of them," Ben reasoned grimly.

As it turned out, they didn't have to go that far. Shortly after they made their first eastward turn, Tikker spotted a lonely wake below them. Ben immediately began a spiraling descent.

"*Mahan,* sure enough!" Tikker said excitedly. "Only three smoke-stacks, see?"

Mallory grunted when he banked the plane far enough to see for himself. "Unless the storm knocked one off *Walker,*" he agreed doubt-fully. "But mainly, she's headed north, toward Baalkpan. *Walker* would be headed west. Yeah, that's *Mahan,* all right. There's her number. Looks even worse than the last time I saw her, but she's under way."

"We're not going to set down, are we?" Ed asked nervously from between the two seats.

"No way. Look at those swells! Let's signal them with the navigation lights."

The sun was setting beyond Java's distant volcanic peaks when *Walker* steamed through the Pulau Sapudi and returned to Aryaal/B'mbaado Bay. The naked tripods of the battle line Homes were silhouetted against the evening sky and the lights of the city. Safe and sound, right where they'd left them. Captain Reddy was dozing in his chair and Keje had gone to the wardroom for a sandwich.

"Just like a bunch of battle wagons moored at Pearl," Garrett quipped, referring to the Homes. "Those guys never know what they're missing when the wind kicks up."

"Maybe so," Dowden agreed, "but small and fast beats slow and fat when bombs and torpedoes are falling out of the sky."

Garrett grinned sheepishly back at him. "Yeah, but we don't have to worry about bombs and torpedoes anymore. The next time we get caught in the middle of a Strakka, tell me again that small and fast beats fat and slow." He gestured at the huge ships in the bay as they drew closer. "Especially since they don't even look like they noticed it."

Appearances were deceiving. The full fury of the storm had passed right over the bay. *Humfra-Dar* had dragged one of its feet and nearly gone aground. Superficial damage had also been sustained by the pagoda structures on all the ships, but the Homes of the People were designed to withstand far worse. Onshore it was a different story. The waterfront ghetto had been knocked flat. Since the buildings there had provided most of the shelter for the AEF, there had been numerous injuries and even a couple of deaths. The rest of the troops had spent an extremely miserable couple of days, exposed to the full violence of the storm. Nevertheless, there were cries of happy greeting as the ship passed through the anchored fleet and neared the pier.

There had evidently been some concern that *Walker* might not fare well against a Strakka of such severity. The concern was better founded than most Lemurians would have believed. They knew she was small, but iron still enjoyed an almost mystical status among them. Surely, with her entire hull made of the mighty metal, *Walker* must be invincible? Some knew better, like Keje and Chack. Adar too. But for the most part, only the Lemurian crew aboard her fully grasped how close the old destroyer had come to disappearing forever. It was a testament to how ferocious the Strakka had been that disquiet over *Walker*'s fate existed at all.

Keje returned to the bridge munching a second sandwich and bearing a cup of "coffee" for the captain. Matt roused almost magically at the smell of the brew and sat, sipping, while Larry Dowden conned the ship alongside the dock. The outward calm he displayed during the maneuver was admirable. On deck, he could hear Gray bellowing at the special sea and anchor detail as they prepared to throw lines to those waiting on shore.

"All stop," said Dowden, with a nervous glance at the captain. "Finished with engines."

Matt spared him a nod. The approach had been fine—slow and careful. The ship's momentum would bleed off sooner than was ideal, leaving a larger gap between her and the dock than would normally be considered perfect, but there was plenty of line. Better to let the line handlers and the capstan heave her in than try to fend off if she came in too fast. That was a losing proposition.

"Lookout reports aircraft at one two zero degrees, Skipper. Range six miles."

Matt nodded, pleased again by the improved quality of the reports from the crow's nest. All of their lookouts were 'Cats now. With their amazing eyesight, they were naturals for the duty. At first, however, their reports had been . . . unusual, to say the least. With time, that changed. Matt glanced at his watch and then out at the darkening bay. Lieutenant Mallory had come very close to disobeying his order not to fly at night.

"He ought to be okay, Captain," said Garrett, sensing Matt's concern. "I bet the bay's pretty clear now. The rough seas probably tore up any of the lizard ships that were still sticking up."

"Yeah," supplied Gray as he entered the pilothouse. He'd discarded his crutch and was getting around almost as well as before. "But now all that junk's out there floatin' around. That cocky flyboy's liable to torpedo himself with a mast or something." He turned to Captain Reddy. "All lines are doubled up and secured, Skipper."

"Very well." Matt upended his coffee cup and grinned wryly. "Mr. Dowden, you have the watch. I'm going ashore to see what we missed."

The makeshift hospital tent had been re-erected behind the entrenchments facing the north wall of the city. It had been used to shelter some of the injured after a desultory daylong drizzle replaced the worst of the storm. Now, the stars shone bright overhead and it was the scene of a relieved reunion of the officers of the AEF. Currently, as was his custom, Matt was receiving individual reports from all the commanders before he addressed the group. Around him, the other officers did the same, less formally. This way they could enjoy a somewhat laid-back visit—which was the preferred Lemurian custom—and everyone would be pretty much up to speed by the time the real meeting commenced.

"So, I'm to believe you made the flight only on Mr. Letts's orders?" Matt asked Lieutenant Mallory, who was next in line. "And you went into the air kicking and screaming with a written protest?"

Mallory shifted uncomfortably. "Not exactly, sir. Mr. Letts did order me to fly, but it's not his fault we got in late. We altered the flight plan a little to increase our search coverage, true, but I'd respectfully point out that we wouldn't have seen *Mahan* otherwise." He shrugged. "We ran into a headwind on the last westward leg."

Matt nodded. "I'm glad you found *Mahan*. Knowing she's safe takes a load off my mind. I just wish you wouldn't cut it so close. You're the only pilot we have."

"Yes, sir. Flying the only airplane. But when we couldn't raise you on the radio we got worried. The last we knew, everybody was at sea in the path of that god-awful storm. I guess we needed to know we weren't suddenly all alone."

Matt studied him in the torchlight. "What would you have done if you found one of us, *Walker* or *Mahan*, in a sinking condition?"

"I . . . don't understand, sir."

"Yes, you do. Say it was *Walker*. No power and low in the water. Just wallowing in the swell." Matt grimaced. "And nothing but the whaleboat, which is, incidentally, all we have left. This afternoon you might've been able to set down, but not this morning. What would you have done?"

The young aviator looked stricken. "I . . . I don't know. Maybe . . ."

Matt interrupted him. "No 'maybe,' Lieutenant. There's absolutely nothing you could've done." He put his hand on Mallory's shoulder. "Nothing. Not if you're a responsible officer. This isn't the world we knew, where you could whistle up some ship to come get us. We're on our own. That's why you and Letts should've waited another day before coming to look for us." He smiled and squeezed the shoulder. "By which time—tomorrow—the radio ought to be fixed. I'm glad you're here, don't get me wrong, and I'm glad you saw *Mahan,* but we can't spare you or that airplane." His smile became a grin. "It's going to have to last the whole damn war." He dropped his hand to his side and nodded toward the chart laid out on a table nearby. Together, they looked down at it. "Now, since you're in a rescuing mood, I want you to take off in the morning—weather permitting—and find *Revenge.* We're going to start on the propeller first thing, but we ought to have the radio repaired by morning. With Riggs gone to Baalkpan, Clancy is chief radio operator and he says with Palmer's help he can get it done. Clancy's already fixed the resonance chamber—used a coffee cup for an insulator!—and he says now that the ship's not pitching her guts out he can re-string the aerial." Matt looked up at Mallory. "By the way, if the radio's not working, you don't fly." He returned his gaze to the chart. "If you find *Revenge* and she needs assistance, with any luck, we'll be able to come and get them." Matt pointed at the chart. "Concentrate here first," he said grimly, indicating a large island surrounded by dozens of smaller ones about halfway between Sumatra and Borneo. "I have a feeling that's where she'll be."

Captain Reddy glanced at the group gathered around them. Many were engaged in animated discussions, while some were relaxing on cushions that had been placed under the awning for their convenience. "It looks like I'm going to be here for a while," he said. "Go get some sleep. You'll need it."

"So," Matt said at last, when the briefings were complete and the "meeting" had been officially under way for some time, "correct me if I'm wrong, but it seems the situation remains unchanged. The battle line is fit for sea, in spite of some slight damage. The B'mbaadan infantry and Rolak's volunteers have been thoroughly integrated into the AEF and are ready to embark. I have every reason to believe my ship will have the use of both engines after tomorrow. Fuel and provisions, as well as some minor repairs, might take a couple more days, but essentially, we're prepared to resume the offensive. Correct?"

"Correct," confirmed Adar. "Essentially."

"Except for Rasik," Rolak growled.

Matt nodded. "Except for Rasik."

"My host will follow you, Cap-i-taan Reddy," Queen Maraan told him, "whatever you decide. We've sworn to do so and that . . . skuggik who lurks behind his walls poses no threat to B'mbaado now. However, Lord Rolak and I have fought together. He is my sword brother—if a slightly elder one." She smiled, baring her perfect teeth. "But Rasik"— she spat the name—"has yet to release the families of Rolak's warriors from the city. He sends excuse after excuse, but it is clear they are his hostages!"

"I fear that is the case," Rolak agreed, still using Chack to interpret. "He believes we won't sack the city with our families inside."

"But we have no intention of sacking the city!" blurted Courtney Bradford. "My God! We have more important fish to fry!"

Rolak looked at him in the low light. "I don't think King Rasik believes that. He has a very narrow view of the world, and it all revolves around him and what he wants. To him, the greatest treasure in the world is the throne of Aryaal. He cannot imagine that anyone else would not want it too."

"But what about the Grik?" asked Ramic-Sa-Ar, High Chief of *Aracca* Home. "Doesn't he fear their return?"

Rolak shook his head. "My . . . spies say he does not. He believes that menace is ended, that they couldn't possibly raise another army like the one we destroyed before his walls."

"But when we showed him the chart—the map showing the extent of the enemy frontiers—he seemed to grasp the peril," Adar interjected sharply. He had acted as emissary in all their dealings with the Aryaalan king.

"Fabrications," Rolak growled. "He believes we make it up—which adds to his paranoia. He believes we intend to carry the war to the Grik, but he does not think they are a real threat. He fears us. Therefore, he keeps the families of my warriors as security against attack. Perhaps he even hopes to lure some of us back into his service. I do not know."

"What about you, Lord Rolak?" Bradford asked in a quiet tone. "Does he hope you will return?" Rolak's gaze rested on the Australian.

"No. He most certainly does not hope that."

"What will you do?" Matt asked after a lengthy silence.

"I will follow you to battle the Grik, lord, as I have sworn to do. But . . . my warriors must remain here. Perhaps to bolster B'mbaado's defense. I cannot ask them to abandon their families to Rasik's mercy. I am sorry."

"There's nothing to apologize for," Matt replied. "I understand completely, as I'm sure the others here do." He glanced down for a moment and then looked back at the Lemurian. "I wish I could offer you the AEF and we'd just storm the city and retrieve your folk, but as Mr. Bradford put it, we've bigger fish to fry." He looked around at the uncomfortable blinking of the gathered officers. "Besides, it might be difficult for many here to fight others of their kind, particularly measured against the greater threat we all face."

"It would be different if we were attacked," explained Keje in a quiet voice. "But we have not been. My warrior soul cries out to assist you, Lord Rolak, but my teaching and my sense of what we risk bids me refrain."

"I do understand," Rolak said. "You sea folk are different. You do not fight without great cause. That is why I believed you so readily when you told me of the greater threat. You're certainly the better choice to lead in that fight now."

"We'll miss your warriors, and you most of all, Lord Rolak," Matt said at last.

"You won't miss me, lord, for I at least will be at your side. I have made an oath."

Matt shook his head. "I release you from it. Stay here and lead your people."

"It's not your place to release me from my pledge, my lord. You cannot do it." Rolak spoke with quiet patience, but there was an edge to his voice. Chack relayed the refusal.

"Then I order it!" Matt retorted with an edge of his own. "As my friend or as my slave, you'll remain here and lead your people." There was a collective intake of breath and then a murmur of approval rippled quickly among those present. Rolak regarded him with wide, staring eyes, then bowed his head in assent.

"As you command, my lord. But now I am even deeper in your debt."

"Well. That's settled," Matt muttered hopefully, suppressing a huge yawn. "What else do we have to cover? I haven't had much sleep lately and it's past my bedtime."

Mank-Lar, soon to be Lord Mank-Lar and captain of the palace guard if all went well, squinted hard into the moonless darkness as he drew closer to the iron ship. There was a muffled *clunk* and a curse behind him. "Quietly, fools!" he hissed at the royal retainers plying the sweeps. It had taken hours to row the large, heavy boat from the river to where the invader was moored and they were almost ready to strike. Mank-Lar didn't know what the Amer-i-caans would do to them if they were discovered, but he knew how the king would react if they failed.

"Of course, Task Leader," came the whispered reply.

Mank-Lar peered back at the ship, still squinting to conceal his highly reflective eyes. A few muted lights would not reveal his ragged cape and dark-furred visage. If anything, they would make it harder for any guards to detect his approach. At the moment he didn't see anyone moving at all and he concentrated on the lights. They didn't flicker like a proper torch and he wondered how they did that. Sorcery, he assumed. It was clear they were not believers. He'd heard how they buried their dead in the ground before Aryaal's very gate.

"Carefully, now," he whispered as they came within a tail of the iron ship's side. He leaned far out over the water and felt along the cool plates until he found what he was looking for. It was a loop of metal protruding from the ship. He knew from looking at it in daylight that there were many others that led all the way to the deck. Quickly, he tied a rope to the loop. The two retainers carefully laid aside the tarp that covered the large object in the bottom of the boat and quietly climbed into the smaller boat they had towed behind them. Mank-Lar knelt and ran his hand along the surface of the object in the dark. *Such a wonderful machine,* he thought. And such a shame to use it so. He didn't know what the sea folk called it, but "fire spitter" seemed appropriate. He had watched from the safety of the walls while this one and others like it had wreaked such havoc on the Grik. It had been as though the Sun God himself spat upon them and swept them aside with his hand. A glorious, glorious machine!

This one had belonged to the sea folk who fought near the river and were overrun. Some Grik had seized the weapon as booty and tried to drag it to the ferry even while the battle raged. When the rout began, the fire-spitter rolled down the embankment, destroying its carriage, and splashed into the river. Mank-Lar had seen where it disappeared. When he told Prince Alcas—now king, of course—the prince commanded him and a small group to venture forth in that dreadful darkness across the sea of carrion and retrieve it at all costs. At the time, right after the battle, not all the carrion were dead and he feared that if he was killed, the Sun wouldn't see him fall and his soul would be doomed to linger there forever, upon that plain of bones. He persevered, however. The reward of Heaven is the Sun God's to grant. The rewards of earth would be granted by the prince.

Wounded Grik weren't his only concern. Patrols of sea folk and B'mbaadans crisscrossed the field all night, searching for their own dead and wounded. They carried torches, however, and were easily avoided. When they found the fire-spitter, still conveniently protruding from the river, they tied on to it easily enough, but quickly discovered it was too heavy to drag back to the city. He had decided to push it back, all the way underwater, with the rope still attached. Then they spent the rest of the night groping in the dark, retrieving as much of the carriage as they could find. These parts they cast into the river some distance from where the main part was hidden. Then they hurried to the city before day and the voracious skuggiks arrived.

They didn't return empty-handed, however. They had found one of the chests full of food for the fire-spitter. When night fell again, after the flocks of skuggiks slunk away or lay in bloated torpor, they went forth once more upon the oozing, reeking field. Treading carefully through the already half-eaten host with a much larger force, they retrieved the prize for their new king.

Only a few of that party were ultimately involved in the plan that the king devised. King Alcas himself had seen, during a moment's lull in his own battle against the traitors, what happened when a fire-spitter was fed too much and was offered fire anyway. Surely the force released by such an act would send the invader's iron ship to the bottom of the bay.

With their spines torn from their backs, the cowardly sea folk would never dare campaign against the distant Grik. They certainly wouldn't attack Aryaal in revenge; their weak sensibilities toward killing other People wouldn't let them. No, they would slink away, never to return, and the king could turn his attention to the traitor Rolak and, ultimately, the Orphan Queen across the bay. Everything would be back to normal, and Mank-Lar would be a lord and captain of much renown. The only thing he regretted was that, once again, the Sun couldn't see his deeds.

He thought he heard something stir in the darkness above and he froze. Muffled footsteps sounded on the iron deck, but they were slow and unconcerned. He resumed his task. As much of the bitter-smelling black food as the thing would hold had already been poured down its mouth. On top of that, six of the copper balls were firmly tamped in place and set with wooden wedges and thick red mud. Only the eye was left open at the back of the tube, so it could see the fire that was offered it. Mank-Lar didn't know how the king knew to do these things; perhaps the information came from spies, but it wasn't his concern. All he had to do was finish the job and he would be rewarded beyond his wildest dreams.

He removed the lid from a widemouthed jar. Inside was sap from the gimpra tree; thick and viscous, and quick to take a spark. Once ignited, it would burn with a fierce, hot flame and nothing he knew of could put it out. He smeared the foul-smelling sap all over the front part of the boat, leaving the back clear where he crouched near the mouth of the fire-spitter. He hoped the eye wouldn't see the fire before he and his helpers got away. He removed the remainder of a coil of rope from a perforated copper box at his feet. On one end of the rope glowed a small orange coal. He blew lightly upon it and inched farther back. With a prayer to the Sun, he pitched the smoldering rope onto the sap.

Chief Harvey Donaghey had the deck. He could count on one hand the times he'd had the duty, but everybody was washed out and, he had to admit, the deck-apes were probably more hammered than the snipes for once. Besides, he didn't mind. It was a beautiful, cool, starry night and it was good to be in the open where he could breathe fresh air for a change. The sound of the blower was reduced to a whisper and the whole ship seemed asleep. Onshore, it was much the same. After the captain came back aboard, everything wrapped up pretty quick. A few fires still glowed by the breastworks, but he imagined that, except for the guards, the whole AEF had knocked out. *Things are gonna start happening soon,* he thought, *and folks are resting up.*

He heard a sound from the amidships deckhouse. Earl Lanier and one of his new monkey-cat mess attendants emerged into the starlight, each carrying a pole. "Not everybody's asleep, I guess," he muttered to himself as the obese cook and his helper neared. "Evening, Earl," he whispered, and nodded at the little black and white 'Cat Earl called Pepper.

"Evenin', P.O.," Lanier grouched. "I'm goin' fishin'," he announced, glancing around. For once, the area was almost clear of sleeping forms. It was cool enough, and after the toil of the storm, nearly everyone wanted the relative comfort of their racks.

"That's fine, Earl. Catch me one too. Just make sure it doesn't eat the ship this time," Harvey warned, absently fingering his pistol. Some of the creatures the cook had dragged aboard from their various anchorages were truly dangerous and most were wildly terrifying. A few had gone ... on the loose. Earl muttered something under his breath and continued toward the rail. Bored, Donaghey followed him. "Hey," he said, about to ask what Lanier was going to use for bait, when he happened to look over the side and saw a shape on the water below. Earl saw it too and for an instant it looked like a small group of Lemurians sitting in a couple of boats smoking a cigar. Just for an instant.

Before their startled minds could comprehend what they saw, the Lemurian in the bigger boat flicked his "cigar" toward its bow. With a flash of light that seared their eyes the forward part of the boat erupted in flames.

"Bloody hell!" Donaghey shouted and reached for his pistol. The small boat rocked as the arsonist jumped in. One of his accomplices raised something to his shoulder and a crossbow bolt whanged off the rail.

"You little bastards!" Lanier screamed when another bolt appeared, its vaned shaft protruding from his wide, drooping belly. "I'm shot!"

"General quarters! General quarters!" Donaghey yelled at the top of his lungs, firing his pistol at the retreating boat. The slide locked back. Empty. He spun to the startled 'Cat named Pepper. "You speak-ee English?" he demanded, the old China hand. Pepper nodded. "Go, chop-chop, ring-ee bell, wake-ee everybody up! Sabe?"

"Aye, aye, Petty Officer Donaghey!" Pepper replied, and raced forward into the dark. Harvey never even noticed that Pepper's English was clearer than his own.

"What the hell's that?" Lanier demanded, pointing at the boat below. The spreading fire illuminated something lying in it.

"Goddamn! It's a gun! I bet those sneaky bastards filled it full of powder and plugged it up, hoping the fire would cook it off!" He started to run for a fire hose, then stopped dead in his tracks. No time. If he was right, that thing could go off any second. It would take several minutes for the water pressure to build. Without a word, he hopped the rail and began climbing down the rungs.

"Where the hell are you going?" Lanier yelled. "I got an arrow in my gut!"

"I doubt it hit anything vital, you fat tub of lard!" Harvey snarled back. "Don't just stand there. Get the hose!"

Lanier waddled in the direction of the closest hose reel and Donaghey resumed his descent. The initial flash of the conflagration had diminished considerably to a steady blaze in the forward third of the boat. He could hear crackling as the wood began to burn. The heat pushed almost physically against him the lower he went and he wasn't sure he was just imagining his skin beginning to blister.

"Hurry up!" he shouted, unsure if the cook even heard him as he gasped for breath in the acrid smoke. Below him, one rung down, he could see through his slitted, watery eyes that a rope had been tied to the ship. With one hand, he reached into his shirt and retrieved a long-bladed folding knife that always hung around his neck on a braided cord. Called a sausage knife, it had a long, skinny blade that was useful for a variety of things. He opened it with his teeth and leaned down to cut the rope that had already started to burn. He was certain he was blistering now and he cried out in pain. He smelled the hair on his arm begin to singe, mingling with the stench of the smoke. He sawed at the rope like a madman. Suddenly, unexpectedly, it parted under his blade and he would have dropped it in the water but for the cord.

The ship's bell began ringing frantically in the dark, followed moments later by the general alarm. Harvey scrambled back up the side of the ship a few rungs to escape the worst of the heat and looked down at the boat. Slowly, lazily, it drifted with the current. Amid the flames he clearly saw the ruddy shape of the bronze cannon barrel as the fire grew around it. From above he heard shouts and curses and a gurgling stream of seawater trickled on the boat. Other hands had joined or taken over for Lanier and they were finally getting water on the fire. It would still take a while for the pressure to build, but it was better than nothing.

Or was it? Even as he watched he knew with a sinking certainty it would never work. The water was just spreading the flames around. Whatever the saboteur had used as an accelerant was acting like gasoline. Worse, the boat wasn't drifting away. The incoming tide had served only to press it more firmly against the ship. All it was doing was creeping slowly aft, snug against the hull.

"Cut the water, you're making it worse!" he shouted upward and with only the slightest hesitation he started back down the rungs. The back of the boat was under him now, where the flames had not yet spread, and he jumped down into it. He fell to the floorboards and came up looking directly into the mud-packed muzzle. Lurching to his feet, he snatched one of the sweeps out of its oarlock and pressed against the side of the ship. Gasping with exertion and bellowing in pain, he heaved with all his might. Slowly at first, but then more easily as momentum conquered mass, the boat began to move.

Coughing, he readjusted his grip and heaved again. Through the tears and sweat that ran in his eyes, he saw he had gained a gap about ten yards wide. Clumsily, he dropped the sweep back into its notch and grabbed the other one trailing alongside. Crouching on his knees, and with his hat pulled down low to protect his eyes, he laboriously managed to turn the boat. With a growing sense of urgency that bordered on panic, he rowed as fast as he could. He heard the yells of the men on deck—quite a few now, by the racket they were making—screaming at him to stop, come back, don't be a fool—but there was no choice. He had no choice.

All he knew, as the flesh on his face and hands began to sear and his vision became a red, shimmering fog, was that he had to row. Nothing else in the entire world mattered anymore except for getting that crazy, stupid bomb the hell away from his ship.

He made it almost forty yards.

Captain Reddy paced the deck beside the number two torpedo mount, back and forth, his hands clenched behind his back. Occasionally he ventured near the smoke-blackened rail and stared at the water below. The angry red horizon that preceded the dawn was a singularly appropriate backdrop to the white-hot rage that burned within him. A quiet circle of destroyermen, human and Lemurian, watched him pace, and Sandra and Bradford were nearby as well, conversing in subdued tones.

On deck, trussed up like hogs, were two Aryaalans. Dennis Silva towered over them with a pistol in his hand and Earl Lanier, shirt off and with a wide bandage encircling his midsection, menaced the prisoners with his fishing pole.

Harvey Donaghey had hit one of them with a lucky shot from his pistol, causing the 'Cat to lose his oar and slowing their escape. By the time the cannon exploded, the saboteurs were far enough away that they weren't directly injured, but they were so startled by the blast that they dropped the other oar over the side. Thus they were quickly discovered by the vengeful whaleboat, wallowing helplessly back toward their intended victim with the tide. By then, the one Donaghey had shot was dead. Garrett commanded the whaleboat and it was all he could do to bring the others back alive. Even so, their capture hadn't been gentle and the Aryaalans watched Matt pace through puffy, swollen eyes, nervously licking their split, bloody lips.

Mank-Lar had told him everything. Why not? It had been an exploit of warriors and had been commanded by his king. It was the way of things. His dishonor was not what he tried to do, but that he had failed. Rasik-Alcas might kill them for that, but even the sea folk would understand they were bound to obey their king . . . wouldn't they? Mank-Lar vaguely understood that the tail-less sea folk might consider it dishonorable that King Alcas had ordered the attack in the first place, particularly since they were not at war. But that was between them and the king, was it not? He himself was just a tool, and it was pointless to deny his role. Regardless, he couldn't escape a growing concern as he watched the brooding leader of his king's enemy.

Larry Dowden approached his captain with care. He'd seen him this way—this intense—only once before, when *Walker* and *Mahan* made their suicidal charge against *Amagi*, so long ago now. It had worked, somehow, but it had also been a reckless moment and he wondered if the captain was on the verge of another one now. He opened his mouth, but hesitated, daunted by the working jaw and the icy green braziers gazing back.

"Captain," he said quietly, "Radioman Clancy says the radio's up.

Lieutenant Mallory requests permission to commence a search for *Revenge*."

Matt looked at his exec for a moment and then nodded slightly. "Very well."

"Aye, aye, sir. Ah, Captain? You said you wanted to begin installing the screw this morning?" Dowden prompted gently. Matt only glanced around for a moment, as if surprised the task wasn't already under way. For the first time he noticed that almost the entire crew was present, grim-faced and angry.

"Right. I guess the men are a little distracted. Have Spanky and the Bosun light a fire under those repair parties." Several of the men held his gaze as it passed across them. "They have their own duties to perform today," he said in a voice that matched his eyes. "I'll take care of this one."

"What should we do with these two, Skipper?" Silva asked, nudging Mank-Lar hard with his shoe. Matt shrugged.

"Don't even need to try them. They've admitted they're enemy saboteurs under orders of their king. But they're without uniforms or even the courtesy of a declaration of war. Hang them."

"I want that little son of a bitch dead!" Matt said in a calm but eerily forceful tone. The gathering was almost identical to the one the night before, only this time it was convened directly behind the massed block of the Second Marines, flanked by Rolak's expatriate Aryaalans and Queen Maraan's Six Hundred. Another entire regiment of B'mbaadan infantry was added as well. Thirty heavily armed destroyermen—not all human—were in the center, anxious to spearhead the assault with fire. The Orphan Queen stood beside Matt, her eyes gleaming with a feral, joyful light.

"It could break the alliance!" Adar pleaded. "Think of the greater threat!" Sandra stood beside the Lemurian Sky Priest and nodded her agreement, but she seemed deeply troubled.

"Why? I haven't asked any of the Homes or Guard regiments from Baalkpan to contribute to the attack." He wore an ironic expression. "I notice none have offered, either, but if they don't want to be in the assault, that's fine."

"What about the Marines? They are drawn from all our people."

Matt looked coldly at Adar. "The Marines are mine. They're all volunteers and they've volunteered for this. I ordered Chack to make sure."

"That still does not give you the right to throw them away on this . . . sideshow!"

Matt's mounting fury exploded. "I'm *not* throwing them away! I'm using them for what they're for! We've been attacked! Suddenly and deliberately and by stealth! Believe me, my people have recent experience with that sort of thing!" His gaze lashed Keje. "We've been attacked!" he repeated. "And I lost a damn good man who died to save my ship. I thought you said it was 'different' if we were attacked? How is it different? I can't tell yet. I assumed it meant that then you might bring yourselves to fight others of your kind. Is that it? Or is it only different if *you* are attacked? You'll personally defend yourselves if you're personally attacked? Where would you be today if *Walker* behaved like that?"

Keje met his gaze, but then looked at Adar and blinked furiously with shame and frustration. Matt continued, his voice angry and sarcastic. "Ever since we met, *Walker* has stood up for you and your people, and she's lost a lot of good men—some to save that damn city I'm about to . . . lose *more* good men going into! But now, when it comes time to stand up for *Walker,* she's not 'one of you,' is she? You almost had me fooled. I was ready to leave Rolak's people to fend for themselves—even after they risked everything to come to our aid. We may have helped them first, but at least they know what gratitude is. Still, I was ready to leave them. Now I know there's *no way* we can leave them here with that madman loose behind those walls. A madman who tried to *sink my ship* after she saved his *ass* because he thought *that* would break the alliance." He grunted. "I wouldn't have believed it yesterday, but now I think he was right.

"If you still think we can just leave here with that maniac free to threaten our friends and our lines of supply, that's fine. You don't have to soil your delicate sensibilities with a morally questionable fight. I will, though, and I'll tell you something else; after what happened last night, 'greater threat' or not, if I don't make this fight the alliance *will* break. If you're all counting on *Walker* to hold you together, you'd better remember one thing. She may be made of iron, but it takes *men* to hold *her* together. Some of those men aren't even all human anymore, but they're still hers, and the ones who tried to destroy her after the sacrifice she made for them have got to *pay!* That's what *my* people say. If you can't see that, you may be 'People,' but you're not *men* and you're not our friends!"

"But—but what if you're killed?" Adar demanded, putting voice to the concerns of many. His face bore no expression, but his words were anguished. "What if Lieutenant Shinya should fall? What will we do then? I understand your anger, even if it is misplaced, I assure you, but to me the Grik threat is the *only* threat. I have sworn—"

Keje held up his hand, interrupting his old friend. "We know," he growled. "Not to rest. What Captain Reddy asks of us is not a diversion from that struggle. It's a task set before us all. Yet another task we must complete in order to finish the greater one." He turned to the others. "He is right. You all know it is true. The Amer-i-caans are our friends! They are our brothers. They have been attacked by a treacherous foe, a foe that is already the enemy of our brother Lord Rolak, whose people have risked everything to come to our aid." He turned back to Matt. "I am sorry, brother. Sorry and ashamed. I *will* fight with you."

"As will I," growled Ramik-Sa-Ar.

"And I," said Geran-Eras.

Tassat-Ay-Aracca looked bemusedly at his father, Ramik.

"I wanted to all along! I—"

Adar stepped forward as if to shush him but stopped and lowered his head. Finally, he raised his eyes, already blinking furiously with shame. "No, brothers. It is I alone who is without honor." He turned to Matt. "I see nothing but the Grik," he said softly, his silver eyes blinking moistly. "At night my dreams are haunted by the lower deck of *Revenge*. The bones, the smells . . . and the eyes of those still living . . ."

He shuddered. "Against the fate that awaits our people, this"—he gestured toward the city—"this is insignificant." He blinked apology. "But you're right. You have been attacked. Lord Rolak has been wronged—as have we all—and many more souls light the heavens because of Rasik's treachery. Souls that would be in this fight yet if not for him. You're right. We cannot just 'leave him here.' He would continue to distract us from our bigger business. Besides, sometimes honor can endure only so much." He drew himself up. "Captain Reddy, you have wronged these chiefs. I alone bear the guilt of perhaps too much zeal for our cause. I made them swear they wouldn't get involved in any Aryaalan . . . adventures. I know now I have been misguided and asked too much of their honor."

Matt wasn't entirely sure if Adar was surrendering because he had to or if he really believed it best. He wasn't certain either if his last statement was an apology or a chastisement. He nodded and grasped Adar's hand. "It's better this way," he assured the priest. "The more we take to the fight, the fewer we will lose." He turned to Keje. Shinya had stepped up beside the Lemurian.

"Thanks. How long before the rest of the forces can be prepared?"

Shinya glanced at Keje and then responded. "An hour, perhaps two, I should think."

Keje nodded. "About that. Not all are ashore, but I doubt we will need all. It will be . . . difficult fighting People instead of animals," he admitted.

"Let's put it this way," Matt answered him grimly. "We saved them from the Grik and yet they threaten to obstruct our war against the common enemy. They've made hostages of their own people and attacked us by surprise—" He stopped and shook his head. "If they'll defend that, then they *are* animals."

Benjamin Mallory hummed to himself through clenched teeth as he struggled to keep the big plane flying in a northerly direction. He'd never flown a PBY in his life before he inherited this one, but for the most part, he had few complaints about its handling—at least from a straight and level perspective. It was no P-40E, or even a P-40B, but it didn't usually take every ounce of his strength to keep it flying in a straight line. Except in a crosswind. As the day wore on and a stiff westerly breeze continued to blow, it was becoming more evident why it had such a big damn rudder. Of course, in some ways the big rudder was part of the problem. It came in real handy if he ever lost an engine—which he knew from personal experience—but it sure put up a hell of a fight in a crosswind. On the other hand, he thought philosophically, if you were born with a big rudder, at least you had a big rudder to make up for it.

"Damn, Tikker," he muttered to his copilot above the droning motors overhead, "I wish your legs were longer. You could give me a hand with this."

"I can give you a hand, boss. Just no feet," Tikker said, looking dubiously down at the distant rudder pedals.

"Smart-ass." Mallory grinned. "You could squirm down there and push 'em with your hands." Tikker blinked at him.

"Your legs are longer than me, my eyes are longer than you. But I can't see through the bottom of the plane. You want me to push pedals or look for ship?"

Ben laughed. He knew that Tikker, like most Lemurians, was extremely literal-minded. He also knew most of the little boogers possessed a highly developed sense of humor and a mischievous streak a mile wide. He didn't know which was in play at the moment. Probably both. "That's okay. I'll go down there and you can fly."

Ed Palmer crawled up between them. "Radio still checks out. But only as long as you don't let the monkey fly . . . sir."

Mallory laughed again. "I swear. You guys ought to trade jobs. I bet you could fly almost as good as Tikker and I *know* he could operate the radio and navigate better than you, Ed."

Ed pushed his clipboard forward so Mallory could look at the charts.

"Where are we?"

"Well, we followed Java west for three hours and we've been flying north-northwest for two. That should put us about here," he said, pointing to a spot just south of Pulau Belitung.

"Okay. That must be it up ahead. That big-assed island with the little white specky ones all around."

Ed squinted through the windscreen. "Damn, you mean we *are* where I thought we are? With all this wind I figured we'd be east."

"Naw, I fudged the headings you gave me." Ben frowned. "Captain said to check these little islands real careful. He figures if the storm drove *Revenge* aground, that's where she'll be."

"What a mess," Ed murmured, looking first at the distant islands and then the chart. "No way she'd have squirmed through, that's for sure."

"Yeah, well," hedged Mallory uncomfortably, "maybe she did. Or maybe she's fine and Rick's still chasing lizards like he was Drake and they were Spaniards."

"Who's Drake?" Ed asked.

"Never mind. British guy."

Tikker leaned forward and squinted until his eyes were tiny slits. "Let me see chart, please," he said, and Ed handed it over. Tikker studied it carefully for a long time and squinted out the windscreen once more. "Very strange," he said and shook his head. "Usually you charts are so good."

"What? Why?"

"I see white islands where chart says should only be water."

Mallory took off his sunglasses and squinted as well. "I don't see anything."

"You push pedals, I look for ship," Tikker said smugly and resumed his study of the horizon. Ed left them and went to the engineer's compartment. One of the few things they'd discovered that still worked in the half-sunken plane when they found it was a thermos. It had been empty at the time, floating in the sandy brown water in the fuselage. Ed rescued it and had used it ever since. The initials "EP" were lightly scratched in the thick aluminum and he was struck by the coincidence since they were the same as his. He often wondered what had become of the original owner. He picked it up and poked his head into the waist gunner's compartment to make sure the other two spotters weren't goofing off. Then he carefully poured a cup of joe into a tin mug and eased his way forward against the jostling motion of the plane.

"Coffee," he announced, slowly extending the cup into Mallory's line of sight.

Ben shook his head. "Can't right now. I need both hands. Thanks, though." Ed only shrugged and took a gentle sip himself. Tikker looked at him and wrinkled his nose. Not very many Lemurians liked real coffee, much less the local brew. Like real coffee, it had a stimulating effect and that's what they used it for: medicine. Not because they liked the taste. The big island was growing larger and many of the smaller ones were easy to distinguish now. Tikker suddenly remembered the binoculars around his neck. He thought they were the neatest things in the world—next to the airplane, of course—but much as he loved them, their technology was still so unfamiliar that he often forgot he had them on. Somewhat embarrassed, he raised them now and adjusted the objective knob. Then he stiffened, and it seemed to Ben every sable hair on his body stood on end.

"What? What do you see?" For a long moment, Tikker couldn't speak. "What is it?" Ben demanded. His copilot's body language had sent a chill of concern down his spine.

"It is not islands where they do not belong," he finally managed. "It is sails. Grik sails."

"Here, give me those," Ben said, taking the binoculars from Tikker's neck. He tried to hold the wheel and the glasses steady at the same time, but found it impossible. He glanced at Tikker, who seemed immobilized by shock. Now wasn't the time for another flying lesson. He handed the binoculars over his shoulder to Ed, who put his cup down on the flight deck in front of him. It immediately began to vibrate violently, "walking" around and sloshing its contents. He raised the glasses to his eyes.

"God a'mighty," he whispered. The entire horizon, from the islands of Pulau Belitung to the distant hint of a smudge that was western Borneo, was dotted with hundreds of dingy pyramid shapes. The water below was still a little foamy and the whitecaps had turned the normally warm, dark blue sea a kind of dirty turquoise, but the hint of red from the enemy hulls made them stand out quite clearly. "God a'mighty," he repeated, a little louder this time and with an edge of panic in his voice.

The intercom crackled and an excited voice reached them from one of the observation blisters. "Ship! Ship! I see ship! Right below! Wake up, you in front! You not see ship?"

Revenge had been through hell. As soon as the size of the storm became apparent, Rick Tolson and Kas-Ra-Ar knew their only hope was to beat north as far as they could and gain as much sea room as possible before the seas grew too large to do anything but run before them. With grim satisfaction, they'd pounded the lone Grik ship with a pair of broadsides as it drew near. Then, leaving the enemy trailing a shattered mainmast and at the mercy of the coming blow, *Revenge* went about. The wind drove out of the west-northwest at first, and the ship shouldered her way through the growing swells far into the Natuna Sea.

For that day and half the night she pounded north, farther than she'd ever been. Past Singapore, in fact, though the chance of anyone seeing her, or caring if they did, was slim. With only her staysails set, she heaved and corkscrewed into the South China Sea as the mounting waves threatened to drive her under with their irresistible force. There were islands in the area too, many islands, but the risk wasn't as great as the almost solid wall that lay to the south. Seams opened and the chain pumps clanked and even the most hard-bitten Lemurian mariners were prostrated with fatigue and seasickness. Finally, when they'd managed as much northeasting as the storm would allow, they wore, and under a bare scrap of her fore-topsail, she ran before the mountainous quartering swell. Rick couldn't believe the height of the sea. It seemed impossible in such shallow water. Occasionally, bits of strange coral and wriggling fish were left in the scuppers when the sea broke over the ship. He half expected her to strike bottom and break her back when in the trough of some of the waves.

The wind and sea whittled her down. Masts and spars and shredded canvas were plucked away bit by bit and the exhausted crew fought like demons to keep the water out. The entire mizzenmast went, along with the maintop, when she was pooped by a mountain of water and several of the crew were lost. The rest of the mainmast, the foretop, and most of the bowsprit were lost the following day when a bolt of lightning struck the ship like a bomb. With only a scrap of the fore course and a single staysail, *Revenge* battled on.

It was in part a testimony, perhaps, to the skill of her hated builders and to the ancient design they'd used. Mostly, however, it was the skill and strength of her officers and crew and their unflagging will to survive and fight that allowed *Revenge* to live to see morning and a calming sea. Just in time. By the end of the final day of the storm's lessening wrath, Pulau Belitung was looming to the south. They dropped both anchors with plenty of scope in the Gaspar Strait, waiting tensely until the ship drug to a stop in the heavy current but lighter swells. There the ship pitched at the end of her cables, waterlogged and shattered, throughout the night and the following day. The crew worked on, repairing what they could with the booming sound of breakers all around.

Rick had worked as tirelessly as any and a close bond was forged between him and the crew. Kas was instrumental, as always, and there was no doubt that if it hadn't been for him, all would have been lost. But it was the symbolism of their Amer-i-caan captain sharing their fate as well as their glory that raised the crew's spirits. Up to that point, Rick had been a popular figure aboard, friendly and competent and raring for a fight. But until then, their greatest challenge had been the Battle of B'mbaado Bay. A great battle and a fine adventure, but *Revenge* had suffered little. Then, throughout their short, successful cruise, *Revenge* had everything her way and their quick, one-sided battles with the Grik had been more play than anything else.

During the storm, however, they'd all suffered deeply. But they'd done it together, as a Home. Captain, crew, and the now strangely less hated ship had worked and fought solely for the common good. None could have survived alone without the others. In spite of everything, *Revenge* was no longer just a ship representing Baalkpan. She'd become a Home. Battered and leaky and in need of much repair, but a real Home nonetheless. And there was no doubt in anyone's mind that Rick Tolson was her High Chief.

That morning, patched and caulked as much as possible, *Revenge* cut her cables and ran down the Gaspar Strait and back into the Java Sea, southeast under as much canvas as she could cram on her reinforced lower foremast. Rick and Kas believed—weather permitting—that they'd limp back into Aryaal in a week or so. Together, they were leaning on the quarterdeck rail, taking turns with Rick's binoculars and studying the nearby islands. The lower, smaller ones had been scoured clean by the storm. Fallen trees and other debris drawn away by the retreating surge floated everywhere, and lizard birds swooped and capered, snatching up dead fish. Rick watched a skuggik, or something similar, standing stoically on a dead tree as it drifted out to sea.

"*Hell* of a storm," he said.

Kas nodded companionably. "I've seen worse, but rarely." The Lemurian grinned and blinked. "And never on anything this small." He pointed at the stranded creature. "Perhaps *he* knows how we feel."

"I wonder if any of the feluccas made it."

Kas's grin quickly faded. "I fear not. They were never designed to ride the Strakka. They are not designed for much at all beyond coastal fishing. We shouldn't have brought them."

"They were a big help. Until we have a larger navy, we may have to use them again." Rick shrugged. "It's war."

Kas looked at him. "I've noticed you Amer-i-caans use that phrase a lot to explain much. You're a war-fighting race. Mine—at least the ones that live upon the sea—is not. Do you find it helps to use the war as an excuse for everything bad that happens?"

Rick returned his stare. "Yeah, I guess so. You like to think that war isn't forever and if it weren't for the war things would be better . . ." He shrugged again. "Besides, it's mostly true—or I hope it is." He shook his head and grinned. "Don't get me wrong, though. I'm having a blast!" Kas looked around them at the devastation and blinked exasperation. Rick chuckled. "Well . . . as Captain Reddy would say"—he screwed his brows into a fair imitation of one of Matt's wry expressions—" 'It's been a tough couple of days!' " They both laughed at the understatement.

Rick's face turned thoughtful. "I am having a blast," he repeated. "I have a command of my own and despite her questionable pedigree, she's one of the most powerful warships afloat. When she's in one piece she's fast, well built—thank God!—and weatherly." Glancing past Kas at one of the many work gangs diligently at their labors, he added, "And she's got the best damn crew any ship like her ever had in this messed-up world. A destroyerman couldn't ask for much more." He paused. "Engines would be nice, but then she wouldn't need her sails and that's part of her charm."

He became serious again. "But that's not what you asked." He sighed. "Yeah, the war's to blame. Those fishermen on the feluccas, they wouldn't have been here if not for the war. They'd have been catching flashies and feeding their families instead of fighting for their lives in a storm they couldn't beat. That's the war's fault, not ours. And before you think that if we weren't fighting the war there wouldn't be one, try to remember *why* we fight. It's fight or die and that's not much of a choice. You *might* die if you fight, but you *will* die if you don't. If you look at it like that, the War isn't an excuse but a blessing. A chance for survival." Rick grew silent and thoughtful for a moment.

"You know, now that I think about it, it *is* different here. What I said before is all a bunch of crap. We can shake our heads and say, 'It's war,' because it's easy and it's what my people are used to. At home, it might even be true sometimes. The war we left behind might've been different, but who's to say? The Nazis and the Japs were *very* bad, but most of the time it's not that black and white. Here? It's the lizards. Period. They're the ones to blame. 'The War' is what we're doing to stop the lizards and when you think of it like that, it makes a good explanation." Rick yawned hugely and then smiled at his friend.

"I'm tired, and I may not be making a lot of sense, but whatever else

I said, I guess what I mean is, if we lost the feluccas, they didn't die for nothing. They were helping fight the War, and in maybe this one and only instance, war is good."

Kas grinned again. "Before the storm came, you certainly seemed to be enjoying it."

Rick grinned back at him. "Well, when something needs doing, it always helps to be good at doing it, and we were so, so good—"

Kas suddenly tilted his head as if listening intently. Rick heard it too. Within minutes, the entire crew of *Revenge* was jumping up and down and pointing gleefully at the sky as the small dark shape of the PBY grew larger and began a rapid spiraling descent. Soon it was skipping tentatively across the tops of the choppy waves until it splashed to a rather abrupt halt some distance ahead of the ship.

Ordinarily, *Revenge* would heave to and lower a boat. They were going to have to think of something else this time, since all the ship's boats had been either lost or badly damaged. This must've become apparent to the flying boat's crew, because as *Revenge* drew near, a small rubber raft appeared in the water under the plane's left wing. Almost as soon as it did, however, it began to deflate.

"Damn flashies," Rick muttered, realizing the fish must have torn the raft apart. "I wonder what now?"

Eventually a man and a Lemurian appeared out of the top of the pilot's compartment and climbed up onto the wing. Slowly, they made their way to the end and crouched there waiting above the float.

"Dangerous," Kas observed.

Rick nodded and called to the helmsman. "Easy there! Don't so much as scratch that plane. Captain Reddy would never forgive us!"

Slowly, *Revenge* wallowed up to the plane. When she was just a few feet off the wingtip, Tikker leaped lightly across. Ed Palmer followed close behind, but with less self-assurance. Waiting hands grabbed him and kept him from falling backward into the water, and his face was drained of color as he stuck out his hand to Rick.

"Man, are you ever a sight for sore eyes!" Rick said happily as he grasped it. Ed returned the greeting with a small, sickly smile of his own, but he seemed distracted. He was looking around at the ship. In spite of the herculean effort to clean her up, her massive damage was still evident. Her deck stood empty of almost anything but her smiling crew. The jagged stumps of her fallen masts jutted forlornly from the quarterdeck and the waist.

"Uh, Captain Tolson," Palmer said hesitantly, using the honorary but still appropriate title for the commander of any ship. "Can you make this thing go any faster?"

Rick Tolson was taken aback by the abrupt question. "Why?"

"Lizards. Coming this way!"

Rick quickly glanced around. Yeah, she was hammered, but with her guns, she still ought to be able to hold off a couple of enemy ships at once, if she had to.

"No, but we ought to be okay. Guns'll keep them off us." He looked at Kas, smiling. "Oh, well, back to 'the War.' And *you* wanted to throw the guns over the side when we started taking water!" he said. Kas began to reply but Palmer interrupted.

"No, damn it!" he said harshly. "You don't understand!"

They stood at the taffrail, staring aft while the horizon filled with enemy sails.

"Does Captain Reddy know about this?"

"I don't know," Ed confessed. "We've been transmitting, but we're pretty far and the atmospherics are lousy."

"How many can fit in the plane?" Rick asked quietly.

"Uh, maybe twenty or thirty of the little guys. Hell, they don't weigh much. The trick'll be finding a place to cram them all," Ed replied.

"They weigh more than you think. They're all muscle." Rick shook his head. "If you flew due east, you could set them on Borneo. With weapons, many would survive the predators and they could easily evade the lizards if they went ashore looking for them. Three-hour round-trip to get back and pick up another load . . ." He sighed. "Not enough time. I'll get you twenty. I don't know how, draw lots or something, and you get them the hell out."

"Twenty besides you and Gandy Bowles? I'll ask Lieutenant Mallory if we can haul that many."

"No," Rick said. "Gandy should leave, but I'm not going anywhere. If we can't all get out, then I stay. It's *my* ship!"

Ed's mouth dropped open and he just stared. He couldn't help it. "Yeah, but, Captain—Rick—there's *two hundred ships* over there, maybe more! I like cat-monkeys a lot, don't get me wrong. I think they're swell, but we *need* you! There's only about a hundred and thirty humans in the whole wide world, as far as we know!"

Rick smiled. "C'mon, Ed. There's more of us somewhere, even if it's just where we came from." He turned and looked upon the wide-eyed, blinking, but otherwise expressionless faces that stared back at him. The faces of his crew. "*Revenge* needs me more."

Six members of *Revenge*'s crew, those most seriously injured in the storm, were carefully swayed over onto the PBY's wing and gently stowed inside. Mallory remained at the controls throughout, cursing and maneuvering the plane against the swells as best he could. When the six were safely transferred, the *Revenge* crew who'd assisted with the operation all scampered back aboard their ship to await the oncoming horde. Even Gandy Bowles, whom Rick practically ordered to leave, elected to remain behind. Ed crawled out to the wingtip once more and Rick Tolson met him just a few feet away with a leather-bound book in his hand. He had to shout to be heard over the engines as the PBY cruised alongside.

"Here's my log. Give it to Captain Reddy! It's a damned exciting read, if I say so myself!"

Ed grabbed his hat before the wind took it over the side. His eyes were stinging. From the salt spray, he told himself. "I'll give it to him," he managed to reply.

"Kas wrote something in there for Keje. They're cousins, you know." Ed nodded. Rick spared a glance to the north. The mass of enemy ships was close enough now that individual forms could be seen upon them. Their garish banners fluttered ominously in the stiff west wind. In the distance, still beyond the horizon, a dark smudge of smoke was vaguely visible. Maybe one of the damn things has caught fire, Ed hoped bitterly. They'd cut it as close as they dared.

"Tell Captain Reddy . . . thanks," continued Rick, handing the book across. "Thanks for the opportunity. It's been a blast. I always knew I was a pirate at heart!" White teeth shone in his tanned, bearded face. "Now get the hell out of here, Signalman Palmer!"

Ed nodded again, and standing as straight as he dared on the swooping wing, he braced to attention and threw Rick Tolson the best salute he knew how. With that, he turned and made his way carefully back to the space between the engines. Mallory throttled back so as not to blow him into the sea, and Palmer dropped down into the pilot's compartment and disappeared.

Calmly, Captain Tolson, commander of *Revenge*, turned to Kas-Ra-Ar. "Clear for action!" he said, the grin still on his face. "Boy, I get such a kick out of saying that!"

"That's it? *Six?*" Mallory demanded. Ed nodded without a word. "*Shit!*" shouted Ben in frustration. "Now I know what the captain meant when he asked me what I'd do!" Ed had no idea what he was talking about, but given the context of the situation, he could make a pretty good guess. "All right," Mallory said at last. "Strap in. As soon as we're airborne, try to raise *Walker* again. You have ten minutes. Then I want you on the nose gun. Tell those 'Cats in the waist to get ready too." He fiddled with the throttles as he turned the plane into the wind. "Maybe if we strafe 'em a few times we'll scare 'em off," he added doubtfully.

The engines roared and the hull pounded and thundered beneath their feet as the plane tried to increase speed, but instead it just seemed to wallow through the choppy swells.

"C'mon! *C'mon!*" Mallory shouted, and slammed the throttles to their stops.

"What's the matter?" Palmer shouted from behind him. Tikker sat, perfectly still, both eyes clenched shut.

"Oh, ah, nothing, Ed. It's just a little rougher than I'm used to!" His voice was vibrating sympathetically with the airplane.

"I'm gonna be sick!" Palmer moaned when the plane pitched nose-first into a larger wave that seemed to arrest all forward motion. "Air-sick and seasick all at once!"

Surprisingly, particularly after the sensation of slowing down, the Catalina suddenly clawed its way out of the water. It clipped the top of another big wave with a resounding boom and a cascade of spray, and then slowly, laboriously, lumbered into the sky.

"Yes!"

At five hundred feet Mallory banked and began a slow turn back toward the crippled ship. The enemy was alarmingly close. Beyond the shock he felt at the sheer number of the things, Ben couldn't imagine how they'd gotten here so quickly. Before the storm, there'd been no evidence such a force even existed—much less was planning to advance. It must have come from somewhere else, close on the heels of the storm, using the very fury of its trailing edge to make them fly. But why now? What was the rush? Ben was certain it was a response to the defeat they'd been handed at Aryaal, but how in blue blazes had the word spread so fast? And how could the enemy have possibly gathered so many ships so quickly? One thing was certain, though; the allied invasion of Singapore was off.

"Get on the horn! We have to tell Captain Reddy!" he cried.

"Maybe that's a little more important than shooting up a few of them?" Ed suggested.

"Sure. But it won't hurt if we do. They don't have anything that can reach us this high, do they?"

"You're asking me? Hell, we're just scouts! We haven't even seen a real battle yet."

"We're about to," Ben muttered. The enemy ships appeared to be making at least eight knots, while *Revenge* was barely making three. Mallory orbited the Catalina above her for several more minutes while Palmer tried to contact the destroyer. The Grik would be in range of *Revenge*'s guns very soon.

"What's the scoop, Ed?"

"I don't know. I think we're transmitting, I don't see why not, but there's a hell of a lot of noise. Probably just out of range." He grunted. "They might be hearing us," he added lamely.

"There's smoke," Tikker said, speaking softly for the first time in a while and pointing at the horizon. "Black smoke. It looks like it's coming from a black island, like a—how you say? Vol-caanno?"

"Volcano," Ben agreed absently. "No shortage of those hereabouts." He continued to crane his neck and stare intently at the drama unfolding below. Never had he felt so helpless, so utterly useless. It was like some horrible nightmare, to stand impotently by while others needed him so desperately and there was absolutely nothing he could do.

Revenge began her fight. Even as he watched, the whole side of the friendly ship disappeared behind a cloud of white smoke. Twelve-pound shot from ten guns shivered the sails of one of the approaching ships, and pieces of debris splashed into the sea around it. It was exhilarating and it felt good to see, but in the face of the descending avalanche, it was nothing. "Give 'em hell, Rick," he whispered. "All right, Ed, get in the nose!" He pressed his microphone. "Waist gunners, I know you haven't had much practice, but you know how to operate your guns. They're packed so tight down there you can't hardly miss, but try to concentrate on killing Grik. You can't do enough damage to enough ships to make a difference. Remember, short, controlled bursts. We might be able to make ammo again someday, but machine-gun barrels are gonna take a while. *Hang on!*"

He banked sharply toward the advancing line and the massive flying-boat thundered over, just three hundred feet above their masts.

"Commence firing!" he shouted. "Just the ones closest to *Revenge*! Damn, what I'd give for a couple of bombs right now!" His last comment was drowned by the staccato bursts of one .30- and two .50-caliber machine guns. The firing in the waist was accompanied by high-pitched squeals of delight. The airframe vibrated more than usual with the recoil of the guns and Ben continued his tight-banking turn to keep his indicated targets in range. Geysers of water marched from ship to ship and then disappeared when the bullets struck wood. Tightly packed Grik warriors were slaughtered in droves.

"Let 'em have it!" Ben screamed. *Revenge* vanished behind another cloud of smoke and this time the foremast of one of the closest ships tottered into the sea. Dragged around by the trailing debris, the ship veered sharply to port and speared into another Grik ship sailing directly alongside. Others slammed into the entangled wrecks from behind and it looked to Ben like a giant chain-reaction pileup on the highway.

"Hell, yes! Outstanding!" he shouted as still more ships added to the catastrophe.

"What are those ones doing?" Tikker asked, pointing. Ben looked. Several ships had broken from the pack and were trying to cut *Revenge* off. If they crossed her bow, the ship's guns wouldn't bear and they'd be free to grapple. Once that happened, it would be all over but the dying.

"New targets!" yelled Ben. "Engage the ships out front! One of them looks different . . . bigger! And the hull's white and gold—not red. I bet it's special somehow. Give it an extra dose!" The nose gun and the port .50 stitched the sea around the unusual ship. Splinters and debris erupted and bodies fell, while others tried to surge away from the impacts. A few even fell into the sea.

"I'm empty!" came a frustrated, keening shriek from aft. So much for controlled bursts. Ben stomped on the right rudder pedal and banked the opposite direction, allowing the starboard gunner a chance.

"Make 'em count!" he snarled. The plane rattled as the other gun resumed fire. Down below, *Revenge* was wreathed in smoke. Bright jets of flame stabbed out at irregular intervals. Several enemy ships were almost upon her and they were being systematically dismantled. Masts crowded with struggling forms fell into the sea and at least one of the enemy was dead in the water, its shattered bow dipping low. So far, none of the enemy had employed their "Grik Fire," however. They seemed intent on coming to grips with *Revenge*, whatever the cost.

"They want her in one piece," Ben surmised aloud. There was nothing he could do about it. Ed's gun had fallen silent in the nose. The PBY wasn't carrying much ammunition—it was never imagined that it would need more than would be necessary to keep a threat at bay while it took off. Much like what had happened right after they discovered it. Now, even as the starboard waist gun continued to stutter, grappling hooks arced through the air, trailing their lines behind them like hundreds of spiders casting their webs.

"Damn it!" Ben exclaimed. His voice cracked. "They want her guns!"

Ed reappeared at his shoulder. "Rick won't let them take her," he said with sad, quiet certainty. Even as they circled, watching with sick fascination, more and more enemy vessels crowded forward like ants upon a stricken comrade. *Revenge* had disappeared entirely within the forest of masts and the only way they could tell her position was by the proximity of the strange white ship and the hazy column of smoke that still rose from the center of the mass. The final waist gun was silent now, but still Ben orbited above. On the decks of the outer ships, Grik waved their swords at them and made taunting gestures.

There was a brilliant flash of yellow fire and a billowing cloud of smoke. Masts toppled outward from the blast like trees on the slope of a volcano and fiery debris rocketed into the sky. The plane was buffeted by the shock wave of the explosion and Ben fought the wheel to regain control. He quickly banked again to see the results through his suddenly unfocused eyes. Eight or ten ships had been in close contact with *Revenge* when she blew herself up. Two were just gone, and three more were smoldering wrecks. Vigorous fires had taken hold on several more and the smoke added to the vast pall now drifting down wind. Of *Revenge* and the white ship that had been beside her, there was no sign.

"That's the style," muttered Ben. His voice was almost a sob. He gently eased back on the controls and the Catalina began to gain altitude.

"Are we leaving now?" Ed asked.

"I guess," Ben replied. "I just couldn't before. Not while there was anybody down there who could see us." Ed nodded understanding. "Besides, the captain . . . everyone will want to know how it ended." He sighed. "One more thing, too. I want to get a solid count of how many ships they have. We're still the 'eyes' of the fleet."

At three thousand feet, Ben circled again while the others counted the enemy.

"Jesus, there's a lot of them. I've lost count twice," Ed said.

"It doesn't have to be perfect. What do you have, Tikker?"

"Three hundred ten, but that's not all I see, that's all I can count. There's more on the horizon." Tikker squinted again. "There's that Volcaanno still." He shook his head. "It looks closer now."

For the first time, Ben really looked to the north where Tikker had spotted the smoke. Sure enough, a solid black column was slanting away to the east. He blinked and rubbed his eyes. "What the . . . ?" He leveled out and pointed the Catalina north, toward the distant smudge.

"What is it?" asked Ed.

"I dunno. It *looks* like . . . but that's impossible." Frozen mercury poured down his back.

"It *is*!" Ed exclaimed excitedly. He was looking through the binoculars now. "It's a ship! A modern ship! Burning coal, by the look of her. That's why all the black smoke." He hesitated and his face assumed a troubled expression. "But what the hell is she doing running around with a bunch of lizards? Look, they're all around her!"

"Maybe they captured her? She had to have gotten here the same way we did. Hell, they nearly got us, remember?"

Ed was still staring intently through the glasses. "Jeez, that's not just any ship, it's a *warship*! She looks bigger than the goddamn *Arizona*!"

The icy mercury running down Ben's back was suddenly joined in his stomach by molten lead. "Give me those!" he said, snatching the glasses away. "Tikker, take the controls!"

The Lemurian stared, wide-eyed, at the wheel in front of him and then grasped it in both of his clawed hands. The tone in Ben's voice told him that any fooling around wouldn't be acceptable. He clenched his teeth and held the wheel as tight and steady as he could. Ben adjusted the objective until the image became crystal clear. His subconscious mind screamed in protest and he almost dropped the binoculars. Even at twelve or fifteen miles the silhouette was unmistakable. He'd seen it before. The last time had been three-quarters of a year before and he'd

260

been standing on *Walker*'s gun control platform with belts of .30-cal over his shoulders.

"This day just gets worse and worse," he said at last.

"What?" demanded Ed.

"You remember that Jap battle cruiser we fought past to duck into the Squall that brought us here?"

"Yeah . . ." Ed's face went white.

"That's her. *Amagi*."

"Son of a *bitch*!" Ed snarled, "I *knew* it! The lizards are *Japs*! Sneaky sons of bitches!"

"We don't know that. The Japs might be lizards."

"What do you mean?"

"The lizards might've captured her. Learned how to use her. We don't know that they're working together. That's how they got their sailing ships, remember?" He looked through the binoculars again. "Trouble is, I don't think we dare get close enough to find out. If they *are* Japs, they're working with the lizards. They'll blow us out of the sky. If they're lizards, it's clear they got the Japs to show them how to operate the ship. They may not have thought they needed to learn about antiaircraft fire, but we're slow as hell. They might still blow us out of the sky. We've got to warn the captain!"

"How close would we have to get . . . to know?"

"Close enough to see if there's Japs or lizards on her. We'd probably be in range by then."

"What about her flag?" Ed asked. "The lizards have all kinds of flags of their own. If they had the ship, they wouldn't leave the 'meatball.'"

"Good point. We might get close enough to see that before they shoot us down." He shrugged. "It doesn't really matter, though. Whatever flag she's flying, we're screwed."

Radioman 1st Class Russell Clancy leaned back in his chair, sipping "monkey joe," in *Walker*'s small, cryptlike radio room underneath the pilothouse. He'd been there all day monitoring the radio and he'd only left once to go to the head. Even then, he'd been reduced to hollering to get somebody to spell him. There was only a skeleton crew aboard. Almost half the human destroyermen were ashore, preparing to attack the city. Most everybody still on the ship was aft, trying to fit the new propeller. His calls to the bridge had been answered, but nobody ever came. That made him mad, since surely they'd heard his yelling—even without the comm. It wasn't like they could have forgotten him. Finally, Reynolds burst into the compartment and told him, "Go! Haul ass!" There was about to be a humongous battle on a shore—they could see everything from the bridge—and he was going to miss it if Clancy didn't hurry up.

That was over an hour ago, and the battle had yet to begin. Occasionally, he stole out the hatch—leaving it open so he could hear—and tried to see up to the north gate of Aryaal, but he wasn't quite high enough. There was a lot of coming and going, though. Troops going ashore from the rest of the fleet. Evidently, the rest of the AEF was pitching in after all. After what had happened, he thought, it was the least they could do. The men were hopping mad over Donaghey's death and the attempt to sink the ship, and Clancy figured that if their friends hadn't come, or worse, tried to stop them, it would have gone down pretty hard.

Clancy was angry as well. He hadn't known Donaghey well—he was a snipe—but he seemed like an all right guy. He wished he was ashore with the others instead of cooped-up waiting for a transmission that never came. That was frustrating too. He *knew* the radio was fine. They'd tested it that morning before the plane flew off. They'd even maintained contact for quite a while as it flew ever farther north. Then, all of a sudden, there was nothing. Just some weird static. It wasn't coming from his end, he was sure, and he doubted that Ed had done anything on his end to cause it. Ed could be a screwball, but he was a pretty good hand with a radio and besides, with the skipper on the warpath, he knew better than to goof around.

A hazy tendril of concern began to creep into Clancy's thoughts. Steve Riggs was in Baalkpan working on a system of communications for the defenses there. With him and Palmer both gone, Clancy would *be* the communications department. Of course, without the radio on the plane, there wouldn't be much need for one. All in all, it had been a pretty nerve-racking day.

"C'mon, Ed," he muttered. "Talk to me."

Suddenly enough to startle him with the irony, he thought he detected something buried in the static. He put his earphones on and began adjusting knobs. There! The unmistakable "beep beeping" began to emerge. Instead of voice, the signal was coming in CW, or Morse code. He snatched up a pencil and began to transcribe the letters as they came.

ZSA ZSA ZSA. (Can you receive?) Over and over again. Clancy quickly tapped back a reply.

ZSB-2. (I can receive. Readability fair.)

ZOE-5-O-J. (I am going to transmit in strings of five-urgent-verify and repeat.)

For an instant Clancy just stared at his key. "What the hell?" he muttered. They'd been transmitting in the clear for so long it didn't make any sense. Why on earth would Ed want to use five-letter code groups?

ZOE-5-O-J, he finally tapped back.

It wouldn't be long now. The bright passion of Matt's rage had ebbed somewhat as the day progressed, and that was probably for the best, he realized. The endless delays of preparing an army for battle had stretched into the midafternoon, and at times he found himself wondering if he really should have waited for the rest of the force to join them. Keje's and even Shinya's estimate of the time it would take to get ready had been overly optimistic. Intellectually, he knew the wait was a small price to pay. Not only would the larger force face less difficulty and take fewer casualties when it stormed the city, but now that it was decided, he believed even more strongly that it was important they all go in together.

The various members of the Allied Expeditionary Force had to learn here and now that they couldn't pick and choose which battles were convenient for them to fight. They were all in this together and if they were going to win this war, they had to share the burden equally.

That didn't mean he felt any less frustrated over the delays. Lord Rolak's force and the Marines still constituted the point of the spear, but Queen Maraan's had been pulled back in reserve and replaced by the Third and Fifth Guards. That's what took the most time. It was believed—probably correctly—that the defenders would fight harder if they knew they were facing their ancestral enemies from across the bay. Matt's destroyer-men had been redeployed as well—much to their disgust. They'd still go in with the "first wave" but more as heavy-weapons support pla-toons than front-line shock troops. Their job would be to shoot archers and commanders with the Springfields and Krags and break up enemy concentrations with the Thompsons and BARs. Either way, they'd be in the thick of the fighting, Matt knew, and they'd use an awful lot of am-munition. And there'd be losses. Of that he was certain. But there was no way he could keep his men out of this fight.

He himself was going in, wounded shoulder or not. Sandra hadn't even tried to stop him, knowing it was pointless. Without a word, she'd almost coldly done her best to completely immobilize his left arm while leaving him as much freedom of movement as she could. Then she went to join her medical staff as they prepared for the inevitable wounded. It hurt him to think she disapproved of what he was doing. He recognized the special tragedy of the losses they would endure in this "sideshow" affair. But he was certain to his core that if they didn't fight today, all would eventually be lost. It was more than just a matter of honor—although there was that as well. And it was more than just the danger of leaving a viper at their backs. It would be this event, he hoped, even more than the battle they'd fought against the Grik, that would forge all the fractious forces of the AEF into a single cooperative fighting force. The day had not started out looking like that would be the case, but this new purpose, this goal, had slowly formed throughout the morning as the other commanders came to realize the nature of the test. If it took this "sideshow" to finally weld the Lemurian people—and their Ameri-can allies—into a united nation of some sort, then so be it.

Lord Rolak was standing beside him, waiting while the final prepa-rations were completed.

"Once more," Matt said. "We'll give them one more chance to lay down their arms and surrender that murdering king. There'll be no time to think about it, no pause for consultations. They'll say yes or no. If they refuse, we attack immediately." Keje nodded solemn agreement. They'd been more than patient. More than fair. Even Adar seemed to have resigned himself to the necessity of the assault. He had embraced the Heavens and blessed the host and most had joined him in the devotional, regardless of denomination. The rites were similar enough, after all, and the bright sun overhead would bear witness to the deeds of B'mbaadans and Aryaalans just as the Heavens would contemplate the actions of the sea folk that day. Now he was as anxious as the others to get on with it. The sooner it was finished, the sooner they could get back to their "bigger business."

Down at the dock, *Walker*'s bell began to ring and her whistle made a sharp exclamation. Matt and his staff turned to look. They saw two men running toward them through the few remaining storm-battered warehouses and the debris of the fishing ghetto. It was half a mile or more, but they were running full out.

"What's that all about?" Matt said aloud. Panting from the unaccustomed exertion, Larry Dowden and Russell Clancy finally lurched to a stop before the captain. Both men saluted, but neither could speak for a moment. "I guess this must be pretty important, Mr. Dowden, for you to leave your posts, run all the way up here, and interrupt our battle," Matt said dryly.

"Yes, sir," Larry gasped, and motioned Clancy forward. "We finally heard from Mallory." Clancy handed over a message form. It was slightly crinkled and blotched with sweat. "I thought you better see that before the fight started," Larry explained.

Matt raised his eyebrows, and then he glanced at the paper in his hand.

REVENGE DAMAGED IN STORM AND BROUGHT TO
ACTION BY SUPERIOR ENEMY FLEET X DESTROYED IN
BATTLE SOUTH PULAU BELITUNG X SIX SURVIVORS ALL

INJURED RETRIEVED BEFORE BATTLE X ENEMY FORCE
ESTIMATED 300 REPEAT 300 PLUS SHIPS COURSE
SOUTH SOUTHEAST 175 DEGREES EIGHT KNOTS X
ENEMY IN COMPANY JAP BATTLE CRUISER BELIEVED
AMAGI X NO SHIT X MESSAGE ENDS

For a long, long moment, Captain Reddy stared down at the rumpled sheet. Over and over he read the words, convinced he'd somehow imagined them. As realization began to dawn and disbelief faded into horror, the implications of what he read descended upon him at last. He doubted if any commander in history had ever received such an unexpected and decisively catastrophic dispatch. It was over, hopeless. Everything they'd worked for, the plans and sacrifice, even the victories they'd gained were for nothing. The "Grand Offensive" to destroy the Grik menace forever now smacked of the hubris of a mouse menacing an elephant with a stick. Three hundred enemy ships—that alone made the odds impossible. They represented more than 150,000 warriors. Possibly many more. And if they really had *Amagi* . . .

He looked at his watch. A little after three. They had about five hours of daylight left and *Amagi*, if she was real, was no more than five hundred miles away. At eight knots, she'd be here in just over two days. He turned to Shinya, who was still standing nearby. For a moment he hesitated, studying the Japanese officer he'd come to rely on so much. He shook his head. Time enough later for doubts like that.

"All officers right here, right now. There's not a moment to lose." Shinya saluted, bewildered, and detailed runners to collect the various commanders. Keje looked at Matt. He sensed the change that had come over his friend and he saw that Dowden and Palmer were visibly upset. He gestured at the paper.

"A message from the flying-boat?"

Matt nodded, reading it yet again.

"Bad news?"

Matt glanced at him and then pitched his voice so no one else could hear. "I think we just lost the war."

＊　　＊　　＊

When the various commanders and chiefs had hastily assembled, Matt regarded them carefully and wondered how to begin. They didn't have time even for this, but if they were to have any chance at all, there could be no lengthy debate. It probably depended most on Queen Maraan and how she reacted. Without her support, all was lost.

"We have no time," he said without preamble. "None." He held up the dispatch so all could see. "*Revenge* has been destroyed. Not in the storm but by the enemy. Right now, more than three hundred of their ships are headed this way. They'll be here in two days."

There were gasps and mumbled protests, but Matt waded through it all. "Even worse, it seems they now have an iron ship of their own. You've all seen what my ship is capable of against the enemy. This ship that has sided with the Grik can destroy *Walker* just as easily."

Now there were shouts of dismay and even an edge of panic. How could it be? Such a ship was surely impossible and if not, how had it come to the Grik? No! It couldn't be. He saw Adar standing as though stricken. His mouth hung open in shock and his eyelids blinked in a furious blur. Forestalling any argument, Matt plowed relentlessly on.

"Imagine a ship newer and more advanced than mine, with more and bigger weapons and almost as large as a Home. That's what we face, combined with the Grik armada. There's *no way* we can stand against it. Not here, not with what we have. Our only hope is to evacu- ate immediately—everybody—from Aryaal and B'mbaado and retreat to Baalkpan as quickly as possible. The enemy is faster than we are, so we have to leave, all of us, no later than tomorrow. If they catch us at sea we'll all be destroyed." He paused and stared directly at Queen Maraan. The usually self-possessed leader of B'mbaado was caught in an unac- customed whirlwind of horror and indecision.

"How?" she asked quietly, her large silver eyes wide with shock. "How can I abandon my country, my home?"

"You must, Your Highness," he answered gently. "Land is not im- portant when it comes to the very survival of your people." He shook his head. "No, I didn't mean that. Of course land is important. But it's an asset you can trade for time while you save the people that matter even more. That's something I was just starting to figure out myself a few months back. I didn't like it, and maybe the way we were doing it was screwed up, but it was our only choice. One of these days, we'll get the land back, Your Majesty, but right now your people need you to lead them to safety, and we desperately need you by our side."

"But how will we take them all? The Homes of the battle line were already crowded with troops."

"We'll pack them in like sand, if we have to. Fill the feluccas to over-flowing. We'll leave no one behind."

"But we will!" she insisted bitterly. "We cannot gather them all, not in so little time! Many do not live in the city. B'mbaado is not a bastion in the wilderness where her people skulk behind walls to protect them from the beasts. There are few dangerous animals on the island and many live in the hills and along the coast!"

"Then you'll have to leave some troops to warn them, to help them hide in the interior. The Grik may not even stay here long, or venture far from the city. Maybe we can send fast ships from time to time, like *Walker* or *Mahan,* to take them off." He shrugged. "Together, at Baalk-pan, we might even beat them if they follow us there, and then we can retake your kingdom. The defenses of Baalkpan are formidable and there are now many guns. But if you stay here, that'll never happen and all will die."

Finally she nodded, and huge, bright tears welled in the eyes of the Queen Protector of B'mbaado. Matt had never even known Lemurians could cry. Slowly, she turned to Haakar-Faask.

"It must be you," she said in a stricken whisper. "You must gather those we leave behind and protect them." Stiffly, she embraced the old warrior, and just as stiffly, glancing around at those nearby, he embraced her back. Matt could tell there was deep feeling between them but they were also highly conscious that they were on a stage in front of many strangers as well as their own people. He heard a sniff from Sandra's direction, but he was filled with admiration.

Safir Maraan backed away from the embrace and struck a pose before the Allied Expeditionary Force. When she spoke, her voice was shockingly loud for such a small creature, but Matt had grown to expect it by now. All Lemurians were just damn loud when they wanted to be.

"My people! My friends! Events have transpired that will force us to leave our kingdom, our homes, for a time. A Grik host advances that all of us combined"—she gestured at all the allied force—"cannot match. We must fall back upon the stronger defenses and more numerous troops of Baalkpan. When the enemy follows us there, we will destroy him and quickly return to reclaim our sacred land." She paused. "The enemy comes quickly. Perhaps not all can be carried away in the time we have, but we will come back! Haakar-Faask will protect the people we leave behind. He will train them to fight and he will lead them against the Grik if he must until we can return to evict the coming scourge or take all away." She paused, but stood even straighter. "If we cannot return in time . . . he will plan a *great* battle! A battle that will be celebrated until the end of time and that the rest of us will think wistfully of until the day we once more join those who fought and hear their deeds in person!"

A great roar went up and, Safir, her eyes still shining, turned to Matt while Chack translated what she said. All Matt could do was shake his head and wonder. He wasn't about to ask right then.

"What about Aryaal?" she asked, the power gone from her voice. "And there are other cities—Kudraang, Kartaj, Bataava—farther up the coast."

"There's nothing we can do for them," Matt replied somberly. "There's not enough time." He glanced grimly at his watch again and then looked at Rolak. The old warrior was standing, shoulders bowed. He knew that just warning his people wouldn't be enough. Rasik would not believe it and all of his people would stay and perish. He and his warriors couldn't leave them to that, and all would die for nothing.

"No time at all," Matt repeated. "Under the circumstances, Queen Protector, I think your troops would be better employed evacuating B'mbaado immediately. Some of the embedded officers might want to remain, however. They might need the experience."

She nodded gratefully, but blinked surprise. Rolak and many others did the same.

"The way I figure it, we have three hours to take Aryaal."

As expected, a last desperate appeal came to naught. Officially, at least. There was no response to the demand for surrender, but when the guns in the breastworks made ready to fire, the defenders on the walls just vanished. With no apparent opposition, the Second Marines and Rolak's force, now called the First Aryaal, moved forward toward the gate. Matt, Keje, and even Adar fell in behind, and five-member squads of destroyermen interspersed themselves among the troops. Silva's squad remained around its captain.

"You believe this . . . nightmare ship truly exists? That it is coming?" Keje asked. "Perhaps your Mallory made a mistake?"

"A mistake like that . . . wouldn't be possible."

"You never told me there was another ship," Adar said, matching their pace.

"We didn't know."

"Then where did it come from, this ship that has changed everything in an instant?"

Matt sighed. "The same place we did. Through the Squall."

"But you know her?"

Matt nodded. "You remember we once spoke of how *Walker* was damaged so badly? And *Mahan* too? *Amagi* did that, by herself."

Adar shook his head. "Then all is lost."

Matt was silent for a moment as they followed the advance. "If we can get to Baalkpan, perhaps not," he said. "*Amagi* is powerful, more powerful than you can imagine. But she can't move on land. She can blow the hell out of the city, but she can't take it. Only the Grik can do that. If we get there first, with all the forces we have, Baalkpan might be able to hold. *Walker* and *Mahan* will try to deal with *Amagi*."

The Marines were near the gate now. So far there'd been no defensive fire at all.

"How can it be that you people, you Amer-i-caans, help us—and yet others of your kind help the Grik?" Adar asked bitterly. "Are your people truly able to think so differently?"

"Why are we attacking a city we saved from the Grik?" Matt countered. "Can you actually think so differently from them? And the Japanese are as different from us as you are from the Aryaalans. Remember, we were at war with them before we came here."

"But—"

"We'll have to pick it up later," said Matt, hitching his belt as best he could and nodding forward.

"Who was winning?" Adar asked quietly, but Matt didn't answer. Ahead, as the first troops entered the city, the distinctive sound of battle reached them from within. Chack shouted something over the din, but what it was, at first, Matt had no idea. Other shouts echoed back, and when Matt and his companions finally passed through the arch, the cause of the confusion was plain. Battle raged in the courtyard and streets beyond, but as yet the Marines weren't involved. Civil war had come once more to Aryaal.

Word of the final ultimatum, complete with the warning of the Grik, had spread like wildfire throughout the city. It began among the defenders at the gate who fled from the guns. Officer after officer—Rasik's handpicked—tried to stem the tide of desertion and many of them were slain. The palace guard tried to stop them too, but when real fighting began, many who were willing to defend the city joined the mutineers when they saw them being killed by the king's personal troops. It was too much. Most were loyal to their city and their king, no matter who he was. That the loyalists had prevailed in the previous fighting was proof enough of that—even if the purges after the first rebellion had been excessive enough to fire indignation and doubt. But as word of the renewed Grik threat continued to spread, they began to realize that the patient invaders outside the walls weren't the real enemy after all. They knew if it hadn't been for the sea folk, the Grik would have had them already. They could never hold them off a second time. Suddenly, to most of the warriors of Aryaal, the survival of their families transcended nationalism and loyalty to a new king they didn't even like.

By the time Lord Rolak entered the city at the head of his column of native warriors, the uprising in the city—at least the northern half—was already practically over. Marines fanned out and created a perimeter inside the gate, but no one so much as threw a rock at them. Beyond the perimeter there was still fighting, but it flared in fits and spurts. It had degenerated mostly into a grudge match now between the various Aryaalan political houses and the palace guard. None of the combatants from any side seemed to want the Marines to get involved. Lord Rolak paced to the great Fountain of the Sun in the center of the plaza and climbed the stepped circle that surrounded it for a better view. From amid the turmoil of fighting and the growing crowd of townsfolk, someone shouted a cheer at the sight of him. Then another. Within minutes, the dwindling sound of battle was overwhelmed by thunderous cheering that surged and echoed off the walls of the city and the royal palace beyond the plaza. Defenders threw down their weapons and many took up the cheer as well.

Rolak was overcome. Matt mounted the steps beside him, grinning for the first time that day. The sound was overwhelming and it only seemed to build as more and more Aryaalans rushed from other parts of the city. The crowd surged, but the Marines kept them at bay. A phalanx of armed Aryaalans—not palace guards but still a well-turned-out force—made its way through the crowd until it reached the Marines' shield wall. Shinya rushed to the point of contact with Chack by his side and after several moments of hand gestures and shouting, a single figure was let through the wall. Chack hurried to Matt and Rolak, with the individual puffing and almost running to keep up. His flowing embroidered robe threatened to trip him.

"Lord Koratin," Rolak said by way of restrained greeting when the pair drew near. Chack automatically translated for Captain Reddy.

"Lord Rolak," Koratin replied, and bowed.

"I understand you are chief advisor to that murdering coward who has stolen the throne," Rolak said. "We were never friends, but I expected better of you."

"It is true, that was my position, my lord. And that is what I tried to do. But my advice wasn't heeded, or even tolerated. The king is quite mad."

"The attempt to sink the iron ship?"

Koratin nodded. "I told him it was madness when I learned his scheme. I even sent three trusted servants to warn you, but they were caught and killed. The palace guard came for me then, but my retainers held them off." He smiled crookedly. "If not for your timely arrival and the chaos that ensued, I would be dead. How delightfully ironic!"

Rolak barked a laugh. "You always were amazingly skilled at survival, Koratin!"

Koratin bowed. "As you can see, it's a useful skill." His face turned grim. "Is it true? The Grik will return?"

"It is true."

"I feared as much. I feared for my younglings—for all the younglings of our people—but the king would not listen. He does not believe the old stories"—he nodded respectfully at Chack—"that for our salvation the sea folk have preserved!"

"Fear still, Koratin. The danger is greater than you imagine. We must all leave this place and become beggars in the north. The sea folk will succor us, but they need our arms more than our bellies, so all who go must be willing to fight, and provocations won't occur."

Koratin was stunned. "But what of our walls? Can we not hold here if the sea folk come to our aid?"

"No." Rolak nodded toward Matt, who stood listening. "Cap-i-taan Reddy has told me how it must be and I believe him."

Koratin turned to look at Matt for the first time. His stare was an appraising one. "So that is the great tail-less leader of the sea folk," he said. "I suspected as much." He bowed low to the captain.

"Where's Rasik?" Matt demanded, eyes flashing.

"In his palace, lord. Yonder." Koratin pointed at the imposing structure beyond the plaza. "He has almost four hundred guards. Quite fanatical, I'm afraid. It will be difficult and costly to storm."

For a long while, Matt said nothing while those nearby waited for his decision. His expression seemed almost yearning as his eyes bored into the palace walls.

"No, it won't," he said at last. Rolak cocked his head and looked at Matt with a questioning blink. "We're not going to storm it. Oh, don't get me wrong—there's nothing I'd rather do than bring the guns in and blow it down around him, and that's what we'd do if we had the time. We'd *take* our time!" he snarled. Calming, he clasped his hands behind his back. "But we don't have the luxury of time, and I'm not going to waste lives getting the little bastard the old-fashioned way. Chack and his Marines will see that no one gets out while you begin evacuating the city."

Chack was confused and surprised. He was first and foremost a destroyerman, after all, and Donaghey was one of his clan. Surely the captain wouldn't leave his death un-avenged—not after he had been willing to break the alliance that morning to take the city. "But what about the king, Captain?" he prodded. "What are we going to do about him?"

"He doesn't leave his palace. No matter what he says or does. Not until everyone in Aryaal and B'mbaado have been evacuated. In the meantime, you'll remain here with half the Marines and keep him bottled up. The other half, and most of the AEF Guard regiments, will be sent immediately back to Baalkpan in feluccas to help prepare the defense." He put his hand on Chack's shoulder. "You and your Marines will be the last ones out of the city. Make sure we don't leave anyone behind that wants to come, even any of Rasik's guards that manage to wiggle loose."

He looked around, sadly, at the city. It really was quite beautiful in an exotic and unfamiliar way. The Aryaalans seemed to love color as much as any of their cousins, but instead of fabric and tapestries, they applied it to the very stone itself. It was too bad he could see it only now, and for so short a time.

"Burn everything. Don't leave anything for the enemy."

"What about the king?" Chack persisted. Matt's expression went cold.

"Except him," he said. "He doesn't believe the lizards will come back. We'll let them convince him themselves." Chack grinned and almost burst out laughing. That would be satisfactory justice to him.

Koratin watched them wide-eyed and shuddered. *Merciful people,* he thought, *in many ways. But not all.* "I will help all I can," he said, his voice very formal.

The captain waved toward Rolak. "Help him. He's in charge here." He took one more look around the plaza and sighed. "I have a ship to fix."

Matt watched the chaos of the exodus while standing on *Walker*'s port bridgewing. It had become the central headquarters for the operation and a steady stream of messengers came and went, bringing news or carrying orders. Lieutenant Mallory joined him there shortly before dark; his plane was alongside *Big Sal* taking on fuel. Now they stood with Adar, Sandra, and Courtney Bradford and stared quietly out upon what looked like the end of the world.

Thousands of terrified refugees, carrying nothing but small parcels of clothing, milled and surged along the waterfront. They were desperate to climb the ramp that led aboard *Humfra-Dar,* and Geran-Eras herself stood at the gangway with a squad of Marines directing the Aryaalan or B'mbaadan passengers toward sections of her ship where they'd be taken in hand by others who would try to accommodate them. Huge bundles of foodstuffs were hoisted aboard and the night was filled with shouts, shrieking infants, anguished cries, and the muffled thunder of countless feet on the wooden dock and deck of the Home. In the distance, flames soared up beyond the walls of Aryaal, as the evacuated portions of the city were put to the torch. Garish flashes pulsed across the bottoms of low clouds that had moved in at dusk, and the light cast an eerie, ruddy glow on the anxious proceedings at the waterfront.

Matt tried to compare the scene to other great national tragedies or evacuations he knew of from history. The sack of Athens, the destruction of Carthage, or the fall of Rome came to mind, as did the burning of Atlanta and Columbia or the evacuation of Richmond. More recently were the newsreels he'd seen of the devastation of Europe and China by the Nazis and Japanese. Each of those calamities was probably as bad or worse, but he hadn't been there to witness any of them firsthand. He was here now, and everything he could see—the suffering, the devastation, the probable extinction of an entire culture—was happening because he'd ordered it. He knew there was no choice, but the magnitude of the disaster wracked him with guilt. They'd come as naive liberators, bent on saving the people of this world from the depredations of a remorseless foe. They were leaving as destroyers, causing more harm than the Grik had yet managed.

With a surprised thankfulness that he couldn't express, he felt Sandra's hand find his in the darkness and he squeezed it gently before letting go. She'd been more reserved toward him that day than their "agreement" required and he still wondered why. Then he looked at Mallory. The young aviator's face glowed grimly in the reflected light. He'd spoken little since he arrived, only confirming with a nod that the dispatch was entirely accurate. There was no mistake. He stood there now, holding *Revenge*'s log in both hands like a sacred treasure. Matt would read it later, when his attention could be spared from the decisions at hand. Right now it would just be too much. He would share it with Keje when the two of them could quietly mourn their dead alone. He cleared his throat. "So, are they Japs, Mr. Mallory? Did you get close enough to see?"

"I guess they probably are. We saw the flags for sure." He grunted. "And then they started shooting at us. The first air burst we saw, we got the hell out."

Matt nodded, deciding not to chastise the flier for the risk he'd taken. "Lucky they didn't let you get closer before they opened fire. Sounds like they got anxious."

"Yes, sir. They must've been pretty surprised to see *us* too."

Matt rubbed his forehead. "Maybe not. We've been transmitting in the clear all this time. Maybe they've been reading our mail. Any transmission at all would've warned them we were here. If they've been listening in, they may even know where Baalkpan is," he added darkly.

"And if that's the case, we won't know until they're almost here whether they're all coming here or they mean to dispatch forces to both places." He ground his teeth. "Damn."

"I'd think *Amagi* would go wherever she thought *Walker* was, Captain," Mallory speculated.

"Maybe. If they know where we are. I wonder if they do?" He paused for a moment and then answered his own question. "Probably. The lizards certainly know we're here." He scratched the stubble on his chin. "But they may not know there are two of us ... Anyway, that answers my question. We have to assume the Japs know, and the last I heard, they don't like us very much. If they figure we're evacuating for Baalkpan they might try to get between us. Make us come to them." He shook his head. "It'll be tough to do at eight knots. I wonder why they're so slow? *Amagi* used to make over thirty."

"Only as fast as the slowest ship?" Bradford opined.

"Yeah, but the lizards are faster than that ... unless maybe *Amagi* is the slowest ship! You're sure it was coal smoke you saw?"

"Positive."

"That may be why we haven't seen her till now—they've been converting her boilers. Coal's a lot more efficient than wood, but not as good as oil. Shorter range and a fair cut in speed. Still . . ."

"Damage," Sandra said suddenly. "We've all been thinking of *Amagi* only in terms of firepower. That's a pretty one-sided comparison. But remember, as bad as she roughed us up, *Walker* and *Mahan* got in some pretty good licks. Maybe enough that she nearly *did* sink!"

"Right," Matt breathed. "We know how tough it's been for us to make repairs. Just think of all the problems they'll have had to face! Every piece of that ship is five times bigger than a comparable part of *Walker*. We've been thinking of that only as an advantage to them, but think of the disadvantages! There's no way they could've fixed a lot of the damage we inflicted. I'm still sure *Mahan* put at least two torpedoes into her. It would've been tough to get her out of a real dry dock and a fully equipped yard this fast!"

Bradford looked at Sandra with a growing, affectionate smile.

"There you go again, my dear. Leaping directly upon the obvious while we mere males flail helplessly at obscure minutia."

"Well, it's a theory," Matt agreed. "We just have to figure out a way to use it, if it's true." He slapped the rail before him in a release of pent-up frustration. "Damn them to hell! How could even the Japs ally themselves with creatures like the lizards?"

"Because they're Japs!" Mallory answered bitterly. "They're *like* the lizards!"

Adar shook his head sadly. So far, he'd said nothing since joining them on the bridge, besides a subdued greeting. Now he spoke. "Lieutenant Shinya is a 'Jaap,' is he not?" Surprised by the question, Matt nodded. Adar sighed deeply. "I spent a short time with him while the Guard regiments were withdrawn from the city. He is overwhelmed with shame. A shame he cannot show."

"Why?" Sandra asked.

Adar looked at her. "Because he is a 'Jaap.' He's seen the Grik for what they are, as have we all, and he asks himself the same question you do, Captain Reddy. It tortures him that his own people might cavort with such evil. It is much like the shame Lord Rolak feels for the things King Rasik has done, only worse." Adar raised his hands in submission. "I do not pretend to understand you humans, not anymore. But Lieutenant Shinya's clan of humans is more difficult to understand than the rest of you in some ways, but even simpler in others. You Amer-i-caans have a delightfully stark conception of the difference between good and evil. In your case, that conception seems to come from how you have individually decided your society will collectively define good and evil." He gazed for a moment at the fire and tumult of the dying city. "I suppose it is fortunate for us that you've decided my people's enemies are the evil ones in this context." He snorted and shook his head.

"From what he has told me, Lieutenant Shinya's people are the opposite of that. In their society, the few or the one—an emperor, I believe?—decides what all of society will consider good or evil and the individuals are forced to accept that decision." He blinked apologetically. "I may be wrong. Lieutenant Shinya, though, I think has always been an individual with a mind of his own, trapped in that society without a voice. At the same time, he is fiercely loyal to his people. Imagine the conflict he faces. He knows it is wrong for his people to support the Grik, but he also knows the decision will have been made for the many by a few."

He looked Captain Reddy square in the eye. "The same thing happens here, but the decisions you make are supported by the majority of your people. You made that clear today. You couldn't rule long or well without that support." He blinked and clasped his hands behind his back. "It seems your decisions are supported by my people as well," he added in the wry tone he'd been practicing. "But as far as *Amagi* is concerned, that may not be the case. The society from which her people come does not allow them to express their views, or even to have any, if they are not consistent with that of their emperor. Is the warrior who fights for evil still evil himself if his society does not see it as such? Perhaps in that way, the 'Jaaps' are more similar to the Grik than we might think. The problem for Lieutenant Shinya still remains. He is a Jaap. You are the sworn enemy of his emperor, and so, in the collective eyes of his people, you are evil. He knows that is not the case. In your eyes, his people are evil. Not just because they support the Grik, but because they attacked you in the world you came from. I've seen how quick you are to anger in the face of such a thing. But in spite of whether you or I—or even he—believes his people in this world are on the side of evil, he cannot believe that all of them *are* evil."

"What will he do?" Matt asked, alarmed. Not because he believed Shinya would turn on them, but because he had, after all, become such an integral part of *Walker*'s family—not to mention the war effort as a whole—and he was worried about him.

"What will he do, indeed?" Adar blinked rapidly. "In any event, I apologize. I did get horribly sidetracked. I believe your original question was 'why would the Jaaps help the Grik?' not 'how will Lieutenant Shinya deal with his conscience?'" He shook his head. "Until we learn more about the Grik, we may never know. They have obviously communicated with each other—which is something we could never do.

Perhaps I was right before and they do have something in common? You said *Walker* and *Mahan* damaged *Amagi* in battle?" Matt nodded. "Well, *Walker* has certainly done a great deal of damage to the Grik." He stopped and looked at the captain with a strange smile on his face. "Perhaps the thing that unites them now is their mutual hatred of you."

Lieutenant Sandison appeared behind them, clambering up the ladder from below. A short, dark-colored Lemurian was with him. A female. She was the liaison from *Humfra-Dar*. Sandison saluted and the little Lemurian imitated the gesture. Matt returned it solemnly.

"Geran-Eras says if she takes on another soul, they'll be standing on each other's heads."

"Very well. She has permission to get under way." Matt had agonized over the decision whether the ships should wait to depart together, or sail independently as soon as they were loaded. He settled on the second alternative. It meant less time they'd be crowded so uncomfortably, but mainly he thought it would actually give them a better chance of escape. If they all headed out together, it increased the possibility that the enemy would catch them together. The mutual protection afforded by numbers would be meaningless against *Amagi*'s guns. Better to split them up. He wasn't worried by the threat posed by any advance scouts. With their big guns, the Homes could repulse even a small squadron of Grik attackers.

"Keje and *Salissa* are next in line," he said. "I want him in Baalkpan as soon as possible to help coordinate the defense. You too, Adar," he added. "Besides, she's the only 'tanker' we have. We'll rig hoses and top off our bunkers while she's taking on passengers. We'll load up on fuel for the PBY while we're at it, just in case. When *Big Sal* gets to Baalkpan, have her fill up again. We might need all the mobile fuel reserve we can get."

A wailing rose from the dock as the ramp to *Humfra-Dar* was blocked. Many might have been separated from their loved ones, or not known there would be other Homes to take them. A panic began to build and several shots were actually fired in an attempt to control the crowd. Adar blinked his distaste.

"It is difficult to believe Amer-i-caans could be as different from the Jaaps as we are from the land folk," he said. "I cannot imagine my people behaving so."

"Give them a break, Adar. They've just lost everything they had in the world. They're at the mercy of people they've distrusted throughout their history to protect them from creatures that'll eat them if they can. Pray you never find out how your people act in a similar situation." Matt gestured at the seething mob. "Besides, those people are the ones that are going to save yours in the end. After we make an army out of them."

"Land folk females do not fight. Many of their males will not."

"They will when they see what's coming," Mallory interjected quietly.

Matt noticed the female Lemurian was still standing there, holding her salute. "You may dismiss your friend now, Mr. Sandison. She'll miss her boat," he said with a small smile. "Do you have a report for me? About progress with the propeller?"

"Ah, yes, sir. Just a moment, sir." He quickly spoke to the 'Cat, and she darted down the ladder. "Lieutenant McFarlane says, 'It's going,' sir. The flashies started chewing through the sail we rigged so the men could work. We're going to have to rig another one. He thinks it's the lights. They're drawing the fish and making them attack the canvas."

"What about the torpedoes?"

"Yes, sir, sorry, sir," Sandison answered guiltily. "We've started back to work on them too." It had been weeks since anyone had tried to figure out what was wrong with the two condemned torpedoes they'd salvaged from Surabaya so long ago.

Matt nodded. "Not your fault. I've handed you plenty of other chores and it didn't look like we'd need them that bad. Until now. Any problems with our three good torps?"

"No, sir, they're fine. All we have to do is wind 'em up. 'Course, we still have the same problem," he added worriedly. "We don't know why they won't hit anything, or if they do, why they won't go off."

"Figure it out, Mr. Sandison."

"We've been trying. We're fooling around with the dud again and Shinya has a couple of ideas." Sandison shrugged. "It's worth a try." Matt frowned slightly and glanced at Adar.

"Shinya?"

"Yeah. He showed up in the workshop ready to work as soon as he came aboard. Said Chack had command of the Marines around the palace, and"—Bernie shrugged, waving at the pandemonium outside—"there's enough troops on the docks." Sandison looked at the captain and read his mind, or he thought he did. "He's okay, sir. He just needs to sort things out."

"By helping you fix torpedoes to sink his countrymen." Matt muttered darkly.

Bernie's eyes widened. "You don't suppose . . . !"

Matt shook his head. "No, but I don't want you leaving him there by himself right now, either. Let him help if he wants, but remind him that by the terms of his parole he's not required to." He looked at Adar again, impressed as usual by the Sky Priest's sensitivity to matters pertaining to human nature that Matt hadn't even noticed. He took solace in the fact that he had quite a lot on his plate just then, but still . . .

"He say anything to you about *Amagi*?" he asked Sandison.

"Well . . . no, sir. But he knows that's why we're working on the torpedoes again. Why else?"

"And you're absolutely certain he's not pulling your chain?" Matt had to ask.

Sandison shrugged. "I know it sounds strange, but he didn't really say anything. Right now he acts like he doesn't care that there's other Japs on *Amagi*. The only thing that seems to matter to him is that she might help the lizards sink the machine shop." The machine shop had been Shinya's refuge ever since being rescued from the sea.

Matt blinked, and Adar barked a laugh in spite of himself.

"You see, Cap-i-taan Reddy? In some ways, much more simple to understand!"

Matt shook his head. "Adar, a while ago you probably described the differences between us and the Japs to me better than anybody ever has, and then you make a comment like that. I'll tell you right now, whatever Shinya's going through isn't going to be simple to understand at all. Least of all to him." Sandison looked worried. He had grown very fond of the Japanese officer.

"Maybe we should, you know, put a guard on him? Shoot, Skipper, he might . . . hurt himself . . ."

"I'm glad you feel that way, Bernie, because on top of everything else, I want you to stick to Shinya like glue. Don't *let* him 'hurt himself.' Understood?"

"Understood, Skipper."

For a while they all stood quietly, staring at the inferno breeding before them—the seething, dying, shattered fragments of all they'd hoped for when their "crusade" began.

"I guess I can understand the Japs wanting to continue their war with us, no matter where we are. It's stupid, but I understand it. Hell, I even sort of feel the same way. Maybe we've just cut each other too deep." Matt shook his head, amazed. "But there's no way you can get me to understand why they'd help the lizards."

*H*isashi Kurokawa, captain of HIMS *Amagi*, stalked slowly back and forth across the battle cruiser's bridge. His hands were clasped behind his back and the red nighttime lighting transformed his round, cherubic features into those of a dark, grimacing Buddha. He paused briefly behind the helmsman, who stiffened nervously under his scrutiny. With a barely audible growl, Kurokawa paced on. If he noticed the tension radiating from each member of the watch as he drew near, he made no sign.

Commander Sato Okada had the watch and he peered warily at the captain as he prowled from station to station. Any minute now he expected *Amagi*'s stocky commander to explode into a fit of rage, triggered by some slight or imagined transgression. Almost twenty minutes had passed since the captain came on the bridge, and lately that seemed to be about the limit. The fits had become so commonplace that they were almost a part of the ship's routine. No one was spared their fury, and Sato himself had probably been on the receiving end of more vitriolic harangues than anyone else on the ship. That was because he often—delicately—told the captain what he actually believed instead of just what he knew the man wanted to hear. More often than not, the disagreements provoked titanic tantrums, and the things the captain said to him in front of other officers and crew were sometimes difficult to bear. But Sato withstood the onslaughts as stoically as he could. The captain believed it was Sato's duty to agree with him, but Sato suspected more and more that his real duty lay in protecting the ship and her crew from the captain.

Right now, for example, he knew Captain Kurokawa was most displeased about their speed, and Sato couldn't make him understand the engineers were doing all they could. The captain wasn't satisfied. Recently, he'd even gone so far as to charge that there were traitors in the engineering spaces. Sato had done all he could to stanch the loss of morale after that accusation came on top of everything else, but the crew was lost, dispirited and afraid. The fear was feeding on the captain's attitude and spreading like a caustic acid.

The lights of their "allies'" ships were all around them on the broad expanse of the sea, clustered about them as if shepherding them along. That infuriated Kurokawa more than anything else. *Amagi* was the most powerful ship in the world. By rights, she should be leading this task force—not groping along trying to keep up. The Grik had slowed their advance so *Amagi* could remain with the fleet, but "keeping up" wasn't what he wanted to do.

Sato glanced at the captain and noticed with a rush of alarm that he was moving in his direction. He braced himself for the onslaught. To his surprise, the captain's voice was quiet, even mild when he spoke.

"I hope you are feeling better, Commander Okada."

Sato gulped and bowed his head slightly. "Yes, Captain. Much better, thank you. It must have been something I ate."

"Of course. I know you are not timid." The captain's face clouded slightly. "Either in the face of the enemy, or my own."

"It is my duty to advise you, sir."

"It is your duty to obey me!" Kurokawa snapped.

"I have always obeyed."

The captain's face clouded still more but, forcibly, he pushed back the threatening storm. When he spoke again, his voice was controlled once more. "Very well. Since you see it as your duty to advise me, how would you do so now?"

Sato looked at the captain, appalled. It was the first time since Kurokawa assumed command that he'd ever asked anyone what they thought. That might be entirely appropriate under most circumstances, but since the Strange Storm, things had been anything but normal. Still, for Kurokawa to actually ask, let alone care, what Sato thought about their situation was most uncharacteristic. It was probably a trap. Something to get him to commit to a course of insubordination.

"On what subject would you seek my advice?" he asked carefully.

"Ah. Of course. I assumed you would have a differing opinion than I on everything we have done. I was correct. Your reports seethe with discontent! Let us limit our discussion to strategy so I might get some sleep tonight!" His face became grim. "I am frustrated with these barbaric 'allies' of ours, as you know. Dreadful creatures, but useful."

Sato had to suppress a shudder at the thought of the Grik. They'd encountered them first at Singapore when they went there for repairs after their battle with the retreating American force. It was then that they discovered something extraordinary had happened to them. Singapore wasn't there! In its place was only a strange village of some sort with a harbor filled with sailing ships—which had attacked them immediately and as apparently automatically as a disturbed hive of bees. Throughout the day and night they fought, killing thousands of the hideous creatures, which continued the assault even as *Amagi* tried to steam away. But the ship had been too badly damaged by the American destroyers and it couldn't outrun the red-hulled ships.

Finally, after they repelled what seemed like countless assaults, a single ship approached but did not attack. Negotiations were established and a bizarre alliance was struck. *Amagi* would join the creatures that attacked her so fanatically such a short time before. In return, she would be provided with fuel, food, and labor for repairs. At the time, even Sato had seen no other alternative. Since that day, however, not a moment went by when he did not regret the choice.

Communication was still difficult, and rudimentary at best. Neither race could form the sounds to actually speak to one another, but had to rely on written *English,* of all things, in order to converse at all. Not that Sato wanted to talk to them. The Grik were loathsome creatures. Vicious and almost mindless in their obsessive ferocity. As far as he could tell, their one motivation was to conquer the world and kill everything else that lived upon it. In spite of how many his forces had killed, he never got any impression the Grik were afraid of them, or even much cared about those that had fallen. There were no funerals, no ceremonies, no mourning for the dead. He never knew for sure—he didn't want to know—but he suspected that they . . . harvested the carcasses of the slain that were not consumed by the suddenly terrible sea. It was surreal, and it was far too much for many of the crew to accept.

And just as quickly and matter-of-factly as the Grik accepted their losses, they accepted the alliance with *Amagi.* They were appropriately appreciative of her power and recognized her as a useful tool. As promised, they assisted in making what minor repairs they could. Once *Amagi* was relatively seaworthy again, the Grik escorted her to Ceylon for further repairs.

Ceylon was another surprise. Okada remembered the great natural harbor of Colombo on the west coast of the island as a major bastion of British empire. Except for a general geographical resemblance, it was gone. Grik architecture tended toward unimaginative utilitarian slabs, contrasted with occasional terrifyingly rendered art relief, reminiscent of some of the more troubling ancient Mexican art he had seen. He was strangely saddened by the absence of the Galle Face Green, the historic promenade used for horse racing, and one of the most ostentatious manifestations of British colonialism in Ceylon. But most striking of all were the hundreds of Grik ships packed into the huge protected bay. At first sight it had been blindingly obvious that a massive buildup for some monumental offensive was under way. An offensive that *Amagi* was now clearly expected to participate in.

Amagi's stay in Colombo amounted to a strange sort of exile. No one went ashore except the captain and a small entourage, and then only when absolutely necessary. The Grik were extremely terrifying. Powerful, consummate predators that gazed upon you always as if speculating on your flavor. Some visits were unavoidable if repairs were to be coordinated, but nobody ever wanted to go twice, and Okada was convinced that the captain used the detail as a punishment. Why else had he been sent so often? In any event, Sato learned much more about the Grik than anyone else, probably even the captain, and began to realize with sick despair just how cheaply they'd sold their souls. Sato and most of the crew detested the Grik, but his initial hope that they would just steam away from their new "friends" was dashed by the realization that *Amagi* could never outrun them in her present state and there was no doubt they would be attacked if they tried.

Amagi had originally been designed to burn coal, so the reconversion wasn't too difficult. But there was so much damage to the engines and boilers that fully repairing them with the facilities at hand was out of the question. The ship's top speed was gone forever. When they saw the size of the fleet in Ceylon, the impossibility of escaping to make their own way was driven dramatically home. For now, there was nothing to do but repair the ship and, in Sato's mind, wait for an opportunity.

So they joined the Grik in their current war of conquest against strange furry folk that resided at sea on large ships, and in the Dutch East Indies. To make matters even more bizarre, the "tree folk"—he believed that was the best translation—seemed to have allied themselves with one of the American destroyers they'd been fighting when they were swallowed by the Strange Storm. It was that discovery, Sato thought, that finally drove Captain Kurokawa mad. If he'd ever had the intention of slipping away from the Grik, it had now certainly passed.

The captain blamed everything that had happened to them on the two destroyers that so arrogantly charged them right before the Strange Storm brought them here. Sato had been secretly stirred by the courage of their crews, but Kurokawa took their escape and the damage to his mighty ship quite personally. Each wound to the ship was matched by one to the captain's pride. That two such outdated and dilapidated vessels could wreak such destruction on *Amagi* was as if house cats had savaged a tiger. And then, as if in punishment, *Amagi* was taken from the world she knew. That was the Americans' fault too. The fact that one of the badly damaged destroyers still existed in this twisted world struck Kurokawa as a personal insult. He was now obsessed with its destruction in an almost Grik-like way, and if it took alliance with such unpleasant creatures to accomplish that goal, so be it.

"What can we do to increase our prestige among those monsters?" Kurokawa asked, waving toward the endless fleet beyond the glass windows of the bridge and returning Okada's thoughts to the unusual conversation.

"Show ourselves to be even more vicious and contemptible than they are, I suspect," Sato said bitterly. The captain considered his words.

"You may not be mistaken. We must put ourselves forward in battle, Commander Okada. Their commander must see our power for himself!" He clenched his fists at his side in frustration. "Which we cannot do if we are so slow!"

Sato tried to avert his captain's mounting rage by changing the subject. "At least now we know the source of the radio transmissions we detected. Not two ships, but a single ship and a plane. The American flying-boat was unexpected."

"Yes. It did a great deal of damage before it flew away." Kurokawa's features reddened. "If our antiaircraft defenses had been better prepared, we could have shot it down and we would not be having this conversation! The Grik would have certainly seen our worth!"

Sato quickly diverted the captain from attacking another part of the crew. "But the enemy ship did much more damage. I understand one of the Grik commanders was killed and his ship destroyed. The survivors of the raid on Surabaya were right about the cannons."

"So it would seem." Kurokawa hesitated. "The Grik will see *Amagi*'s worth if they face many more of those." He glanced at the clock on the bulkhead. For the first time, Sato thought he saw nervousness behind the captain's eyes. "Soon I must cross to the 'flagship.'"

Sato waited a moment before he spoke. "Must you take Captain Kaufman with you this time? He might be even more valuable to us now, and each time he is in the presence of those creatures, he ... slips ... a little more."

Kurokawa regarded him with a hard gaze. "Pity for the enemy, Commander Okada?"

Sato's expression hardened as well. "Empathy for an officer who saw his crew *eaten* by our 'allies,' Captain Kurokawa. Even the Grik spoke highly of his bravery, after a fashion. He did not surrender; he was overwhelmed."

Kurokawa waved his hand dismissively. "I do not care. I can write English," he said distastefully, "as most naval officers once had to. Speak to him, though. Find out why he said nothing about a flying-boat. If he knew of it and did not speak, I want him to regret it deeply!" He smiled. "Perhaps we will return him to his former masters, eh?"

Sato shuddered, and once more changed the subject. He was getting good at maneuvering the conversation to keep his commander's temper in check. "Will you tell the Grik your assumptions based on *all* the radio traffic we intercepted? Before the enemy resumed transmitting in code?"

Kurokawa looked at him. "Of course. It is valuable information and they will see it as such." He smiled. "That we've somehow divined it will surely raise us in their estimation."

Sato took a deep breath and glanced around at the other men on the bridge. He knew they were straining to hear, but doubted they could understand much. In spite of that, he spoke barely above a whisper. "Before we reveal that we can send and receive messages over long distances, let alone where we think the American base might be, would it not be best to speak to the Americans first?"

Kurokawa's eyes bulged and he screamed, "You would *speak* to the *enemy*?!"

Sato forced his voice to remain calm and low. "Captain, please! Let me speak!" he said. "First, would it not be best to conceal the technology of radio from ... our 'allies' as long as we can? Once they know of its existence, we will have irretrievably lost an advantage. They will want its secrets and we will have difficulty withholding them."

Taken aback, Kurokawa lowered his voice. "But what good is it to keep the secret? *We* have no one to talk to!"

"That may not always be the case! Besides, we have two aircraft of our own. The spotting planes! They have radios!"

Amagi had lost one of her spotting planes in the battle that brought her here—ironically when a Japanese dive bomber went out of control and crashed directly atop her amidships ten-inch turret, destroying it as well as the plane and catapult on top of it. But she still had two planes left. Both were obsolete, short-range biplanes. Nakajima Type 95 E8Ns, to be precise. They were single-engine affairs and carried one huge float under the fuselage and a couple of smaller ones under the wings. They were good, reliable, low-maintenance airplanes with all-metal structures covered by fabric. The two-man crew sat in individual open cockpits where they would never have to worry about being too comfortable to keep their eyes open. Perfect for observation planes. Probably the best kind of planes they could have right now, since they were so simple. But they were certainly not fighters.

Kurokawa still seethed constantly over the loss of their much more capable plane, the Aichi Type Zero E13A1 that had been turned into flaming confetti along with quite a lot of other very useful equipment, weapons, ammunition, and fuel—Kurokawa didn't consider the men—when the crippled plane smashed into his ship. Okada mourned every scratch *Amagi* suffered and every life she lost, but practically speaking, under the circumstances, he'd trade the Type Zero for the Type 95s any day.

"True, but we have hardly any fuel for them," the captain snapped bitterly. He waved his hand. "Enough for a few short flights. Most of our reserve was destroyed by the Americans' cowardly torpedo attack . . . And That Imbecile Who Crashed Into My Ship!" The entire bridge watch tensed for a moment, waiting to see if the captain's loud imprecations toward the dead pilot would manage to snare anyone else. Remarkably, they sometimes did.

"But the Americans obviously *do* have aviation fuel—and probably fuel oil as well!" Okada interjected. "It should have been easy for them to get. Is that not why we were intent on conquering the Dutch East Indies in the first place?"

"We shall still!" roared the captain and Sato recoiled. "What would you have me do? *Beg* the Americans for *fuel*?!" Kurokawa seethed. "The situation may have changed somewhat, but I still have my orders! To assist in the capture of the Emperor's objective!"

Sato couldn't stop himself. "But, Captain, the Emperor is not *here*! Assisting the Grik in *their* objective would not, I think, please His Majesty! They are . . . hideous barbarians! Inhuman monsters! The Americans at least are people!" He lowered his voice, hoping the captain wouldn't explode. He desperately wanted to crack Kurokawa's apparently maniacal shell.

"I think we should speak to them—before we help the Grik wipe them out! I must tell you, Captain, I fear this course we've embarked upon is without honor! It's not of the Way! I implore you, sir, let us detach ourselves from this unwholesome alliance! We could tell the Grik we've had another breakdown—they would surely believe that—and when we have only a few escorts, we could easily break away!"

Sato braced himself for the hurricane of rage that was sure to follow his outburst. Instead, Kurokawa only stared at him, his expression cold as ice. "Commander Okada. Your suggestion regarding the radio is well taken. I will endeavor to relate our suspicions about the enemy base without disclosing that secret. But hear me! The Empire of Japan is *at war* with the United States of America, and that war will be prosecuted whenever and wherever our forces meet! I have no illusions that the Grik are our friends, but they are not our enemies either. I will use their assistance to achieve our ultimate objective, and that objective is the destruction of any American or allied force within the Malay Barrier. Is that understood?" Sato could only nod. "Good," continued Kurokawa in a mounting voice, "because according to this Kaufman, the Grik have already destroyed one of the destroyers that crippled my ship and that leaves only one for me! I *will have that ship* if I have to chase it around the *world*! Is that understood? I will capture it or send it to the bottom. It makes no difference to me. That is what my orders prescribe and *my* honor demands! And if you utter one more suggestion that I should treat with the enemies of the Emperor, I will have you executed for treason!"

With that, Captain Kurokawa spun on his heel and exited the bridge. Sato Okada could only stare after him, shaking with frustration and terror.

Captain David Kaufman, U.S. Army Air Corps, sat on an inverted bucket in a darkened compartment somewhere deep in the Japanese ship. He had nothing to read, nothing to do with his hands. Nothing at all to divert his mind during the endless hours of solitude between the infrequent visits of his captors. It was dank and stuffy and smelled of old paint and oily machinery. The deck beneath his feet vibrated slightly and there was a dull roar from the engines, although he didn't know if he was forward or aft of the engineering spaces. If he hadn't already been out of his mind, the sensory deprivation and boredom would certainly have done the trick. All he could do was sit on the bucket, alone, and relive the horrible memories of the events that brought him to this place.

If only he'd left well enough alone. It was clear from his most recent interrogation that *Walker* was still afloat. If he hadn't seized control of *Mahan*, she'd have rejoined her sister and he would be safe among his own kind. Safe for a while, at least, he corrected. He'd seen the size of the Grik armada when the Japanese "rescued" him from the Grik commander. Even without *Amagi*, there was no hope for *Walker* now. He must have been totally out of his mind when the Japanese came. Hunger, terror, and the shock of his circumstances had left him a jibbering wreck. He'd been feverish when he arrived in Colombo and he'd almost thought he imagined *Amagi* in the bay, but when he saw the Japanese officers from where he was chained, naked, at the base of Tsalka's throne, he was sure the madness had entirely overwhelmed him. After everything else that had happened to him, to see *Japs* there too . . . He fought like an animal, slashing with his teeth, his fingernails—anything he could use. Either they'd kill him or he'd wake up from his nightmare at last. Knocked unconscious, he was brought aboard *Amagi*.

As his senses returned, he was given clothes and fed, and for a brief time he clung to his Japanese guards like saviors. They kicked him and cuffed him and treated him worse than an animal, but he didn't think they'd eat him. For a while, that was enough. Then the questions started. In spite of the fact that they had rescued him from the Grik, a distant sense of propriety made him try to reveal only his name, rank, and serial number. After all, his saviors were still the enemy, weren't they? His questioners beat him. He was so far gone physically and mentally, and so glad they'd saved him from the Grik, he almost felt that he deserved the torment—felt almost guilty that he wanted to keep things from them. His resistance was short-lived and he told them everything he knew.

Mahan was lost. She must be. Most of her crew had been with him, and then the other Grik ships went after her. Shorthanded as she was, and in her condition, there was no way she could have repelled the thousands that rounded the southern point of Nias and headed toward the anchorage where he left her. Everyone who'd been aboard her was now certainly dead and it was all his fault. His only slight consolation was that *Mahan* had apparently burned and sunk. At least the lizards hadn't gotten their hands on her.

He told them everything he knew about *Walker* too, but he didn't know enough to satisfy them, so the beatings resumed with even greater vigor than before. He must have almost died. He remembered little of what happened, only that the torture suddenly stopped and there was an officer in the compartment. He passed out. Later, he remembered being carried to his cell and he was even visited by a doctor. Slowly, he healed. The days passed without notice and he managed to keep some idea of the time only by the meals they brought him. Therefore he knew that about a week had passed before he had his first visit by the officer.

Since then the officer had appeared several times, never giving his name, only his rank—commander. But he was solicitous and kind and he was someone to talk to. Twice when he came, they'd blindfolded him and taken him to the Grik. He was terrified that they were giving him back to them, but they only used him to translate messages that the Grik and the Japanese captain passed to one another. He'd learned quite a lot about the situation that way, not that it would do him any good. Besides, he'd been so relieved when they returned him to his cell that he found he forgot much of what he'd translated. Even in spite of his fear, however, Kaufman yearned for the man to come.

With a rasp of gears and a metallic *clunk,* the hatch swung wide and the compartment was bathed in the light of the passageway. It hurt his eyes and he squinted as a man stepped inside. Another light came on, from a single bulb overhead. A switch in the passageway activated it. The officer said something in Japanese and the hatch was closed and secured. As always, now that they were alone, the officer wrinkled his nose at the stench from the other bucket, in the corner. Kaufman didn't even notice the smell anymore. Still squinting, he hastily stood.

"Good morning, Captain Kaufman," said the man in pleasant, if badly accented, English.

"Is it morning?" Kaufman asked eagerly.

"Yes. Just dawn." Sato paused, watching the nervous twitch that had taken control of the prisoner's pale, waxy face. That was new. "I have not come to take you to the Grik," he hastily assured him. "You are well?"

Much of Kaufman's tension ebbed, but the twitch remained. "I am, thank God. I mean, thank God . . ." He shuddered, and Sato nodded understanding.

"I too am glad," he muttered. "But I have to ask you a question."

Kaufman nodded and straightened his shoulders. "Of course."

"Yesterday, our . . . the fleet we are a part of was involved in action with an enemy ship . . ." Kaufman tensed again and his expression was one of anguish. "It wasn't the American destroyer," Sato mercifully assured him. "It was a captured Grik vessel that the enemy had supplied with cannons. They were most effective. Many Grik ships were destroyed." He paused and watched to see how Kaufman reacted to that. He wasn't surprised to see a fragile smile and he had to struggle not to match it. "Regrettably, from an intelligence standpoint, the ship was destroyed. Nothing was recovered, but there is testimony from the survivors on nearby ships that there was one human, perhaps two, on board the enemy ship. We can only conclude they were countrymen of yours." Sato hesitated when he saw the prisoner's stricken look. "For that, you have my condolences. What I must ask you, however, is whether or not you were aware of the existence of an American flying-boat?"

Kaufman's eyes went wide and, if anything, his twitch became more violent. He began scratching the left side of his face unconsciously. "Well, yes, I am . . . I mean, I was. You mean you've seen it?" Sato nodded and Captain Kaufman closed his eyes and smiled with genuine relief. "My God. So Mallory made it after all!" He stopped and looked at Commander Okada. "We found it on the beach. The plane, that is. It was shot up and half sunk, but Mallory and a couple other fellas got it flying. The Grik nearly got them! Anyway, I sent it on to Ceylon to bring out an escort for *Mahan*." He stopped and his face was stricken. "But he couldn't have gone to Ceylon . . . could he?"

"Why did you never mention the plane before?"

Kaufman glanced vacantly around. "Nobody asked. I just figured it was lost. The Griks that got after it saw it that day." He looked imploringly at Sato. "I'm sorry. I would have told you, I swear! I just never thought it was still around!" He sat back down on his bucket and rubbed his twitching face, staring at Sato through his fingers with red-rimmed eyes. "Please," he whispered. "Don't beat me anymore."

Sato stared down at the prisoner, sickened. As much with Kaufman as with himself. "You won't be beaten," he said. He glanced back at the hatch to make sure it was still dogged. "This plane," he said, "has a radio." It wasn't a question, but a statement of fact. "So too does the American destroyer. If I could arrange it so you had access to a radio yourself, could you contact either of them?"

Kaufman looked down at the floor. "I don't have a codebook," he said quietly.

"That doesn't matter. If I am able to arrange a radio, you would be able to speak in the clear."

"What would you want me to say?"

Sato shook his head. "I do not know yet. That would depend on a number of things . . . What I want to know now is can you do it? Do you think they would listen to you?"

"I doubt Reddy would," he said grimly, and Okada recognized the name of the destroyer's commander. "I doubt he trusts me. I know he doesn't like me. Mallory, though . . ."

"Mallory is the pilot of the flying-boat?"

"Yes. At least he was. I think I could talk to him. Maybe he'd talk to Reddy . . ." Kaufman looked up at Sato. "Why?"

"Perhaps no reason. But let us keep this between ourselves." He waited until he saw Kaufman nod. "In the meantime, is there anything I can do for you?"

For a long moment, the aviator didn't reply. He just stared at Sato with astonished eyes. Finally, he spoke.

"Light. Leave the light on, please."

Sato nodded. "Anything else?"

Kaufman blinked and looked vaguely around the compartment. "Something to read," he pleaded. "I don't care what it is."

Big Sal left at dawn. Slowly, majestically, the giant wings spread and the sweeps were stowed. Matt watched her go with tired eyes and de-cidedly mixed emotions. *Big Sal* or Keje had always been there, some-where nearby, almost since they came to this world, and he knew he'd miss them and worry about their safety. *Aracca* Home was being loaded now, and in the distance he saw the first smoke of the fires that would consume B'mbaado City. He realized with regret that he'd never even visited the Orphan Queen's palace, and now it was being destroyed. At least not all of it would be lost. Several feluccas had been detailed to take away B'mbaado's greatest treasures. He wished the same could have been done for Aryaal, but Rasik still hoarded them to himself, locked in the royal palace. Matt realized that the vengeance he'd chosen had contributed to that loss, but lives were more important. His conscience wouldn't suffer much when all was said and done.

His coffee cup was empty and Juan was nowhere in sight. Garrett had the watch and so he decided to try and find some, and maybe grab something to eat. That reminded him he'd been too busy to check on Earl Lanier and he grimaced at the thought. Sandra had told him the cook would be fine. The shaft hadn't penetrated beyond his impressive layer of fat. But Matt should have checked.

Thinking of injuries . . . Experimentally, he tensed a muscle in his shoulder to see what he could get away with. To his surprise, it seemed considerably better. Time to pester Sandra again about getting the dressings removed. He was sick of running around trying to do everything with one hand. He knew Sandra was asleep, though. For now, he'd leave her alone.

First get something to eat, and then go aft. He figured it wouldn't hurt to see for himself how the work on the propeller was shaping up. Progress there had him more worried than he cared to admit. They'd finally been forced to lay off work last night when the flashies tore through a second sail. Spanky himself was in the water and they nearly got him. Hopefully they'd make up for lost time in the light of day. He didn't like the idea of the world falling on top of them when they had a half-installed screw. With two engines, three boilers, and a full bunker of fuel, he would feel a lot more confident in the face of what was coming.

For the moment at least, everything was well in hand on shore, and the evacuation had taken on a more orderly atmosphere. The panic of the night before had subsided, despite the fact that time was increasingly short. Perhaps it was the daylight that eased people's fears. *Walker*'s crew was making preparations for getting under way and, except for the propeller, there were no difficulties in that regard. For the first time in longer than he could remember he faced no pressing decisions that he alone could make. They'd all been made already, and now there was nothing left to do but watch while others carried them out and hope it wasn't all for nothing. It left him somewhat at a loss. He couldn't shake the feeling there was something left undone. Pondering his unease, he descended to the wardroom. There he found Courtney Bradford, alone and sleeping in a chair at the table. His head was tilted back and his mouth was open. Loud snores filled the compartment.

There was a coffee cup on the table, but by the smell of the room, coffee hadn't been in it. Matt sighed and poured some lukewarm coffee for himself from a carafe. Then he opened the portholes on either side of the wardroom to let the warm morning air circulate within. Bradford's snore caught in his throat and he opened his eyes and blinked. Matt sat across from him and emptied the carafe into the Australian's cup. Then he gestured at it.

"That's got to stop, Courtney," he scolded him gently. "It sets a bad example."

"'m not in the Navy," Bradford grumbled. "And even if I was, it would be the Royal Australian Navy, which, I might remind you, certainly does not persecute the occasional tot."

"Your 'tots' are no longer occasional. Alcohol's not allowed on U.S. Navy ships, but so far I've turned a blind eye because of your . . . unusual status . . . and because, until lately, you've been discreet." He rubbed his eyes and cleared his throat. "I need you sober, Mr. Bradford. I need you sober and clearheaded all the time. We're all going to need our wits to survive." He smiled slightly. "And I've come to rely heavily on yours."

Bradford snorted and sipped from his cup. Grimacing, he set it aside. "I'm not much good to anyone, I'm afraid." He spoke with a still muzzy voice. "Sometimes I think there is really not much point. No matter what we do, we are continually faced with ever greater obstacles." He covered his face with his hands. "I grow so weary and . . . I miss my son quite dreadfully, you know."

Matt leaned back. Bradford had never spoken of a son. Like most of them, he hadn't said much at all about what he'd left behind. Bradford shook his head and sat up straighter. "Oh, he's alive, for all I know. Flying Hurricanes for the RAAF, in England." He frowned. "For all I know. The trouble is, I don't know for sure and I never, ever will." He glared at Matt. "We Australians still have somewhat closer ties to the mother country than you Yanks, and even though we were considerably farther away, the threat posed by Hitler struck a little closer to home. My son volunteered to fight against him almost a year and a half ago." He glanced down at his cup and took another reluctant sip. "Adar always talks about the 'greater threat'—we all do, and we've certainly been proved right in this instance. But while my son and most of the rest of the world were confronting the Nazis, you Yanks were busy antagonizing the Japs."

He paused, and turned visibly inward. Then he held up his hand. "I apologize," he said at last. "That was unfair. I was about to ask why you should care a damn what the Japs did in China when I recognized my own hypocrisy. Why should England? Or why should anyone care about Poland, you could say. Perhaps I am a bigot, after all, although I've always loved the Malays. And now the Lemurians . . . God help me, I do love the little buggers . . ." He stifled a hiccup and coughed.

"I suppose I have at times resented you Yanks for not helping my son fight the Nazis. That made it all very personal, don't you see? Of course you do. But the Japs are just as bad and they are physically much closer to home. What they did in Nanking . . . They actually bombed Australia, did you know?" Matt nodded patiently. One of *Walker*'s sisters, the *Peary*, had been sunk by the Japanese in Port Darwin. "So I suppose it makes little difference," Bradford mumbled. "You Yanks are fighting Hitler now—or were—whatever. My point is, the reason that's the case is that the Jappos and the Nazis are allies. You said you couldn't understand why the Japs would help the Grik? If they are on the same side as Hitler, there's no telling what they might do."

"That's a good point, Mr. Bradford, although war can certainly force you to make some awfully unusual friends. Uncle Joe's no saint."

"True, but Stalin shared with us the dubious distinction of being one of the Attacked, not the Attacker. In this instance at least. I won't belabor Poland, or mention Finland for the moment." He crossed his arms on the table and laid his head down. He wore no hat, and a long wisp of thinning hair trailed down almost into his cup. "I just miss my boy," he said at last.

"I understand," Matt said around a lump that had formed in his own throat. "I miss my folks. I wonder sometimes how they are and what they're doing. As far as they know, *we're* dead. It's pretty tough some-times." Bradford raised his head and looked at him with red-rimmed eyes. "Everyone aboard must feel the same way," Matt continued. He gestured at the cup, and by inference, what had been in it before. "But we can't find solace in that. If we do, we lose." He shrugged. "We might lose anyway, but we owe it to our people here on *Walker,* as well as our new friends, to do our very best, and wallowing in booze and self-pity's not the way." Bradford's eyes flared with anger, but Matt continued on. "The war back home will be won or lost—there's nothing we can do about that. I hope your son survives, but if he doesn't, he'll have died for a good cause that he actually chose. In the meantime, we have our own war to fight, against an enemy that's just as bad as Hitler—maybe worse in a way—and our odds of survival are even worse as well. But we have to go on—not only for ourselves but for the people who trust us. Human and Lemurian."

Bradford's anger had disappeared and he sat staring at his hands. "What do you want from me?" he asked quietly.

"Ease off on your 'tots,' " Matt replied. "Other than that, what I want you to do—what I need you to do—is to keep on being the same cheer-ful, irreverent, awkward—brilliant—pain in the ass you've been since the day you came aboard. The men—our allies too—like you, Court-ney, and they count on you in ways you can't imagine. I do too. If they think you've lost hope, then they might too." He stood.

"I came down here wondering what I was forgetting, what I've ne-glected to do with everything else that's been going on. I just realized what it was. Sometimes, even when we're in a group, people get to feel-ing like they're all alone. It's like you're sitting on the track and there's a freight train headed your way and there's nothing you can do to stop it. All you can do is look around and hope *somebody* knows what the hell they're doing. Even while the train's bearing down, you gain strength from your comrades, not only from their courage but from the real-ization that you're not the only one that's scared to death. At the same time, you need to believe that the one person you hope and pray has all the answers, really, really does." He smiled. "And so, I'm going to take a leisurely stroll. Walk around the ship and look at parts of it I haven't seen with my own eyes in weeks—and I'm going to *act* like I've got a pair of aces up my sleeve."

Bradford stood as well. His face was apologetic, and he toyed with the cup on the table, not meeting Matt's eyes. "What can I do?"

Matt shrugged. "Like I said, pretty much the same. Be seen. Do an autopsy on a skuggik on top of one of the torpedo mounts, for all I care. Just talk strange and say weird stuff." He grinned. "Be yourself."

"If you really think it'll help . . ."

Matt nodded. "If Jim Ellis were here, he'd be doing much the same thing. It's kind of the executive officer's job. But he's not and I don't think Larry Dowden can pull it off."

"Why not? He seems a capable young officer."

"Oh, he's that, but he's way too honest." Matt's grin began to fade. "Spanky and the Bosun'll keep things from falling apart, but if we have to tangle with *Amagi* again, they'll need all the help they can get. In more ways than one."

Walking slowly aft, Matt offered smiles and encouragement to the busy, hardworking destroyermen. As he passed under the amidships gun platform, he noticed Silva putting some of the Lemurian crew through gunnery drill on one of the four-inch-fifties overhead. The 'Cats bent themselves to the task with a will, enthusiastically traversing the gun and chittering to one another in their own tongue—as well as a broken English. Silva's bellowed instructions and threats sounded apoplectic, but there was a satisfied grin on his face. Passing by the galley, Matt snatched up the last sandwich from a platter full of crumbs just as Ray Mertz turned with a tray heaped with fresh ones he'd just made. He set it down hastily and wiped his hands on his shirt.

"Morning, Mertz. How's Lanier today?"

A chair groaned inside the galley as a great weight lifted from it. "Sufferin' sore, Captain," Lanier said around a mouthful of food as he appeared in the window. "Sufferin' sore." He gestured at the greasy bandage around his middle that could be seen through his open shirt.

"But not too sore to feed the men, I see," Matt observed.

Lanier took on a pious look. "No, sir. Never. Ravenous bastards, too, sir—beggin' your pardon. Never a word of thanks neither, but I toil away regardless." He gave a murderous look to Mertz. "Whaddaya mean, givin' that stale damn thing to the captain? Especially after Rodriguez . . ." He paused, catching himself. Matt was already chewing a bite.

"What did Rodriguez do to it?" he finally asked when he swallowed. Lanier looked stricken.

"He, uh, knocked it off onto the deck." He cringed. Matt looked down for a moment where the sandwich had probably lain and let the tension build. Then he chuckled.

"Must not have been there long, or the roaches would have carried it off." He took another bite.

"Uh, no, sir, Captain! Not long," Lanier said with evident relief. He speared Mertz with another seething glare. Then he turned back to Matt and proudly beckoned him to behold the glorious pile of newly constructed sandwiches as though he was displaying a work of art. "There you go, Captain. Take your pick! Eat two! You're too skinny as it is, if you don't mind me sayin', sir."

"Don't mind if I do," Matt said, selecting another sandwich from the pile. Earl beamed. Unhurried, Matt transferred it to his still-immobilized left hand and, munching on the first one, he continued aft.

"You idiot!" Earl cursed quietly and slapped Mertz on the side of the head. "It's a good thing the captain likes my cookin' or you'd be in a hell of a mess."

"But you *told* me to pick it up!" Ray protested.

"I didn't tell you to give it to the captain!"

Matt heard the exchange and a genuine smile replaced the false one he had worn. *In spite of everything,* he thought again, *some things never change.* He passed the number one torpedo mount, where some 'Cat and human torpedomen were checking the pressure in the air flasks and accumulators. The flasks had been empty for the last few months— which was customary when the torpedoes weren't needed. Now they were full. Sandison had asked him that morning if he could perform quarterly maintenance on the operable fish and Matt agreed, so long as all three would be ready when *Walker* got under way. By the time he reached the number four mount, he could already hear Spanky's curses from the fantail. The engineer and the Bosun were supervising their respective divisions in—hopefully—the final process of installing the propeller. Gray's men were trying to keep the sail tight against the hull so no flashies could get past and Spanky's snipes were controlling the now submerged screw with taglines. A heavy cable descended into the water from a makeshift boom, down between the supports for the propeller guard, and Dean Laney was reluctantly preparing to go back into the water. Astern, a far more orderly procession than the night before was mounting the ramp onto *Aracca*'s deck and a smoky haze had descended from the nearby burning city.

It was already warming up and Spanky wiped sweat from his brow. He was vigorously chewing a quid of something that caused a distinct bulge in his cheek. "What's that in your mouth?" Matt asked.

Surprised, Spanky turned and saw the captain. "Good morning, Skipper," he said and saluted with a grimy hand. He shifted his chaw speculatively. "I'm not rightly sure. Something Chack came up with. He said it was 'courtesy of King Rasik.' They use it for some kind of holy stink-weed or something hereabouts. It looks like a yellow tomato leaf, but it sorta tastes like tobacco." He shrugged. "Anyway, some of his boys were poking around near the palace and found a warehouse full of the stuff. They sent down what must be a ton of it last night."

"Has it made anybody sick?"

"Silva's been chewing it steady, ever since it came aboard, and he's okay so far."

Matt chuckled. "I'm surprised Silva would chew anything Chack recommended—after last time."

Spanky joined him in a laugh. "So you knew about that?"

"Of course." Matt grinned.

Chack had Silva chewing every dead leaf he could find, trying to find some replacement for his precious tobacco. The process left Dennis ill enough to waste a shell on an easy shot against a Grik ship. Silva did not endure ridicule gladly, and Matt was certain that was when the scheme between Risa and Silva—to embarrass Chack—had been hatched.

"Maybe with a real, good-faith tobacco substitute, Silva will forgive Chack and quit pretending to carry on with his sister. I need Chack sharp, and I know that drives him nuts."

Spanky nodded vigorously. It drove him nuts too and he was almost sure Silva *wasn't* pretending. "Order 'em to stay away from each other," he urged.

"Can't. Other than Chack, the 'Cats don't think it's a big deal even if they are . . ." He shuddered. "And I can't start giving orders against frat-ernization between our people. We need each other too much." Matt fumed. "Besides, then that bastard Silva would have won. He would've forced me to call his bluff. No. He can put more significance and mean-ing in an arched eyebrow—" He snorted a laugh, his face red, and shook his head. He gestured at the work with his second sandwich in his hand. "How's it going?"

"Slower than I'd hoped," Spanky replied, glad to change the subject. "But we'll have it shipped by this afternoon. The screw is almost in po-sition. Once it's there, we slide it on the shaft and bolt it down. Easy as pie in dry dock, but a little more involved under the circumstances."

"That's cutting it pretty close. If the enemy scout ahead, some of them could be here by tonight."

Spanky's expression grew solemn. "Yes, sir. We're going as fast as we can."

Matt patted him on the arm. "Of course you are." He looked ashore, at the teeming mass of Lemurians waiting to board *Aracca*. The haze was thicker toward Aryaal, although the massive fires of the night be-fore had dwindled. To the northeast, B'mbaado City was engulfed in flames. It looked like hell, and it was all so very familiar. Less than a year ago, they'd steamed out of what the maps showed as this very bay in the face of an overwhelming invasion. Of course, somehow that happened in an entirely different world. Regardless, the sense of impending doom was very much the same. Also, fantastically, it was once again the Japanese they were running from. It was as though *Walker* was condemned to repeat the same event in increasingly warped realities, over and over until the end of time. Or until fate finally caught up with her.

Spanky followed his gaze and then spoke more quietly so those nearby couldn't hear. "Would we be running if it weren't for the Japs?" he asked, reading Matt's mind. His voice was bitter. "The boys are tired of running. They were used to winning for a change."

Matt nodded. "I know. It was a good feeling, wasn't it?" He sighed. "Yeah, we'd still have to run. There's too many of them this time, even without *Amagi*. If we make it back to Baalkpan we'll have a chance." He raised his voice. "Keep up the good work. When you get finished, this old bucket'll be the fastest thing in the world again. The Japs are down to eight knots, after the last time they tangled with us. If they want a rematch, we'll run rings around 'em!"

There were tired but determined growls of approval, and Matt grinned at the men's spirit. Inside, he was sick with dread.

A little after noon, Matt watched *Aracca* fade into the haze to the east. They were cutting it close indeed. *Nerracca* was now alongside the pier and was quickly filling with the increasingly nervous refugees. They would have to pack them in tighter than ever before, but Tassat-Ay-Aracca assured him they'd find a place for everyone. When last he checked, Spanky'd said the screw was finally in place. Now all that remained was to bolt it down—a laborious and dangerous underwater procedure, but one that wouldn't take much longer. All the feluccas were gone and the last company of Chack's Marines was marching down the harbor road. They would come aboard *Walker*.

Alone in his palace now, except for his most fanatical followers, Rasik-Alcas, king of Aryaal, continued to rave and threaten and occasionally even plead for his people not to leave him. None of the few who remained on the pier could hear him, but it wouldn't have made any difference if they had.

Ben Mallory was up, scouting the enemy approach. He'd sent a warning a few minutes earlier that advance elements of the enemy fleet, a dozen ships, were less than fifty miles away. The rest seemed to be coming on hard not too far behind. Hundreds of ships could be seen in the distance, more spread out than before since they were no longer confined between Belitung and Borneo.

Matt ordered Mallory to fly back in the direction of Aryaal until he was out of sight of the lizards, and then proceed toward Baalkpan. Nakja-Mur's city would need constant reports, and Matt wanted to resume direct communications with Baalkpan. In case the Japanese were able to find their direction by radio, however, he forbade any further transmissions by the PBY except in an emergency. Once home, they could monitor *Walker*'s transmissions. If the enemy still didn't know about Baalkpan, Matt didn't want to tell them now.

Every day they had to prepare was precious. He even toyed with the idea of broadcasting continuously from *Walker* while steaming away down the Lesser Sunda Islands. Then they could go silent and run up around Celebes and down to Baalkpan from the northeast. It would lengthen the enemy's lines of supply and leave them no idea where their quarry was, but it was an awfully long way and Matt wasn't sure he even had the fuel to do it. Besides, they'd have no way of knowing if the enemy took the bait. Better to stick with the original plan and just try to get around them undetected. That was going to be hard. Even if she left right now, *Nerracca* would risk discovery by the advance force. The greatest danger of that would come after dark, however, and maybe then the massive ship could avoid being seen.

"Marines are coming aboard now, Skipper," Lieutenant Garrett reported, "and *Nerracca* says she'll be ready to shove off within the hour."

"Anything new from Spanky?"

"At least another hour, maybe more. They had to pull Laney out. He was nearly unconscious. The flashies must've figured out something's in the sail and they're beating the hell out of it."

Matt nodded and winced. He remembered Laney's bruises from the last time. "Very well. Have *Nerracca* get under way as soon as she's able. Don't wait for us. We'll catch up. We can move faster than she can even with only one engine if we have to."

Garrett shifted uncomfortably. "We'll risk losing the screw if it's not bolted on tight, Skipper."

"I'm aware of that, Mr. Garrett. I'm sure Spanky is too. But we aren't going to bug him anymore. If it comes down to it and we have to move before he's ready, then we will. I'd rather risk losing the screw than the ship."

Dennis Silva had made some dumb choices in his life, but this one took the cake. He'd volunteered to go in the water and finish the job after Laney was hauled back aboard, but even then he was less than enthusiastic. Laney looked like they'd dragged him out of a Shanghai bar after he told a dozen Royal Marines the king was queer. He was black and blue with bruises again, and at first he could barely move. It was obvious that swimming with the flashies, even with the sail as protection, wasn't going to be a walk in the park. There was nothing for it, though. When Laney finally opened his eyes, they settled challengingly on Silva. Not a word was spoken, but the implication was clear. The snipes had done their part. Now it was the deck-ape's turn. As one of the only said "apes" qualified in a suit, Silva had to pick up the slack. There was *no way* the mighty Dennis Silva would admit he was afraid to do anything a damn snipe would do, and as soon as the helmet sealed out the smoky air of the harbor, over the side he went. That was less than half an hour ago and already he was beginning to think that a fight with a dozen Marines would have been a good trade.

Even over the sound of the bubbles and his breathing, he could *hear* the bony-headed flashies thumping the canvas around him. Occasionally, when he strayed too close to the sail, one struck close enough to hit him. It felt like a pile driver. It was like being hit by a dud torpedo, he imagined, except the flashies didn't weigh as much. After two or three such blows, he thought he had a broken rib. One blow struck him on the elbow and he dropped one of the precious baseball-sized nuts. He had to go down into the bottom of the sail to retrieve it, and it took forever because every time he reached for the damn thing, a fish would strike nearby and launch it. He finally got it only because it was literally bounced into his left hand by a strike. His right arm was still numb from his shoulder to his fingertips.

"Funny bone, my ass," he grumbled. Raising himself back up on a level with the screw, he began threading the nut onto the final remaining stud. Nearby in the murk hung a giant wrench suspended by a rope from above. With the nut screwed down as far as he could turn it with the clumsy gloves of the diving suit, he reached up for the wrench. A blow from directly behind drove him facefirst into the screw. He grunted from the pain that spread between his shoulder blades and he had to blink to clear the tears that sprang to his eyes. He was also nearly deafened by the bell-like *clang* of the helmet striking the bronze propeller. "Son of a bitch!" he muttered through clenched teeth. "I think it was a Buick, officer!"

He grabbed the wrench again and began to tighten the nut. Another off-center hit in his back drove the wind out of him for a moment, but he doggedly continued his task. The fish were becoming more aggressive. They'd been doing this long enough—the flashies had to be convinced there was something in the sail. Something good to eat. Or maybe the sound or the bubbles stirred them up. Whatever the case, Silva was ready to get out of the water.

The nut was tight at last and he grabbed the wrench with both hands and heaved down as hard as he could. "Done, dammit!" he gasped.

Suddenly, a bright, silvery-shape about four feet long ricocheted off the side of his helmet and drove headfirst into one of the propeller blades with a distinctive muffled *gong*. For an instant, the hideous thing just hung there, stunned by the impact with the ship. Silva was just as stunned with shock and terror that one of the things was in there with him. Then it began to recover. Quickly, he grabbed it by the tail and yanked it toward him. Catching it by the head, he sank his fingers into its eyes on each side of its skull and held on for dear life when it began to thrash. It was incredibly powerful and it took all his strength to keep its gnashing jaws away from him. He didn't dare turn it loose. Instead, he grasped his hose and yanked it frantically as hard as he could. That was the signal to pull him up. Even as he began to rise, it dawned on him with a flash of terror that if one of the damn things had gotten in, so could others. The seconds between that realization and the instant his head broke water were the most viscerally frightening of his life.

He clenched his eyes shut until he was hauled entirely out of the water and he lay crouching on the fantail beside the depth charge rack. Slowly his breathing returned to normal and he began to wonder why no one had cracked his helmet. The fish thrashed spastically in his grasp. Oh. With some difficulty, he stood and took two steps over to the little three-inch antiaircraft gun and, with all his might, he bashed the fish against the barrel again and again. Finally, when its thrashing had been reduced to a faint twitch, Silva threw it hard against the deck. Only then did someone venture close enough to help him remove the helmet.

He looked at the shocked, wide-eyed expressions all around him. Some began to edge closer. Spanky was above him, leaning on the aft deckhouse rail, chew in his mouth. He just shook his head. Then Silva saw that Laney had retreated as far aft as he possibly could, until he stood wedged between the depth charge racks where they angled together near the jackstaff. He still had a blanket draped across his bruised shoulders and his jaw hung slack.

"There you go, Laney!" Silva bellowed, managing to leer at the machinist mate and gesturing grandly at the fish. "I brung you a present!"

By the time the sail was jettisoned and *Walker* was ready to get under way, *Nerracca* was a blur in the smoke as she worked downwind across the bay. Black puffs of smoke rose from *Walker*'s numbers three and four stacks and joined the baleful pall drifting eastward from the two gutted cities. The pier was almost empty except for the line handlers, and even they quickly deserted it when their chores were done. Only Chack and Safir Maraan, Queen Protector of B'mbaado, remained behind. She'd insisted on being the last of those leaving to set foot on this land, even if she now stood on Aryaalan soil. It was the symbolism of the act, Matt knew, as he watched the pair staring across the bay toward the flames that roared above B'mbaado City. Rolak had wanted to stay, but the bulk of his troops had embarked on *Big Sal* and Matt wanted him with them. He and Queen Maraan had become very close, but she had a functioning staff to ride herd on her people. Rolak didn't. He would have to create one on the fly. And so the Orphan Queen remained behind, the last representative of both their peoples. Gently, Chack touched her arm and with him in the lead so she could, in fact, be the last, they finally came aboard. Once behind the railing, she leaned against it, arms outstretched, as if reaching for her island home. In an almost singsong chant that hushed all chatter around her, she spoke:

"I shall not forget you, Haakar-Faask, or those whom you shall lead. No matter how long it takes, even if it costs my life, this I swear to you: I shall return!"

Slowly, the breeze and the ebbing tide moved the ship into the bay. The new propeller got an immediate trial when Matt gave the order: "Port engine, ahead one-third. Right ten degrees rudder." The deck began to vibrate under their feet, and everyone noticed immediately that the vibration was slightly different than it had ever been before. Not bad, just different. An uncertain smile crossed Dowden's face and he looked at Matt with his eyebrows raised. It was as if the propeller had brought a little of *Mahan*'s personality along with it and *Walker*'s distant sister was somehow helping her escape the relentless enemy.

"All ahead one-third," Matt commanded when *Walker*'s nose swung around to point away from the smoke-dimmed sun approaching the distant peaks of Java.

"Recommend course zero eight zero," Larry Dowden said.

"Very well. Make your course zero eight zero. Increase speed slowly to two-thirds." Matt was still testing the "feel" of the new screw. The blower noise began to increase. Unseen, Sandra Tucker had climbed the ladder behind him.

"Request permission to come on the bridge," she inquired as softly as she could and still be heard. Ever since she'd helped Matt prepare to storm Aryaal, she'd been somewhat distant. More proper, but cool.

"Permission granted," he said and she walked to the starboard bridgewing not far from where he stood. She leaned on the rail, staring aft. After a moment Matt joined her.

"I'll take care of Queen Maraan," she volunteered. "God, did you see them just now? I thought I would bawl."

"I was hoping you would," Matt said quietly. "With Rick dead, and Alan and Steve in Baalkpan, she can have their quarters. How many attendants did she bring aboard?"

"Only three. She understood the accommodations on *Walker* are less opulent than she's accustomed to." A ghost of a smile touched Sandra's lips.

"Well, I guess they can hot-bunk, or maybe we can cram a cot in there."

Sandra nodded. "I'll figure something out," she said in a low, sad voice. She stared down at the water for a long moment as it swished by below. "I feel like somebody I was trying to save just died on my operating table."

"I know what you mean," Matt agreed.

She sighed. "Maybe you really do." She was quiet again as he stood there beside her. "I'm sorry for the way I acted before you went into the city," she said at last.

"Nothing to apologize for."

"Yes, there is. I acted very badly and there's no excuse at all. I understood why you had to go into Aryaal—why everyone did—but I was mad because you were going to risk your life. And like any idiot girl, I took my anger out on you—the person I was most concerned about." She coughed a little from the smoke. "Not very professional, or even very adult. But I couldn't help myself. I nursed you back to health after your terrible wounds, and there you were, about to run yourself through the meat grinder all over again." She managed a slight smile. "It all seemed so ungrateful. Thank God it wasn't a meat grinder . . . this time."

"I'm not ungrateful," he murmured. Sandra shook her head.

"I know that. That's not the point." She glanced quickly over her shoulder at the bridge watch and lowered her voice even further. "Look, I know we had a deal, that we wouldn't let our feelings show—and I know, deep down, it's the right thing to do. But sometimes it's so hard.

Particularly when I've seen you shattered and had to put you back together. I didn't know what I'd do if you got hurt again. Or worse. I didn't think I could take it. I was being selfish and I'm sorry."

He wanted to hold her then, to console her. To tell her everything would be all right, even as the smoke of defeat stung their eyes. But he couldn't. Not here. Not now.

"Do we have any chance at all?" she asked finally in an almost plaintive tone. Matt could see there were tears in her eyes. He wondered what she meant by that. Did she mean love? Or survival?

"Yes," he finally answered, hoping his voice sounded more sure than he felt. "Yesterday I wouldn't have given odds, but today? Yes. We've managed to evacuate thousands of people from two cities, something I thought we'd never pull off. And *Walker* has her legs back under her again. That by itself has sure improved my frame of mind. Yesterday, when I read Ben's dispatch, all I could focus on was *Amagi* and how powerful she is. I was in shock, I guess. Part of it was losing *Revenge*, but mainly I just couldn't believe *Amagi* had somehow followed us here. It was too damn much. Then, when we were talking about it last night, you reminded me of *Amagi*'s vulnerabilities. You gave me hope, Sandra. Since then I've been thinking about *our* advantages for a change. There aren't very many, I'll be honest, but we do have a few. With luck, they'll be enough and someday we'll come back to this place and the people who live here will return."

Sandra was shaking her head. "I think you do know how I feel. You fought just as hard to save this place and its people as I've fought to save the wounded those battles have sent me. You thought you had it done, but then . . . the patient took a turn for the worse." She looked at him. "I feel like we're caught in a nightmare that never ends. It just seems that, no matter what . . ." She stopped. "These Lemurians, these people—they're *good* people, aren't they?"

Matt nodded. "For the most part, I think they are. Just like most of the folks back home are good. There're always exceptions."

"So we just have to keep on trying, don't we? No matter what."

He looked at her for a moment and smiled. "Like you said, the patient has taken a turn for the worse, but he's not dead yet. We can't ever give up as long as there's hope." Affectionately, and fully aware of the irony, he slapped the railing under his hand. His gaze swept aft, where he saw the distinctly satisfying wide, churning wake that only two engines could make. "And as long as we have this tired, worn-out heap of rusty baling wire . . . hope will survive." Matt started to turn back to his chair. The new screw was behaving itself and he wanted to increase speed. He stopped and looked at the nurse. "Speaking of hope and baling wire, don't you think it's time to unstrap my wing? It itches something fierce."

Unseen by the captain and the nurse, in the deepening evening gloom of the pilothouse, the members of the bridge watch surreptitiously glanced at one another and tried to hide their grins. With everything else that was going on, at least the captain and his girl had made up.

Walker caught *Nerracca* long before the giant ship drew abreast of the Sapudi Islands and she slowed her exuberant sprint to a crawl. There were no lights showing on either vessel. The only illumination came from the stars and the tiniest sliver of moon in the clearing sky. Far astern, above the two destroyed cities, a faint ruddy glow remained. *Walker*'s Lemurian lookout spotted *Nerracca*'s darkened shape with his keen eyes as they came alongside. A human might have missed her. Together, the last two ships to leave B'mbaado/Aryaal Bay worked east into the Bali Sea until they made their turn north, past the Kangean group. It took all night to get that far, and it was in the first gray light of morning that Matt studied the charts with Larry Dowden, who'd just resumed his watch.

Matt had slept little—again—and his eyes felt like gritty balls of lead. He'd been on edge all night, poised for battle because he half expected to encounter enemy pickets in the dark waters of the Bali Sea. If the enemy had pushed very hard, using the brisk west wind that still prevailed, the twelve ships of the advance force could have slanted down between the Sapudis and Kangean. If the entire invasion fleet was indeed headed for Aryaal, that would have been its only chance to stop them before they got into the Java Sea.

The wind had been good to *Nerracca* too, though, and as heavily loaded as she was, she managed a solid five knots throughout the night. Even so, at five knots it was an awful long way to the Makassar Strait. Matt didn't like to think about what might happen if part of the Grik armada was headed for Baalkpan instead. If that was the case, by the time *Nerracca* and *Walker* reached the strait, they might find themselves caught *behind* the enemy fleet. There wasn't much they could do about that but plod slowly onward and hope for the best.

Juan arrived in the pilothouse with the morning coffee and Matt gratefully accepted a refill. He reflected idly for a moment on how accustomed he'd grown to that particular ritual. Like all the routine activities that somehow carried on aboard his ship in spite of everything, it was a comforting taste of normalcy. The weird part was, ever since they ran completely out of "real" coffee and Juan was forced to make do with the local stuff, the morning brew had actually improved. In some corner of his mind, Matt still remembered the taste and smell of the coffee his mother used to make, and there was no comparison between that nostalgic ideal and what he was drinking now. But Juan's new coffee was unquestionably better than it had been when he had the "real" stuff to ruin. Matt's tired mind attempted to grasp the significance of that even while he tried to concentrate on the chart, but all he could come up with at the moment was that either he was actually beginning to get used to "monkey joe" or Juan's coffee had been even worse than he realized. He straightened, shaking his head.

"I'm going to stretch out for a while, Mr. Dowden. Continue 'steaming as before.' Your course is zero two zero. Wake me if . . ." He shrugged and addressed the pilothouse at large. "Mr. Dowden has the deck and the conn."

"Aye, aye, sir," Dowden replied. He turned to the helmsman. "This is Mr. Dowden. I have the deck and the conn . . ."

Even as Larry spoke, Matt was descending the ladder. Down the companionway and into his quarters, he had no conscious memory of how he arrived, sitting on his bunk and taking off his shoes. It had been a particularly grueling couple of days, physically as well as emotionally. The bad thing was, despite what he'd said to Sandra, it was only liable to get much worse.

"Captain to the bridge!"

Matt's eyes opened with a start and he rolled over and looked at the speaker on the bulkhead. Had the summons really come or had he only imagined it? His brain was still foggy with the unpleasant and, as usual, quickly receding remnants of the elusive dream. It was uncomfortably hot and stuffy in the compartment and his shirt was soaked with sweat. He'd been so tired when he finally turned in that he hadn't even clicked on the little fan. The light was still on too, and he wondered how long he'd slept. Rolling to a sitting position, he pressed the comm stud.

"Bridge. This is the captain . . . Did you just call me?" His voice was rough and his mouth was dry.

"Yes, sir. This is Mr. Garrett. You're needed on the bridge."

Surprised that it wasn't Larry Dowden's voice, Matt quickly looked at his watch. 1700. Somehow, he must have been asleep for almost nine hours and Dowden was probably in his own rack by now. As the Lemurian recruits were trained to the point they could competently exercise the duties of those they'd lost, *Walker* had finally been able to return to a normal watch rotation. So had her bridge officers, now they no longer had to wear so many other hats as well. Matt pressed the stud again.

"On my way."

He pulled his shoes back on and quickly ran a comb through his hair. Dampening a towel in his tiny basin, he wiped the sleep from his eyes and moistened his face. Contemplating his razor for just a moment, he decided it could wait until he knew what the situation was. With the exception of Courtney Bradford, himself—and Sandra Tucker of course—virtually the entire crew now sported beards. The quality of each beard varied with the men's individual ability to grow one, however, and a few were a little sparse. The razors on the ship would last only so long and he wasn't going to force the men to shave, but he did require they keep themselves trimmed. His own determination was to remain clean-shaven as long as he possibly could and he disliked appearing with stubble. It was his little ritualistic way of showing daily defiance toward the adversity they faced.

Sensing it was important somehow, he picked up the razor after all. His officers knew he preferred to take the few extra minutes to make himself presentable. It never hurt for the men to see, no matter how desperate the situation, their skipper was always calm enough to hold a razor to his face. If time was critical enough to prevent him from doing so now, Garrett would have made that clear. He did hurry, though, and in just a few minutes he was climbing the ladder at the rear of the pilothouse. As he did so, he was surprised how rested and vigorous he felt. The long sleep had done him a world of good, but in spite of that he couldn't ignore the growing dread that welled inside him. He always felt apprehensive when called to the bridge unexpectedly, but the fact that they were in the middle of the Java Sea, in broad daylight, only made his concern more acute. He knew his officers had probably conspired to let him sleep as long as he could and it would have taken something fairly serious to disturb him. In their current situation, things went from "fairly serious" to "catastrophic" pretty damn quick.

"Captain on the bridge!" Garrett called. He was waiting for him by the chart table.

"As you were. What's up, Mr. Garrett?"

"Surface contact, Captain," he said. "You can see it better from the fire-control platform." The gunnery officer led him up the next ladder to the platform above the bridge. Matt followed slowly, still hampered by the use of only one arm. His plea the evening before had come to naught, but Sandra had promised to take another look at his shoulder today. Then she would make her decision. He hadn't seen her yet today, having been asleep for most of it. Slightly winded, he gained the platform and joined the lieutenant beside the useless range finder.

"Port bow," Garrett suggested, and pointed. "On the horizon. *Nerracca* saw them first and signaled. Her lookouts are a lot higher than ours. It didn't take long for us to see them, though."

Matt raised his binoculars and peered through them for a moment, adjusting the objective. *Walker* and *Nerracca* were in one of those rare parts of the Java Sea in which absolutely no land could be seen in any direction. They would soon raise the islands off the southern coast of Borneo, but for now there was nothing. The afternoon was bright and almost completely clear. A few high clouds scudded hastily overhead in the direction of Borneo. Evidently the wind had finally shifted back out of the south.

Matt focused carefully at the point where the sea met the sky and as he stared, he began to discern towering, dirty-white sails outlined against the light blue background. There was no doubt about it. Even as he concentrated on holding the binoculars steady, more and more of the ominous shapes resolved themselves in the distance. It wasn't just the advance element of the enemy fleet they'd been avoiding either. There were far too many. In spite of the heat, icy tendrils clutched his heart and radiated outward, across his chest and down his back. Far in the distance, beyond the ever more crowded horizon, Matt thought he could see a hazy column of black-gray smoke drifting away to the north and up toward Borneo and the Makassar Strait. He lowered the binoculars until they hung suspended from the strap around his neck.

"They must've seen us," he observed. "At least *Nerracca*. Her masts are twice as tall as theirs."

"Yes, sir. It's hard to tell, but it looks like they've altered course since I first saw them. Right before I called you. Should I sound general quarters?"

Matt shook his head. "Not yet. But please do have Mr. McFarlane, Mr. Dowden, and the Bosun report to the bridge immediately."

"Aye, aye, Captain."

Ten minutes later, Matt gently tapped the chart with his index finger. "We're here," he said to the small group that had quickly gathered on the bridge. Then the same finger stabbed down a little to the northwest of their position. "The enemy is there. There's no longer any question in my mind that they know where Baalkpan is. There's no other reason for them to come this way." His lips formed a rueful smirk. "Just like we feared, the Japs must've been 'reading our mail.' Monitoring our transmissions." The smirk changed to a snarl. "And they ratted us out to the lizards. Regardless whatever other 'inducements' the Grik might have used to get the Japs to help them, they told them about Baalkpan because they wanted to." He shook his head, genuinely amazed. The Japanese were the enemy and when it came to *Amagi*, he had to admit it was even kind of personal. But he still found it hard to believe they would actively, voluntarily, help the Grik. Fleetingly, he wondered how *Amagi*'s more junior personnel felt about that. Pointless to speculate. He looked at each of those present. "Whether this force represents the bulk of the enemy fleet or not is impossible to say just yet, but it's certainly a sizable fraction of it. *Nerracca*'s lookouts have counted upwards of a hundred ships so far." He paused and took a deep breath. "And there's definitely a column of dark smoke rising from somewhere within or beyond the enemy force. We have to assume that smoke represents *Amagi*."

"But . . . when Lieutenant Mallory reported the advance force nearing Surabaya, he also sighted a significant number of enemy ships on an identical course less than thirty miles behind them," Dowden stressed.

"Yeah, but as I've been concerned all along, if they really have more than three hundred ships, they have more than enough to send a 'significant number' in two directions at once. It seems that's what they've done."

"We gotta warn Baalkpan!" Spanky said, around a mouthful of the yellow leaves.

"That's happening right now. I just hope they can hear us. We're still pretty far away." He frowned. "I told Clancy to ask for confirmation when he gets through. Radio silence is pointless at this stage. They clearly know where we're going."

Dowden's face suddenly went white with dreadful realization. "What are we going to do about *Nerracca*?"

Matt nodded slowly. "Precisely. What *are* we going to do? *Walker* can easily outrun the enemy, but obviously *Nerracca* can't. She's gained almost a knot, with this good wind on her starboard quarter. For her, that's really moving. Right now the lizards are beating into the wind, but once they turn north after passing these islands here"—he pointed again at the chart—"she won't have a chance. She might not anyway." He nodded toward the distant ships. "As you can see, they have the angle on us."

"Damn it, Skipper!" Gray growled with frustration. "What can we do? There's seven or eight thousand people on that ship!"

Matt glared at him. "That's what I was going to ask you!" He rubbed his eyes and looked at the others. "Gentlemen, we've *got* to come up with something, and we've got to do it now!" McFarlane's face wore a thoughtful expression. "Spit it out, Spanky!"

"Well, you said *Nerracca*'s making six knots."

"Thereabouts."

"If we light off the number two boiler, *Walker* can make thirty for a while. Hell, we could sustain twenty-eight if nothing pops." He glanced around at the expectant faces. "That's a hell of a lot of horsepower."

"You mean, rig a *tow*?" Matt breathed. Spanky nodded.

"But will it be enough?" Garrett asked skeptically. "I know *Nerracca*'s mostly wood, but her hull is incredibly thick and she's . . . *huge*! Especially with all those people on board, I bet she weighs twenty thousand tons!"

"Probably more," Spanky said.

"Could we add enough to her speed to make it worth the effort?" Matt asked, but Spanky shook his head.

"Skipper, I got no idea. I don't know what else we can do."

"I'm all in favor of giving it a try," said Gray, "but we don't even have a cable big enough. What are we gonna pull her with, kite string?"

"*Nerracca* has heavy cable," Garrett said, thinking aloud. "Hell, her anchor cable is three feet thick."

"Right," said Gray, "and what are we gonna secure it to? There's not a cleat on the ship that would stand strain like that!"

Spanky glared at the Chief. "Then figure it out, Fitz! You're in charge of the deck divisions. You're always reminding us of that! Rigging the tow is something you're going to have to solve! Distribute the load to more than one cleat—you can come up with something!"

Gray nodded. "That might work," he said. "I'll see what I can do."

"There's going to be other problems, Captain," Larry Dowden warned.

Matt sighed. "I know, Mr. Dowden. We'll just have to solve them, won't we?" For a moment he watched the distant armada creeping slowly but inexorably closer to the point far ahead that he'd calculated *Walker* and *Nerracca* must reach before the enemy did. "We don't have any choice."

Pete Alden stood on one of the many balconies surrounding Nakja-Mur's Great Hall. The branches of the mighty tree that soared from the top of the impressive structure provided some much-appreciated shade. Still, it was hot and humid and it had been a long, grueling day. He wiped sweat from his eyes and took a sip of some sour-sweet nectar that had been offered him by a member of the High Chief's expanded staff. Pete grimaced at the taste, as well as the situation. In the distance, down at the pier, he made out *Mahan*'s disheveled form. Still wounded by all she'd been through and badly battered by the storm, she'd crept painfully into Baalkpan Bay just two days before. She looked muddy with rust and her missing 'stack and searchlight tower gave her a gap-toothed appearance. Her steering had been repaired before she left Ary-aal and her bridge was a bridge again, but there sure weren't any bells and whistles.

Jim Ellis had made his report and it still felt sort of weird having an officer come to him. Letts had administrative command—after Nakja-Mur, of course—but he'd been off inspecting the wellhead and retrieving the launch from upriver when *Mahan* arrived. It had finally been determined that Tony Scott must have fallen prey to a "super lizard," an ambush hunting descendant of Allosaurus, according to Bradford. The things were rare and Pete had never seen one, but by all accounts they were one of the few "dinosaurs" of this region that weren't stunted. The Lemurian scouts had discovered tracks and blood on the pipeline. The monster must have been lying in wait for passing prey, hunkered slightly back in the dense foliage along the trail when Scott came ambling by. It was a terrible loss and Pete shuddered to think about how it must have been. Even so, the irony of the coxswain's death wasn't lost on him.

Anyway, since Pete had operational command of Baalkpan's defenses, Jim cheerfully reported to him when he arrived. There wasn't even the tiniest hint that Mr. Ellis considered it inappropriate and Pete was grateful for that. The irony of a naval lieutenant in command of a destroyer reporting to Mrs. Alden's son was even more bizarre, to him at least, than the way poor Scott had gotten it. Ever since then, though, Jim had been down at the dock working night and day, with hundreds of Lemurian "yard-apes" crawling all over his ship. By Nakja-Mur's command, every possible assistance, regardless of expense, was placed at the disposal of the young lieutenant and his wounded destroyer.

Nakja-Mur had certainly stepped up to the plate; Alden had no complaints about that. He no longer questioned what things cost. The High Chief had finally completely grasped the concept of total war, and everything else had dimmed to insignificance. Nothing was as important to him as saving his city and its people and he'd do whatever it took. With Letts's help, the High Chief of Baalkpan had blossomed into a kind of bureaucratic prodigy. In a government like that of the United States, Nakja-Mur would have been performing all the duties usually associated with the secretaries of state, commerce, agriculture, public works, and war. He didn't really know doodly-squat about any of those things, but he was smart enough to know it, and he delegated all the hands-on work to people who did. He just made sure the wheels were greased and he arbitrated disputes. He was also a genius at sorting out priorities and making sure the most important projects got the assets they needed the quickest. He relied heavily on Alden and Letts to advise him as to which projects those were, but since Baalkpan's defense and the support of the AEF were almost everybody's top priority, there was rarely any disagreement between them.

The exception to this unity of purpose was still represented by what Letts called the Run Away Party, which was enjoying a resurgence that began with *Fristar*'s return and was reinforced by the terrible news that the offensive was turning into a desperate retreat. The "Run-Aways" were still a minority since most of them had, of course, already run away. But Alden figured that as soon as the new scope of the threat they faced became known, the Run-Aways would gain many converts. There was no Lemurian president, or anything of the sort, to rule the collection of independent Homes and peoples from other "land" Homes that had gathered at Baalkpan. The leadership was more like some sort of screwy legislature of equal representatives. Kind of like the city-state setup of ancient Greece, Alden thought. Unlike the captain, Pete didn't know much about history—beyond that of the Marine Corps—but he'd heard of the Spartans and he knew about Thermopylae. He hoped they weren't facing a similar situation. He knew one of the problems the Greeks had faced was an inability to work together. But Nakja-Mur chaired all the meetings since he was High Chief of the "Host" Home. Hell, throw in speaker of the house while you're at it, Alden thought. So far he'd managed to keep everybody's eye on the ball.

Pete gazed out across the city below and wondered yet again at the ingenuity of the people here. Instead of walls to protect them from predators, like the Aryaalans used, they had opted for a raised-platform architecture that allowed them to sleep safely at night, when those predators were most likely to visit. The problem with that type of defense, however, was it was useless in the face of an invading army. That was a threat Baalkpan had never had to contend with before, and Alden could sympathize with the growing panic felt by those who heard the news brought by the flying-boat the evening before.

A brief attempt was made, at first, to control the news of *Revenge*'s loss and the forced evacuation of Aryaal and B'mbaado in the face of an exponentially increased threat. That effort didn't last long. Nakja-Mur felt compelled to share the information with the other chiefs and the news leaked out as quickly as that. When Steve Riggs came to Pete and said a fishmonger near the pier told him less than an hour after the meeting of the chiefs that the entire AEF had been destroyed, Pete knew something had to be done. He and Steve immediately went to Nakja-Mur and told him they had to make an announcement *now* and tell the people *everything*—not just that the AEF was in retreat but that they were bringing thousands of new allies to defend Baalkpan. Otherwise, by morning there wouldn't be a single Home in Baalkpan Bay and half the city would be empty. Nakja-Mur made the announcement. Soon the hysteria began to subside, but in its place remained a deep anxiety.

Baalkpan did have more allies now, besides the B'mbaadans and Aryaalans. Several more Homes had arrived since the AEF set out and word of the Grik menace was spreading fast. It was generally agreed they were facing a repeat of the prehistoric, almost mythical conflict that drove the People from paradise. Those who knew of the Great War in the west believed Baalkpan and the Homes that answered her call were doing great work on behalf of all the People to stamp out this terrible scourge. It was known and appreciated that Baalkpan had split its own defenses in order to take the fight to the enemy. But few foreign warriors came to Baalkpan's aid.

A few hundred came from across the Makassar Strait on Celebes, from a small colony city called Sular. The Sularans were nervous from the start about the ambitious battle plan and had sent no representatives to the conference. Once the offensive began, they were convinced it would meet disaster, and their entire population evacuated to—of all places, Pete thought—Manila. That was where many of Baalkpan's people had gone as well. But the Sularan warriors who remained behind were among the most fanatical converts to the tactics Alden taught. There weren't enough of them to defend Sular but, possibly ashamed of the rest of their people, they were determined to fight the Grik. They had, in fact, been preparing to move to Aryaal with the next transport.

Manila was the largest known land outpost of the Lemurian People, in terms of numbers, and it shared a religion and heritage with the people of Baalkpan. Led by a High Chief named San-Kakja, the Manilos sent food and promised workers and warriors to bolster the defenses of their sister city to the south. The warriors would also learn the new ways of war being taught there. San-Kakja dared not send too many troops because he feared that if the war went poorly and Baalkpan fell, it would be only a matter of time before the enemy came to Manila, and he had his own defenses to prepare. His city was open to any and all refugees, however, and it was to Manila that all of Baalkpan would eventually retreat if they were forced to—and if they were able. Pete hoped the promised troops would arrive in time.

The people of the seagoing Homes had been helpful as well, serving as transports for goods and refugees. It was a dangerous passage, since they risked the attention of the mountain fish, a few of which were known to dwell in the deeper parts of the Celebes Sea. Normally, these creatures weren't a threat to a Home—that was one of the reasons the ships were so large in the first place. Mountain fish were certainly *capable* of destroying a Home, but they only rarely ever tried. Perhaps it was because the Homes of the People were almost as big as they were and they just didn't think of them as food, or maybe they thought the Homes were other mountain fish. Whatever the reason, the only time they seemed aggressive toward them was, unfortunately, at this time of year. It was mating season for the mountain fish and instinctual urges triggered aggressive and possibly territorial reactions toward the Homes precisely because they thought they were other mountain fish. Of course, no one knew for certain. In any event, even though the Homes that plied back and forth between Baalkpan and Manila provided no troops for Baalkpan's defense, the aid they delivered was doubly appreciated because of the risk involved.

Pete harbored no illusions that the Homes would help defend Baalkpan if the Grik came this way. They'd definitely been a help, but like *Fristar,* few of the Homes' people or High Chiefs could understand why the people of Baalkpan—or any land Home, for that matter—would choose to defend, well, *land* in the first place. They considered it regrettable and inconvenient that the Ancient Enemy had found them again and some boasted that if they'd been aware of the offensive against the Grik they might have been willing to participate. But if the Grik learned where Baalkpan was and came to threaten it directly, they would undoubtedly flee. Why not? Unlike their ancestors, the sea folk weren't tied to the land. They could just move on whenever the Grik became a threat. Nakja-Mur tried to convince them it was different this time. The Grik now had ships that could follow, wherever they went. What would they do when they faced the Great Eastern Ocean? Would they continue to flee until they fell off the world? In this instance at least, his pleading was to no avail.

Alden didn't really much care. He wanted only dedicated soldiers under his command. Maybe it was the Marine in him, but he wasn't interested in using troops to keep an eye on other troops that didn't want to fight. Besides, if the Grik did come, the Homes would be needed to evacuate the last of Baalkpan's noncombatants—though there weren't many of those left. Most who hadn't already fled or been sent away had been training to become soldiers and Marines even while they worked on the city's defenses.

As he'd reported to the captain, those defenses were impressive. Much of the works were visible from where he stood on Nakja-Mur's balcony. Baalkpan had a wall now, ten feet high and made of hard-packed dirt. Reinforced with timbers from the surrounding jungle, it completely surrounded the city. A wide, deep moat was at its base and beyond that was an impressive killing ground full of sharpened stakes and entanglements. Heavy guns like those they'd armed the Homes with faced the bay, where they could bear on enemy ships. Dozens of the smaller twelve-pounder guns, like those that had been aboard *Revenge*, protected the approaches from the land. Behind them were the mortar emplacements. All the guns had overhead protection from plunging crossbow bolts and nowhere could the enemy get close enough to the walls to use their firebomb throwers without coming under direct artillery fire. There were multiple magazines for ammunition storage and extra wells had been dug to improve their water supply—not just for drinking but for fighting fires. Tons of food had been prepared and preserved and, even if most was fish, there should be enough for many months.

On the promontory overlooking the mouth of the bay, Lieutenant Brister had overseen the construction of a fort in the shape of a pentagon, much like those that proved so effective in the eighteenth and nineteenth centuries. Like its predecessors, this one was festooned with heavy guns that covered the harbor entrance and there were defenses around it similar to those that encircled the city. There were also sufficient provisions within that it could hold for quite a while if it was ever cut off from Baalkpan. Brister had named it Fort Atkinson, after *Mahan*'s captain who'd been killed in the battle with *Amagi*. Brister had admired Captain Atkinson very much. He was proud of the fort and Pete was too. He was proud of everything they'd done to prepare for a possible attack. Now, as he stood waiting for Nakja-Mur to join him for their afternoon bull session, he fervently prayed that all the defenses he'd helped design and build and all the citizen-soldiers he'd trained would never face the test they'd been preparing for.

A tapestry separating the balcony from the Great Hall parted, and Nakja-Mur strode through to join Sergeant Alden with his own goblet of nectar in his hand. His face was expressionless, as usual, beyond a small, clipped frown that didn't reveal his teeth. His shoulders sagged and his tail drooped and it was clear he was exhausted.

"Good afternoon, Gener-aal Aalden," he said by way of greeting.

Pete grimaced. He hated it when Nakja-Mur called him that, especially in front of others. "Good afternoon, Nakja-Mur, U-Amaki Ay Baalkpan."

"Preparations continue to proceed well?" Nakja-Mur asked.

Pete shrugged. "Well enough. We started building up the overhead protection for the batteries today, now that we know about *Amagi*." He shook his head. "Not that it'll do much good against ten-inch guns. That's one thing we never planned for. I've also started working on more shelters for troops and medical facilities. It's mostly revetments to protect from fragments, but it's better than nothing."

"These ten-inch guns are very bad?"

Pete nodded. "They're more than twice as big as *Walker*'s."

"But the guns you helped build for my people are as well."

"True," Alden agreed, "but as we've discussed many times, those guns, as powerful as they are, are still no match for *Walker*'s in range, power, or accuracy. I wish they were, but we just don't have the facilities to make anything like that yet. As for *Amagi,* her guns are bigger still than the best we've been able to make and they can shoot ten times as far."

Nakja-Mur nodded solemnly. "You're saying we have no real defense against this *Amagi*? Not even now that there are two of your fast iron ships?"

"No. As you can surely see for yourself, *Mahan*'s in no shape for a fight. Jim's killing himself trying to get her ready and hopefully he'll have time. But even if *Walker* and *Mahan* were brand spanking new, they'd be no match for that damn thing. We'll think of something. We have to. But right now I sure don't know what it'll be. Pray, I guess."

Nakja-Mur nodded. "I will certainly do that," he said. "I will pray that it never comes. It may not, you know," he added hopefully.

Just then, Ed Palmer was escorted onto the balcony by a pair of Nakja-Mur's guardsmen, who paused and waited to be summoned close. Ed accompanied them and Pete's heart sank when he saw the signalman's ashen face.

"My guess is," Pete said before Ed spoke a word, "we should have been praying already."

A skeptical but willing Tassat-Ay-Aracca supervised the passage of a fat, looped hawser to *Walker*'s fantail as the destroyer lay hove-to in the massive ship's lee. The heaviest cables that could be secured were attached to four mooring stanchions, two on each side of *Walker*'s aft deckhouse. The cables were rigged aft, outboard, and draped across the top of the propeller guards. Once they were secured to *Nerracca*'s cable, the connection point was allowed to trail fifty yards astern. Hundreds of hopeful faces lined the Home's catwalk railing and watched while the work was completed. A party of Marines under Chack's direction accomplished much of the labor. Now that he was back aboard ship, he'd quickly reverted to his position of bosun's mate. When completed, Gray reluctantly gave his approval to the unorthodox rig. The strain on *Walker*'s hull would be immense, but it was all they could manage in the time they had.

Slowly, with hot exhaust gases rippling above three of her stacks, *Walker* surged ahead to take up the slack. The cable rose, dripping, from the depths, and with a nerve-racking, trembling groan the old four-stacker added her thrust to *Nerracca's* sails. Gray was on the aft deck-house scrutinizing the cables as the strain began to build and Spanky was below, monitoring the engines and the boilers. Matt paced back and forth between the port wing and the aft bridge rail. From that position he could see *Nerracca*, the length of his ship, and the enemy as well. He called a slight course correction to Larry Dowden, who stood at the helmsman's side. It had been carefully stressed to Tassat that *Nerracca* must follow exactly in *Walker's* wide wake. The frothing violence of that wake was unprecedented as the RPMs of the twin screws rapidly built.

Garrett appeared at Matt's side. "Thank God the sea's not running very high, Captain," he said. "We could break her back if it was."

Sandra and Queen Maraan stepped out onto the weather deck below. The queen looked up at him with her wide silver eyes.

"Thank you, Cap-i-taan Reddy, for what you are trying to do. Many of my people are aboard that ship."

Matt shifted uncomfortably and nodded. The queen had spoken in almost perfect English. He knew Chack was still teaching her, but Sandra might have told her what to say. Regardless, it was obvious she'd wanted to say it. "We'll do our best, Your Highness," he replied. "We're doing all we can."

"Seven knots!" came the cry from the wheelhouse. "We're starting to gain a little!"

Slowly, agonizingly, the speed mounted while *Walker* bucked and heaved like a greyhound dragging an elephant. Triumphantly, they passed eight knots. Then nine. The enemy force grew closer, but they were still on a slower tack. *Amagi* wasn't, however. As slow as she was, she still wasn't dependent on the wind, and she shouldered her way forward through the temporarily slower ships. The column of dark smoke grew ever more distinct and the lookout had reported her pagoda-like superstructure on the distant horizon.

Ten knots seemed to be it, for once they reached that speed, no amount of labor on *Walker*'s part was able to increase it. The sun was beginning to set, but the Grik were much closer now. Soon they'd know if it would be a stern chase or a fight. Matt tried to estimate how fast the enemy could sail with the wind directly astern. He'd seen them make at least twelve knots once before, but that was with the wind slightly abaft the beam, a square-rigger's best point of sailing. If *Walker* could somehow manage to keep this speed all the way to Baalkpan, and if they could squeeze past the foremost ships that were straining to cut them off, Matt didn't think the Grik could catch them. On the other hand, *Amagi* would soon be in range of her big guns. With darkness falling, she wouldn't have a target, though, would she? Once she got behind them, she'd never catch up either. Not if eight knots was all she had.

A couple of Grik ships, either because of better seamanship or cleaner hulls, were drawing ahead of the pack. Matt had a good eye for geometry and there was no way *Walker* would drag *Nerracca* past those two, at least.

"Sound general quarters," he ordered at last. The raucous "gong, gong, gong" reverberated throughout the ship and hats were exchanged for helmets. Matt knew the consensus was that no one wanted to go in the water with a life jacket on, but he ordered them worn regardless. Sandra suggested that the possibility a crewman might be eaten was more than offset by the protection against crossbow bolts and flying debris that the jackets afforded them. The Lemurian destroyermen hated the jackets even more than the humans did. In their case it was because, for the most part, they were way too big. They wore them nonetheless.

Bernard Sandison was the last to report, as usual. He had the farthest to go from where he was supervising the preparation of the torpedoes. He plugged in his headset, turned to the talker, and gave a thumbs-up sign.

"All stations manned and ready, Captain," Reynolds said aloud.

"Very well. Who's in the crow's nest?"

"Bosun's Mate Chack, sir."

Matt nodded. Early on, Lieutenant Garrett had worked very closely with the burly young Lemurian. He'd picked up ranges well. Matt didn't have the perspective of the lookout, but those two lead ships were obviously in range. He wanted to knock them out before they got dead ahead, when only the number one gun would bear. "Inform Mr. Garrett he may commence firing when ready," he said.

On the fire-control platform, Garrett listened to Chack's report as it came through his earpiece. He echoed it to Sandy Newman, who was operating the mechanical fire-control computer. "Load one, two, and four. Range to target four O double O. Angle is zero six zero, speed seven knots."

"On target!" chorused the director and the pointer.

Garrett knew they didn't have the ammunition to waste on an "up ladder." Since there was still some visibility, he would fire a single salvo and hope they could correct from there. Chack had good eyes; he should spot the fall of shot.

"One round each, salvo fire. Commence firing!"

The salvo buzzer alerted the bridge crew and a moment later the ship shook perceptibly with the booming roar of three four-inch guns. In the deepening twilight the tracers quickly converged on the target. A bright, rippling flash erupted amidships of the first enemy ship and a chorus of exultant shouts rose up. Matt was excited as well. Chack was right on the money.

"Silence!" bellowed Chief Gray on the fo'c'sle, right behind number one. "Grab that damn shell, Davis, before it goes over the side!" His yell was loud enough that half the ship must have heard.

Still grinning, Matt turned to the talker. "By all means let's have some quiet so the men can do it again."

The next ship in line was destroyed almost as quickly, but it took two salvos instead of one. It must have maneuvered to avoid the sinking, burning hulk in front of it. More ships were cracking on, though. It was as though the destruction of the first two only spurred the rest to greater effort. Reynolds spoke up. "Captain, Mr. Garrett recommends we go to single shots, alternating the guns. We may not sink 'em every time but we ought to slow them down."

"Agreed," Matt said. "We don't have enough shells to fire even once at every ship out there." For the next several minutes there was a steady booming, going from forward, aft, and then forward again. In the deepening gloom, the sea off the port bow was littered with burning ships they'd hit. Garrett was judiciously targeting only the ones that might cut them off and it looked like the strategy was working. Matt scanned the sea to port to see if he could tell how close *Amagi* was, but it was impossible to say. The sun had set behind the Grik fleet and *Amagi*'s pagoda was lost in the hundreds of silhouetted sails. But at that very instant, a bright flash of light erupted a little farther to the north than he'd been looking. It seemed closer than he expected, too.

"Captain!" cried Reynolds. "Lookout reports *Amagi* has opened fire!"

"I saw it!" Matt answered. "Right full—" He stopped. "Belay that! Keep your rudder amidships! Maintain current heading!" *Walker* couldn't make any evasive maneuvers at all. Not while she had *Nerracca* in tow.

"My God," Dowden muttered. "We're a sitting duck!"

Matt turned to him. "Mr. Dowden. I believe your action station is the auxiliary conn, aft. Why don't you get there as quickly as you can?"

"Aye, aye, Captain! Sorry!" Dowden muttered, and without another word, he bolted for the ladder. Before he even reached it, eight enormous waterspouts marched across the sea, the closest about fifteen hundred yards off the port quarter. The impacts were widely spaced, across a square mile of ocean. They must be near *Amagi*'s maximum range.

Matt turned to the talker, judging the wind. "Make smoke! Signal *Nerracca*; no lights at all!" Another enemy salvo rained down, a little closer than the first but no less scattered. Thick columns of black smoke gushed from *Walker*'s stacks and drifted northward, toward the enemy. The light was failing fast, but what little there was would be right on *Walker* and *Nerracca*. The smoke might help a little, but all by herself, there was no way the old destroyer could pump out enough to cover something the size of a small island. He hollered up at Garrett on the fire-control platform. "What's it look like ahead?" Matt could no longer see any Grik ships other than those that were afire. Unlike the ones that invested Aryaal, these were not lit from stem to stern with lanterns. "Do you think we can get clear if we cease firing? Our gun flashes will give them a target."

"No, sir," Garrett replied. "There's a couple more of the bastards that might get close. If they throw a firebomb on us or *Nerracca,* the Jap'll really have a target!"

"Very well. Try not to shoot unless you have to, though." He glanced aft. Even through the smoke and the darkness, the massive white sails of the Home seemed painfully bright. Another salvo from *Amagi* lit the night. A few moments later he watched as the bright underwater flashes sent more geysers into the air. The pressure of the explosions pounded his ears and seemed to suck the air from his lungs. Closer still, and they weren't using armor-piercing shells this time. They wouldn't need them; high explosive would be far more devastating. He looked down and caught a glimpse of Queen Maraan, Bradford, and Sandra on the weather deck looking up at him. Sandra must have been trying to keep the other two out from underfoot. Otherwise, he imagined she'd be on the bridge. Suddenly he realized he wanted her there. "Come on up!" he shouted over the roar of the blower. "Just stay on the wing, if you please." The three quickly scrambled up the ladder and stood beside him.

"Well done, Captain!" Courtney cried, grasping his hand and shaking it. "You've been giving those lizards quite a thrashing! And those Jappos are just killing fish!"

"I would never have believed the power of the Jaap's guns, if I hadn't seen it for myself!" Safir Maraan breathed. "Are we safe from them here?"

Another salvo rumbled in. This time they were going to be close. Even over the sound of the blower, the heavy, ripping-canvas sound could be heard. The majority of the salvo sent spume into the air less than a hundred yards to port. One was inside of thirty and the terrible force of the blast sent heavy pieces of shrapnel crashing into the side of the ship as a high-pitched shriek rent the air. One went ridiculously long and exploded without effect two hundred yards off *Walker*'s starboard quarter.

One hit *Nerracca* in the port bow at the base of the forward tower and tripod mast. It detonated with a tremendous explosion and a roiling ball of flame. Splinters and shell fragments rained into the sea for hundreds of yards and splintered wood sprayed the destroyer. Wood, and pieces of God knew how many refugees. The queen held her hand over her open mouth in a very human gesture of horror and Courtney Bradford clasped her protectively to his side. Matt realized he'd done the same with Sandra and he immediately released her and spun back inside the wheelhouse.

"Damage report!" he demanded.

A few moments later Reynolds recited the litany. "Minor flooding in the aft engine room! Half a dozen holes in the port side, anywhere from the size of a quarter to one that looks like a boot. Only a couple are on the waterline and they think they can get them plugged pretty quick." Reynolds listened for a moment. "The number four torpedo mount looks like Swiss cheese and one of the 'Cats bought it. Three wounded are on their way to the wardroom." Matt looked out where Sandra had been standing, but she was already gone. The salvo buzzer rang and the numbers one and two guns fired almost simultaneously at a pair of Grik ships that were edging too close. The express-train rumble of another Japanese salvo neared and Matt dashed back onto the bridgewing. Mountainous splashes straddled *Nerracca* and one erupted near *Walker*'s fantail but evidently didn't explode. Sheets of water cascaded down on the men on the aft deckhouse and the crew of number four. Another explosion on *Nerracca* lit the night not far from where the first one hit. The enormous forward sail began to burn.

"All ahead flank!" Matt yelled. The bridge watch exchanged nervous looks, but the order was relayed. *Walker*'s stern crouched even lower and the thrashing wake threatened to swamp the fantail. If *Walker* hadn't been constrained, she would have been kicking up a rooster tail six feet over the stern. The terrible vibration they'd almost gotten used to suddenly tripled, and the old destroyer wheezed in agony as she loyally strained to do what was asked of her.

"Captain!" Reynolds called, "Lieutenant McFarlane says we don't have the fuel for this—to make it to Baalkpan—even if she doesn't tear her guts out. His words, sir."

"We don't have to do this all the way to Baalkpan! We just have to get away from *that*!" Another forest of splashes appeared close by the struggling ships. *Nerracca*'s forward sail was fully engulfed now. Flaming debris and clouds of sparks drifted downwind. Some fell on *Walker*'s deck and men and Lemurians scurried about, kicking the burning fragments over the side. Even over all the noise and turmoil, a great, high-pitched, moaning wail arose from the stricken Home as the suffering and terror there passed endurance.

Chief Gray appeared on the port bridgewing. He cast a fixed, stony glance where Bradford was trying to console the weeping queen. The sight of Safir Maraan—usually so stoic and strong—in such a state almost broke his resolve. But he steeled himself for what he had to do and stepped before the captain. "It's no use, Skipper," he said quietly.

"No!" Matt snarled, just as quiet but from within a furious rage. "We can't leave them here! There's *thousands* . . . !" Suddenly, his mind's eye saw a bright, sunny day with high, drifting clouds overhead—and *Exeter*'s barnacle-encrusted bottom rolling toward the sky while shells fell on the men struggling in the water. Then, all over again, it was *Encounter*'s turn, and he watched as the gallant British destroyer disappeared under a marching haze of foam. At last there was *Pope*, mortally wounded and low by the stern while the white-painted buzzards with red spots on their wings circled overhead. *Pope*, like all the others, was in *Walker*'s wake, but *Walker* wasn't the one who'd left her. It was Matt who had done that. Finally, in the midst of all this horror, the nightmare he could never remember came to his waking eyes. He knew it was the thing that had driven him all this time to save all that he could. It pushed him to crusade against the Grik and it fueled his hatred of them once he came to know what they were. They were the physical personification, in this twisted alien place, of the remorselessly inhuman juggernaut that had hounded *Walker* here in the first place. The Grik had become the Japanese. And now *Amagi*, the arch-villain of the nightmares that tortured his sleep, had chased them into hell itself to finally finish the job.

His eyes had taken on a cold inner light when he refocused them on the Chief and spoke in a soft, but almost manically precise tone. "We Are Not Leaving Anyone Else Behind." Gray took a step back. Even given the situation, he was surprised by the captain's intensity. Matt's eyes still didn't leave him. Finally he called over his shoulder. "Speed?"

"We almost had eleven knots there for a minute, Skipper, but now we're down to nine—and falling." Another salvo plummeted down and multiple explosions convulsed *Nerracca*. Her forward tripod teetered and fell, taking with it much of the pagoda tower it straddled. Fire was spreading toward the center sail. *Walker* shook from end to end like a giant hand had slapped her. Shell fragments rattled the amidships gun platform and the two stacks forward of it. They sounded like heavy hail on a tin roof.

"Lieutenant McFarlane says we have to back it down, Captain!" Reynolds pleaded. His voice was almost a squeak. He was hearing constant reports now from all over the ship, detailing all the things that were breaking. And yet, right there in front of him was the captain, who seemed set on a course of action that would only redouble those reports. Reynolds was caught in the middle. He felt like he was the only person on the entire ship that was getting information from every perspective, because he wasn't entirely sure the captain was even listening anymore. He was terrified. Regardless, he dutifully passed the rest of Spanky's urgent message. "He says pressure's dropping on the number four boiler. He thinks the feed-water pump is crapping out. He also thinks that last near miss might've shaken something loose inside it."

"We're down to six knots!" shouted Norman Kutas, who was monitoring their speed. In addition to losing a third of her own propulsion, *Nerracca* was getting heavier as tons of seawater poured inside her through gaping holes and opened seams. As tough as the Homes of the

People were, they were never designed to absorb the type of punishment *Amagi* was inflicting.

For a long, torturous moment, Matt said nothing. He just continued to stare at Gray with a look of inexorable determination. The salvo buzzer rang again and the number one gun fired into the night. Then . . . he blinked. It was as though the nightmare that had surged from his subconscious mind was suddenly subverted by the one he was living now.

"Secure from flank," he said in a subdued voice.

"Captain!" shouted Sandison from the starboard bridgewing, "Small craft are coming alongside!" Matt raced to join him and peered over the rail. A shoal of small double-ended sailing craft, about thirty feet long, were struggling to catch up with the destroyer. Matt immediately recognized them as boats the People used to hunt the gri-kakka. Much like human whaleboats of the past, they carried the hunters close enough to strike their prey with a lance. Most Homes carried dozens of the extremely fast things and launched them from the large internal bays Matt had first seen on *Big Sal*. The gri-kakka boats were packed to overflowing.

"Get boarding nets over the side!" Matt shouted. "Slow to two-thirds!"

Immediately, as soon as the nets were rigged, boat after boat thumped alongside and terrified Lemurians swarmed up to the deck. Most were younglings.

"What the hell are they doing?" Gray demanded.

"They're trying to get as many off as they can!" Matt shouted. "Get down there and start packing them in!"

Gray was stunned. "But how many can we hold?"

"As many as they send us! Now get your ass down there and get them below! We have to keep the ship trimmed and you're the only one that can do it. Use all the help you need!" The Bosun dashed toward the ladder. Matt realized Queen Maraan had joined him. With her black fur and clothing she was almost invisible in the dark. Only her silver eyes and the tears matting the fur around them were visible, reflecting the light of the fire that raged aboard *Nerracca*. More shells shrieked down and churned the sea.

"You risk much," she said in a soft, sad voice.

"I'm risking everything," he told her truthfully. Even he realized it now. One lucky hit and *Walker* and everyone aboard her would be blown into quickly sinking fragments. A few would survive in the water long enough to know they were being eaten. And then *Amagi* and the Grik armada would continue remorselessly toward Baalkpan with little more than poor, crippled *Mahan* to stand in the way. *Nerracca* was doomed no matter what. Probably the only reason *Amagi* was still shooting at her was that her fires gave the Japanese gunners a target in the distant dark. There was always the chance they would hit the American destroyer. "Sometimes you just don't have any choice."

The gri-kakka boats scurried back and forth, ferrying people as fast as they could while *Walker* still heaved on the cable. It made the transfer more difficult, but they had to remain under way to keep as much distance as possible between themselves and *Amagi,* as well as the approaching Grik. Also, if *Nerracca* went dead in the water, she would be a sitting duck and the Japanese gunners would finish her in a matter of minutes. As it was, Matt began gently altering course as radically as possible, trying to throw some errors into the enemy fire control. It was very subtle because they couldn't do much, but the number of hits *Amagi* scored began to decline. Still, the shells continued to rain down and Matt had to wonder why the enemy was expending so much of their limited ordnance. Evidently, whoever was in command over there wasn't willing to risk any possibility that his prey would escape. Even temporarily.

Another nearby salvo tossed *Walker* like a cork. So far, she'd taken no direct hits, but the damage from near misses and shell fragments was becoming critical. The wardroom was filling with wounded but, miraculously, no more of her crew had been killed. That luck didn't extend to the refugees. Almost a dozen had been scythed down on *Walker*'s deck, and many more died when two of the gri-kakka boats were pulverized by a direct hit alongside. Refugees filled *Walker*'s lower decks and every crevice and compartment was packed to overflowing. Even the sweltering engineering spaces were full of panting Lemurians and the air was filled with a desolate, terrified keening sound and the smell of soggy fur and voided bowels.

"Keep packing them in," Matt ordered the Bosun when he came to report.

"It's turning into hell down there, Captain," Gray replied.

Matt nodded grimly. "Just put them wherever you can. It sure beats the alternative."

Gray nodded. "If they fill up the main deck, she'll capsize," he warned. "We're already so low in the water with all the extra weight that we're taking water through holes above the waterline. Damage control can't even get to them with all the bodies down there."

"I know. Are the pumps keeping up?"

"So far—" Gray was interrupted by the bark of the number three gun. The Grik were closing on them now and all guns were in local control, firing at nearby targets of opportunity. The sea to port was scattered with burning hulks. *Amagi* had slipped aft somewhat, until now she was off *Nerracca*'s port quarter. She was closing, though, since their own speed had diminished so much. She had advanced through most of the Grik that accompanied her until, by the flashes of her guns, they saw few lizard ships remaining between them. Most of the main Grik force had caught the favorable wind and were closing on the port bow. Matt realized bitterly that if it hadn't been for those early hits, their scheme to pull the Home clear of danger would probably have worked.

Both the ships were heavier now. Behind them Matt saw that *Nerracca* was horrifyingly low in the water. All of her masts and sails were aflame, as was virtually everything on or above her main deck from stem to stern. The only people escaping now came from the bays low on her hull. Even that couldn't last much longer. Soon they would be underwater.

"Four knots!" Kutas yelled shrilly over the roar of the tortured blower and the rattling cacophony of the exhausted ship. Several falling shells struck *Nerracca* simultaneously and rocked the hulk with what seemed like a single massive detonation. One shell went long and exploded just off *Walker*'s starboard bow. Matt, Safir, and Bernie Sandison were all knocked off their feet by the concussion, and fragments sleeted into the side of the bridge and the splinter shield on the number one gun. Leo Davis went sprawling and two of the Lemurian loaders were swept away.

Then, as those on the bridge gained their feet, they were hurled backward against the chart house and *Walker* erupted forward like a racehorse from the gate. Matt staggered up, climbing the conduits on the bulkhead. Reynolds was down, but conscious, and he was scrambling to put his headset back on. His helmet was nowhere to be seen.

"Report!"

"The cable parted!" Reynolds cried.

"Did it burn through?"

"No, sir. Mr. Dowden says it was cut! One of those whaleboats of theirs did it!"

Matt's shoulders sagged. "Come about. Right full rudder. Get me the crow's nest."

"Chack's on the line, Captain."

"Ask him how many boats are in the water with people in them." There was a momentary pause while *Walker* churned back toward the burning Home.

"Chack says the one that cut the cable is the only one under way. All the others have unloaded and been cast adrift."

"Rudder amidships. Slow to one-third," Matt ordered the helmsman. "We'll pick up the people in that last boat."

"Aye, aye, sir."

The final gri-kakka boat came alongside while Matt stared ahead at the burning, wallowing wreck. *Nerracca* was so low in the water now that there was no way anyone else could have escaped through her launch bays. Whoever cut the cable must have been on the last boat out. He had no idea how many Lemurians *Walker* had taken aboard, but surely there were still thousands left behind, trapped between the inferno above and the rising water below.

"All aboard, Captain," Reynolds reported quietly. "They've jettisoned the boat and are securing the nets now." The darkness to the south-southwest lit up again with another mighty salvo. The bastards were *still* shooting at *Nerracca*!

"Helm, make your course one six zero, all ahead full," Matt ordered.

Sandison looked at him hesitantly. "Captain . . . Baalkpan's almost due north."

"I'm well aware of that, and so is the enemy. They'll expect us to hightail it there as fast as we can because that's probably what we ought to do. There's no moon and once we're out of *Nerracca*'s glare, no one will ever see us." As if to punctuate his point, *Amagi*'s latest salvo erupted in the sea behind them, on and around the helpless Home. None of the shells came close to the destroyer and Matt didn't even flinch when they detonated.

"That's not what we're going to do?" Sandison asked. His eyes were wide. In spite of the rage that threatened to engulf him, Matt almost laughed at the young officer's expression.

"No, Bernie, we're not. We'll use this excellent moonless night to our advantage for another purpose. We're going to steam south until we arrive off *Amagi*'s starboard beam and then we're going to turn directly toward her. At that point you, Mr. Sandison, are going to slam our last three working torpedoes into her goddamn side."

Bernie gulped. "Aye, aye, sir."

"The enemy ship is destroyed, Captain," Sato Okada said quietly but urgently. He was standing beside Kurokawa on *Amagi*'s bridge. The middle distance was awash with flames, both from their allies' ships and from the giant Tree Folk vessel. "I recommend we cease firing and conserve ammunition." Kurokawa turned to him and regarded him intently. His eyes reflected the flames of the burning ships like little mirrors, and Sato suspected with a shudder that that's what they were. Mirrors to his soul.

"The American destroyer? Do you think we got it?"

"Impossible to say. As soon as it began to tow the bigger ship directly away from us, it was lost to view." Sato almost shrugged. "There were many explosions. Perhaps she was hit. Right now, however, we are wasting ammunition."

"Oh, very well, Commander," Kurokawa growled. "You may cease firing. We will steer toward the wreckage and see for ourselves. If we did not sink the American ship, we almost certainly damaged it. She will fly as fast as she can to her lair and we will catch her soon." He paced the length of the bridge as though lost in thought while Sato gave the order to stop the bombardment of the burning, sinking hulk. A moment later he returned to Sato's side. Strangely, there was a smile on his face. "A most impressive display for our allies, I should think," he said. "None of them could stop the enemy ship, and yet we did it with contemptuous ease. I expect a greater say in matters after this!"

Sato bowed, but he cleared his throat. When he spoke, his voice was brittle. "Before it grew too dark, the lookout reported that the enemy ship seemed to be packed with refugees. Civilians."

"So? It was to be expected. They have evacuated Surabaya." The captain's gaze grew intent once more. "They are the enemy, Commander Okada. You would do well to remember that." His expression became coldly philosophical. "Besides, we gave them a quicker and more honorable death than the Grik would have afforded them."

Sato turned away to conceal his disgust. "Honorable," he whispered.

"We've outpaced our escorts for once," Kurokawa said with satisfaction as he glanced astern. "I expect the flagship will signal us shortly, as soon as it catches up. When it does so, you will inform me at once. I will be in my quarters."

Sato bowed and, to his immense relief, the captain left the bridge. Staring at the distant glare, he wondered about what he had seen. When the report came that the American destroyer was actually *towing* the enormous enemy ship, once again something stirred within him. Rather than make an easy escape, the destroyer had done everything she could to aid her slower consort. *That* was honor. They may be the enemy, but Sato could still find it within himself to respect them for what they'd done. He wondered why Kurokawa could not. His hatred had blinded him to everything but revenge. Something was fundamentally wrong with this entire situation, but he had no idea what to do about it.

Effectively invisible, *Walker* steamed south at twenty-five knots with a bone in her teeth and blood in her eye. Chack remained in the crow's nest, occasionally calling out a range and bearing to the target whenever *Amagi* fired her guns, but that didn't last much longer. Finally, she wearied of wasting ammunition and her salvos at last ceased. Chack's reports grew farther apart and less certain as he tried to pick the battle cruiser from among the stars she obscured. *Nerracca* was still an inferno behind them, but it was clear by now, even to the enemy, that no one could possibly survive aboard her. Matt was staring at her with a profound sense of loss and failure. He wondered if she would never sink and end the agony at last.

His reverie was interrupted when Chief Gray escorted a young Lemurian female onto the bridge. Her fur was scorched and it was impossible to tell what color it had been. She was also entirely naked except for a towel someone had given her to replace her lost kilt. In spite of her disheveled appearance, she looked vaguely familiar. As soon as she saw him, she threw herself upon the wooden strakes of the wheelhouse and clasped his leg below the knee. Matt looked at Gray for an explanation.

"That's Tassat's daughter, Tassana," the Bosun said, his rough voice almost cracking. "I bet she's about thirteen." Matt looked back down at her. Now he remembered. She'd been present at some meeting or other, there to attend her father, Tassat-Ay-Aracca, *Nerracca*'s High Chief. She began to shake with sobs as she clutched him. "She was on the last boat out," Gray continued. "She helped cut the cable herself, with an axe. Her dad told her to."

"Tassat?" Matt asked quietly.

Gray shook his head. "He didn't make it."

Of course he didn't. The ebullient Lemurian would never have abandoned his Home while there was anyone left aboard. He might not have even then. A further wave of sadness swept over Matt and he knelt beside Tassana. Queen Maraan joined him there and embraced her.

"You save so many, at such great risk," Tassana murmured through her tears. "My father bade me honor you with his final words to me. Honor all *Walkers* for their courage. *Nerracca* Clan . . ." Her voice caught with a shudder. What few of *Nerracca*'s people that still lived no longer had a Home. ". . . *Nerracca* Clan never forget," she finally managed. Queen Maraan gently rocked her back and forth as Tassana began to cry again. She soothed her while Matt continued to kneel beside them, unable to speak. To him it seemed so terribly wrong for anyone to be grateful to him. So many had died. He stood and Safir helped Tassana to her feet. The Bosun started to lead her away.

"How many did we save?" Matt asked him. Gray shook his head.

"I have no idea. They're packed away below like those damn Vienna scum weenies. Eight hundred? Maybe more." He looked Matt in the eye. "We couldn't have taken many more anyway, Skipper. Not and stayed afloat." Matt said nothing and Gray gently led Tassana toward the ladder. Matt turned and found Queen Maraan's shining eyes fixed upon him.

"B'mbaado will never forget what you've done for us either, Cap-i-taan Reddy," she said. She motioned at the night. "You go now to try and strike a blow against *Nerracca*'s murderers and I would be a part of that." She shook her head. "But I am of no use to you here." She paused. "My people believe that the God of the Great Light that burns during the day does not see the deeds that take place when he is not above. I do not know if that is true or not. But the souls of *Nerracca*'s dead have already been carried skyward by the pyre. They know what has happened and they will watch what is yet to be. Whether the Sun sees them or not, He will hear of *Walker*'s deeds and He will honor you as well." She smiled at him then. "I am shamed by my inaction. With your permission, I will go where I may be of help. I will join your mate in the wardroom and see if I may assist with the wounded."

"Of course," he said. "I'm sure that—" He stopped. What had she just said? "Lieutenant Tucker would appreciate the help, and the

company. Please ask her to make a quick report as soon as it's convenient." Bowing her head, Queen Maraan left the bridge.

"Captain, lookout reports a surface contact bearing one one zero
degrees. Range about eighteen thousand. He's not completely sure, sir,
but he thinks it's her."

"Very well. Helm, make your course one four zero. Reduce speed
to two-thirds." He caught a couple of raised eyebrows at that. "Don't
worry, gentlemen. That bastard doesn't have a clue we're here. We're
going to get in as close as we can and I don't want him to spot our wake.
We'll keep the steam up in case we have to jump."

Sandison was double-double-checking his headset connection to
Randal Hale, who was the captain of the number one torpedo mount
behind the amidships deckhouse on the starboard side. Hale's station
was directly atop the mount. Beneath him, nestled in their tubes, the
final three operating MK-15, twenty-one-inch torpedoes in the entire
world patiently waited, their safety pins removed. There had probably
never been any more lovingly treated and carefully maintained torpedoes in the history of the Asiatic Fleet and they'd been painstakingly
tested for every conceivable defect. Each of the three weapons was
a marvel of technology and precise engineering and was, pound for
pound, the most complicated piece of machinery aboard the entire
ship. Not to mention the fact they'd cost the War Department of the
United States more than ten thousand dollars apiece.

And nobody really trusted them to work.

There were many theories as to why the American torpedoes had
performed so dismally. Much of the problem was undoubtedly due to
the fact that prior to the war, destroyer and submarine crews were allowed very little practice in their use. They were fantastically expensive
and the budget for the Asiatic Fleet in particular was extremely tight.
Bernie Sandison, however, as well as his division, was convinced the
problem was far more insidious. At Balikpapan, they'd *seen* the foam-
ing wake of one of their torpedoes end directly amidships of a Japanese
transport at the height of that confusing fight. To their amazement, it
didn't explode. On other occasions they'd been positive that the weap-

ons ran true, but in spite of their certainty, their efforts and risks weren't rewarded. Destroyermen on other ships, not to mention submariners, complained bitterly about similar experiences. It was obvious there was something fundamentally wrong with the MK-15 and -14 torpedoes. There were really only two possible mechanical explanations. Either the torpedoes were running too deep or something was wrong with their magnetic detonators. Maybe both.

With the captain's permission, Bernie had set the last three fish to run about half as deep as the manual prescribed. The worst thing that could happen, theoretically, was that they'd explode against *Amagi*'s side instead of underneath her like they were designed to do. The damage wouldn't be as great, but at least they should hit the target. That left only the problem of the MK-6 magnetic exploders. The MK-14 submarine torpedo they'd salvaged in Surabaya had actually struck a ship and failed to go off and *Walker*'s torpedomen were highly suspicious that it had to do with the MK-6. Bernie and his men, as well as Shinya, had been all over the damn things. The best they could figure was since the weapons were designed to explode magnetically, not enough thought had gone into what was essentially the backup contact detonator. Shinya was accustomed to the evidently far superior Japanese torpedoes and he'd seen it first. The contact detonators on the American torpedoes weren't robust enough to operate properly when they struck the side of a ship at close to fifty knots.

If that was indeed the case, the torpedoes America had taken to war were hamstrung by a no-win situation. If they went too deep, which Bernie was positive they did, the magnetic exploder failed to operate. If they actually hit the target, they wouldn't explode because the contact detonator often malfunctioned. That would explain a lot and, if true, it was a miracle that any U.S. torpedoes had gone off since the war began. Sandison had taken his case to the captain late the night before and he'd agreed to let them try to beef up the contact exploder on one of the fish. It was a risk, because they might only ensure it wouldn't go off, but nobody wanted to fire the last fish they had and just trust to luck, as they had in the past. They had to try something.

Lieutenant Sandison continued to worry as he made his final preparations. Self-doubt constantly warred with his conviction that he'd been right to make the modifications. He knew his division had done everything humanly possible to ensure that the attack would succeed. But if he was wrong . . .

Chack finally reported that he was certain the target was *Amagi* and there were no Grik between them and the enemy. The range had dwindled to less than four miles—well within the range of the torpedoes—and so far there was no indication the Japanese even suspected they were there. A hush fell over the crew. Creeping up on a battle cruiser in the dark wasn't a tactic they'd ever trained for or ever dreamed they'd use. The normal procedure was to race in at top speed and fire torpedoes from the maximum range of about eight miles. This method was . . . surreal.

Walker continued her leisurely approach, her bow-on aspect presenting the smallest possible target in the pitch-dark night. The tubes were rigged out at a thirty-degree angle and awaiting the command. Now that Chack was sure, he was calling constant corrections. Bernie didn't need them now. Even he could see the massive ship looming ahead, a malignant black outline against a wash of stars beyond. He tracked the target with his torpedo director. Nine thousand, eight thousand, seven thousand yards, and still they narrowed the gap. *Amagi* was making barely eight knots and her course was constant. She was a sitting duck. The range was becoming almost ridiculously close when Captain Reddy finally spoke.

"Mr. Reynolds, remind Mr. Garrett not to open fire unless I give the command, but be ready if I do." He looked at Bernie Sandison and, even in the darkness, Bernie thought he detected a ferocious, predatory gleam in the captain's eye. "Fire your torpedoes, Mr. Sandison."

"Aye, aye, Captain." Bernie addressed Randal Hale in a brisk, nervous voice. "Mount one: Fire one! Fire three! Fire five!"

With each new command, there was a *thump-chuff!* and a sharp flash of yellow light aft as the small black-powder charge within each tube expelled the torpedo. The brightly polished weapons shone only as long dull shadows as they arced into the sea and entered the water amid a gray, concave splash.

"Helm, left full rudder. Come about to course one zero zero."

"Aye, aye, sir. Left full rudder," confirmed the helmsman. "Making my course one zero zero!"

As the destroyer heeled to starboard, Matt went out on the port bridgewing and waited for the stern to come around. This would be the most critical moment. If anyone on *Amagi* saw the impulse charges go off and looked hard in their direction, they'd probably see the ship as she turned broadside-on for a moment. Soon *Walker* steadied and Matt heard the helmsman announce he'd achieved his course. He raised his binoculars to watch the enemy ship. He couldn't see the torpedoes and he felt strangely cheated, even though he knew it was for the best. If it was too dark for him to see the telltale trails of bubbles, then the Japs couldn't see them either. Uh-oh, something was happening. Even as Matt stared at *Amagi*, a searchlight flared to life. Then another.

"All ahead flank!" Matt shouted into the pilothouse. The launch must have been seen after all. The searchlights stabbed at the darkness in their general direction, but for the moment they concentrated on an area to port. Then another light came on and almost instantly, *Walker* was seared by the harsh, bright glare.

"Commence firing!" Matt yelled. "Target their searchlights!" Garrett must have heard him because the salvo buzzer rang even before Reynolds relayed the order. Number two and number four fired together and the tracers lanced into the night. Another salvo left the guns before the first was halfway there.

"Come left ten degrees!" Matt said and raised his glasses again, trying to see through the blinding light. He knew the course change would make *Walker* a larger target, but he wanted the number one gun in the fight. When the next salvo fired, it joined the others. The other two lights had found them now, and then yet a fourth. One suddenly winked out, however, and Matt supposed they must have gotten a hit. "How long on the torpedoes, Mr. Sandison?" he demanded.

"Another minute, Captain." The torpedo officer had taken station on the port torpedo director—not that there was anything left to direct. He just had to see . . .

Other lights lit the battle cruiser, gun flashes from her secondary armament. The first splashes fell about two hundred yards to starboard and a little aft. The second group of enemy shells raised geysers just off the port beam and shell fragments peppered *Walker*. *Amagi's* secondaries weren't nearly as large as her main battery, but they were bigger than anything *Walker* had. The ship staggered under the force of a direct hit aft, and the sound of the explosion and the screams of refugees were deafening. The ship recovered herself, however, and continued her frantic sprint. Another blast, farther aft, and *Walker* shuddered in agony.

"Torpedoes?!"

Sandison's eyes flicked to the stopwatch in his hand.

"Now!"

The lights went out.

Matt snapped the binoculars to his eyes in time to see a bright, slashing pulse of fire rising from *Amagi's* waterline, just aft of amidships. A jet of sparks vomited from her stack and illuminated the rising cloud of smoke caused by the blast. The searchlights that just moments ago had been so remorselessly fixed on the destroyer were now askew, throwing eerie, smoke-dense beams in all directions.

"*Yes!*" shouted Bernie as his relief surged forth. Not what they'd hoped for, but one hit out of three was better than their average to date. He was pretty sure he knew which one it had been. Cheers erupted all over the ship. Cheers of relief and vindication.

"Secure from flank! Come right ten degrees. Let's get some distance while she decides whether or not to sink. If she doesn't, I'd just as soon we were out of range when they get their priorities straightened out. Cease firing main battery."

A few more desultory shells landed in *Walker's* wake, but without the searchlights to guide them the Japanese gunners fired blind. However much damage they'd caused, the torpedo attack had taken them completely by surprise. By the time the searchlights began scanning for *Walker* again, she had disappeared completely into the dark.

Matt slowly let out a breath. "Damage report?"

"That last hit tore hell out of the guinea pullman," Reynolds said, referring to the crew's berthing space situated above the propellers. "Lots of refugee casualties in there." He paused. "There's some flooding in aft general storage and the steering engine room . . . There's people in there too."

Matt was staring aft at the amidships deckhouse. He couldn't see much in the darkness except for the occasional white T-shirt and hat dashing through the smoke that still poured from under it. "What about the hit amidships?" he asked.

The talker nodded. "The Chief says there were a lot of 'Cats hunkered under the deckhouse. He has no idea how many bought it. The galley's a wreck, but Lanier made it okay." Reynolds blinked. "He was in the head. Mertz and the cat-monkey mess attendant are both wounded." The talker paused again, listening. "Oh, goddamn!" he exclaimed in an indignant voice. "Beggin' your pardon, Captain."

"What else?"

"Those Jap bastards got the Coke machine!"

Matt almost laughed. The last of their Cokes had been gone for weeks—all except one that was stashed in his own quarters. He doubted he'd ever drink it. The machine itself had remained a source of pride to the crew, in a strange, black-humor sort of way. They may have been lost on a hostile, alien—other—earth, but by God, the Coke machine still worked. The men would take that news disproportionately hard. Compared to the other sacrifices he'd seen that night, the destruction of the Coke machine seemed pretty ridiculous. He had to maintain appearances, however.

"Well, let's just hope it was worth it. I think the Japs would trade a dozen Coke machines for the hole we put in their guts."

He looked back at the distant ship. There was a fire aboard her now and it might have been his imagination or even just wishful thinking, but it seemed she was listing to starboard. He wanted more than anything to stay, to see for sure if they'd banished this particular demon once and for all. But deep down in his heart, he couldn't bring himself to believe it. One more fish would have done the job. He was certain of that. He should have let Sandison alter them all. He shook his head. Another mistake. One thing was sure, however. Whether *Amagi* sank or not, *Walker* had hurt her badly. The sparks from her stack had come from a boiler, one that was burning coal, so they were bound to have slowed her down, at least. And maybe, just maybe, they had managed to kill whoever it was who was responsible for what she'd done to *Nerracca*.

"Take that, you son of a bitch," he muttered under his breath. Then he raised his voice. "Helm. Make your course zero two zero. We've still got to get through the lizards and I'd just as soon we didn't run into any if you don't mind." He turned to Reynolds. "We'll have the searchlights on just as soon as we're sure we're out of *Amagi*'s range. The main battery won't fire on any lizards we see unless they give us no choice. We have to conserve ammunition." He finally walked over and sat in his chair. "Besides," he added quietly, "we've got a lot of shook-up folks on board. It's probably time we gave them a break."

He rubbed his eyes and spoke once more: "Help Clancy compose a full report of tonight's action, Mr. Reynolds, and transmit it to Baalkpan. Then tell Lieutenant Mallory I want him in the air as soon as it's light enough to fly. Give *Amagi*'s current position and tell Ben to see if she's still afloat or not, and what she's doing if she is. But whatever he does, he *will* stay out of range of her antiaircraft weapons. Make sure he understands that's an order."

At almost dawn, but long before Matt would have personally considered it "light enough to fly," the loud engines of the big flying-boat droned by overhead in the darkness. He had Radioman Clancy send Ben the additional instruction to check on *Aracca*. *Walker* had steamed past her a little before three in the morning and flashed a brief account of the battle. *Aracca*'s High Chief, Ramik-Sa-Ar, was Tassat's father and most of the people on the two Homes were related. Matt hated to break the news like that, but he had little choice. With her heavy load of survivors aboard, *Walker* was taking more water than her pumps could keep up with. *Aracca* was far enough ahead of the Grik that she should be safe from pursuit, but Matt wanted Ben to make sure.

Tsalka glared across the water as Kurokawa's launch returned to his ship. "You know, General, I grow increasingly weary of that creature."

General Esshk hissed agreement. "I begin to understand why those who joined us in the Great Hunt in the past have ultimately fallen prey themselves. If they were as grasping and unpleasant as that one"—he gestured at the retreating boat—"it is no wonder the Hij of old turned them out and hunted them to extinction." Tsalka agreed, but he knew there was more to it than that. Despite the Ancient Way, that whoever hunts together may partake of the meal, he knew it was difficult for any predator to share its prey. The tail-less, almost toothless Hij he had just endured was not one he would care to dine beside.

"Their iron ship is damaged again and it will move even slower now," Tsalka mused. "But it is still wondrously powerful. I heard the tales of how it destroyed our Uul before it joined the hunt. Last night, I saw how it did so. Magnificent!"

"Most impressive," Esshk hedged. "But to strike from such a distance! Where is the challenge . . . the sport in that? It is the hunt that counts. The harvest is secondary."

Tsalka looked at him with his slitted yellow eyes. "Indeed. But it is not very sporting when the prey consumes the hunter. This prey has teeth! I do not desire another catastrophe such as befell our hunters at the walled city. Such a thing has never happened before and it will not happen again. The Celestial Mother would not be pleased and neither would I." He gazed at the lumbering iron monstrosity. Black smoke belched from its middle as it burned the coal that somehow pushed it along. There was other smoke still, from the wound it suffered last night, and Tsalka perceived a slight list. Despite its amazing power, the Tree Prey had friends who could damage it. The thought gave him pause. They had damaged a thing that multiple vigorous assaults by his own race did not scratch. Insufferable as the Hij leader of the iron ship folk might be, Tsalka was beginning to suspect that he was right about one thing: the Grik needed them, and might need them very much if the Grand Swarm was to meet with success. The thought rankled, and yet it might be true. The Tree Prey had grown into Worthy Prey in their own right, but with friends such as they had . . . the slow iron ship of the new hunters might have to make the difference.

Initially, as was customary, the new hunters had been treated with proper disdain. That was appropriate, since they were the newest hunters in the pack. But things had changed. The prey fought well. They had flying things to help them, as well as an iron ship of their own. Much as he disliked the idea, Tsalka admitted it was probably wise to heed the council of a creature—however distasteful—who knew how to counter such things. For the first time, that morning he had actually paid attention to what the iron ship leader had to write.

"You and I are Hij, General Esshk," he said. "We can look back upon the Uul-life with fondness and nostalgia. That was our time for the hunt to be sport. That time is past. I joined the Swarm because I was bored and there has not been a Grand Swarm in my lifetime. I wanted to see it for myself. Although I appreciate your courtesy, command is yours, of course. But I flatter myself that my advice may have some value."

General Esshk bowed low and hissed respectfully. "Your wisdom is renowned, Lord Regent. As always, I crave your counsel."

"Very well then. We must look to the welfare of our Uul. They are our children, General, and they will do what we ask of them. But we may need to protect them from their own exuberance. I do not think there has ever been a hunt quite like this before, and to avoid learning too much about what the Tree Prey and their friends know about thwarting the hunter, I would not hesitate to strike them from farther than I can see, if I could. We must use the iron ship to our utmost advantage because I suspect there will be very little sport to this hunt in the end."

"We both already agree on that, so what is your counsel?"

"Only this: that we postpone this hunt. We should return to the Walled City—Aryaal, I believe? There we should repair the iron ship and summon more Uul. We will gather our strength and when we advance it will be with all our might, at the head of a Swarm such as the world has never seen!"

Captain Hisashi Kurokawa was in a towering rage when he returned from his visit aboard the painfully bright, white-painted ship, and he was seething when he stormed onto the bridge. For quite some time, as much as possible, the bridge watch stood silent, fearing that any sound or voice would draw the captain's wrath. He had already had last night's lookouts arrested and put in irons. They should have seen the American destroyer and had their searchlights on her sooner. Now his ship was even further crippled. With the flooding of another fireroom and the certain destruction of two more boilers, *Amagi* would be even slower than before. He tried to explain to the stupid lizards that his ship *had* to have proper repairs, that she couldn't continue to steam all over the place with half her insides open to the sea. If he could just *fix* her, she would be faster than any ship afloat.

But they just stood there and stared at him as he wrote his demands. Acted as if the inconvenience of his ship's damage was *his* fault! He had suggested that if some of the red ships of their lower class had been screening him, the torpedo wouldn't have gotten through, but that got a stony response. Finally he left, half convinced that he would open fire on the Grik leader's ship as soon as he returned to his own. He still yearned to do so, but there were more than two hundred other Grik ships close by. If he gave in to the impulse to destroy their leaders, surely the others would swarm his ship. Not only would that ruin all his plans, but he would certainly be killed. No, the time would come. For now, he would content himself with finding fault with those who were at his mercy. Commander Okada had the watch, just as he did last night when they were damaged. He would start with him.

"Captain?" came a tentative voice from the bridgewing lookout's position.

"Yes, what is it?" he snapped.

"A signal from the Grik flagship." Like all their technical writing, the Grik used English for their signal flags. Kurokawa assumed there was some connection to the ships they built, since they looked very eighteenth-century British. Regardless, using English to communicate with the monsters was convenient, even if it rankled.

"Well, what does it say?" he snarled impatiently.

"Ah . . . the fleet will come about and join our 'brethren' who have already surely taken the Walled City. There, we will refit and repair all our ships and wait for more hunters to join the Swarm."

"So," grumped Kurokawa, "they listened after all." His mood brightened perceptibly. "Helmsman, bring us about." He smirked. "And do be careful not to smash any of our 'allies.'"

The next hour was awkward for Okada because the captain never left the bridge. He almost never stayed that long, and most of the watch was nervous to the point of distraction—particularly when Kurokawa stepped near their station. But the entire fleet had changed its course, and despite the fact that the damage to *Amagi* was probably responsible, the captain acted like he had achieved some sort of victory.

"Captain!" a talker suddenly blurted nervously. "The lookout reports sighting the American flying-boat, almost directly overhead!"

Kurokawa and Okada both raced out onto the bridgewing with their binoculars. Sure enough, floating lazily above, droning motors lost in the cacophony of *Amagi*'s abused machinery, was the PBY Catalina.

"Damn them!" shouted Kurokawa. He looked around. "Why isn't anyone shooting at them?"

"They are out of range. If you want to waste ammunition to no effect—for all to see—we certainly can."

Kurokawa's gaze slashed at Okada. Then he raised his binoculars toward the Grik flagship. Some of the "officers" were clearly staring at the plane—the damn things had phenomenal eyes—and some were looking right back at him.

"Commander Okada," he said in a menacing tone, "we must destroy that plane."

Okada was incredulous. "But . . . how?"

"We will use one of our planes, of course."

"But, Captain! Those planes are some of our most precious assets and we only have enough fuel for a couple of flights. Also, as you your- self pointed out, they are not fighters, they are spotting planes. They are lightly armed, and I'm not even sure they are fast enough to *catch* the American plane."

Kurokawa's round face regarded Okada without expression. "You, Commander, will choose a flight crew for the fastest of the two planes, if there is any difference. You will have it only half filled with fuel since it needn't go far. That should improve its speed and will save fuel as well. You will then tell the crew that they will destroy the American plane or they need not return. Finally, if they are not in the air in ten minutes, they will be shot." He snorted. "Remember, our 'allies' are watching."

All Okada could do as he raced aft was mutter, "Madness!" under his breath.

"There they are!" Tikker shouted excitedly long before Ben Mallory could see anything but water and sky. By the time the leading edge of the enemy armada was visible to the pilot, Tikker already had an an- swer to one of their questions. The Grik had turned around. "They go home!" he shouted with glee.

"I doubt it." Mallory sighed. "I bet they're headed for Aryaal. They'll set up a base there and hit us when they're ready. Question is, why aren't they ready now? Do you see any sign of *Amagi*?"

"I'm afraid so," said Tikker with disappointment. "There is a large, dark shape farther ahead with smoke rising above it. It seems smoky all over, so maybe it is badly damaged. But we are still too far to tell."

"There's nothing for it then. We have to take a closer look."

"Sure," said Ed Palmer, standing in his usual place at the rear of the flight deck, "but I'm relieved for *Aracca*'s sake."

"You and me both," sighed Ben. "She might have made it, but if they'd still been coming on even at eight knots . . . Well, *Walker*'s report about what happened to *Nerracca* . . ." Everyone nodded. There was no reason to go on.

It was convenient that the PBY had full tanks of oxygen when they found it and Ben had them use some now, so they could get above the antiaircraft weapons. The seals on the masks didn't work too well because even Ben and Ed had fur on their faces now, but there was plenty of oxygen for the few minutes they would need it. They would barely scratch the surface. There was almost a ten-hour supply. Ben pulled back on the wheel and slightly advanced the throttles. Before long, they were cruising at 18,000 feet—the big plane's maximum service ceiling. Now the Japanese could shoot at them all they wanted, but the chances they'd hit anything were infinitesimal. Ben was betting they knew that too and wouldn't want to waste ammo in front of their "friends."

Ed was back in one of the observation blisters, staring straight down with his binoculars. At over three miles, the visibility wasn't what he would have liked, but it was good enough. *Amagi* had been hard hit and she had a distinct list to starboard. Gray smoke from extinguished fires still rose to join the black smoke from her stack. Unfortunately, she was still clearly under way and in no apparent danger of sinking. They'd done all they could and she was still afloat. Ed didn't think they'd get another "surprise" chance like the one last night, and they were out of torpedoes anyway, weren't they? There was no way *Walker* and *Mahan*, even together, could stop her in a stand-up gunnery duel. They would have to think of something else.

Fortunately, it looked like they were going to have time to do that. *Walker* had clearly pounded the Grik fleet the night before. Several ships could be seen under tow, while more than a dozen had apparently been abandoned as beyond repair, or unable to make the voyage to Aryaal. A couple didn't look too bad to Ed. He'd mark their positions. Maybe they could come out and tow them in. There was no telling how many ships *Walker* sent to the bottom. Regardless, however many Grik ships the old destroyer sank or damaged the night before, it was an insignificant percentage of the whole. If the Grik had wanted to, they could have come straight on. They would be mauled, but they would probably win. But they weren't coming on. Just like what they had originally taken to be the "leading edge" of the Grik fleet, *Amagi* had reversed her course. Like those of the hundreds of sailing ships around her, the battle cruiser's rather jagged, uneven wake proved she was headed back in the direction of Aryaal.

Perhaps *Amagi* was the reason they'd stopped! After last night, they might think they had to have her and if that was the case, they might attempt major repairs! That could take a long, long time. There was no question the Grik threat would only grow during that period, but if *Walker*'s desperate torpedo attack hadn't destroyed *Amagi*, it had certainly bought them some time. Time they desperately needed.

Ed relinquished his vantage point to the Lemurian waist gunner and made his way forward. After he relayed his observations and deductions to Ben, he returned to his post at the radio and began signaling *Walker* with the news. Ben flew on a while longer, taking in the scope of the enemy fleet, then banked the plane until it pointed in an almost due-northerly direction. Once the battle cruiser was safely behind them, he began a slow descent. At 7,000 feet, the Catalina's most efficient cruising altitude, he leveled off and asked Ed for some coffee. They'd already secured the oxygen masks.

Ed poked his head up between the two seats on the flight deck. "Sure thing. I'll have some too." He looked at the sable-furred Lemurian. "How 'bout you?" Tikker just grimaced and shook his head.

"Just give it a chance," urged Ben. "It'll grow on you."

"Like a great, hideous tumor, I suspect," retorted the 'Cat. They all laughed. Suddenly there was a sound like heavy gravel being thrown hard against the plane's aft fuselage, followed by a high-pitched shriek.

"What the *hell*!"

"Plane! Plane! Behind us shooting!" came the panicked cry from one of the Lemurians in the waist.

"Shoot back at him!" Mallory bellowed as he instinctively shoved the oval wheel forward to the stop. With the nose pointed at the sea—too close—he slammed the throttles forward and began banking right. He had no idea what was on their tail except it must have come from *Amagi*. That meant it was an observation plane of some sort and had to be dragging floats. The thing was, the Japanese had seaplane versions of almost all their first-line fighters—including the notorious Zeke. If that was what was after them . . . All he could do was what he'd done. The dope coming out of China and the Philippines was that the Zeke couldn't dive, and if it did it had a hard time turning right against the torque of its radial engine. "Ed," he shouted over the roar of engines, the rattling moan of the stressed airframe and the screech of terrified Lemurians, "get an eyeball on that guy and see what we're up against!"

Palmer dragged himself aft and upward. It seemed like forever before he reached the waist gunner's compartment, but when he did, he was greeted by a dreadful sight. Daylight streamed through a dozen bullet holes in the ceiling of the compartment and he knew there were probably many more aft. The Plexiglas in the starboard observation blister was shattered and a hurricane of wind swirled around him. There were brains spattered all over the forward bulkhead and the deck, and blood seemed to have been smeared over every surface with a mop. The dead Lemurian was sprawled in the middle of the aisle, his partner curled in a fetal position on the port side of the bulkhead, rocking back and forth and emitting a keening moan. Ed barely controlled his reflex to retch and snatched the headset off the live Lemurian. "Snap out of it!" he yelled, somewhat shakily. He leaned into the intact blister. First he looked down—he couldn't help it—at the rapidly approaching water. He was no pilot, but *he* damn sure would have been pulling up by now. He took a deep breath and faced aft. Nothing but sky. Their maneuver should have caused their pursuer to overshoot and dump some speed before trying to match their turn. He should have been able to see it.

More "gravel" slammed into the plane. Many of the impacts were quieter that the first and he felt them more than heard them. They must have been in the wings. A final burst sounded directly overhead and it ended with an explosion of sound up forward.

"Goddamn it! What the hell is he?" Mallory screamed.

Ed lunged to the shattered blister, his hat instantly disappearing in the slipstream. Through squinted and watering eyes, he caught a glimpse of a winged shape swerving from starboard to port. He leaped back across the dead Lemurian and finally caught a good view of their tormentor. "It's a *biplane*," he cried into his borrowed microphone, incredulously. "Radial engine and three floats. One big one under the fuselage and two smaller ones under the wings. I swear to God it looks like a Stearman with floats! Two crew—pilot and spotter. The spotter has a gun too." Ed grabbed hold of the .50-caliber machine gun in its pintle mount and prepared to open fire. There were flashes of light from the Japanese spotter's gun before the plane began to bank toward them for another run. The PBY had the lead in their race to the deck, but the biplane was almost as fast and much more agile. Ed looked behind him for an instant, checking to see if the gun in the damaged blister was okay. He blinked. "Uh, Ben . . . I see smoke. Are we on fire?"

Even as Ben's mind absorbed Ed's report and he realized they were under attack by a lowly "Dave" or, to be more specific, a Nakajima Type 95, at present he was too busy to respond with anything more than "Shoot him!" He was trying to pull the big plane out of the dive he'd put it in while listening to the starboard engine, almost directly over Tikker's head, tear itself apart.

"Help me with the stick, Tikker! We've gotta get her nose back up!"

"Yes, yes!" agreed the copilot. "But the engine!" Everything Ben had taught him flew in the face of what they were doing right now.

"I know," Ben yelled to be heard over the calamitous uproar, "but we can't pull out with only one engine." He motioned over his head while he pulled back on the wheel. "I think the Japs must've knocked a jug off her—a cylinder. That's what that god-awful racket is, a piston flailing around, on the loose, banging the crap out of the jugs on either side." He shook his head and snorted, an almost rueful expression joining his clenched-teeth concentration. "I wouldn't have thought a Dave would have the firepower to do that."

"That kill engine?" Tikker asked nervously, looking up at the clattering monstrosity mere feet above his head. Oil was leaking everywhere, running back along the wing, spraying from the cowling, pouring a growing stream of gray-white smoke.

"Maybe," Ben replied. "Right now I just hope it has enough horsepower to keep us from getting wet!" From behind them, they heard the staccato and felt the vibration of one of the .50s opening up. He glanced nervously up at the engine and then at the gauges. Temperature was through the roof, oil pressure was nonexistent. RPMs were dropping . . . He looked at the altimeter and saw it was no longer spinning. With a sigh, he realized they'd begun to level off. Now, if they could shake or shoot down the enemy plane, they'd be all right. He began to give the order to shut down the starboard engine when it suddenly erupted in a bright fireball of greasy yellow flames.

"Shit!" screamed Tikker. "Fire! Fire! We on fire! We burn! Goddamn!"

"Cut the fuel!" yelled Ben. "Activate the fire extinguisher and feather the prop!"

Tikker quickly obeyed. He closed the valve that allowed fuel to flow to the burning engine and hit the extinguisher, but in growing panic he scanned the control panel.

"I cut fuel and use extinguisher like you tell me—like you *show* me! But you never show me feathers for prop!"

If Ben hadn't been so terrified, he would have laughed. As it was, he simply reached over and feathered the prop himself and watched while the blades turned edge-on, somewhat reducing the drag of the now dead engine. Thankfully, the flames had almost entirely flickered out as well. A fuel line must have been hit too, and as fuel and oil sprayed on the increasingly hot engine . . . Ben and Tikker both sighed with relief when the last tendrils of flame disappeared. One disaster averted. Now what? Throughout the battle in the cockpit, they'd heard intermittent firing from aft and Ben wondered how Ed's battle was going. So far, the enemy had scored no further hits, but they were still on the defensive. That didn't sit well with Mallory's personality or fighter training. The question was, what else could they do? He glanced at the airspeed indicator; with the port engine at full throttle, they were barely hovering around ninety knots. He thought a Type 95 could do about a hundred and fifty, so they weren't going to outrun him.

He berated himself. That's exactly what he should have done from the start, if he'd known what was after them. The Japanese pilot must have used their leisurely exploration of the enemy fleet to work himself into what he thought was a one-chance attack. If Ben had thrown the throttles to the stops and slowly *climbed,* they would have had a forty-knot and ten-thousand-foot advantage. As it was, he, Lieutenant Benjamin Mallory, trained fighter pilot, had been bested in his first aerial combat by what was essentially an obsolete trainer with floats. It didn't matter that he'd assumed the enemy was far more capable. He shouldn't have assumed anything. Hindsight could hurt.

"Ed," he called over the intercom.

"Thanks for remembering me," came the sarcastic reply. "I see you have at least stopped our uncontrolled plummet to the sea and the smoke's not quite as bad."

"Sorry about that," Ben replied in his best upper-crust British accent. "One of our engines developed a bit of a . . . stitch and we thought it best to let it rest a while. We only have one other one, you know." His voice turned serious. "What's our troublesome little friend been up to?"

"He's been coming in on our flanks, trying to get an angle on our engines, I guess. His last few tries have been to port. I guess he knows the other one's out."

"How are things back there?"

"One of the gunners is dead. I've been alone back here most of the time. I finally got the other one to snap out of it and he's doing okay. I think he got a piece of the bastard on his last attack. He's on the port side. Starboard's a little unpleasant."

"Understood."

"Other than that, things are about the same. We're a long way from home and almost out of ammo."

"Can the gunner back there handle things for now?"

"Well . . . I guess."

"Good. Then I want you in the nose turret."

"The *nose* turret! Ben, this guy hasn't come anywhere near the nose since he started."

"That's about to change. Give all your bullets to the port gunner and tell him to hammer away the next time that Jap gets in range. He's got all the bullets in the world, got it?"

"Sure, but . . ."

"That's when I'm going to lower the wing floats."

"What! Damn, Ben! That'll just slow us down even further. We'll be sitting ducks!"

"No, listen! If he thinks we're about to set down, he'll pull out all the stops. He has to *shoot* this plane down to destroy it. Once we're down, he can shoot at it till he runs out of fuel or bullets—which he has to be getting low on—and not do any appreciable damage unless he gets another lucky hit on an engine. Besides, he's bound to know our marksmanship would improve dramatically. Hitting a moving target from a stationary one is a lot easier than moving versus moving."

"Are we going to land on the water?"

"Not unless we have to," Ben confessed.

"Why not? It sounds like the perfect plan. We'd have all the advantages. If we don't shoot him down, we just wait till he flies away." Ben cleared his throat.

"We set down only if we have to. Honest to God, I don't think I can get this crate off the water with one engine. Half the time I don't know how I do it with two. You keep forgetting—I'm not a seaplane pilot. I'm still making most of this up as I go."

Ed groaned. "Okay, Ben. I'm with you. And here comes our little friend, right on cue."

"Get in the nose, Ed. As soon as he starts shooting, I'm lowering the floats. Anything could happen after that."

Ed rushed forward. When he arrived, he was reminded just how much he hated the nose turret. It was built for guys a lot smaller than he was and it seemed like a stupid design. He had actually given it a lot of thought and believed he could have come up with something better. The first change would have been the emplacement of something more powerful than a measly .30-cal. It might have been a little cramped with a .50, but they could get a smaller guy. If they got a smaller guy to work the plane's radios and help with navigation, that would be fine too. He put on the headset and racked the bolt, chambering a round.

"Aaaa-eeesh!" cried the gunner in the waist. "I chop him up good that time! Shoot up tail! Maybe kill gunner. Get even for my friend!"

"Where'd he go?" questioned Ben.

"Straight out, away. Direction . . . nine . . . nine clocks?"

"You get that, Ed? I think it's working. Keep your eyes peeled."

"I got it." Palmer strained his eyes through the cloudy Plexiglas. The plane and all its components had been through so much, looking for a plane through the turret was like looking for a minnow in four feet of murky water.

In any event, it took much longer than any of them expected for the Dave to get around in front of them. Maybe it was being careful, or maybe it truly was damaged and had lost some speed. Whatever the reason, when Ed first saw the enemy plane, it was already closer than they'd hoped to spot it, but it was doing exactly what they'd expected: going for the PBY's remaining engine from the front.

"There he is," Ed announced, more calmly than he felt. "I can't judge distance through this crummy glass, though. You're going to have to tell me when he's in range."

"Uh, he's already shooting at us, so whenever you're ready . . ."

"Have you seen this can of ammo down here?" he demanded hotly. "This *one* can of ammo? I need him closer!" A few bullets began to strike the plane.

"He's getting closer!"

"Just a few more seconds!" Ed could see the plane clearly now. If it was damaged aft, he couldn't tell, but it was coming straight in, yellow flashing from its single forward firing machine gun. More bullets were hitting the PBY and Ben's voice grew more insistent. Even Tikker's voice rose in an indignant shriek. Ed paid no attention—even when one bullet grazed the curved Plexiglas mere inches in front of his face. He was concentrating on the sights. They were crude and pretty much limited to known ranges, but he aimed carefully at the steady target of the biplane's round engine, raised the sights a little, and started to fire. He wasn't using short bursts like he ought to have; he was trying to hose out a solid wall of lead that the seemingly flimsy biplane couldn't survive. Evidently, by the sounds of impact, that's what the enemy hoped as well.

Finally, exultantly, he saw a flash and a gout of smoke erupt from the Dave's engine, and the plane seemed to wobble as if the pilot was struggling for control. Ed let out a whoop, but an instant later the firing pin in the .30-cal snapped on an empty chamber. "I'm out!" he yelled over the comm.

"Relax," shouted Ben in return. It sounded like he was talking over a hurricane. "He must be empty too, or you wrecked his gun."

Ed studied the oncoming plane. Sure enough, the shooting had stopped . . . but why was he still coming on? The Japanese pilot was clearly having trouble keeping the plane in the air. He ought to have been headed for the deck where he could set down on the water and call for help. The last thing in the world he should be doing was struggling to maintain altitude and trying to keep his nose pointed right at the PBY as the distance between them closed . . . Ice water poured down Ed Palmer's back. "He's gonna ram us!" he shouted. "The crazy bastard's gonna ram us with his plane!"

"Where is he?" Ben's voice sounded almost as panicked as his own. "The windscreen is gone! All I've got is my sunglasses, but blood keeps getting in my eyes. Tikker doesn't even have sunglasses! You have to tell me, Ed!"

"Oh, God! . . . Okay! He's eleven o'clock low, so I doubt you'd see him over my turret anyway. We're closing pretty fast, so whatever you do, do it *now*!"

In the space of an instant, Ben Mallory made up his mind. Up and away would make them a bigger, slower target. Up and toward might do the same thing, but it was better. Down and away was probably the worst choice he could make. It would give the enemy time to fine-tune his aim. No, down and toward would surprise the enemy and he'd have no time to adjust. "Hold on!" he screamed.

Ed watched it all from the confines of the turret, almost removed somehow from the trauma of the moment. When Ben actually turned *toward* the suicide plane, his panic reached a point of almost surrealistic calm. Analytical. He thought he knew what Ben was trying to do and whether it was inspired by madness or brilliance he didn't know, but it seemed to be working. Suddenly, the Type 95 was clearly visible trailing smoke and angling for the spot the PBY would have been in just a few seconds. The big bright red circles clearly contrasted with the dark green paint. Ed almost thought he could see the pilot's face. It looked like they were clear. Then, with a tight, rolling maneuver that the big flying-boat could never match, the agile biplane flipped on its back, the light gray bottom of its big central float flashing in the sun, and slanted toward them again. Even if he'd had time to warn Mallory, he wouldn't have known what to say.

Someone must have warned him, or maybe he saw it himself, because the Catalina suddenly banked right as hard as he'd ever felt it—back toward the enemy again—but this time it was too little, too late. Ed closed his eyes when he felt the jarring impact and saw the first flash of the fireball.

It was midafternoon when *Walker* steamed into Baalkpan Bay and the usual midday squall had just passed. By the time they gazed upon the city in the steamy light, they could clearly see the many changes that had been made since they'd left. Fort Atkinson loomed above them at the harbor entrance; its big guns with their gaping mouths would be a formidable deterrent to a rational enemy. But the Grik weren't rational. They would be slaughtered, but chances were they'd get past the fort.

Around the city, they saw a high earthen rampart, reinforced with heavy timbers and faced by obstacles and entanglements on both sides of a wide moat. More heavy guns poked from embrasures and there was good killing ground before them. While they watched, work was under way to reinforce the overhead protection beyond the rampart—particularly over the guns. Pointless against *Amagi*'s main battery, of course, but it might help against secondaries or fragments. Beyond the fortifications, Matt saw little change to the city he'd come to think of almost as home, but the fortifications themselves made a profound difference.

In the distance, tied to the old fitting-out pier, was *Mahan*. A wisp of smoke coiled from her number one stack and she seemed to be nearly half covered by Chief Gray's new light gray paint scheme. Matt knew Jim wouldn't be goofing around with paint if a lot of his ship's other issues hadn't already been resolved.

By contrast, if the city and its surroundings looked different now than they had when *Walker* led the Allied Expeditionary Force to raise the siege of Aryaal, the destroyer had changed just as much. Gone was her own dazzling light gray paint. Instead, the elderly ship was almost a uniform orange color, with heavy, darker streaks down her sides. Harsh red rust shone through the smoke-blackened sections, and the large numbers, 163, that had stood so tall and proud at her bow were nearly obliterated. Clusters of splinter wounds and a few larger holes were visible in her flanks, and streams of water coursed over the side as beleaguered pumps struggled to force it out of the overloaded, battered hull. Alone she would have been a dismal, dispiriting sight, but the hundreds of hollow-eyed, bedraggled Lemurians packing her top-heavy deck gave testimony to the greater tragedy.

Because of her arrival, even with all the preparations under way, thousands of people were on hand to witness her slow approach to the dock. The contents of the radio message detailing the events of the night had rapidly spread. There was no reason to conceal the fact that *Nerracca* and most of the people aboard her were lost. It would have been a greater shock to the morale of the defenders if they'd known nothing until *Walker* came in alone. The one thing that mitigated against total despair was the obvious fact that *Walker* had put up a hell of a fight and had saved as many as she could. So strong was the Lemurian faith in the old destroyer's power, they felt sure if *Walker* looked this bad, surely *Amagi* was in much worse condition—if she had in fact survived. Most of them couldn't conceive of the difference between the two ships' relative size and power, and *Walker*'s daring, vengeful counterattack had been duly reported as well. It was still a somber crowd that waited to greet the survivors.

Finally, a sharp, congratulatory *toot! toot!* and a cloud of steam issued from *Mahan*'s repaired whistle and the trancelike immobility of the crowd was broken. Dockworkers shouldered their way through and positioned themselves to catch lines thrown by destroyermen on the ship. Up close, *Walker* looked even worse and the smoke and steam that rose from her aft stacks resembled nothing so much as an exhausted gasp. Gangplanks were rigged and the stunned survivors began to disembark. Some were met by family or acquaintances who had already arrived on *Humfra-Dar*. *Big Sal* was in the bay but hadn't yet reached the dock. No one aboard her would have any idea what had taken place. *Walker* flew only a cryptic signal as she churned past her lumbering old friend. "Glad to see you. Must off-load passengers before we sink."

Most of the survivors weren't met by anyone. They just wandered around in small, confused groups as though in a daze. Most were females or younglings who'd lost everything they ever knew. They'd suffered the trauma of leaving their homes and had nearly been killed at sea. Many of their loved ones were dead. Now they were cast on the shores of an unknown, alien land. Fortunately, someone in a position of authority had their wits about them, and squads of troops were detailed to gently take the refugees in hand. With as little fuss as possible, they were led away. At the urging of officers, the crowd began to disperse and return to their now even more insistent chores. When a lane was cleared, the wounded were carried ashore. There were quite a few.

Matt watched from the port bridgewing while Sandra supervised below. Beside her still was Queen Maraan, giving support and encouragement to the injured—no matter where they were from. Matt's admiration for the Orphan Queen had grown even greater than before. He knew she was a strong and respected leader to the people of B'mbaado, but she'd also shown herself to be wise and compassionate to her former Aryaalan enemies and strangers as well. He was certain she'd be a major unifying figure and a force to be reckoned with in the events that were to come. Beside him stood Chack, watching as well. The young Lemurian was tired but surprisingly alert after spending virtually the entire night in the crow's nest. Matt nodded toward the queen.

"Go give them a hand if you want," he said with a small smile. "Or you can hit the rack. It's your choice."

"If it makes no difference to you, Cap-i-taan, I will help the ladies." He grinned.

"That's fine, but be back aboard by the first watch. We've got a hell of a mess and the Chief's going to need your help. Try to get some sleep between now and then. It's going to be a busy night."

"Aye, aye, Cap-i-taan." Chack saluted him and bailed down the ladder. Matt shook his head. Very carefully, he tried to stretch. Not long before they opened Baalkpan Bay, he'd finally convinced Sandra to remove the rigid strapping that held his arm immobilized. He felt no pain at all from his ribs and the wound through his shoulder had healed remarkably well. That seemed to be the case with every patient treated with the infection-fighting goo. Sandra knew where it came from now—fermented polta fruit that was further processed in some seemingly mystical way—but she still didn't know what made it work and she yearned for a microscope to study it with. Matt didn't care what the stuff was so long as it worked and he was eager to get his considerably atrophied arm back in service. He stretched a little farther, tensing the muscles, and tried to raise the arm from his side. Salvos of pain shot in all directions, and with a wince he let the arm drop. The pain lingered, throbbing with heat, but as it began to subside, he tried again.

"Ahh!"

Deciding to delay his therapy a little longer, he looked back down at the dock. A procession of Guardsmen dressed in the colors of Nakja-Mur's clan had arrived and Nakja-Mur himself was ascending the gangway with Alan Letts and Jim Ellis. Despite the mess and the chaos on deck, Chief Gray managed to assemble a side party to receive them and the sound of his bosun's pipe twittered from below. A few moments later, the two men and the rotund Lemurian leader were admitted to the bridge. Out in the open air, salutes were exchanged and Jim and Alan extended their hands in heartfelt relief. To Matt's surprise, Nakja-Mur enveloped him in a crushing embrace.

"Ah!" Matt said again, clenching his eyes shut.

"I am so glad you and your ship did not die!" the High Chief exclaimed in much improved English. He was oblivious to the pain he'd accidentally caused.

"Me too," Matt agreed, once he could trust his voice. "*Nerracca* wasn't so lucky."

Nakja-Mur nodded grimly. "A terrible thing. I am deeply grieved and angered by its loss. As I am for *Revenge*." Matt remembered that almost the entire crew of *Revenge* had come from Baalkpan.

"*Revenge* died well, Nakja-Mur," he said quietly. "She destroyed hundreds of the enemy. The families of her people can be proud."

"They are," the High Chief confirmed. "As am I. But pride is mixed with sorrow."

"Of course."

Nakja-Mur gestured at the pier where the last of the wounded were being taken away. "You saved many from *Nerracca*."

"As many as we could. Tassat is a hero. He's the one that made it possible, by sending them over in the gri-kakka boats. When all was lost, it was his daughter herself who cut the cable that doomed her father but saved everyone else. A hell of a thing."

Nakja-Mur nodded. "Indeed. She and all her people will be welcome in my clan if they desire. They will probably go back to *Aracca*, but . . . they are welcome." He stopped for a moment but then looked up into Matt's eyes. It was time to get to the point. "Do you think you destroyed the iron ship of the enemy?" he asked urgently. Of course, by asking the question, Nakja-Mur confirmed Matt's fear as he looked again at the empty pier where the PBY should have been tied several hours before. So it hadn't just been moved ashore for repairs.

"Well, in that respect, it seems we have good news and bad," Matt hedged.

"I must know." The Lemurian pressed him. "Did you destroy that terrible ship?"

Matt finally exhaled and shook his head. "No," he said at last and watched the humans' faces fall. Nakja-Mur only blinked. "We got in a damn good lick and she wasn't in good shape to start with—but Ben's last report had her listing but afloat and under way."

Letts shook his head. "And it's not just the Japs. There's still tens of thousands of those damn lizards coming right at us. It's going to be tough with or without the Japs."

"We must have a council tonight," Nakja-Mur declared distractedly. "By then, with your Maall-orry's help, we will know exactly what we face, as well as when the blow will fall."

"No," Matt said. "That's more of the bad news—as well as the good." He gestured toward the empty pier. "It looks like the plane didn't make it. The last word we had was that *Amagi,* as well as the entire enemy fleet, has turned around and is headed for Aryaal. Signalman Palmer speculated it was damage to *Amagi* that influenced them to delay their attack, so at least we bought a little time. How much is anybody's guess." His voice became even grimmer. "Without the plane, it'll be harder to figure out." He looked at Jim and offered a brittle smile. "Right back where we started. Outnumbered, and no air cover."

"How can you be sure the plane is lost?" whispered Nakja-Mur, devastated.

"It should have beaten us here by two or three hours at least, and there hasn't been any radio contact since right after what I told you." He paused. "If you still want a meeting tonight, that's fine, but"—he gestured around at the ship—"I've got a lot of work to do between now and then. I'll see you tonight, Nakja-Mur."

"And I respectfully recommend," added Jim Ellis, "that we continue to prepare as if, as far as we know, they're coming straight on."

The High Chief blinked agreement. "We all have much to prepare." He turned to go, but then looked back at Matt. "I am *very* glad you did not die, Cap-i-taan Reddy."

"I think he kind of missed you, Skipper," Letts said when Nakja-Mur had gone. "I know I sure as hell did!"

They all glanced down the ladder to see Lieutenant Sandison clomping up the rungs. His clothes and hands were covered with grease and he'd smeared some across his nose. When he looked up and saw the officers gathered above him, his expression became apprehensive.

"What is it, Mr. Sandison?" Matt asked, his eyebrow arched at Bernie's apparent mood.

"Uh, final report on the condemned torpedoes, Captain."

"So soon?" Matt wasn't being sarcastic. He was genuinely surprised that the torpedo officer had come up with an answer so fast now that he was working on it again. Bernie visibly flinched. He did think the captain was being sarcastic. What's more, he thought he had every right to be.

"Well, sir, you may remember there were two of them," he temporized. Matt nodded.

"I believe I remember that number being mentioned," he said.

"And that they were submarine torpedoes . . ."

Matt nodded again, making a "come on" gesture with his hand. The fact they were submarine torpedoes didn't really matter. The MK-14s were virtually identical to the MK-15s designed for destroyer use, except they were shorter and had a shorter range. They were even identical down to the fact that they had all the exact same problems. They could still be used in *Walker*'s launchers, however. "Get on with it, Mr. Sandison."

"Uh, yes, sir. Well, one of them is totally wrecked. The one they pulled out of the side of that Dutch freighter. That's the one that had me looking at the exploders. Maybe we can use it for a pattern someday, for parts, but it's done for. It's just too badly damaged to repair."

"That's pretty much what you told me before," said Matt a little impatiently. "I assume you have news about the other torpedo?" Sandison nodded his head, looking miserable. "Well? What's the matter with it?"

"Nothing." He took half a step back.

"*Nothing?!*"

"Yes, sir. Nothing, as far as Lieutenant Shinya and I can tell. We've been all over that thing and we just can't find anything wrong with it." He held up his greasy hands.

"If there's nothing wrong with it, why would it have been con- demned? Especially the way everybody was screaming for torpedoes?"

"Well, Captain, I got to thinking... maybe it wasn't really condemned."

"What the hell are you talking about?" Ellis interrupted. "Of course it was condemned! I was there when we swiped them, remember? They both had tags—"

Sandison shook his head. "No, sir, they *didn't* both have tags. This one didn't. That's why we never could figure out where to start looking for a problem."

"But—" Ellis stopped. "Then why was it in there *with* a bunch of condemned torpedoes?"

Sandison took a deep breath and then let it out. "Because it's old. It's not a MK-14 submarine torpedo; it's an MK-10!"

"What diff—" Alan Letts slapped his forehead. "Of *course!*" He turned to Captain Reddy. "The MK-10 is an S-Boat torpedo—an *old* S-Boat torpedo! The newer fish won't fit in the oldest subs we have—" He corrected himself, "I mean *had.* So they gathered up all the MK-10s to save them just for the older boats. They probably wound up with one running loose in Surabaya and stuck it with the rejects!"

Sandison was nodding. "That's what I was thinking."

Matt looked at him. "There's *nothing* wrong with it?"

"No, sir."

"We can use it?"

"Yes, sir. MK-10s are slow, but they bloody well *work.* They don't have any damn MK-6 exploders!"

Matt shook his head and closed his eyes, then opened them again and looked at nothing in particular. "We sure could've used it last night!"

"Yes, sir," Sandison agreed, miserable.

Matt patted him on the shoulder. "Not your fault." He glanced aft. "Thank Lieutenant Shinya for his assistance, but ask him to report to Mr. Alden to resume his primary duty of helping train Lemurian troops. We're going to need all we can get." He maneuvered Sandison slightly aside. "Please do discuss our . . . concerns about Mr. Shinya with Mr. Alden."

"Certainly, Captain."

After everyone returned to their duties, Matt found himself alone on the starboard bridgewing, staring out across the busy bay. He glanced at his watch. He'd tried not to allow himself to hope the PBY might still make it. If it lost an engine and Ben was flying very carefully it could conceivably arrive hours late. But no matter how he stacked it, he just couldn't justify the amount of time that had passed.

"Don't give up," came a soft voice beside him. He turned to see Sandra standing there, folding her bloody apron. She looked exhausted.

"On the plane? I'm afraid there's not much choice."

"I wouldn't write them off just yet, but that's not what I mean. I mean don't give up on what you've started here; this 'crusade' of yours to save the Lemurians—and, incidentally, us—from the creatures of whatever species that could do what was done to *Nerracca* last night." She sighed and looked at him almost apologetically. "I admit, at first I was skeptical we could accomplish much and afraid that we'd bitten off more than we could chew—especially after the Battle of Aryaal. But then I saw something happen. In spite of all the blood and suffering, or maybe even because of it, all these disparate peoples began to come together, to fight for a common cause. And all that happened because of you." She shrugged. "So we won a few battles by the skin of our teeth. So we lost a campaign. So we got kicked out and thousands of people died! Think about it: we saved many thousands more people than we lost—than would have been saved if we'd never acted." She paused, looking at him. Searching. "Eventually, the Grik and *Amagi* will come here. We will have prepared as best we can and the biggest, most horrifying battle ever waged on this entire planet will take place. And you know what? We're going to *win*! We'll win because we'll have an army of many cultures fighting for a common ideal, an army that's been trained to win. We'll win because of the memory of Aryaal and Baalkpan burning on the horizon, and we know the alternative to victory. And we'll win because of what happened to *Nerracca*. People, Lemurians, will remember, and they'll rally to that!" She glanced around and saw no one looking, then raised both hands and put them on his shoulders. "And we'll win because you'll be leading us." Her voice was intent. "You have to believe that!"

He smiled at her wistfully. "I believe almost every single thing you just said, except for one thing: I'm not as sure as you are that we'll win." Sandra seemed thoughtful for a moment, as if considering his words, then looked at him with a strange expression.

"The same 'not sure' the PBY will return? More? Less?"

"I'm a little more sure than that." His voice lowered. "Sandra, the plane is lost."

"Sure?"

He was becoming a little annoyed, and was about to say, "Sure," when he saw the impish look on her face. Then his gunnery-damaged hearing caught it too—about the same time the other human destroyermen did, and he realized that even Sandra had been relying on the excited reactions of Lemurian crewfolk on the fo'c'sle. The bells on both ships began to ring and the whistles blew. What had been rather somber destroyermen and dockworkers now leaned on the rails and shouted or waved their hats in the air. They could see the plane now, out over the bay. It was running on only one engine, but they'd seen that the day it first arrived. Something was different this time, though.

"Pipe down!" bellowed the Bosun loud enough for the crews of both ships to hear. He leaned over the side. "Stow that crap and get some men in Scott's launch!" Gray caught himself and looked up at the captain. Matt nodded, making it official. From now on, the big launch would be named after *Walker*'s former coxswain. Everyone had learned of his death as soon as they tied up and many were deeply saddened by the loss. The news came as yet another blow after the last few days they'd endured. Sandra took it hard; he'd saved her life. But, oddly, Silva seemed the most affected. Everyone knew the two men were friends, but as soon as Nurse Cross was seen telling him the news, he disappeared entirely.

The PBY labored as close to its usual landing area near the pier as it could get, but apparently exhausted, it seemed to give up. The plane's nose was a little high, and the tail of the boat-hull dragged on the water until the plane just stalled, and with a thundering boom, pancaked almost to a stop on the mercifully calm water. It was as close to a controlled crash as the plane and its crew could probably survive. The exuberance of a moment before turned to a collective horror at the condition of the plane, and dread over the condition of the crew.

The starboard propeller was feathered and the cowling was riddled with holes and black with smoke. Virtually the entire plane was full of holes, for that matter, and even if they weren't very big, they seemed to concentrate in critical areas—where people had been. The cockpit windscreen was shot away, as were both the observation blisters. A few holes even crazed the nose turret. As for the rest of the plane, the wings had taken enough hits for fuel to be dripping from numerous places, in spite of the self-sealing tanks. Exotic colors dappled the water where the drops fell. The canvas control surfaces, particularly on the port side of the tail, were ravaged, and the aluminum skin around them seemed riddled by shrapnel. Most terrifying, and frankly amazing, of all was that beyond the port wing float, three or four feet of the wingtip were missing, as was the entire port aileron, as if they'd been bitten off by a shark. The float itself was unsupported, but just by hanging there it kept the wing out of the water. At least here, in the calm.

"My God," murmured Sandra, her smile fading away. "How did they ever make it?" Matt was wondering to himself how many actually had. Scott's launch throttled up and headed for the plane even as its remaining engine wound down. It wasn't even going to attempt an approach to the pier. One of *Mahan*'s launches raced to assist. While they watched, three bloody forms were removed from the plane and loaded in Scott's launch. One was clearly human. They were joined by a human and a 'Cat and when they were aboard, the launch throttled up and headed for the pier, where an ambulance cart awaited. Nurse Karen Theimer, whom they'd left in Baalkpan, had taken to heart her directive to continue working to establish an efficient hospital and ambulance corps.

Three of the launch's passengers were whisked away on the 'Cat-drawn cart, while the others painfully scrambled across *Walker's* gangplank. A few moments later, they both stood before Matt, Sandra, and a growing number of officers from both ships. Probably only Chief Gray's imposing presence could have kept the rest of the crew at a respectful distance.

Ed Palmer saluted and Jis-Tikkar nervously copied the gesture. He'd never met Captain Reddy before. Ed's voice was exhausted and full of delayed stress when he spoke.

"Captain Reddy, I must report the successful completion of our mission to observe the enemy fleet and report their course and disposition." He sighed. "I must also report that Lieutenant Mallory was badly wounded in the head and shoulder and both of our waist gunners were killed." The Lemurian elbowed him sharply and Palmer rolled his eyes. "Acting copilot trainee Jis-Tikkar was also bravely wounded during the action." Tikker proudly tugged on his right ear, displaying the neat, round 7.7-millimeter hole. Matt nodded in appreciation of the Lemurian's sacrifice, then returned his attention to Ed.

"What happened?"

"We got jumped by a plane." Palmer continued his tale in the face of astonished expressions, detailing everything from the first shot to the last. When it came time to describe the final act, his own expression turned to one of incomprehension.

"He just rammed into us, Skipper. Deliberately. The fight was over. There was nothing either of us could do to the other, but despite everything Ben could do—he almost got us clear—that Jap still managed to hit us. As he tore into our wing, though, the wing must've ripped open his fuel tank. He was already on fire and he just blew up. That's where all the damage on the port side came from and that's when our other waist gunner bought it."

"Is that when Mr. Mallory was incapacitated?"

"Well, no, sir, he was already wounded. Bad scalp wound and shot through the shoulder. But he was still flying until about an hour ago. He was getting woozy from blood loss, so I got him out of the chair and patched him up. He . . . sorta told us what to do after that." Matt blinked.

"Am I to understand that you, Signalman Palmer, flew and landed that plane?"

"No, sir," answered Ed distinctly. That left only one other possibility. Matt looked incredulously at the Lemurian standing as tall and straight as he could—and coming up to Ed's shoulder. "He sat on two parachute packs and I worked the rudder. It was . . . a little uncoordinated at first, but we got the hang of it." Matt grinned at what had to have been a monumental understatement.

"Very well, and well done. Now, both of you get some rest. With Mr. Mallory laid up, you two will have your jobs cut out for you coordinating repairs to the plane." He paused. "By the way, you're both promoted. I just have to figure out what to. Carry on."

"Aye, aye, Skipper," replied Ed with a tired grin of his own. He pointed at the plane. "We'll get some rest, but I recommend you get somebody to drag that thing up on the beach before it sinks."

When everyone had returned to their duties, or in Ed and Tikker's case, gone ashore to their berths, Matt found himself almost alone with Sandra again. Almost, because they'd been joined by Courtney Bradford. Together they watched while hundreds of Lemurians heaved on ropes, dragging the battered plane ashore. The exotic city of elevated pagoda-like structures with their slightly eastern flair was now strangely familiar and certainly a welcome sight.

"Remarkable!" Courtney exclaimed.

"Indeed," agreed Matt. "Remarkable in every way." He looked at Sandra and smiled. "Everything that's happened since we got to this world. Remarkable deeds accomplished by remarkable people, both humans and 'Cats." He shook his head, looking back at the plane. "And that's why I won't give up and why, eventually, we'll win." He snorted. "We may not live to see it, and this city will probably look worse than that plane, but if the enemy comes here, we'll beat them here and then wherever else we have to because, in the end, we have no choice—and it's the right thing to do."

EPILOGUE

*I*sak Rueben, Gilbert Yager, and Tab-At emerged into the light. They'd gone to their berthing space only to discover their racks were wrecked, along with most of the others, and so, on a whim, they decided to expose themselves to the outside world for the first time in several days. They resembled disoriented, grimy moles, squinting and sniffing at the unaccustomed evening sunlight. Gradually, their eyes began to adjust. All around was frantic activity. Rapid repairs were under way, being performed by the ship's crew and dozens of Lemurian yard workers. The Mice had a lot of work as well, but they'd just stood eight consecutive watches and Spanky ordered them to take one off and get some sleep. That order was going to be difficult to follow. Everywhere they looked they saw extremely noisy activity.

Right in front of them, the perforated number four torpedo mount was being disassembled. It was destroyed beyond repair, but they could salvage the steel. An incessant staccato clanging came from everywhere as tortured plates were beaten back into shape, and arcs of fire soared in all directions as the welders went to work. Air hoses and torch lines snaked underfoot and the smell of hot steel and burning paint filled the air along with bilingual curses. To Isak, the scene looked more like the scrapyards of hell than the deck of a ship that might ever fight again.

Slowly, they worked their way forward through the jostling workers, trying to avoid being knocked down, burnt, or crushed. They made it under the shade of the amidships gun platform, but things were just as hectic there. Lanier was sitting on a stool, watching protectively while repairs were made to the galley. The shredded Coke machine lay in state on its back off to one side. For a wreath, somebody had decorated the dead machine with a silk lei they'd brought from Pearl when they joined the Asiatic Fleet. The compressor and tubing had already been removed. Lanier was guarding a platter of sandwiches on his lap. By the crumbs around his mouth, an undetermined number no longer required his protection.

"Here," he said, offering the plate as the Mice squeezed past. His voice held little of its usual acerbic impatience. It just sounded . . . sad. "Nothin' but sammiches for a while, till the galley's fixed. Thank God they didn't get the refrigerator! No fresh bread—you better eat one of these!" he insisted. When all three Mice accepted one, Lanier continued talking, shaking his head mournfully. "Made these with the last of the bread. Now we're gonna be tryin' to choke down that local shit until I get my oven back."

"It could'a been worse," Yager said, taking a bite. "How's Mertz?"

Lanier waved his hand. "Got a piece of shrapnel in his ass, and a couple more in the back of his leg. Lost a finger too, and he thinks it's a big deal. Hell, he's got nine more. No, the worst part is, besides the Coke machine, the damn Japs got my spice locker! The last black pepper in the whole wide world's just . . . gone! Sneakiest stunt they've pulled since Pearl Harbor!" Lanier's tone began to return to normal as he seethed. "Bastards!"

Tabby was surprised by the cook's priorities, but Isak and Gilbert both nodded solemnly. "It's a hell of a thing," Isak agreed. "How's your gut feelin', Earl?" Lanier glared up at him.

"None of your goddamn business, snipe!" He straightened up on the stool as best he could and pulled his shirt closed over his grimy bandage. "Now you've stolen the best sammiches I had left, why don't you quit goofin' off and get back to work! I can't fix the whole ship by myself!"

They crossed the deck and ducked under the bridge beside the radio shack. Clancy was inside with the hatch open. His earphones were on his head and he nodded as they passed. Who knew what he was listening for. Going through the hatchway that led onto the foredeck, they emerged into sunlight again. Finally they'd found a place that hadn't been damaged the night before—beyond a few dents and scratches from shell fragments—and so, for now at least, it was probably the quietest place on the ship. They crawled up under the splinter shield of the number one gun and stretched out in the sparse shade beneath it.

"Laan-yeer is a strange man," Tabby observed at length. "He think whole ship—just so he have galley."

"Yeah," Isak agreed from beneath his right arm, which rested across his eyes. "But we're sort of the same way, I guess. Nothin' really matters except our boilers. Spanky has it tough. He has to worry about the boilers *and* the engines. Other stuff too. Chief Gray's like that with the topsides. But that's just the way it is. Everybody has a particular part of the ship that it's their job to take care of. Nobody could do it all."

"Except the cap-i-taan," Tabby said thoughtfully. "He have to worry about everything. Not just all ship, but *everything*."

They lay quietly for a moment, listening to the racket from aft.

"Yeah," Yager breathed at last. "I sure wouldn't want his job."

Read on for an excerpt from Book III in
the exciting *Destroyermen* series by Taylor Anderson

Coming from Roc in February 2009

*T*here was a new rumbling sound below, but it went unnoticed by the eight-year-old girl swaying in the sailcloth hammock. Her slumber was already filled with the incessant rumbling and groaning of the working hull and the endless, hissing blows of the pounding sea. Then came another rumble and another, each more insistent than the last. Still she didn't stir from her dream. In it, she'd been swallowed by a leviathan, just as she'd dreaded since before the strange voyage ever began. Every night, as soon as the lids closed over her large, jade-colored eyes, the same terrible dream came again. She was in the very bowels of the leviathan and the rumbling, hissing roar was the sound of its belly digesting the ship. The voices came—there were always voices—excited, urgent. Voices in a tone entirely appropriate. Of course there would be dreadful voices in a dreadful dream. She knew what would happen next . . .

She was facedown on the thundering deck and only her tangled bedding protected her delicate nose from the fall. Her eyes were instantly open, but she could barely see. The only illumination in the stateroom came from the meager light of a gimbaled lantern on the far bulkhead. Slowly emerging from the dark nightmare of a moment before, she began to understand she'd entered another. The deck felt wrong, its motion contradicting what she'd come to perceive as normal. She still heard the voices and although the words were muffled, they were louder and shrill with alarm. One word she clearly understood sent a spasm of primal terror through her heart: "Leviathan!"

The rumbling groan intensified and the deck heeled hard beneath her. She had the impression the ship was rising up, much of the noise coming from the mighty timbers of its very bones, stressed beyond endurance. With a screech of agony and a splintering crash, the stress fell away like a broken spring and she tumbled against the aft bulkhead that suddenly became the floor. With a sickening, wallowing lurch, the stateroom righted itself, but then quickly tilted down toward the bow. She hugged her knees to her chest and sobbed.

The stateroom door crashed open and her heart leaped with relief to see the wispy form of her tutor, Master Kearley, stumble into the room.

"My lady!" he cried, over the rising pandemonium in the passageway.

"Master Kearley! Oh, Master Kearley!"

"There you are, child," he exclaimed in a more normal tone. He even paused to straighten the lapels of his frock coat. "Come along quickly— no, do not hesitate to dress! A simple shawl will do."

She was accustomed to following his orders and she did so now without thought, snatching her shawl from the hook by the door and quickly draping it around her shoulders.

"And your bonnet too, I suppose," he instructed. Obediently, she took the bonnet from its place beside the shawl and pulled it down over her long golden locks.

"What has happened?" she asked tremulously.

"Come," he said. "I will tell you what I know as we go, but we must hurry."

The darkened passageway swirled with kaleidoscopic scenes of shadowy panic. Shrieks of terror rent the air and bustling shapes surged aft against the increasing cant of the deck. An indignant roar rose above the turmoil and the girl thought she recognized the voice of Director Hanes. Even his exalted status couldn't protect him from the animalistic instinct of the throng. The metallic *sheeng!* of a sword leaving its scabbard quickly silenced the dignitary.

"Hurry!" Kearley prompted as they wove, hand in hand, toward a companionway. "We have struck a leviathan—or it has struck us. It makes no difference. The ship will quickly founder. Her back is broken." The girl sobbed again and her terror threatened to overcome her. The nightmare was true after all.

"Make way, there!" Kearley shouted at the broad back of a man blocking the ladder. "Are you unmanned? Don't you know who this is?"

The big man whirled and made a fist, preparing to strike the frail scholar. His eyes were wide and white with fear, his huge, disheveled black mustaches almost covering his entire mouth. Before he released the panicked blow, however, he recognized the small form below him.

"Yer pardon, young miss!" He almost squealed with contrition. "Clap onto me back and I'll plow us a road!"

Kearley grabbed a handful of belt with one hand and took the girl's wrist with the other. Together, they fought their way up the choked companionway and onto the tilting quarterdeck. Once there, to the girl's surprise, the big man stooped and swept her off her feet.

"We must put her in a boat this instant!" he cried. His voice had returned to what was surely a more normal growl.

"My thanks, good sir," Kearley replied. "I appreciate your assistance." The man spared him an incredulous glance. Now that he recognized the girl, there was no question he would die to save her.

The girl was oblivious to the exchange. Around her in the darkness there was no longer any doubt: her terrible dream had come to life. Helpless canvas flailed and snapped and the once fascinating scientific intricacy of the rigging was a hopeless mare's nest of tangled lines. A constant, deadly hail of blocks and debris fell from above. Beyond her immediate surroundings, she dimly saw the bow, twisting and bent, jackknifing ever upward until the bowsprit pointed at the sky. The fragile paddle wheels on either side, amidships, resembled twisted flowers, shorn of their petals. Steam and smoke jetted from the funnel. In the center of this catastrophe, the deadly sea coursed into the ship.

Then, past the bow, coal dark against the starry horizon, she saw a monstrous form. It was clearly the great leviathan that had destroyed the ship—possibly entirely by accident. It may have simply risen from the depths, unknowing and unconcerned, to inhale a cavernous lungful of air. Perhaps only then did it discover the water bug on its back. No matter, it noticed it now. Even as the girl watched with unspeakable dread, the island-sized creature completed its leisurely turn and came back to inspect the wounded morsel in its wake. The big man saw it too.

"Into a boat!" he bellowed, carrying her to the larboard rail, where a dozen men frantically tore at the quarter-boat tackle. "Make way, damn ye! Can ye not see who I bear?" A wide-eyed young officer motioned them through the gathering throng that regarded the boat with frantic, greedy eyes.

"Are you a sailor?" the officer demanded of the big man. "You are not one of the crew."

"I was a sailor once," he admitted. "And a soldier. I'm a shipwright now, bound for the yard at the company factory."

The officer considered. "Right. Take her aboard under your protection. As soon as you launch, you must hold the boat close so we may put more people aboard." He cast an appraising glance. "You do look strong enough."

Before the girl could form a protest, she was hoisted over the rail by the man's powerful arms and deposited in the boat. Quick as a goat, he followed her and turned to accept the bundles hastily passed to him. A sailor jumped aboard too, encumbered by a double armful of muskets, which he quickly stowed. The girl found her voice.

"Master Kearley!" she wailed. "Master Kearley, you must come too!"

"I will, my dear," came a muted cry beyond the desperate mass. "Lower away!"

The boat dropped swiftly to the water and struck with a resounding smack.

"Fend off, you lubbers!" came the cry from above. "Hold her steady, now! I will send them down two at a time on the falls!" The big man looped a rope around his powerful forearm and pulled with all his might while the seaman pushed against the hull with an oar.

"Let 'em come!"

The girl gave voice to such a sudden, piercing, gut-wrenching shriek of terror that for an instant, in spite of their own fear, everyone froze to look. A massive cavern had opened before them, wide enough to swallow half the ship. Amid a chorus of muted screams, it clamped down on the settling bow with a thunderous, rending crash. The mainmast toppled forward and fell against the darkened mass. More screams came when the mizzenmast also thundered down upon the horrified humanity on the quarterdeck.

"Master Kearley!"

With a terrible grinding, crunching sound, the titanic jaws gaped open and closed once more on the pulverized forward section of the ship. Far in the distance, a monumental explosive splash of mighty flukes crashed down and with a convulsive jerk, the entire ship lurched bodily away from where the tiny boat bobbed in the choppy sea.

"Master Kearley!" shrieked the girl with a desolate, perfect anguish while the rest of the ship was shattered by the impossible strength of the beast. The boiler burst with a thunderclap roar and a swirling, scalding gout of steam. Further enraged by the discomfort this might have caused, the leviathan redoubled its attack. Terrible screams and splintering timbers filled the night, but soon all that remained was the surging sound of the agitated sea.

The seaman who brought the muskets had gone over the side, so there was no hope for him. The girl collapsed into the bottom of the boat and wept with disconsolate abandon. For a while, the big man could do nothing except stare into the empty, endless night. Occasionally, his gaze fell upon the ragged, pulsing stump of his left arm. The rest of it had been snatched away so suddenly and with such force that all he remembered feeling was a tug and a pop. Now his life was coursing into the sea and he already felt the loss. Shaking himself, he snatched his belt from his waist and wound it tightly around the stump. Shortly, the cascade reduced to a trickle, but, light-headed, he sat heavily in the boat and looked down at the sobbing girl.

"Little miss," he croaked, and the girl slowly raised her sodden eyes to regard him. "Your ladyship . . . I truly hate to impose, but if ye could see clear to bind me a bit better, I might be of more use to ye."

Seeing his terrible wound, the girl recoiled for an instant, but then scrambled lightly across the seats to his side.

"I will do what I may," she assured him bravely through her tears, "but I am no surgeon."

"That's a fact," he agreed with a wan smile, "but I've no doubt ye could be if ye wished." As gently as she could, the girl tightened the tourniquet and then rummaged for something to use as a bandage. She finally settled for the sleeve on his other arm.

"They will search for us, won't they?" she asked while she worked.

"Of course they will, lass."

"Will they find us?"

The big man's smile faded completely and he gazed out at the dark, endless swells. They'd lost contact with their consorts some nights back, but that happened all the time. The other two ships wouldn't grow concerned until several days after they reached the factory dock and the doomed ship and her important cargo still had not arrived. They'd traveled only half the distance to their destination, so it would be weeks before they were considered overdue. Months before the news reached home and a search was mounted. The wind and current would drive them quickly westward, far beyond the lanes traveled by men.

He blinked and then looked down into the huge, trusting eyes that seemed to pierce his calloused soul.

"Of course they will, Your Highness."